The first romance stories **Stephanie Laurens** read were set against the backdrop of Regency England, and these continue to exert a special attraction for her. As an escape from the dry world of professional science, Stephanie started writing Regency romances, and she is now a *New York Times*, *USA Today* and *Publishers Weekly* bestselling author.

Stephanie lives in a leafy suburb of Melbourne, Australia, with her husband and two daughters, along with two cats, Shakespeare and Marlowe.

Visit Stephanie Laurens online:

www.stephanielaurens.com

www.facebook.com/AuthorStephanieLaurens

D0321276

A
Rogue's Proposal

Stephanie Laurens

piatkus

PIATKUS

First published in the United States in 1999 by Avon Books,
An imprint of HarperCollins Publishers USA
First published in Great Britain in 2007 by Piatkus
This paperback edition published in 2007 by Piatkus
by arrangement with Avon

9 10

Copyright © Savdek Management Proprietory Ltd. 1999

The moral right of the author has been asserted.

A CIP catalogue record for this book
is available from the British Library.

ISBN 978-0-7499-3719-5

Typeset by Action Publishing Technology Ltd, Gloucester
Printed and bound in Great Britain by
Clays Ltd, St Ives plc

Papers used by Piatkus are from well-managed forests
and other responsible sources

ROM
Pbk

Piatkus
An imprint of
Little, Brown Book Group
Carmelite House
50 Victoria Embankment
London EC4Y 0DZ

An Hachette UK Company
www.hachette.co.uk

www.piatkus.co.uk

The Bar Cynster Family Tree

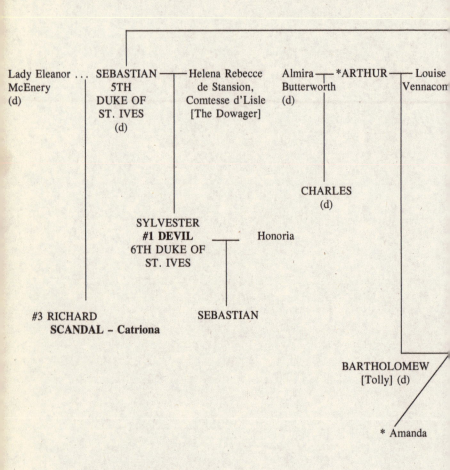

Lady Eleanor ... SEBASTIAN —— Helena Rebecce   Almira —— *ARTHUR —— Louise
McEnery   5TH   de Stansion,   Butterworth   Vennacom
(d)   DUKE OF   Comtesse d'Lisle (d)
                 ST. IVES   [The Dowager]
                 (d)

                                                  CHARLES
                                                  (d)

        SYLVESTER
        #1 DEVIL   ——   Honoria
        6TH DUKE OF
        ST. IVES

#3 RICHARD   SEBASTIAN
SCANDAL – Catriona

                                          BARTHOLOMEW
                                          [Tolly] (d)

                                                        * Amanda

THE BAR CYNSTER SERIES
#1 Devil's Bride
#2 A Rake's Vow
#3 Scandal's Bride
MALE CYNSTERS named in capitals * denotes twins

* GEORGE —— Horatia
Rotherwell

Augusta – Herbert
Marquess of
Huntly

MARTIN —— Lady Celia
Hammond

SPENCER
#2 VANE – Patience

**#4 HARRY
DEMON**

RUPERT
GABRIEL

ALASDAIR
LUCIFER

* Amelia

SIMON

Henrietta

Mary

Heather   Elizabeth   Angelica

Chapter One

March 1, 1820
Newmarket, Suffolk

Unfettered freedom! He'd escaped.

With an arrogant smile, Harold Henry Cynster – Demon to everyone, even to his mother in her weaker moments – drew his curricle to a flourishing halt in the yard behind his Newmarket stable. Tossing the reins to his groom, Gillies, who leaped from the back of the elegant equipage to catch them, Demon stepped down to the cobbles. In a buoyant mood, he ran a loving hand over the glossy bay hide of his leader and scanned the yard with a proprietorial eye.

There was not a scheming mama or disapproving, gimlet-eyed dowager in sight.

Bestowing a last fond pat on his horse's shoulder, Demon headed for the open rear door of the stable. He'd left London at midday, unexpectedly content to have the breeze blow the cloying perfume of a certain lascivious countess from his brain. More than content to leave behind the ballrooms, the parties, and the myriad traps the matchmaking mamas laid for gentlemen such as he. Not that he'd found any difficulty in evading such snares, but, these days, there was a certain scent on the breeze, a presentiment of danger he was too experienced to ignore.

First his cousin Devil, then his own brother Vane, and now his closest cousin, Richard – who next of their select band of six, the Bar Cynster as they were called, would fate cause to trip into the arms of a loving wife?

Whoever it was, it wouldn't be him.

Pausing before the open doors of the stable, he swung around, eyes squinting in the slanting sunlight. Some of his horses were ambling in the paddocks with their lads in close attendance. On the Heath beyond, other stables' strings were exercising under the eyes of owners and trainers.

The scene was an exclusively male one. The fact that he felt entirely at home – indeed, could feel himself relaxing – was ironic. He could hardly claim he didn't like women, didn't enjoy their company. Hadn't – didn't – devote considerable time to their conquest.

He couldn't deny he took pleasure in, and derived considerable satisfaction from, those conquests. He was, after all, a Cynster.

He smiled. All that was true. However . . .

Whereas the other members of the Bar Cynster, as wealthy, well-born gentlemen, had accepted the fact that they would marry and establish families in the timehonored tradition, he had vowed to be different. He'd vowed never to marry, never to tempt the fate with which his brother and cousins had fenced and lost. Marriage to fulfill society's obligations was all very well, but to marry a lady one loved had been the baneful fate of all male Cynsters to date.

A baneful fate indeed for a warrior breed – to be forever at the mercy of a woman. A woman who held one's heart, soul and future in her small, delicate hands.

It was enough to make the strongest warrior blanch.

He was having none of it.

Casting a last glance around the neat yard, approving the swept cobbles, the fences in good repair, Demon turned and entered the main stable housing his racing string. Afternoon stables had already commenced – he would view his exercising horses alongside his very capable trainer, Carruthers.

Demon was on his way to his stud farm, located three miles farther south of the racecourse in the gently undulating countryside bordering the Heath. As he had every intention of avoiding marriage for the term of his natural life, and the current atmosphere in London had turned fraught with the Season about to start, and his aunts, as well as his mother, fired with the excitement of weddings, wives and the consequent babies, so he'd elected to lie low and see out the Season from the safe distance of his stud farm and the unthreatening society of Newmarket.

Fate would have no chance to sneak up on him here.

Looking down to avoid the inevitable detritus left by his favored darlings, he strolled unhurriedly up the long central alley. Boxes loomed to his left and right, all presently empty. At the other end of the building, another pair of doors stood open to the Heath. The day was fine, with a light breeze lifting manes and flicking long tails – his horses were out, doing what they did best. Running.

After spending the last hours with the sun warming his shoulders, the stable's shadows felt cool. A chill unexpectedly washed over the back of his shoulders, then coalesced into an icy tingle and slithered all the way down his spine.

Demon frowned and wriggled his shoulders. Reaching the point where the alley widened into the mounting area, he stopped and looked up.

A familiar sight met his eyes – a lad or work rider swinging a leg over the sleek back of one of his champions. The horse was facing away, wide bay rump to him; Demon recognized one of his current favorites, an Irish gelding sure to run well in the coming season. That, however, was not what transfixed him, rooting his boots to the floor.

He could see nothing of the rider bar his back and one leg. The lad wore a cloth cap pulled low on his head, a shabby hacking jacket and baggy corduroy breeches. Baggy except in one area – where they pulled tight over the rider's rear as he swung his leg over the saddle.

Carruthers stood beside the horse, issuing instructions. The lad dropped into the saddle, then stood in the stirrups to adjust his position. Again, corduroy strained and shifted.

Demon sucked in a breath. Eyes narrowing, jaw firming, he strode forward.

Carruthers slapped the horse's rump. Nodding, the rider trotted the horse, The Mighty Flynn, out into the sunshine.

Carruthers swung around, squinting as Demon came up. 'Oh, it's you.' Despite the abrupt greeting and the dour tone, there was a wealth of affection in Carruthers's old eyes. 'Come to see how they're shaping, have ye?'

Demon nodded, his gaze locked on the rider atop The Mighty Flynn. 'Indeed.'

With Carruthers, he strolled in the wake of The Flynn, the last of his horses to go out on the Heath.

In silence, Demon watched his horses go through their paces. The Mighty Flynn was given a light workout, walking, trotting, then walking again. Although he noted how his other horses performed, Demon's attention never strayed far from The Flynn.

Beside him, Carruthers was watching his charges avidly. Demon glanced his way, noting his old face, much lined, weathered like well-worn leather, faded brown eyes wide as he weighed every stride, considered every turn. Carruthers never took notes, never needed any reminder of which horse had done what. When his charges came in, he would know precisely how each was faring, and what more was needed to bring them to their best. The most experienced trainer in Newmarket, Carruthers knew his horses better than his children, which was why Demon had pestered and persevered until he'd agreed to train for him, to devote his time exclusively to training Demon's string.

His gaze fastening once more on the big bay, Demon murmured, 'The lad on The Flynn – he's new, isn't he?'

'Aye,' Carruthers replied, his gaze never leaving the horses. 'Lad from down Lidgate way. Ickley did a runner – leastways, I assume he did. He didn't turn up one morning and we haven't seen him since. 'Bout a week later, young Flick turned up, looking for a ride, so I had him up on one of the tetchy ones.' Carruthers nodded to where The Flynn was trotting along, pacing neatly with the rest of the string, the small figure on his back managing him with startling ease. 'Rode the brute easily. So I put him up on The Flynn. Never seen the horse give his heart so willingly. The lad's got the touch, no doubt about that. Excellent hands, and good bottom.'

Demon inwardly admitted he couldn't argue. 'Good,' however, was not the adjective he'd have used. But he must have been mistaken. Carruthers was a staunch member of the fraternity, quite the last man to let a female on one of his charges, let alone trust her with The Flynn.

And yet. . .

There was a niggle, a persistent whisper in his mind, something stronger than suspicion flitting through his brain. And at one level – the one where his senses ruled – he *knew* he wasn't wrong.

No lad had ever had a bottom like that.

The thought reconjured the vision; Demon shifted and inwardly cursed. He'd left the countess only a few hours ago; his lustful demons had no business being awake, much less raising their collective head. 'This Flick . . .' Saying the name triggered something – a memory? If the lad was local, he might have stumbled across him before. 'How long's he been with us?'

Carruthers was still absorbed with the horses, now cooling before walking in. 'Be two weeks, now.'

'And he pulls his full load?'

'I've only got him on half-pay – didn't really need another hand with the stablework. Only needed him for riding – exercising and the gallops. Turned out that suited him well enough. His mum's not well, so he rides up here, does morning stables, then rides back to Lidgate to keep her company, then comes up again for afternoon stables.'

'Hmm.' The first horses were returning; Demon drew back into the stable, standing with Carruthers to the side of the mounting area as the stable lads walked their charges in. Most of the lads were known to him. While exchanging greetings and the occasional piece of news, and running knowledgeable eyes over his string, Demon never lost sight of The Flynn.

Flick ambled at the rear of the string. He'd exchanged no more than brief nods and occasional words with the other lads; amid the general camaraderie, Flick appeared a loner. But the other lads seemed to see nothing odd in Flick; they passed him as he walked the huge bay, patting the silky neck and, judging from the horse's twitching ears, murmuring sweet nothings with absolute acceptance. Demon inwardly cursed and wondered, yet again, if he could possibly be wrong.

The Flynn was the last in; Demon stood, hands on hips, to one side of Carruthers in the shadows, shadows rendered even deeper by the sudden brilliance of the westering sun. Flick let the bay have a last prance before settling him and guiding him into the stable. As the first heavy hoof clopped hollowly on the flags, Flick looked up.

Eyes used to the sunshine blinked wide, finding Carruthers, then quickly passing on to fix on Demon. On his face.

Flick reined in, eyes widening even more.

For one, tense instant, rider and owner simply stared.

Jerking the reins, Flick wheeled The Flynn, sending Carruthers a horrified glance. 'He's still restless – I'll take him for a quick run.' With that, she and The Flynn were gone, leaving only a rush of wind behind them.

'What the—!' Carruthers started forward, then stopped as the futility of any chase registered. Bemused, he turned to Demon. 'He's never done anything like that before.'

A curse was Demon's only answer; he was already striding along the alley. He stopped at the first open box, where a lad was easing the girth strap on one of his heavier horses.

'Leave that.' Demon shouldered the startled lad aside. With one tug and a well-placed knee, he recinched the girth. He vaulted into the saddle and backed the horse, fumbling with the stirrup straps.

'Here – I can send one of the lads after him.' Carruthers stepped back as Demon trotted the horse past.

'No – leave it to me. I'll straighten the *lad* out.'

Demon doubted Carruthers caught the emphasis; he wasn't about to stop and explain. Muttering, he set out in hot pursuit.

The instant his mount cleared the stable door, he dug in his heels; the horse lengthened his stride from trot to canter to gallop. By then, Demon had located his prey. In the far distance, disappearing into the shadows thrown by a stand of trees. Another minute and he'd have lost her.

Jaw setting, he struggled with the stirrups as he pounded along. Curses and oaths colored the wind of his passage. Finally, the stirrups were lengthened enough; he settled properly into the saddle, and the chase began in earnest.

The bobbing figure on the back of The Flynn shot a glance behind, then looked forward. A second later, The Flynn swerved and lengthened his stride.

Demon tacked, trying to close the gap by cutting diagonally across – only to find himself careening toward a stretch of rough. Forced to slow and turn aside, he glanced up – and

7

discovered that Flick had abruptly swung the other way and was making off in a different direction. Instead of shortening, the distance between them had grown.

Jaw clenched, eyes narrowed, Demon forgot about swearing and concentrated on riding. Within two minutes, he'd altered his initial plan – to ride Flick down and demand an explanation – to simply keeping the damned female in sight.

She rode like a demon – even better than he. It didn't seem possible, but...

He was a superlative rider, quite possibly the most accomplished of his day. He could ride anything with four legs, mane and tail anywhere, over any terrain. But Flick was leading him a merry dance. And it wasn't simply the fact that his horse was already tired or that he rode much heavier than she. The Flynn was tired, too, and was being ridden harder; Flick was fleeing; he was only following. But she seemed to merge with her mount in that way only other expert riders could understand.

He understood it and couldn't help admiring it grudgingly, even while acknowledging he had not a hope in hell of catching her.

Her. There was no doubt of that now. Lads did not have delicate shoulders and collarbones, swanlike necks, and hands that, even encased in leather gloves, looked small and fine-boned. As for her face, the little he'd glimpsed above the woollen muffler wound about her nose and chin had been more Madonnalike than manlike.

A female called Flick. In the distant recesses of his brain, a memory stirred, too insubstantial to catch and hold. He tried to coax it further into the light, and failed. He was sure he'd never called any female Flick.

She was still a good two furlongs ahead of him, maintaining the distance with ease. They were riding directly west, out onto the less frequented stretches of the Heath. They'd sped past a number of strings out exercising; heads had come up to watch them in surprise. He saw her glance around again; an instant later, she swerved. Grimly determined, Demon squinted into the setting sun and followed in her tracks.

He might not be able to ride her down, but he'd be damned if he'd lose her.

His resolution had, by now, communicated itself quite effectively to Flick. Making a few choice observations about London-bound rakes who came up to their stud farms with not a moment's notice and then proceeded to get in the way, to throw her off her stride, to plunge her into a ridiculous fluster, she irritatedly, and not a little frantically, reviewed her options.

There weren't many. While she could easily ride for another hour, The Flynn couldn't. And the horse Demon was on would fare even worse. And, despite the knot of sheer panic in her stomach, there wasn't any point fleeing, anyway.

She would, one way or another, either now or only marginally later, have to face Demon. She didn't know if he'd recognized her, but in that frozen instant in the stable when his blue gaze had raked her, she'd got the impression he'd seen through her disguise.

In fact, the impression she'd got was that he'd seen right through her clothes – a distinctly unnerving sensation.

Yet even if he hadn't realized she was female, her impulsive reaction had made a confrontation unavoidable. She'd run – and she couldn't possibly explain that, not without giving him, and his memories, far too many hints as to her identity.

Catching her breath on a hiccup, Flick glanced back; he was still there, doggedly following. Turning forward, she noted their location. She'd led him west, then south, skirting the stables and paddocks edging the racecourse, then heading farther onto the open Heath. She glanced at the sun. They had at least an hour before twilight. With all the others back at the

9

stables settling horses for the night, this part of the Heath was now deserted. If she found a spot where they were reasonably screened, it would be as good a place as any for the meeting that, it now seemed, had to be.

Honesty was her only option. In truth, she would prefer it – lies and evasion had never been her style.

A hundred yards ahead, a hedge beckoned. Her memory provided a picture of what lay beyond. The Flynn was tiring; she leaned forward and stroked the glossy neck, whispering words of praise, encouragement and outright flattery into his ear. Then she set him for the hedge.

The Flynn soared over it, landing easily. Flick absorbed the jolt and wheeled left, into the long shadows thrown by a copse. In the space between the hedge and the copse, screened on three sides, she reined in and waited.

And waited.

After five minutes, she started to wonder if Demon had looked away at the crucial moment and not seen where she'd gone. When another minute passed and she sensed no ground-shaking thuds, she frowned and straightened in her saddle. She was about to gather her reins and move out to search for her pursuer when she saw him.

He hadn't jumped the hedge. Despite his wish to catch her, wisdom – care for his horse – had prevailed; he'd gone along the hedge until he'd found a gap. Now he cantered up through the late afternoon, broad shoulders square, long limbs relaxed, head up, the sun striking gold from his burnished curls, his face a grim mask as he scanned the fields ahead, trying to catch sight of her.

Flick froze. It was tempting – so tempting – to sit still. To look her fill, and let him pass by, to worship from afar as she had for years, letting her senses feast while she remained safely hidden. If she made no sound, it was unlikely he would see her. She wouldn't have to face him unfortunately, there were too many hurdles along that road. Stiffening her spine, taking a firm grip on her unruly senses, she lifted her chin. 'Demon!'

His head snapped around; he wheeled aggressively, then saw her. Even at that distance, his gaze pinned her, then he scanned her surroundings. Apparently satisfied, he set his grey trotting toward her, slowing to a walk as he neared.

He was wearing an elegant morning coat of a blue that matched his eyes; his long thighs, gripping the saddle skirts, were encased in tight buckskin. Ivory shirt, ivory cravat and gleaming Hessians completed the picture. He looked what he was – the very epitome of a London rake.

Flick kept her gaze fixed on his face and wished, very much, that she were taller. The closer he came, the smaller she felt – the more childlike. She was no longer a child, but she'd known him since she had been. It was hard to feel assured. With her cap shading her face, her muffler over her nose and chin, she couldn't imagine how he might see her – as a girl still with pigtails, or as the young lady who'd trenchantly avoided him. She'd been both, but she was neither now. What she was now was on a crusade. A crusade in which she could use his help. If he consented to give it.

Lips firming beneath her muffler, she tilted her chin and met his hard stare.

Demon's memories churned as he walked his horse into the copse's shadow. She'd called him 'Demon' – only someone who knew him would do that. Images from the past jumbled and tumbled, glimpses through the years of a child, a girl, who would without a blush call him Demon. Of a girl who could ride – oh, yes, she'd always ridden, but when had she become a maestro? – of a girl he had long ago pegged as having that quality Carruthers described as 'good bottom' – that open-hearted courage that bordered on the reckless, but wasn't.

11

When he stopped his horse, nose to tail with The Flynn, he had her well and truly placed. Not Flick. Felicity.

Eyes like slits, he held her trapped; reaching out, he tugged the concealing muffler from her face.

And found himself looking down at a Botticelli angel.

Found himself drowning in limpid blue eyes paler than his own. Found his gaze irresistibly drawn to lips perfectly formed and tinged the most delicate rose pink he'd ever seen.

He was sinking. Fast. And he wasn't resisting.

Sucking in a breath, he drew back, inwardly shocked at how far under he'd gone. Shaking free of the lingering spell, he scowled at its source. 'What the damn hell do you think you're about?'

12

Chapter Two

She tilted her chin – a delicate, pointy little chin. Set as it was, it looked decidedly stubborn.

'I'm masquerading as a stable lad, in your stables, so—'

'What a *damn fool* lark! What the *devil*—'

'It's *not* a lark!' Her blue eyes flashed; her expression turned belligerent. 'I'm doing it for the General!'

'The General?' General Sir Gordon Caxton was Demon's neighbor and mentor, and Felicity's – Flick's – guardian. Demon scowled. 'You're not going to tell me the General knows about this?'

'Of course not!'

The Flynn shifted; tight-lipped, Demon waited while Flick quieted the big bay.

Her gaze flickered over him, irritated and considering in equal measure, then steadied on his face.

'It's all because of Dillon.'

'Dillon?' Dillon was the General's son. Flick and Dillon were of similar age. Demon's most recent memories of Dillon were of a dark-haired youth, swaggering about the General's house, Hillgate End, giving himself airs and undeserved graces.

'Dillon's in trouble.'

Demon got the distinct impression she only just avoided adding 'again.'

'He became involved – inadvertently – with a racefixing racket.'

'*What?*' He bit off the word, then had to settle his mount. The words 'race-fixing' sent a chill down his spine.

Flick frowned at him. 'That's when jockeys are paid to ease back on a horse, or cause a disruption, or—'

He glared at her. 'I *know* what race-fixing entails. That doesn't explain what *you're* doing mixed up in it.'

'I'm *not!*' Indignation colored her cheeks.

'*What* are you doing masquerading as a lad, then?'

Her soft blue eyes flashed. 'If you'd *stop* interrupting, I'd be able to tell you!'

Demon reined in his temper, set his jaw, and pointedly waited. After a moment's fraught silence, blue eyes locked with blue, Flick nodded and put her pert nose in the air.

'Dillon was approached some weeks ago by a man and asked to take a message to a jockey about the first race of the season. He didn't see any reason he shouldn't, so he agreed. I suspect he thought it would be a lark – or that it made him more involved with the racing – but he agreed to carry the message to the jockey, then didn't. Couldn't. He got a chill and Mrs. Fogarty and I insisted he stay in bed – we took away his clothes, so he had to. Of course, he didn't say *why* he kept trying to struggle up. Not then.'

She drew breath. 'So the message didn't get passed on. It was an instruction to fix the race, so the race, therefore, wasn't fixed. It now seems that the man who approached Dillon was working for some sort of syndicate – a group of some description – and because the race wasn't fixed and they didn't know it, they lost a lot of money.'

'Men came looking for Dillon – rough men. Luckily, Jacobs and Mrs. Fogarty didn't like their style – they said Dillon was away. So now he's in hiding and fears for his life.'

Demon exhaled and sat back in his saddle. From what he

knew of the unsavory types involved in race-fixing, Dillon had good cause to worry. He studied Flick. 'Where's he hiding?'

She straightened, and fixed him with a very direct look. 'I can't tell you – not unless you're willing to help us.'

Demon returned her gaze with one even more severe, and distinctly more aggravated. 'Of *course* I'm going to help you!' What did she think he was? Beneath his breath, he swore. 'How's the General going to take it if his only son is charged with race-fixing?'

Flick's expression immediately eased; Demon knew he couldn't have said anything more convincing – not to her. More devoted than a daughter, she was intensely protective of the ageing General. She thought the world of him, as did he. She actually nodded approvingly.

'Precisely. And that, I'm afraid, is one of the things we especially fear, because the man who hired Dillon definitely knew he was the General's son.'

Demon inwardly grimaced. The General was the preeminent authority on English and Irish Thoroughbreds and revered throughout the racing industry. The syndicate had planned well. 'So where's Dillon hiding?'

Flick considered him, one last measuring glance. 'In the tumbledown cottage on the far corner of your land.'

'*My* land?'

'It was safer than anywhere on the Caxton estate.'

He couldn't argue – the Caxton estate comprised just the house and its surrounding park. The General had a fortune invested in the Funds and needed no farms to distract him. He'd sold off his acres years ago – Demon had bought some of the land himself. He shot a glance at Flick, sitting comfortably astride The Flynn. 'My horses, my cottage – what else have you been making free with?'

She blushed slightly but didn't reply. Demon couldn't help

but notice how fine her skin was, unblemished ivory silk now tinged a delicate rose. She was a painter's dream; she would have had Botticelli slavering. The idea brought to mind the painter's diaphanously clad angels; in a blink of his mental eye, he had Flick similarly clothed. And the tantalizing question of how that ivory skin, which he'd wager would extend all over her, would look when flushed with passion formed in the forefront of his brain.

Abruptly, he refocused. Good God – what was he thinking? Flick was the General's ward, and not much more than a child. How old was she? He frowned at her. 'None of what you've said explains what *you're* doing here, dressed like that, working my latest champion.'

'I'm hoping to identify the man who contacted Dillon. Dillon only met him at night – he never saw him well enough to recognize or describe. Now Dillon's not available to act as his messenger, the man will have to contact someone else, someone who can easily speak to the race jockeys.'

'So you're hanging around my stables morning and afternoon, hoping this man approaches *you*?' Aghast, he stared at her.

'Not *me*. One of the others – the older lads who know all the race jockeys. I'm there to keep watch and overhear anything I can.'

He continued to stare at her while considering all the holes in her story. Clearly, he'd have to fill them in one by one. 'How the hell did you persuade Carruthers to hire you? Or doesn't he know?'

'Of *course* he doesn't know. No one does. But it wasn't difficult to get hired. I heard Ickley had disappeared – Dillon was told Ickley had agreed to act as messenger for this season, but changed his mind at the last. That's why they approached Dillon. So I knew Carruthers was shorthanded.'

Demon's lips thinned. Flick continued. 'So I dressed

appropriately' – with a sweeping gesture, she indicated her garb – 'and went to see Carruthers. Everyone in Newmarket knows Carruthers can't see well close to, so I didn't think I'd have any difficulty. All I had to do was ride for him and he'd take me on.'

Demon swallowed a snort. 'What about the others – the other lads, the jockeys? They're not all half-blind.'

The look Flick bent on him was the epitome of feminine condescension. 'Have you ever stood in a working stable and watched how often the men – lads or trainers – look at each other? The horses, yes, but they never do more than glance at the humans working alongside. The others see me all the time, but they never look. *You're* the only one who looked.'

Accusation colored her tone. Demon swallowed his retort that he'd have to have been dead not to look. He also resisted the urge to inform her she should be grateful he had; just the thought of what she'd blithely got herself into, squaring up to expose a race-fixing syndicate, chilled him.

Race-fixing syndicates were dangerous, controlled by men to whom the lives of others meant little. The lives of people like Ickley. Demon made a mental note to find out what had happened to Ickley. The idea that Flick had set herself up as Ickley's replacement was enough to turn his hair grey. Gazing at her face, on her openly determined expression, it was on the tip of his tongue to terminate her employment immediately.

Recollection of how her chin had set earlier made him hold the words back. Pretty little chin, delicately tapered. And too stubborn by half.

There was a great deal he did not yet know, a great deal he didn't as yet understand.

The horses were cooling, the sun slowly sinking. His mount shifted, coat flickering. Demon drew breath. 'Let's get back, then I'll go and see Dillon.'

17

Flick nodded, urging The Flynn into a walk. 'I'll come, too. Well, I have to. That's where I change clothes and switch horses.'

'Horses?'

She threw him a wary glance. 'I couldn't turn up for work riding Jessamy – *that* they'd certainly notice.'

Jessamy, Demon recalled, was a dainty mare with exceptional bloodlines; the General had bought her last year. Apparently for Flick. He glanced at her. 'So?...'

She drew breath and looked ahead. 'So I borrow the old cob you let run on your back paddock. I don't ride him above a canter, if that. I'm very careful of him.'

She looked up. He trapped her gaze. 'Anything else you've borrowed?'

Big blue eyes blinked wide. 'I don't think so.'

'All right. We'll ride these two back, then you climb on the cob and head off. I'll leave in my curricle. I'll drive home, then ride out and join you. I'll meet you by the split oak on the road to Lidgate.'

She nodded. 'Very well. But we'll need to hurry now. Come on.' She leaned forward, effortlessly shifting The Flynn from walk, to trot, to canter.

And left him staring after her. With a curse, he dug in his heels and set out in her wake.

He reached the split oak before her.

By the time she appeared, trotting the old cob, long past his prime, down the middle of the road, Demon had decided that, whatever transpired with Dillon, he would ensure that one point was made clear.

He was in charge from now on. She'd asked for his help; she would get it, but on his terms.

From now on, he'd lead and *she* could follow.

As she neared, her gaze slid from him to his mount, a

raking grey hunter who went by the revealing name of Ivan the Terrible. He was a proud and princely beast with a foul, dangerous, potentially lethal temper. As the cob drew closer, Ivan rolled one eye and stamped.

The cob was too old to pay the slightest attention. Flick's brows, however, rose; her gaze passed knowledgeably over Ivan's more positive points as she reined in. 'I *know* I haven't seen him before.'

Demon made no reply. He waited – and waited – until she finished examining his horse and lifted her gaze to his face. Then he smiled. 'I bought him late last year.' Flick's eyes, suddenly riveted on his face, widened slightly. She mouthed an 'Oh,' and looked away.

Side by side, they rode on, the cob doggedly plodding, Ivan placing his hooves with restless disdain. 'What did you tell Carruthers?' Flick asked with a sidelong glance. When they'd returned to the stable, Flick had been in the lead. Carruthers had been standing, hands on hips, in the stable door. From behind Flick, Demon had signalled him away; Carruthers had stared, but, as Flick had trotted The Flynn up, he'd stood aside and let her pass without question. By that time, Carruthers and the nightwatchman, a retired jockey, had been the only ones left in the stable.

Handing his mount to the nightwatchman to unsaddle, Demon had set about mollifying Carruthers.

'I told him I knew you as a brat from near Lidgate, and you'd feared that, recognizing you, I'd terminate your employment immediately.' The twilight was deepening; they jogged along as fast as the cob could manage. 'However, having seen you ride, and being convinced of your fervent wish to work my horses, I said I'd agreed to let you stay on.'

Flick frowned. 'He came in and all but shooed me off – said he'd settle The Flynn and I should get on home without delay.'

'I mentioned that I knew your sick mother and how she'd

worry – I instructed Carruthers that you shouldn't pull duties that will keep you late, and that you should leave in plenty of time to reach home before dark.'

Although he was examining the scenery and not looking at her, Demon still felt Flick's suspicious glance. It confirmed his opinion that she didn't need to know about the other instructions he'd issued to his trainer. Carruthers, thankfully not an imaginative or garrulous sort, had stared at him, then shrugged and acquiesced.

They left the road and turned into a sunken track between two fields. The cob, sensing home and dinner, broke into a trot; Ivan, forced to remain alongside, accepted the edict with typical bad grace, tossing his head and jerking his reins every few yards.

'He's obviously in need of exercise,' Flick remarked.

'I'll give him a run later.'

'I'm surprised you let him get into such a bad temper.'

Demon stifled an acid retort. 'He's been here, I've been in London, and no one can ride him but me.'

'Oh.'

Lifting her gaze, Flick looked ahead to where the track wended into a small wood; she fell to studying the trees.

From under his lashes, Demon studied her. She'd examined his horse so thoroughly she probably knew his every line, yet she'd barely glanced at him. Ivan was indeed a handsome beast, as were all his cattle, but he wasn't used to taking second place to his mount. Which might seem arrogant, but he knew women – girls and ladies, females of any description – well.

It wasn't simply that she hadn't looked. His senses, well honed through his years on the prowl, could detect not the slightest flicker of consciousness – the minutest suggestion of awareness – in the female riding beside him.

Which, in his experience, was odd. Distinctly odd.

The fact that her lack of awareness was focusing his to a remarkable degree hadn't escaped him. It didn't surprise him; he was a born hunter. When the prey didn't take cover, he – at least that part of him that operated on instinct first, logic second – saw it as a challenge.

Which was, in this case, ridiculous.

There was no reason a girl like Flick, raised quietly in the country, should be aware, in any sexual sense, of a gentleman like him – especially one she'd known all her life.

Demon frowned, tightening the reins as Ivan tried to surge. Disgusted, the big grey snorted; Demon managed not to do the same.

He still had no idea precisely how old she was. He glanced her way, covertly confirming details he'd instinctively noted. She'd always been petite, although he hadn't seen her in recent years. In her present incarnation, he'd only seen her atop a horse, but he doubted her head would clear his shoulder. Her figure remained a mystery, except for her definitely feminine bottom – a classic inverted heart, sleekly rounded. The rest of her was amply disguised by her stable lad's garb. Whether she wore bands about her breasts, as did many devoted female riders, he couldn't tell, but her overall proportions were nice. Slim, slender – she might well be delectable.

On the way back to the stables, she'd tugged her muffler up over her nose and chin so the swath hid most of her face. As for her hair, she'd stuffed it under her cap so thoroughly that, beyond the fact it was as brightly golden as he recalled, he couldn't tell how she wore it. A few short strands had slipped free at her nape, sheening against her collar like spun gold.

Looking forward, he inwardly frowned. It wasn't simply that there were lots of things he didn't yet know about her that bothered him. The very fact he wanted to know bothered him. This was Flick, the General's ward.

General Sir Gordon Caxton had been his mentor in all

matters pertaining to horses since he'd been six. That was when, while visiting with his late great-aunt Charlotte, he'd first met the General. Thereafter, whenever he'd been in the locality, he'd spent as much time as possible with the General, learning everything he could about breeding Thoroughbreds. It was due to the General, to his knowledge freely shared and his unstinting encouragement, that he, Demon, was now one of the preeminent breeders of quality horseflesh in the British Isles.

He owed the General a great deal.

A fact he could never forget. He comforted himself with that thought as he trotted beside Flick into the trees beyond which stood the old cottage.

Once a tenant farmer's home, it was now one step away from a ruin. From the rutted lane meandering up to its warped and sagging door, the structure looked uninhabitable. Only on closer inspection could one discern that the roof of the main room was still mostly intact, the four walls enclosing it still standing.

With an imperious gesture, Flick led the way around the cottage. Briefly raising his eyes to the skies, Demon fol lowed, entering a grassy clearing enclosed by trees. A sharp whinny greeted them. Eagerly, Flick urged the cob on. Looking across the clearing, Demon saw Jessamy, a pretty golden-coated mare with pale mane and tail and the most exquisite conformation he'd ever seen. She was tethered on a long rein.

Ivan saw Jessamy, too, and concurred with Demon's assessment. Still held on tight rein, Ivan reared and trum-peted. Only excellent reflexes saved Demon from an embarrassing unseating. Smothering an oath, he wrestled Ivan down, then forced him to the other side of the clearing, ignor-ing the combined, slightly insulted stares of Flick, Jessamy and the cob.

Dismounting, Demon double-tied Ivan's reins to a large tree. 'Behave yourself,' he ordered, then turned away, leaving the stallion, head up, staring with complete and absolute absorption across the clearing.

Having turned the cob loose, Flick dumped her saddle on a convenient log and gave Jessamy, who clearly adored her, a fond pat. Then, with another imperious, beckoning wave, she led the way around the far side of the cottage.

Muttering beneath his breath, Demon strode after her.

He rounded the cottage – Flick was nowhere in sight. A lean-to had been tacked onto the cottage on that side. The lean-to hadn't survived as well as the cottage – its outer wall was crumbling and half its roof had disappeared. Flick had ducked through an opening, a door that had never been planned. Hearing her voice in the main room beyond, Demon ducked beneath the canted beams; easing his shoulders through the narrow space, he stepped silently through the debris and entered the cottage proper.

And saw Flick standing beside Dillon Caxton, who was sitting at one end of an old table, blankets wrapped about his shoulders. She was bent over him; as Demon entered, she straightened, frowning, her hand on Dillon's brow. 'You don't have any sign of a fever.'

Dillon didn't respond, his eyes, large and dark, framed by long black lashes, fixed on Demon. Then he coughed, glanced at Flick, then at Demon. 'Ah ... hello. Come in! I'm afraid it's rather cold in here – we daren't light a fire.'

Mentally noting that the cottage was *his* property, Demon merely nodded. In such flat countryside, smoke could easily be traced, and smoke rising from an area thought to be uninhabited would certainly attract attention. Holding Dillon's increasingly wary gaze, he strolled the few paces to the other end of the table, to a stool that appeared sufficiently robust to support his weight. 'Flick mentioned that there were gentlemen about whose company you were keen to avoid.'

Color flooded Dillon's pale cheeks. 'Ah, yes. Flick said

23

you'd agreed to help.' With one long-fingered hand, he combed back the thick lock of dark hair that fell, in perfect Byronic imitation, across his brow, and he smiled engagingly. 'I can't tell you how much I appreciate it.'

Demon held Dillon's impossibly innocent gaze for a moment, then hitched up the stool and sat, declining to mention that it was for the General's sake, and Flick's, that he was involving himself in a mess that, as an owner of racing Thoroughbreds, he'd much rather hand straight to the magistrates.

Dillon glanced up at Flick; she was frowning slightly at Demon. 'Flick didn't say how much she's told you—'

'Enough for me to understand what's been going on.' Resting his arms on the table, Demon looked at Dillon and didn't like what he saw. The fact that Flick was hovering protectively at Dillon's shoulder contributed to his assessment only marginally; much more telling were his memories, observations made over the years, and the facts of the current imbroglio, not as Flick had innocently described them but as he knew they must be.

He didn't doubt she'd faithfully recounted all she'd been told; the truth, he knew, was more damning than that.

His smile held the right degree of male camaraderie to appeal to a youth like Dillon. 'I'd like to hear your observations direct. Let's start with your meeting with this character who asked you to carry a message.'

'What do you want to know?'

'The how, the when, the where. The words.'

'Well, the when was nearly three weeks ago, just before the first race of the year.'

'Just before?'

Dillon nodded. 'Two days before.'

'Two days?' Demon raised his brows. 'That seems awfully short notice to arrange a fix, don't you think? The general

24

consensus is that these syndicates lay their plans well in advance. It's something of an imperative, given the number of bookmakers and other supporting characters necessarily involved.'

Dillon's eyes blanked. 'Oh?' Then his smile flashed. 'Actually, the man did say they'd had another messenger – Ickley – he used to work at your stables – lined up to do the job, but he'd changed his mind. So they needed someone else.'

'And so they came to you. Why?'

The single word startled Dillon, then he shrugged. 'I don't know – I suppose they were looking for someone who knew their way about. Knew the jockeys, and the places to go to rub the right shoulders.'

Flick settled onto a stool. She was frowning more definitely, but her frown was now aimed at Dillon.

'Why did you imagine this man didn't just ask you to point out the particular jockey and speak to him himself?'

Dillon's brows drew down sharply; after a moment, he shook his head. 'I don't follow.'

'Surely you wondered why it was necessary for this man to have a messenger at all?' Demon trapped Dillon's gaze. 'If the messages were innocent, why did the man need to hire you – or anyone – to deliver them?'

Dillon's trademark smile flashed. 'Ah, but the messages weren't innocent, you see.'

'Oh, I do see,' Demon assured him. 'But you didn't know that before they hired you, did you?'

'Well ... no.'

'So why didn't you simply tell this man where he could find the jockey? Why be his go-between?'

'Well, because ... I suppose I thought he might not want to be seen ... well, no.'

Demon recaptured Dillon's gaze. 'No, indeed. How much

25

did they pay you?'

Every drop of blood drained from Dillon's face; his eyes grew darker, wilder. 'I – don't know what you mean.'

Demon held his gaze unblinkingly. 'This would not, I suggest, be a good time to lie. How much did they pay you?'

Dillon flushed.

Flick sprang to her feet. 'You took *money*?' Behind her, the stool clattered on the flags. 'You took money to carry a message to fix a race?'

The accusation in her tone would have made the Devil flinch; Dillon did not. 'It was only two ponies – just for the one message. I wasn't going to do it any more. That's why they got Ickley.'

'Any *more*?' Flick stared at him. 'What do you mean 'any more'?'

Dillon's expression turned mulish; Flick leaned both hands on the table and looked him in the eye. 'Dillon – *how long*? How long have you been taking money to carry messages for these men?'

He tried to keep silent, tried to withstand the demand in her tone, the scorn in her eyes. 'Since last summer.'

'Last *summer*?' Flick straightened, shoving the table in her agitation. 'Good God! *Why*?' She stared at Dillon. 'What on earth possessed you?'

Demon held silent; as an avenging angel, Flick had a distinct advantage.

Turning sulky, Dillon pushed back from the table. 'It was the money, of course.' He attempted a sneer, but it bounced off Flick's righteous fury.

'The General gives you a very generous allowance – why would you want more?'

Dillon laughed brittlely and leaned his arms on the table. He avoided Flick's outraged stare.

Which did nothing to soothe her temper. 'And if you

needed more, you know you only had to ask. I always have plenty . . .' Her words trailed away; she blinked, then her eyes blazed. She refocused on Dillon. 'You've been gambling at the cockfights again, haven't you?' Scorn – raw disgust – poured through her words. 'Your father forbade it, but you couldn't leave it be. And *now*—!' Sheer fury choked her; she gestured wildly.

'Cockfighting's not that bad,' Dillon countered, still sulky. 'It's not as if it's something other gentlemen don't do.' He glanced at Demon.

'Don't look at me,' Demon returned. 'Not my style at all.'

'It's disgusting!' Flick looked directly at Dillon. 'You're disgusting, too.' She whirled and swooped on a pile of clothes set on an old chest. 'I'm going to change.'

Demon glimpsed the blue velvet skirts of a stylish riding habit as she stormed past him out into the ruined lean-to.

Silence descended in the main room; Demon let it stretch. He watched Dillon squirm, then stiffen his spine, only to wilt again. When he judged it was time, he quietly said, 'I rather think you'd better tell us the whole of it.'

Eyes on the table, on the fingertip with which he traced circles on the scratched surface, Dillon drew a shaky breath. 'I ran messages the whole autumn season. I owed a cent-per-cent in Bury St. Edmunds – he said I had to pay up before year's end or he'd come and see the General. I had to get the money somewhere. Then the man – the one who brings the messages – found me.' He paused, but didn't look up. 'I always thought it was the cent-per-cent who nudged him my way, to ensure I'd be in a position to pay.'

Demon thought that very likely.

Dillon shrugged. 'Anyway, it was easy enough – easy money, I thought.'

A choking sound came from the lean-to; Dillon flushed. 'Well, it was easy last year. Then, when the man brought the messages for the last few weeks of races, I told him I wouldn't do it any more. He said, 'We'll see,' and I left it at that. I didn't expect to see him again, but two nights before the first race this year, he found me. At a cockfight.'

The sound from the lean-to was eloquent – mingled disbelief, frustration and fury.

Dillon grimaced. 'He told me Ickley had balked, and that I'd have to do the job until they could find a 'suitable replacement.' That's how he phrased it.' Dillon paused, then offered, 'I think that means someone they have some hold over, because he said, bold as brass, that if I didn't agree they'd tell the authorities what I'd done, and make sure everyone knew I was the General's son. Well, I did it. Took the message. And the money. And then I got sick.'

Demon could almost have felt sorry for him. Almost. The flies in the ointment were the General, and Flick's sniff of disillusionment that came from behind him.

After a moment, Dillon wearily straightened. 'That's all of it.' He met Demon's gaze. 'I swear. If you'll believe me.'

Demon didn't answer. Forearms on the table, he steepled his fingers; it was time to take charge. 'As I see it, we have two objectives – one, to keep you out of the syndicate's way until, two, we've identified your contact, traced him back to his masters – the syndicate – and unmasked at least one member of said syndicate, and have enough proof for you to take to the magistrate, so that, in turning yourself in as a witless pawn caught up in a greater game, you can plead for leniency.'

He looked up; Dillon blanched, but met his gaze. A moment passed, and Demon raised his brows.

Dillon swallowed, and nodded. 'Yes, all right.'

'So we need to identify your contact. Flick said you never saw him clearly.'

Dillon shook his head. 'He was always careful – he'd

come up to me as I was leaving the pit in the dark, or come sidling up in the shadows.'

'What's his height, his build?'

'Medium to tall, heavy build.' Dillon's frown lifted. 'One thing recognizable is his voice – it's oddly rough, like his throat is scratched, and he has a London accent.'

Demon nodded, considering. Then he refocused. 'Flick's idea is the only reasonable way forward – we'll have to keep watch about the tracks and stables to see who approaches the race jockeys. I'll handle that.'

'I'll help.'

The statement came from behind him; Demon glanced around, then rose spontaneously to his feet. Luckily, Flick was coldly glaring at Dillon, which allowed him to get his expression back under control before she glanced at him.

When she did, he met her gaze impassively, but he remained standing.

He'd guessed right – her head didn't top his shoulder. Bright, guinea-gold curls formed an aureole about her face; without muffler or cap, he could see the whole clearly, and it took his breath away. Her figure, neat and trim in blue velvet, met with his instant approval. Sleek and svelte, but with firm curves in all the right places. He could now take an oath that she must have worn tight bands to appear as she had before; the swells of her breasts filled the habit's tightly fitting bodice in a distinctly feminine way.

She swept forward with an easy, confident grace, then bent to place her neatly folded stable lad's outfit on the chest, in the process giving him a reminder of why he'd first seen through her disguise.

He blinked and drew in a much needed breath.

She looked like an angel, dressed in blue velvet.

A still very angry angel. She ignored Dillon and faced Demon. 'I'll keep your stables under surveillance – you can

29

watch the other stables and other places I can't go.'

'There's no need—'

'The more eyes we have watching, the more likely we'll be to see him. And I'll hear things that you, as the owner, won't.' She met his gaze steadily. 'If they recruited Ickley, there's a good chance they'd like to hobble one of your runners – you'll have quite a few favorites in the races this season.'

The Flynn, among others. Demon held her gaze, and saw her chin firm, saw it tilt, saw defiance and sheer stubborn will flash in her eyes.

'That's right,' Dillon concurred. 'There's a lot of Newmarket to cover, and Flick's already been accepted as one of your lads.'

Demon stared, pointedly, at him; Dillon shrugged. 'She's in no danger – it's me they're after.'

If Demon had been closer, he would have kicked Dillon; eyes narrowing, he was tempted to do it anyway. Only the fact that he hadn't yet determined how Flick saw Dillon – if she reserved the right to kick him to herself, and would fly to Dillon's defense if he administered any of the punishment Dillon so richly deserved – kept him still.

Dillon glanced at Flick. 'You could even try riding for some of the other stables.'

Flick looked down her nose at him. 'I'll stick to Demon's stable – he can look over the others.'

Her tone was cold and distant; Dillon shrugged petulantly. 'You don't have to help if you don't want to.'

He looked down at the table and so missed the fury that poured from Flick's eyes. 'Just so we're perfectly clear,' she stated, 'I am only helping you because of the General – because of what having you taken up, without any evidence of a syndicate to redeem you in any way, will do to him. *That's* why I'm helping you.'

Head high, she swung on her heel and stalked out.

Demon paused, looking at Dillon, now staring sulkily at the table. 'Stay here. If you value your life, stay out of sight.'

Dillon's eyes widened; with a curt nod, Demon followed Flick into the deep twilight.

He found her saddling Jessamy, her movements swift and jerky. He didn't offer to help; he suspected she could saddle up blind – indeed, he wasn't at all sure she wasn't doing that now.

Hurt and anger poured off her; disillusionment shimmered about her. Propping his shoulders against a convenient tree, Demon glanced across the clearing to where Ivan was still standing in exactly the same pose as an hour ago – staring at his new lady love.

Brows quirking, Demon turned back to Flick. Her head was just visible over Jessamy's back. He considered the halo of gold, the delicate features beneath.

She was furious with Dillon, hurt that he hadn't told her the truth, and shocked by the details of that truth. But, once her fury wore thin, what then? She and Dillon were of similar age; they'd grown up together. Precisely what that meant he didn't know, but he had to wonder how accurate her last assertion was. Was she risking her reputation *only* for the General? Or for Dillon as well?

He studied her, but couldn't decide. Whatever the answer, he would shield her as best he could.

He looked up at the stars, just starting to appear, and heard a sniff, instantly suppressed. She was taking a long time with her saddle girths.

'He's young.' Why he felt compelled to excuse Dillon he couldn't have said.

'He's two years older than me.'

How old did that make her? Demon wished he knew.

'What do you think happened to Ickley?'

Demon silently considered; he didn't imagine her ensuing

silence meant she didn't expect an answer. 'Either he's gone to ground, in which case the last thing we'd want to do is flush him out, or . . . we'll never know.'

She made a small sound, like a hum, in her throat – a muted sound of distress.

Demon straightened away from the tree; in the gathering gloom, he couldn't see her face clearly. At that moment, she stepped back from Jessamy's side, dusting her hands. He strolled around the mare. 'You can continue at my stable for the time being – until we catch sight of this con tact.' If any avenue had offered, he'd have eased her out of his stable, out of Newmarket itself until all danger was past. But. . .her stubbornness was a tangible thing.

She turned to face him. 'If you try to get rid of me, I'll just get a job in another stable. There's more than one in Newmarket.'

None as safe as his. 'Carruthers will keep you on until I say otherwise.' Which he would the instant they located Dillon's contact. 'But you'll be restricted to riding track, morning and afternoon.'

'That's the only time that matters, anyway. That's the only time outsiders aren't looked at askance about the Heath.'

She was absolutely right.

He'd been going to give her a boost to her saddle; instead, features hardening, he reached for her, closed his hands about her waist and lifted her.

Lust flashed through him like liquid heat – a hot urgency that left him ravenous. He had to force himself to set her neatly in her saddle, to let go, to hold her stirrup while she slipped one small boot into it.

And not drag her back down, into his arms.

He wanted her in his bed.

The realization struck like a kick from one of his Thoroughbreds, leaving him winded and aching. Inwardly shaking. He looked up – and found her looking down at him.

She frowned and shook her reins. 'Come on.' Wheeling Jessamy, she trotted out of the clearing.

Demon swore. He crossed the clearing in three strides, yanked at Ivan's reins, and then remembered the double knots. He had to stop to undo them, then he vaulted to the saddle.

And followed.

Chapter Three

Demon rose before dawn the next morning and rode to his stable to view the morning gallops – and to keep an eye on Flick and her bottom. He felt distinctly aggrieved by the necessity of rising so early, but ... the thought of her, the angel in blue velvet, thundering about disguised as a lad, with all the potential calamities that might ensue, had made dozing off again impossible.

So he stood in the thin mist by Carruthers's side and watched his horses thunder by. The ground shook, the air trembled; the reverberations were as familiar as his heartbeat. The scene was a part of him, and he a part of it – and Flick was in it, too. She flew past, extending The Flynn, exhorting him to greater effort, leaving the other horses behind. Demon's breath caught as she flashed past the post; he felt her thrill – a flaring sense of triumph. It shivered through him, held him effortlessly, then he drew breath and forced himself to look away, to where his other work riders were urging their mounts along.

The fine mist glazed the shoulders of his greatcoat; it darkened his fair hair. Flick made those observations as, slowing The Flynn, she glanced back to where Demon stood. He was looking away, a fact she'd known, or she wouldn't have risked the glance. He'd been watching her almost without pause since he'd arrived, just after she'd taken to the Heath.

Luckily, cursing beneath her breath only reinforced her disguise. But she had to suppress all other signs of agitation so she didn't communicate her sudden nervousness to The Flynn. She'd always felt breathless whenever Demon was about; she'd anticipated some degree of awkwardness, the remnants of her childhood infatuation with him. But not this – this nerve-stretching awareness, the skittery sensation in her stomach. She'd buried deep the suspicion it had something to do – a great deal to do – with the breathstealing shock she'd felt when he had lifted her to her saddle the previous evening. The last thing she wanted was for The Flynn to make an exhibition of himself under Demon's expert eye. He might see it as a God-given sign to change his mind and relieve her of her duties.

But riding track with him watching proved a far greater trial than performing for Carruthers alone, despite the fact the old curmudgeon was the most exacting trainer on the Heath. There was a certain sharp assessment in Demon's blue gaze that was absent from Carruthers's eyes; as her nervousness grew, she had to wonder if Demon was doing it deliberately – deliberately discomposing her – so she'd make some silly error and give him a reason to send her packing.

Thankfully, all her years of riding had taught her to hide her feelings well; she and The Flynn put on a good show. Wheeling the big bay, she headed back to the stable.

Demon nodded his approval when she walked The Flynn in and halted him in the mounting area. Kicking free of the stirrups, she slid down the horse away from Demon and Carruthers. An apprentice hurried up; he grabbed the reins before she could blink, before she could think, and led The Flynn off to his box, leaving her facing Carruthers, with Demon beside him.

'Good work.' Demon's blue eyes held hers; he nodded curtly. 'We'll see you this afternoon. Don't be late.'

Flick's tongue burned; she had, until now, unsaddled and brushed down The Flynn herself. But her disguise demanded meekness; she ducked her head. 'I'll be here.' With that gruff declaration, she swung around and, remembering at the last not to walk stiffly, sauntered up the alley to where the cob stood dozing by the door. She scrambled up to her saddle and left without a backward glance – before temptation could get the upper hand.

Behind her, she heard Demon ask Carruthers some question – but she could still feel his gaze on her back.

After seeing Flick safely away, Demon repaired to the coffee-house in Newmarket High Street favored by the members of the Jockey Club.

He was hailed the instant he crossed the threshold. Returning greetings right and left, he strolled to the counter, ordered a large breakfast, then joined a group comprised mostly of other owners at one of the long tables.

'We're exchanging predictions for the coming season.' Patrick McGonnachie, manager of the duke of Beaufort's stable, turned to Demon as he sat. 'Currently, of course, we've five times the number of winners as we have races.'

'Sounds like a fresh crop,' Demon drawled. 'That'll keep the General busy.'

McGonnachie blinked, then caught his meaning – if horses that hadn't won before made it to the winner's circle, the General would need to investigate their pedigree. McGonnachie shifted. 'Ah, yes. Busy indeed.'

He looked away up the table; Demon resisted pressing him. McGonnachie, in common with all of Newmarket, knew how close he and the General were. If there was any less-than-felicitous whisper going the rounds concerning the General, McGonnachie wouldn't tell him.

So he ate and listened to the chat about the table, and

contributed his share. And bore with easy indifference the good-natured ribbing over his activities in London.

'Need to change your style if you don't want to miss your chance,' Old Arthur Trumble, one of the most respected owners, nodded down the table. 'Take my advice and spend less time lifting the skirts of London's *mesdames*, and more dealing with the business. The higher the standing of your stud, the more demanding it'll be.' He paused to puff on his pipe. 'And Lord knows, you look like taking the Breeder's Cup this year.'

Two others took immediate exception to that prediction, leaving Demon with no need to reply. He listened, but detected no further suggestion of rumors concerning the General other than McGonnachie's earlier hesitation.

'Mister Figgins is back – did you hear?' Buffy Jeffers leaned forward to look around McGonnachie. 'Sawyer ran him in the first – he couldn't wait to see if that leg would hold up, but it did. So your Mighty Flynn will have some decent competition. The handicaps won't be the walk-over they might otherwise have been.'

'Oh?' Demon chatted with Buffy about The Flynn's chances, while his mind raced on a different track.

He had wondered how Dillon's syndicate had expected to fix the first race of the year. Run before the start of the spring season, the early races were used to trial horses, generally those new to racing. If that was the case, then fixing meant making sure one specific horse came first, which meant influencing how at least a handful of other horses ran. Bribing multiple jockeys required more money, and was more hazardous, than the alternative way to fix a race. But the other method required one outstanding runner – a crowd favorite.

'Tell me,' Demon asked, when Buffy paused for breath. 'Did Mister Figgins win? You didn't say.'

'Romped in,' Buffy replied. 'Showed the pack a clean pair of heels all the way down the straight.'

Demon smiled and let their talk drift into other spheres.

At least he now knew how the syndicate operated; they must have cursed Mister Figgins all the way down the straight. Mister Figgins was the horse the fix should have been applied to; the syndicate would have assumed he'd lose, and their tools – however many bookmakers they'd seduced into their game – would have offered good odds on Mister Figgins, taken huge bets, and, in this case, suffered mammoth losses. That was the one drawback with that method – it could seriously backfire if the bribe wasn't in place, if the race wasn't properly fixed.

Which explained why Dillon was in serious trouble.

After breakfast, in company with the others, Demon strolled across the street and into the Jockey Club. The hallowed precinct was as familiar as his home; he spent the next hour wandering the rooms, chatting to stewards, jockeys and the racing elite – those gentlemen like himself who formed the hub of the English racing world.

Time and again in his idle chats, he sensed a start, or hesitation – a quick skirting around some invisible truth. Long before he ran into Reginald Molesworth, Demon knew beyond doubt that there were rumors afoot.

Reggie, an old friend, didn't wait to be asked. 'I say,' he said the instant they'd exchanged their usual greetings, 'are you free? Let's go get some coffee – The Twig and Bough should be pretty quiet about now.' He caught Demon's eye and added, 'Something you need to know.'

An easy air hiding his interest, Demon acquiesced; together with Reggie, he strolled out of the club and down the street. Ducking his head, he led the way into The Twig and Bough, a coffeehouse that catered more to the genteel elements of the town than to the racing set.

Their appearance left the two serving girls gawking, but the proprietress preened. She quickly bustled out from behind her counter as they claimed seats at a table against the wall. After taking their orders, the woman bobbed and hurried away. By unspoken understanding, Demon and Reggie chatted about inconsequential, tonnish London matters until their coffee and cakes arrived, and the little waitress left them.

Reggie leaned over the table. 'Thought you'd want to know.' He lowered his voice to a conspiratorial whisper. 'Things are being said regarding the household at Hillgate End.'

Impassive, Demon asked, 'What things?'

'Seems there's some suspicion of races not being run the way they should. Well, there's always talk every time a favorite loses, but recently . . .' Reggie stirred his coffee. 'There was Trumpeter and The Trojan here last season, and Big Biscuits, Hail Well and The Unicorn at Doncaster. Not to mention The Prime at Ascot. Not so many that it's certain, but it doesn't take a man o' business to work it out. A lot of money changed hands over those losses, and the offered odds in every case. . .well, it certainly gives one to think. And that was just the autumn season.'

Demon nodded. 'Is it official?'

Reggie grimaced. 'Yes and no. The Committee think there's a definite question, and they want answers, thank you very much. At present, they're only looking at last autumn, and it's all been kept under wraps, which is why you might not have heard.'

Demon shook his head. 'I hadn't. Is there any reason to think it went on last spring as well?'

'I gather there is, but the evidence – meaning the offering of odds that could only be considered deliberately encouraging – is not as clear.'

'Any guesses as to the Committee's direction?'

Reggie looked up and met Demon's gaze. Reggie's father was on the Committee. 'Yes, well, that's why I thought you

39

should know. The jockeys involved, of course, are all as close as clams – they know it's the devil of a case to prove. But it seems young Caxton's been seen about, chatting to the jockeys involved. As he's not previously seemed all that interested in rubbing elbows with the riders, it was noticed. The Committee, not surprisingly, wants to talk to the youngster. Trouble is' – Reggie pulled one earlobe – 'the boy's off visiting friends. Given he is the General's son, and no one wants to unnecessarily upset the venerable old gent, the Committee decided to wait until Caxton junior got back, and take him aside on the quiet.'

Reggie sighed and continued. 'Good plan, of course, but when they made it, they imagined he'd be back inside of a week. That was two weeks ago, and he's still not back. They're uneasy about fronting up at Hillgate End and asking the General where his son is – they'll hold their hand as long as they can. But with the spring season in the offing, they can't wait forever.'

Demon met Reggie's deceptively innocent eyes. 'I see.'

And he did. The message he was getting was not from Reggie, not even from Reggie's father, but from the all-powerful Committee itself.

'You don't have any ... ah, insights to offer, do you?'

After a moment, Demon said, 'No. But I can see the Committee's point.'

'Hmm.' Reggie shot Demon a commiserating look. 'Not hard to see, is it?'

'No, indeed.' They finished their coffee, paid, then strolled outside. Demon paused on the step.

Reggie stopped beside him. 'Where are you headed?'

Demon shot him a glance. 'Hillgate End, where else?' He raised his brows. 'To see what the situation there is.'

'They all think I don't know.' General Sir Gordon Caxton sat in the chair behind his desk. 'But I follow the race results better than most and although I don't get out to the paddocks much these days, there's nothing wrong with my hearing when I do.' He snorted.

Demon, standing before the long windows, watched his longtime friend and mentor fretfully realign his already straight blotter. He'd arrived a quarter of an hour before, and, as was his habit, had come straight to the library. The General had greeted him with open delight. To Demon's well-attuned ear, the General's heartiness had sounded forced. When the first rush of genial exchanges had faded, he'd asked how everything was with his friend. The General's superficial delight evaporated, and he'd made his admission.

'Whispers – and more. About Dillon, of course.' The General's chin sank; for a long moment, he stared at the miniature of his late wife, Dillon's mother, that stood on one side of the desk, then he sighed and shifted his gaze to his blotter once more. 'Race-fixing.' The words were uttered with loathing. 'He might, of course, be innocent, but ...' He dragged in an unsteady breath, and shook his head. 'I can't say I'm surprised. The boy always lacked backbone – my fault as much as his. I should have taken a firmer stand, applied a firmer hand. But ...' After another long moment, he sighed again. 'I hadn't expected this.'

There was a wealth of hurt, of confused pain, in the quietly spoken words. Demon's hands fisted; he felt an urgent desire to grab hold of Dillon and iron him out, literally and figuratively, regardless of Flick's sensitivities. The General, despite his lumbering bulk, shaggy brows and martial air, was a benign and gentle man, kindhearted and generous, respected by all who knew him. Demon had visited him regularly for twenty-five years; there had never been any lack of love, of gentle guidance for Dillon. Whatever the General might imagine, Dillon's situation was no fault of his.

The General grimaced. 'Felicity, dear girl, and Mrs.

41

Fogarty and Jacobs all try to keep it from me. I haven't let them know there's no need. They'd only fuss more if they knew I knew.'

Mrs. Fogarty had been the General's housekeeper for more than thirty years, and Jacobs, the butler, had been with him at least as long. Both, like Felicity, were utterly devoted to the General.

The General looked up at Demon. 'Tell me – have you heard anything beyond suspicions?'

Demon held his gaze. 'No – nothing more than this.' Briefly, he stated all he'd heard in Newmarket that morning.

The General humphed. 'As I said, it wouldn't surprise me to learn Dillon was involved. He's away staying with friends – if the Committee's agreeable to wait until he returns, that would be best, I suspect. No need to summon him back. Truth to tell, if I did send a summons, I couldn't be sure he wouldn't bolt.'

'It's always been a mystery how Dillon could be so weak a character when he grew up alongside Felicity. She's so . . .' The General stopped, then smiled fleetingly at Demon. 'Well, the word 'righteous' comes to mind. Turning her from her path, which you may be sure she's fully considered from all angles, is all but impossible. Always was.' He sighed fondly. 'I used to put it down to her parents being missionaries, but it goes deeper than that. A true character – steadfast and unswerving. That's my Felicity.'

His smile faded. 'Would that a little of her honesty had rubbed off on Dillon. And some of her steadiness. She's never caused me a moment's worry, but Dillon? Even as a child he was forever in some senseless scrape. The devil of it was, he always looked to Felicity to rescue him – and she always did. Which was all very well when they were children, but Dillon's twenty-two. He should have matured, should have grown beyond these damned larks.'

Dillon had graduated from larks to outright crime. Demon stored the insight away, and kept his lips shut.

He'd promised Flick his help; at present, that meant shielding Dillon, leaving him hidden in the ruined cottage. Helping Flick also, he knew, meant shielding the General, even if that hadn't gone unsaid. And while he and Flick were doubtless destined to clash on any number of issues in the coming days – like the details of her involvement in their investigations – he was absolutely as one with her in pledging his soul to spare the General more pain.

If the General knew where Dillon was, regardless of the details, he would be torn, driven by one loyalty – to the industry he'd served for decades – to surrender Dillon to the authorities, while at the same time compelled by the protective instincts of a parent.

Demon knew how it felt to be gripped by conflicting loyalties, but he'd rather leave the weight on his shoulders, where it presently resided, than off-load the problem onto his ageing friend. Facing the windows squarely, he looked over the neat lawns to the shade trees beyond. 'I suspect that waiting for Dillon to return is the right tack. Who knows the full story? There might be reasons, mitigating circumstances. It's best to wait and see.'

'You're right, of course. And, heaven knows, I've enough to keep me busy.' Demon glanced around to see the General tug the heavy record book back onto the blotter. 'What with you and your fellows breeding so much Irish into the stock, I've all but had to learn Gaelic.'

Demon grinned. A gong sounded.

Both he and the General glanced at the door. 'Time for lunch. Why not stay? You can meet Felicity and see if you agree with my assessment.'

Demon hesitated. The General frequently invited him to lunch, but in recent years, he hadn't accepted, which was presumably why he'd missed seeing Felicity grow up.

He'd spent the previous evening dredging his memory for every recollection, no matter how minute, trying to find some balance in his unexpectedly tilting world. Trying to ascertain just what his role, his standing, with this new version of Felicity should be. Her age had been a pertinent consideration; physically, she could be anything from eighteen to twenty-four, but her self-confidence and maturity were telling. He'd pegged her at twenty-three.

The General had now told him Dillon was twenty-two, which meant if Flick was two years younger, then she was only twenty. He'd been three years out, but, given the General's assessment, with which he concurred, she might as well be twenty-three.

Twenty-three made her easier to deal with, given he was thirty-one. Thinking of her as twenty made him feel too much like a cradle-snatcher.

But he still couldn't understand why he hadn't sighted her in the last five years. The last time he'd seen her was when, after importing his first Irish stallion, he'd come to give the General the relevant information for the stud records. She'd opened the door to him – a short, thin, gawky schoolgirl with long braids. He'd barely glanced at her, but he had remembered her. He'd been here countless times since, but hadn't seen her. He hadn't, however, stayed for a meal in all those years.

Demon turned from the window. 'Yes, why not?' The General would attribute Demon's break with long-standing habit to concern for him, and he would be half-right at that.

So he stayed.

And had the pleasure of seeing Felicity sweep imperiously into the dining parlor, then nearly trip over her toes, and her tongue, deciding how to react to him.

Which was only fair, because he had not a clue how to

44

react to her. Or, more accurately, didn't dare react to her as his instincts suggested. She was, after all – despite all – still the General's ward.

Who had miraculously grown up.

In full light, dressed in ivory muslin sprigged with tiny green leaves, she looked like a nymph of spring come to steal mortals' hearts. Her hair, brushed and neat, glowed like polished gold, a rich frame for the distinctive, eerily angelic beauty of her face.

It was her face that held him, compelled him. The soft blue of her eyes, like a misty sky, drew him, urging him to lose himself in their gentle depths. Her nose was straight, her brow wide, her complexion flawless. Her lips begged to be kissed – delicately bowed, soft pink, the lower lip full and sensual, they were made to be covered by a man's.

By his.

The thought, so unequivocal, shocked him; he drew breath and shook free of the spell. A swift glance, a rake's appraisal of her figure, nearly had him in thrall again.

He resisted. The realization that he'd been bowled over for the first time in his life was enough to shake him to his senses. With his usual grace and an easy smile, he strolled forward and took Flick's hand.

She blinked and very nearly snatched it back.

Demon quashed the urge to raise her quivering fingers to his lips. He let his smile deepen instead. 'Good after noon, my dear. I do hope you don't mind me joining you for lunch?'

She blinked again, and shot a quick glance at the General. 'No, of course not.'

She blushed, very slightly; Demon forced himself to ignore the intriguing sight. Gracefully, he led her to the table. She claimed the chair by the General's left; he held it for her, then strolled around the table to the place on the General's right, directly opposite her.

The placement couldn't have been more perfect; while chatting with the General, it was perfectly natural that his gaze should frequently pass over her.

She of the swanlike neck and sweetly rounded shoulders, of the pert breasts encased in skin like ivory silk, their upper swells revealed by the scooped neckline of her gown. She was perfectly prim, perfectly proper, and perfectly delectable.

Demon's mouth watered every time he glanced her way.

Flick was very aware of his scrutiny; for some mystical reason, the touch of his gaze actually felt warm. Like a sun-kissed breeze touching her – lightly, enticingly. She tried not to let her awareness show; it was, after all, unsurprising that he found her appearance somewhat changed. The last time he'd seen her, she'd been fifteen, skinny, scrawny, with two long braids hanging down her back. He'd barely registered her existence – she'd stared at him and hadn't been able to stop.

That was the last time she'd allowed herself the liberty; thereafter she made sure that whenever he called, she kept out of his sight. Even if she glimpsed him, she'd force herself to walk the other way – precisely because her impulse lay in the opposite direction. She had far too much pride to stare at him like some silly, lovestruck schoolgirl. Despite the fact that was how he made her feel – hardly surprising, as he'd been her ideal gentleman for so many years – she had a strong aversion to the notion of mooning over him. She was quite sure he got enough of that from other lovestruck girls and all the lovestruck ladies.

She had absolutely no ambition to join their ranks.

So she forced herself to contribute to the conversation about horses and the coming season. Having grown up at Hillgate End, she knew more than enough about both subjects to hold her own. Demon twice tripped over her name, catching himself just in time; she manfully – womanfully – resisted glaring at him the second time it happened. His eyes met hers; one brow quirked and his lips curved teasingly. She pressed her lips tight shut and looked down at her plate.

'Could you pass the vinegar, m'dear.'

She looked for the cruet set only to see Demon lift the bottle from the tray further down the table. He offered it to her; she took it – her fingers brushed his. A sharp shock lanced through her. Startled, she nearly dropped the bottle but managed to catch it in time. Carefully, she handed it to the General, then picked up her knife and fork and looked down at her plate. And breathed slowly in and out.

She felt Demon's gaze on her face, on her shoulders, then he turned to the General. 'The Mighty Flynn's shaping well. I'm expecting to have another two wins at least from him this season.'

'Indeed?'

The General was instantly distracted; Flick breathed a touch easier.

Demon kept the conversation rolling, not a difficult task. Much more difficult was keeping his gaze from Flick; his attention, of course, remained riveted. Ridiculous, of course – she was twenty, for heaven's sake.

But she was there, and utterly fascinating.

He told himself it was the contrast between Flick the righteous, who dressed as a stable lad and single-handedly set out to expose a race-fixing syndicate, and Felicity, the delicate and determinedly proper Botticelli angel.

It was a contrast designed to intrigue him.

'Perhaps,' he said as they all stood, the light luncheon disposed of, 'Felicity would care to take a turn about the lawns?'

He deliberately phrased the question to give the General an opening to support him. He needn't have bothered. Flick's head came up; she met his gaze.

'That would be pleasant.' She glanced at the General. 'If you don't need me, sir?'

'No, no!' The General beamed. 'I must get back to my books. You go along.'

He shooed them toward the open French doors; Demon caught his eye. 'I'll drop by if I have any news.'

The General's eyes dimmed. 'Yes, do.' Then he glanced at Flick and his smile returned. Nodding benignly, he headed for the door.

Leaving Flick by her chair, staring at Demon. He raised a brow, and gestured to the French doors. 'Shall we?'

She came around the table but didn't pause by his side, didn't wait for him to offer his arm. Instead, she walked straight past, out of the open doors. Demon stared at her back, then shook his head and followed.

She'd paused on the terrace; as soon as he appeared, she led the way down the steps. With his longer stride, he easily caught up with her as she strolled the well-tended lawn. He fell in beside her, sauntering slowly, trying to decide what gambit would work best with an angel. Before he could decide, she spoke.

'*How* am I supposed to hear any comments or see anyone approaching the riders in your stables when I barely spend a moment *in* them?' She cast a darkling glance his way. 'I arrived this morning to discover The Flynn already saddled. Carruthers sent me straight out to take The Flynn around for an extended warm-up' – her eyes narrowed – 'so he wouldn't still be restless at the end. And then *you* bundled me out of the stable as soon as I rode back in.'

'I assumed you would need to get back here.' He hadn't, but it was a good excuse. He slanted her a mildly questioning glance. 'How are you covering your absences early morning and afternoon?'

'I often go riding first thing in the morning, so that's nothing unusual. If Jessamy's missing from the stable, everyone assumes I'm somewhere about, enjoying the morning. Just as long as I'm

48

back by lunchtime, no one would think to worry.'

Slowing as they passed into the shade of the old trees edging the lawn, Flick grimaced. 'The afternoons are more difficult, but no one's asked where I ride off to. I suspect Foggy and Jacobs know Dillon's not off with friends, but somewhere close – but if they don't ask, then they can't say if questioned.'

'I see.' He hesitated, inwardly debating whether to take her hand and place it on his sleeve, forcing her to stroll with him rather than lead the way. But she'd tensed when he'd taken her hand before, and she'd nearly dropped the vinegar. Suppressing a grin, he opted for caution. 'There's no reason you can't loiter around the stables after the morning gallops. Not having any chores should give you a freer rein.' He had no intention of rescinding the orders he'd given Carruthers. 'However, there's no sense in dallying after afternoon stables. At that time, most of the jockeys and hangers-on retire to the taverns.'

'There's no reason I can't slouch about the stables until they leave.'

Demon inwardly frowned. There was a mulishness in her tone, a sense of rigid purpose in her stance; both had been absent earlier. Earlier in the dining room, when she'd been Felicity, not Flick. Flick was the righteous crusader, Felicity the Botticelli angel.

Slowing, he considered a swath of daffodils nodding their trumpets in the breeze. The odd bluebell and harebell were interspersed, creating a spring carpet stretching under the trees and into the sunshine beyond. He nodded toward the show. 'Beautiful, aren't they?'

An angel should respond to natural beauty.

Flick barely glanced at nature's bounty. 'Hmm. Have you learned, or heard, anything yet?' She looked into his face. 'You did go into town this morning, didn't you?'

49

He suppressed a frown. 'Yes, yes and yes.'

She stopped and looked at him expectantly. 'Well?'

Frustrated, Demon halted and faced her. 'The Committee is waiting for Dillon to return to have a quiet word with him over a number of races last season where the suspiciously priced crowd-favorite didn't win.'

Her face blanked. 'Oh.'

'Indeed. The slumgudgeon didn't even realize that, as he hadn't made a habit of hobnobbing with the riders before, people would notice when he suddenly did.'

'But ...' Flick frowned. 'The stewards haven't come asking after him.'

'Not the stewards, no. In this instance, they weren't required – any number of the Committee have probably called on the General in the last weeks. Easy enough to learn whether Dillon is here or not.'

'That's true.' Then her eyes flew wide. 'They haven't said anything to the General, have they?'

Demon glanced away. 'No, the Committee sees no reason to unnecessarily upset the General, and as yet, they have no proof – just suspicions.'

He looked back as Flick sighed with relief. 'If they hold off until Dillon can return—'

'They'll hold off as long as they can,' he cut in. 'But they won't – can't – wait forever. Dillon will have to return as soon as possible – the instant we get enough information to prove the existence of the syndicate.'

'So we need to make headway in identifying Dillon's contact. Are the rumors of race-fixing widespread?'

'No. Among the owners and trainers, yes, but amongst others, less so. Some jockeys and stable lads must have suspicions, but they're unlikely to voice them, even to each other.'

Flick started to stroll again. 'If there's no open talk, no rumors abounding, it's less likely someone will let something slip.'

50

Demon didn't reply; Flick didn't seem to notice. Which, to him, seemed all of a piece. Right now she didn't seem aware of him at all – she seemed to regard him as a be nevolent uncle, or some creature equally benign. Which was so far from the truth it was laughable.

It was also irritating.

The Botticelli angel of the dining room, the one who had delicately shivered at his touch, and trembled when his fingers brushed hers, had vanished.

She glanced at him. 'Perhaps you could start with the jockeys whose mounts failed last season. I assume, if they've taken a bribe once, they'll be more likely to be approached again?'

'Ordinarily, yes. However, if they've been questioned, however elliptically, by the stewards, one can guarantee their lips will be sealed. With a license in the balance, no jockey's going to incriminate himself.'

'There must be some action you can take while I keep watch in your stables.'

Demon's eyes widened; he only just stopped himself from replying caustically with rather more information than she needed. 'Never mind about me. I'm sure I'll find some useful avenue to explore.' He'd already thought of several, but he had no intention of sharing his views. 'I'll make a start before I look in on the afternoon's work.'

'You could investigate any touts or hangers-on lurking about the other stables' strings.'

'Indeed.' Demon couldn't help himself – eyes hardening, his gaze openly intent, he lengthened his stride, swung to face her, and halted.

Sucking in a breath, she stopped precipitously, all but teetering in her effort not to run into him. She looked up, blue eyes widening in surprise.

He smiled down at her. 'I'll be watching you, too.' He held her gaze. 'Don't doubt it.'

She blinked; to his chagrin, not a flicker of awareness – the consciousness he was deliberately trying to evoke – showed in her soft blue eyes. Instead puzzlement filled them. She searched his face briefly, then shrugged, stepped aside and walked around him. 'As you wish, although I can't see why. You know I can handle The Flynn, and Carruthers never misses a stride.'

Swallowing a curse, Demon swung on his heel and stalked after her. It wasn't The Flynn that concerned him. Flick clearly considered him unthreatening. While he had no wish to threaten her, he definitely wanted her in his bed, which ought, in his book, to make her nervous, at least a bit wary. But no – not Flick.

Felicity was sensitive – Felicity was sensible. She had the good sense to be aware of him. Felicity had some degree of self-preservation. Flick, as far as he could tell, had none. She hadn't even recognized that he was not a benign uncle, and definitely not the sort of man to be managed by a mere chit.

'It won't,' he enunciated, regaining her side, 'be The Flynn's performance I'll be watching.'

She glanced up and met his eyes, her frown more definite. 'There's no need to watch me – I haven't parted company with my saddle for years.'

'Be that as it may,' he purred, 'I assure you that watching you – keeping my gaze firmly glued to your svelte form as you trot about perched on one of my champions – is precisely the sort of behavior that's expected of a gentleman such as I.'

'Be that as it may, watching me when you could be observing the hangers-on is silly. A wasted opportunity.'

'Not for me.'

Flick humphed and looked ahead. He was being deliberately difficult – she could sense his aggravation, cloaked though it was, but she had no idea what had caused it, or why he was making less sense than Dillon. She strolled on. And continued to ignore the fluttery sensations assailing her stomach, and the insistent flickering of her nerves. Along with the other unwanted, unwelcome remnants of her girlish obsession with him.

He'd been her ideal gentleman since she'd been ten and had found a book of Michelangelo's works in the library. She'd found one sculpture that had embodied her vision of a handsome male. Except that Demon was handsomer. His shoulders were wider, his chest broader and more finely muscled, his hips narrower, his legs longer, harder – altogether better defined. As for the rest, she'd surmised from his reputation that he was better endowed there, too. His easygoing attitudes, his love of horses and his involvement with the world of horse racing had all served to deepen her interest.

She hadn't, however, ever made the mistake of imagining he returned it, or ever would. He was eleven years her senior, and could have his pick of the most beautiful and sophisticated ladies in the ton; it would be foolish beyond permission to imagine he would ever look at her. But she would marry one day – one day soon; she was very ready to love and be loved. She was already twenty, waiting, hoping. And if she had her way, she would marry a gentleman exactly like Demon. He, however, was an unattainable idol, entirely beyond her reach.

'This' – she gestured – 'shady contact of Dillon's. Presumably he's not a local. Perhaps a search of the hotels and inns—'

'I've already got that in hand.'

'Oh.' She glanced up and met Demon's gaze; for a moment, his blue eyes remained sharp, keen, then he looked ahead.

'I'll check, but it's unlikely we'll find much by that route. This is, after all, Newmarket, a place that abounds in inns and taverns, and that attracts its fair share of shady characters, most of whom aren't local.'

Flick grimaced and looked forward – they'd ambled through the gardens. The stables lay ahead, framed by a series

53

of wooden arches over which wisteria grew. Stepping onto the path leading beneath the arches, she mused, 'This contact – who would he be? One of the syndicate, or another pawn?'

'Not one of the syndicate.' Demon strolled beside her, his strides long and lazy, his hands, somewhat surprisingly, in his trouser pockets. His gaze was on the gravel. 'Who ever they are, the syndicate won't want for money, and the last thing they'd risk is exposure. No – the man will be a hireling. Perhaps a permanent employee. That, for us, would be best.'

'So once we identify him, we'll have the best chance of following him back to his masters?'

Demon nodded. Then he looked up and stopped. They'd reached the end of the arches.

Flick glanced up, squinting into the sunlight that shone from over his shoulder. He was looking at her; she couldn't see his features, but she could feel his gaze, could sense his sheer physical presence through every pore. She was used to working with large horses; standing near him reminded her of them – he exuded the same aura of potent physical power, which could, if provoked, be dangerous. Luckily, neither horses nor he posed any danger to her. Inwardly lamenting her continuing sensitivity, she raised a hand and shaded her eyes.

And looked into his.

Her breath caught; for an instant, she felt disoriented – unclear who she was, who he was, and how things really were. Then something shifted in the blue; she blinked, and regained her mental footing. Yet he continued to look at her – not precisely seriously, but intently, the expression in his eyes one she neither recognized nor understood.

She was about to raise a brow when, his gaze still steady on her face, he asked, 'Now you know the full story of Dillon's involvement, do you regret agreeing to help him?'

'Regret?' Considering the question, she raised both brows. 'I don't think the concept applies. I've always helped him –

he's made something of a career of getting into unexpectedly complicated scrapes.' She shrugged. 'I always imagined he'd grow out of them eventually. He hasn't yet.'

Demon considered her face, her open expression, the honesty in her soft blue eyes. They didn't tell him how she felt about Dillon; given her apparent resistance to him, he had to wonder if Dillon was the cause. When she and Dillon were together, she was the dominant party – the one in charge. She'd grown accustomed to Dillon being dependent on her – it was possible she liked it that way. There was no doubt she liked to lead.

Which was all very well, but . . .

'So,' she blinked up at him, 'what do you imagine will happen next?'

He raised his brows. 'Probably not a lot.' At least, not in his stables. 'However, if you do stumble on any clue, I will, of course, expect to be notified immediately.'

'Of course.' She lowered her hand and turned toward the stables. 'Where will you be?'

Investigating far and wide. 'Send a message to the farm – the Shephards always know where to find me.'

'I'll send word if I hear anything.' She stopped at the edge of the garden and held out her hand. 'I'll see you at the stable in a few hours.'

Demon took her hand. He lifted his gaze to her eyes – and fell into the blue. Her fingers lay, trusting, quiescent in his grasp. He considered raising them, considered brushing a lingering kiss upon them, considered . . .

Madness and uncertainty clashed.

The moment passed.

He released her hand. With an elegant nod, he turned and, jaw setting, strode for the stables, more conscious with every stride of a demonic desire to capture a Botticelli angel – and take her to his bed.

Chapter Four

The next days passed uneventfully; Flick swallowed her impatience and doggedly watched, doggedly listened. She rode morning and afternoon track work every day, then slouched about the stable for as long as she could in the mornings, and until all the stable lads left in the evenings. After three days, the only suspicious character she'd spotted had proved to be one of the lads' cousins, visiting from the north. The only surprising information she'd heard concerned the activities of some redheaded barmaid.

As he'd intimated, Demon had attended all the track work religiously – he'd watched her religiously, too; her sensitivity to his gaze grew more acute by the day. She'd sighed with relief when, within her hearing that morning, he'd told Carruthers that he'd be spending the afternoon about the other stables looking over the competition.

So at three o'clock, she left the General nodding over his records and set off on Jessamy for the cottage – Felicity garbed in her blue velvet riding habit – feeling less trepidatious, certainly more sure of herself. No longer wary of what she might face at the stable.

Dillon was in the clearing when she rode up, the cob placidly munching nearby. She reined in and slid out of her saddle, turned on her heel and marched into the cottage to change – without a single glance at Dillon. He'd have the cob saddled and bridled, and Jessamy unsaddled and tethered, by the time she came out.

She hadn't spoken to him since she'd learned the truth. Every time she'd come by, he'd tried to catch her eye, to smile and make amends.

Struggling out of her velvet skirts, Flick humphed. Dillon was being excessively careful around her – he could be careful for a while more. She hadn't forgiven him for deceiving her – she hadn't forgiven herself for being so gullible. She should have guessed; she knew he wasn't that innocent any more, but the idea that he could have been so comprehensively stupid hadn't entered her head.

Smoothing her curls, she crammed her cap over them. She was exceedingly tired of putting right Dillon's wrongs, of easing his way, but ...

She sighed. She would continue to shield Dillon if the alternative was upsetting the General. Distress wasn't good for him, as Dr. Thurgood had made very clear. Assuring his tranquility was also one way she could repay him for all he had given her.

A home – a secure, stable place in which to grow up. A steady hand, a steadier heart, and an unwavering confidence in her.

She'd come to Hillgate End a confused seven-year-old, suddenly very much alone. Her Aunt Scroggs, with whom her parents had left her in London, had not been willing to keep her when her temporary need had turned permanent. No one had wanted her until, out of nowhere, the General, a distant connection of her father's, had stepped in, smiled kindly upon her, and taken her into his home.

In the country, where she loved to be, close to horses – her favorite animal.

Coming to Hillgate End had changed her life forever, and all for the better. Even though she hadn't been a pauper, as a child, who knows where she might have ended without the

General's kindness, without his care? Thanks to the General, she'd ended here, with a happy life and every opportunity. She owed him a great deal.

Drawing a deep breath, she stepped out of the lean-to. Dillon was waiting, holding the cob, saddled and bridled, close by the log she used for mounting. Flick eyed him steadily as she crossed the yard, but she refused to let him catch her eye. Despite her affection for the General, Dillon, at the moment, she simply endured.

She mounted, gathered the reins, and jogged off without a word.

At least Demon had got the truth out of Dillon. Even though she'd felt foolish for not having seen the inconsistencies in Dillon's story, she could only be glad of Demon's intervention. Since he'd agreed to help, despite his ridiculous insistence on watching her, she'd sensed a lightening of the weight that until his arrival had rested solely on her shoulders. He was there, sharing the load, doing, like her, whatever he could to spare the General. Regardless of anything else, it was a distinct relief.

Reaching the road, she set the cob trotting. At the stable, a lad had The Flynn saddled and waiting; she checked the girths, then with the lad's help, jumped up to perch high on the bay's back. He was used to her now, to the croon of her voice; with the merest urging, he trotted to the door.

Carruthers was waiting. 'Take a long walk, then a gentle trot, at least six, then walk him again and bring him in.'

Flick nodded and clicked the reins. Afternoon work was always easy; not every trainer even bothered.

She paraded with the rest of the string, listening to the natter of the lads and riders about her, simultaneously scanning the nearby verges of the Heath where the watchers – the hangers-on and the touts, spying out the form for bookmakers or private clients – congregated.

As usual, she was the last to walk her mount in, so she could watch to see if any outsider tried to speak to a rider. None did; no one approached any rider in Demon's string, nor the strings from nearby stables.

Disappointed, starting to question whether she would ever see or hear anything useful, she slid from the saddle and let the stable lad lead The Flynn away. After a moment, she followed.

She helped the lad unsaddle, then left him cleaning the manger while she fetched the feed, then the water. The lad moved on to the next horse he looked after. Flick sighed, and The Flynn turned his huge head and nudged her.

Smiling crookedly, she patted his nose. On impulse, she climbed the box wall and perched atop it, leaning her shoulder against the stable's outer wall. She scanned the boxes, listening to the murmurs and conversations – mostly between lads and their equine charges.

The Flynn nudged her legs; she crooned at him, grinning when he hurrumphed and nodded.

'Oh, fer Gawd's sake – take a hike! I doan wanna hear what you've got ter say, so just piss off, why doan yer?'

Flick straightened so abruptly that she nearly fell off the wall. The words sounded so clear – then she realized she was hearing them through the stable wall. The speaker – she recognized the dulcet tones of one of the top race jockeys – was outside.

'Now, now. If'n you'll just hear me out—'

'I tol' you – I doan wanna hear nuthin' from you! Now push off, afore I set ol' Carruthers on yer!'

'Your loss.'

The second speaker had a scratchy voice; it faded away.

Flick scrambled off the wall and tore through the stable, dodging lads with buckets and feed all the way up the alley. They swore at her. She didn't stop. She reached the doors;

hugging their edge, she peeped out.

A heavy figure in an old frieze coat was lumbering away along the edge of the Heath, a cloth cap pulled low over his face, his hands sunk in his pockets. She could see little more than Dillon had.

The man was heading for the town.

For one moment, Flick stood in the yard, juggling possibilities. Then she swung around and hurried back into the stable.

Demon ambled into his stable at the end of the working day. Soft snorts and gentle whinnies punctuated breathy sighs as stable lads closed their charges in their boxes. The reek of horse was absolute; Demon barely noticed. He did notice the old cob quietly dozing in one corner, a few handfuls of hay and a bucket close by. Glancing left and right, Demon strolled down the alley.

He stopped by The Flynn's box; the big bay was settled and contentedly munching. Strolling on, he came upon Carruthers, inspecting a filly's hoof.

'Where's Flick?'

Carruthers glanced at him, then snorted. 'Gone orf, already. In a pelter, he was. Left his cob – said he'd fetch it later.' He looked down at the hoof he was tending.

Demon held back a frown. 'Did he say anything else?'

'Nah!' With a deft flick, Carruthers pried a stone free. 'Just like the other lads – couldn't wait to get to the Swan and lift a pint.'

'The Swan?'

'Or the Bells.' Carruthers let the horse's leg down and straightened. 'Who knows with lads these days?'

Demon paused; Carruthers watched the filly test the hoof. 'So Flick headed into town?'

'Aye – that's what I'm saying. He usually heads off home

to Lidgate, quiet as you please, but today he beetled off into town.'

'How long ago?'

Carruthers shrugged. 'Twenty minutes.'

Demon bit back an oath, swung on his heel and strode out of his stable.

He didn't find Flick in the Swan or the Bells, both respectable inns. He found her in the smoke-filled snug of the Fox and Hen, a seedy tavern down a narrow side street. Nursing a full pint pot, she sat sunk in a corner, surrounded by ale-swilling brutes three times her size.

She was trying to look inconspicuous. Thankfully, a dart game was in full swing, and many patrons were still rolling in; the rabble were presently distracted and hadn't started looking around for likely victims.

Jaw set, Demon grabbed a pint from the harassed barman and crossed the room, his size, accentuated by his heavy greatcoat, allowing him to cleave a passage through the crowd. There were others of his ilk present, gentlemen hobnobbing with cits, rubbing shoulders with half-pay officers and racecourse riffraff; his appearance attracted no undue attention.

Reaching the corner table, he ignored Flick's huge eyes. Setting his pot down with a definite click, he sat opposite her. Then he met her gaze. 'What the hell are you doing here?'

She glared at him, then flicked her gaze to the next table, then back.

Nonchalantly picking up his pint, Demon sipped, scanning the tables beside them. The nearest held two men, hunched over the table, each with a pint before him. They'd both looked up at the dart game; as Demon turned away, they looked down and resumed their conference.

Meeting Flick's eyes, Demon saw them widen meaningfully. Leaning forward, she hissed, 'Listen.'

It took a moment to focus his hearing through the din, but once he had, he could hear well enough.

'So which horse and race are we talking about then?' The speaker was a jockey, one Demon had never hired and only knew by distant sight. He doubted the jockey knew him other than by name, but he kept his face averted.

'Hear tell you're down to ride Rowena in the Nell Gwyn Stakes in a couple o'weeks.'

The second man's voice, deep and grating, was easy to distinguish beneath the raucous din. Demon lifted his eyes and met Flick's; she nodded, then shifted her attention back to their neighbors.

The jockey took a long pull, then lowered his pot. 'Aye – that's right. Where'd you hear? It's not about the course yet.'

'Never you mind where I heard – what you should be concentrating on is that because I did hear, you've an opportunity before you.'

'Opportunity, is it?' The jockey took another long, slow drink. 'How much?'

'Four ponies on delivery.'

An eruption of cheers from the dart game had both men looking around. Demon glanced at Flick; eyes wide, she was watching their man – the contact. Under the table, he nudged her boot. She looked at him; he leaned forward. 'If you don't stop staring, he'll notice and stare back.'

She narrowed her eyes at him, then lowered her gaze to her ale – still untouched. There was another roar from the dart game; everyone looked – even Flick. Swiftly, Demon switched their glasses, leaving his half-full pot for her to nurse. Lifting hers, he drained half; the brew at the Fox and Hen left a lot to be desired, but sitting in a snug amid this sort of crowd nursing a full pot for more than five minutes was enough to invite unwanted attention.

The dart game had concluded. The cheers died and every-one returned to their drinks and conversations.

The jockey looked into his pot as if seeking guidance. 'Five ponies.'

'Five?' The contact jeered. 'You're a mite full of yourself, me lad.'

The jockey's expression hardened. 'Five. I'm the one on Rowena's back that race, and she'll start it prime favorite. The bets'll be heavy – real heavy. If you want her out of the winner's circle, it'll cost you five.'

'Hmm.' It was the contact's turn to seek inspiration from his ale. 'Five? If you want five, you'll need to keep her out of the places altogether.'

'Nah.' The jockey shook his head. 'Can't do it. If she finishes outside the places, the stewards'll be on my tail, and a whole monkey wouldn't be worth that. I ain't about to blow my license for you. Even bringing her in second well, I can do it, but only because Cynster's got a prime filly in the race. Rowena's better, but I can slot her behind the Cynster filly and it'll look all right. But unless there's another runner we ain't seen yet, they're the only possible winners. No way I can drop Rowena out of the places.'

The contact frowned, then drained his pot. 'All right.' He looked the jockey in the eye. 'Five ponies for a no win – is it a deal?'

The jockey hesitated, then nodded. 'Deal.'

'*Aaargh!!*' A bellowed war cry erupted through the noise. Everyone turned to see a furious brute break a jug over his neighbor's head. The jug shattered, the victim slumped. A fist swung out of nowhere, and lifted the assailant from his feet.

And it was on.

Everyone leapt to their feet; chairs crashed, pots went flying. Bodies ricochetted off each other; some thudded on the floor. The melee expanded by the second as more and more patrons launched themselves into the fray.

Demon swung back. Flick, eyes huge, was on her feet in the corner. With an oath, he swept the pots from their table and set it on its side. Reaching across, he grabbed her shoulder. 'Get down!'

He forced her down behind the makeshift barricade. One hand on her cap, he pushed her fully down. 'Stay there!'

The instant he removed his hand, her head popped up. He swore and reached for her; her already-wide eyes dilated.

He swung around just in time to weave back from a hefty fist. It grazed his jaw – and ignited his temper. Regaining his balance, he plowed a fist into his assailant's gut, then followed with a solid right to the jaw.

The huge walloper teetered sideways, then back, then crashed onto his back amid the ongoing brawl.

'Demon!'

Ducking, he threw his next attacker, managing to shift his feet enough so the bruiser landed against the wall beyond Flick, rather than on top of her.

A jarvey staggered free of the central melee and swung his way. The man met his eyes and stopped, swaying on his feet, then turned and charged back into the heaving mass of bodies and flailing fists.

'Stop it, yer mongrels!' The barman jumped up on the counter, laying about him with a besom. To no avail. The brawlers were well away, enjoying themselves hugely.

Demon looked around. The only door from the snug was diagonally across from their corner, beyond the heaving mass of the fight. The wall to their left hosted two grimy sash windows; thrusting aside tables and chairs, he reached the nearest, forced the catch free, then heaved. After an initial resistance, the sash flew up.

Turning back, he grabbed Flick by the collar, unceremoniously dragged her from her hiding place, then manhandled her out of the window. She tried to climb daintily out; he grabbed her and pushed. She hissed and batted at his hands – he kept grabbing and pushing. She hesitated halfway out, deciding which foot to place where; he slapped a hand beneath her bottom and shoved.

She landed in an inelegant sprawl on the grass.

Flick dragged in a breath; curses burned her tongue, but she didn't have breath enough to utter them. Her bottom burned, too; her cheeks were aflame. Both sets. She glanced back. Demon was halfway through the window. Swearing weakly, she scrambled to her feet, dusting her hands on her thighs – she didn't dare touch her posterior.

The other sash window flew up, and more patrons piled out. Demon appeared beside her; grabbing her elbow, he shoved her away from the inn as others started using their escape route. An orchard rolled down an incline away from the inn – with Demon at her heels, Flick slipped between the trees. The twilight was deepening. Behind them, through the now open windows, they heard shouts, then the piercing whistles of the Watch. Glancing back, Flick saw more of the inn's customers scrambling through the windows, hurrying to disappear down the orchard's slope.

'Come on!' Demon grabbed her hand, taking the lead, lengthening his stride so she had to scurry to keep up. She tried to wriggle her hand free; he flung her a scowl, tight ened his grip, and strode on even faster. She cursed; he must have heard but gave no sign. He dragged her, skipping, half-running, to the end of the orchard, to where a seven-foot wall blocked their way.

He released her as others joined them and immediately started climbing the wall. Flick eyed the wall, then edged closer to Demon. 'Is there a gate anywhere?'

He glanced at her, then nodded to the others scrambling up and over. 'Doesn't look like it.' He hesitated, then stepped to the wall. 'Come on – I'll give you a leg up.'

Bracing one shoulder against the wall, he formed a cup with his hands. Balancing one hand on the stones, the other on his shoulder, Flick placed her boot in his hands.

He pushed her up. It should have been easy; The Flynn's back was nearly as high as the wall. But the top of the wall was hard and narrow, not smooth and slippery like a saddle. She managed to get half over, with the wall digging into her middle, but her legs still dangled down.

Blowing out a breath, she braced her arms, straightened her spine, and searched with her boots for purchase. But with her hips on the wrong side of the wall, if she straightened too much, she risked falling back down. And if she didn't straighten enough, she couldn't reach any toehold. She teetered, like a seesaw, on the top of the wall.

From beneath her came a long-suffering sigh.

Demon's hand connected with her bottom again. He hefted her up; in the most flustered flurry of her life, cheeks all flaming again, she quickly swung one leg over the wall and sat.

And tried to catch her breath.

He grabbed the wall beside her and hauled himself up. Easily. Astride the wall, he raked her with a glance, then swung his leg over and dropped into the lane.

Flick dragged in a breath and swung her other leg over, then wriggled around and dropped down – before he felt compelled to help her again. She picked herself up and dusted her hands, aware to her toes of the assessing gaze that passed over her. Lifting her head, she met his eyes, ready to be belligerent.

He merely humphed and gestured down the lane.

She fell in beside him, and they strolled to the road. There were too many others about to risk any discussion. When they reached the road, Demon nudged her elbow and nodded up a lane leading to the High Street. 'I left my curricle at the Jockey Club.'

They changed direction, leaving the others behind.

'You were supposed to send word to me the instant you learned anything.'

The words, deathly soft, lethally restrained, floated down to her.

'I would have,' she hissed back, 'once I had a chance. But who could I send from your stable? Carruthers?'

'Next time, if there's no one to send, bring the message yourself.'

'And miss the chance of learning more – like today?'

'Ah, yes. Today. And just how do you imagine you would have survived if I hadn't arrived?'

She studied the small houses lining the road.

'Hmm, let's see.'

His purr sank deeper, sliding beneath her skin. Flick resisted an urge to wriggle.

'First we have the question of whether, quite aside from the brawl, you would have escaped notice, given you'd bought a pint and couldn't drink it. Your disguise would have disintegrated rather quickly, revealing to all the fact that the General's ward, Miss Felicity Parteger, was slumming in the Newmarket stews dressed as a lad.'

'It was an inn, not a stew.'

'For a lady found in it, the difference is academic.'

Flick humphed.

'And what might have happened if you'd survived the brawl, with or without being knocked senseless, and landed in the arms of the Watch? One can only wonder what they would have made of you.'

'We'll never know,' Flick hissed. 'The important thing is that we've identified Dillon's contact. Did you see which way he went?'

'No.'

She halted. 'Perhaps we should go back—'

Demon didn't stop; he reached back, grabbed her arm, and hauled her forward so she marched beside him. 'You are not following anyone anywhere.' The look he shot her, even muted by the gloom, still stung. 'In case it's escaped your notice, following a man like that to his customary haunts is liable to be dangerous for a gentlewoman.'

His clipped accents gave the words a definite edge. As they swung into the High Street, Flick put her nose in the air. 'You got a good look at him and so did I. We should be able to find him easily, then find out who he works for, and clear up this whole mess. It's our first real discovery.'

After a moment, he sighed. 'Yes, you're right. But leave the next step to me – or rather Gillies. I'll have him go through the inns and taverns – our man must be putting up at one of them.'

Demon looked up as they crossed the High Street; the Jockey Club stood before them. His horses were tied to a tree under the porter's watchful eye. 'Get in. I'll drive you back to the stable.'

Flick strolled to the curricle and climbed up. Demon went to speak to the porter, then returned, untied the reins, and stepped up to the box seat. He backed the horses, then set them trotting with an expert flick of his wrist.

As they headed down the High Street, Flick tilted her chin. 'You'll tell me the instant Gillies discovers anything?'

Demon reached for his whip. The black thong flew out and tickled his leader's ears. The bays stepped out, power in every stride. The curricle shot forward.

Flick grabbed the rail and stifled a curse.

The whip hissed back up the handle, and the carriage rocketed along.

Demon drove back to the stable without uttering a word.

Chapter Five

After dinner that evening, Demon retired to the front parlor of his farmhouse to consider the ramifications of all they'd learned. Frowning, he paced before the fireplace, where a small blaze cheerily danced.

His thoughts were not cheery.

He was deeply mired in them when a tap sounded on the curtained window. Dismissing it as an insect or misguided sparrow, he didn't pause, didn't rouse from his reverie.

The tapping came again, this time more insistent.

Demon halted. Raising his head, he stared at the window, then swore and strode across the room. Jerking the curtains aside, he looked down on the face that haunted his dreams. 'Dammit – what the *devil* are you doing *here*?'

Flick glared, then mouthed, 'Let me in!' and gestured with her hands for him to lift the sash.

He hesitated, then, muttering a string of epithets, opened the catch and flung up the sash.

He was presented with a gloved hand. 'Help me in.'

Against his better judgment, he did. She was dressed in breeches – not her stable lad attire but a pair of what looked to be Dillon's cast-off inexpressibles, which fitted her far too well for his equanimity. Flick clambered over the sill and into the room. Releasing her hand, he lowered the sash and redrew the curtains. 'For God's sake, keep your voice down. Heaven only knows what Mrs. Shephard will think if she hears you—'

'She won't.' With a dismissive wave, Flick stepped to the settee and sank down on one arm. 'She and Shephard are in the kitchen – I checked.'

Demon stared at her – she stared ingenuously back. Deliberately, he thrust both hands into his trouser pockets – against the temptation to lay them on her. 'Do you often flit through the twilight dressed like that?'

'Of course not. But I didn't know whether I'd be able to reach you without knocking on the door. Luckily, I saw your shadow on the curtains.'

Demon clamped his lips shut. There was no point expostulating that her calmly knocking on his front door and asking his housekeeper, a matronly woman with sharp eyes, to show her into his parlor would have been unwise; she would only argue. Swinging on his heel, he strode back across the room; in the circumstances, the least he should do was put some real distance between them.

Regaining the fireplace, he turned to face her, propping his shoulders against the mantel. 'And to what do I owe the pleasure of this visit?'

Her eyes narrowed slightly. 'I came to discuss the situation, of course.'

He raised one brow. 'The situation?'

Flick held his gaze for a moment, then looked down and, with patent determination, removed her gloves. 'It seems to me that what we learned today raises a number of issues.' Laying the gloves on one thigh, she raised her hands and ticked each point off on her fingers. 'First and foremost, if another race is to be fixed, should we warn the authorities? However' – she proceeded to her next finger – 'there's the consideration that if we tell the stewards, they may alert the contact and he'll simply disappear, along with all connection to the syndicate. If that happens, we'll lose any chance of redeeming Dillon. Even worse' – she moved to her next finger – 'if we inform the stewards and they question that man, it sounds, from what Dillon said, that he'll simply implicate him, and very likely cast him as the instigator of the scheme, thus protecting the syndicate from exposure.'

Lifting her head, she looked across the room at the long, lean figure lounging, all brooding elegance, against the mantel. If she'd harbored any doubts that he intended to curtail her involvement in their investigations, his present attitude dispelled them; resistance poured from him in waves. His eyes, his attention, were fixed on her, but he showed no inclination to respond. She tilted her chin. '*So*, are we going to inform the authorities?'

He continued to study her intently, unwaveringly, but he said nothing. Lips thinning, she raised a brow. '*Well*?'

'I haven't yet decided.'

'Hmm.' She ignored his clipped, definitely pointed tone. 'That man offered the jockey one hundred and twenty-five pounds – a small fortune for a race jockey. It seems unlikely the jockey will change his mind.'

He humphed; she took it as agreement.

'Which means your horse is almost certain to win.' Eyes wide, she met his gaze. 'That places you in a rather awkward position, doesn't it?'

He straightened; before he could speak she went on. 'It's a horrible fix – with Dillon to rescue on the one hand, and your responsibilities to the Jockey Club on the other. I suppose it's a clash between loyalty and honor.' In the same even tone, she asked, 'Which will you choose?'

Hands sunk in his pockets, he stared at her, then looked down and paced before the fire. 'I don't know.' He shot her a glance, one dark with irritation. 'I was considering the matter when you came through the window.'

His look was lightened by a hint of curiosity; she grinned. 'I came to help.' She ignored his derisive snort. 'We need to weigh things up – consider our options.'

'I can't see any options.' He continued to pace, his gaze on the floor. 'That one of my horses is involved is irrelevant – it simply makes things worse. Having learned of an attempt to fix a race, my duty as a member of the Jockey Club is clear. I should inform the Committee.'

'How absolute is that duty?'

The glance he sent her was hard. 'As absolute as such things can be. I could not, in all honor, let a fixed race run.'

'Hmm. I agree it's impossible to let a fixed race *run* – that's quite out of the question. But ...' She let her words trail away, her gaze, questioning, fixed on Demon.

He halted, and looked her way. Then he raised a brow. 'But can I—' He broke off, his gaze on her, then briefly inclined his head. 'Can *we* legitimately withhold the information until closer to the race, to give ourselves time to follow this contact back to the syndicate?'

'Exactly. That race is next month – more than a couple of weeks away. And the stewards could stop it even if we told them just before the start.'

'Not quite, but if we hold back the information until the week before the race, it would leave us five weeks in which to trace the syndicate.'

'Five weeks? That's plenty of time.'

Demon suppressed a cynical humph. Flick's face was triumphantly aglow; although it was partly at his expense, he had no wish to dim it. When she'd come through the window, he'd been thinking solely in the singular; he was now talking in the plural. Which was what she'd intended; *that* was why she'd come.

Now she sat, perched victorious on the arm of his settee, one boot swinging, a satisfied smile in her eyes. Her understanding of the honor and responsibilities involved in his position intrigued him. She understood racing, the fraternity and its traditions – not something he'd encountered in a woman before.

But discussing such matters with a sweet innocent felt odd. Especially late in the evening, in his front parlor.

Entirely unchaperoned.

He resumed his pacing – this time, in her direction.

'*So*' – she almost bobbed in her eagerness – 'how do we find the man we saw this evening? Shouldn't we be trying to locate him?'

He halted beside her, his gaze on her face. '*We* are. At this instant, three of my men are rolling around the town, searching the inns and taverns.'

She beamed at him. 'Excellent! And then?'

'And then . . .' He reached for her hand; she surrendered it readily. Smoothly, he drew her to her feet. 'Then we follow him' – holding her gaze, he lowered his voice to a deep purr – 'until we learn all we need to know.'

Trapped in his gaze, her hand in his, eyes widening, she mouthed an 'Oh.'

He smiled intently. Wrapping his fingers about her hand, he waited, just a heartbeat, until she trembled.

'We'll find the contact and follow him.' His lids veiling his eyes, he lowered his gaze to her lips, soft, sheening, succulent pink. 'Until he leads us to the syndicate – and then we'll tell the stewards all *they* need to know.'

When he spoke of 'we' he didn't mean her – but he'd tell her that tomorrow; no need to mar the night.

Raising his lids, he recaptured her gaze, marvelling at the softness of her clear blue eyes. The two of them stood, handfast, gazes locked, mere inches distant, with her trapped between the settee and him. Without conscious thought, he shifted his fingers, brushing the backs of hers.

Her eyes widened even more; her lips parted slightly. Her breath hitched—

Then she blinked, and narrowed her eyes. Frowning, she tugged her hand free. 'I'll leave you now.'

Blinking himself, he released her.

She stepped sideways, heading for the window.

He followed. Close.

She glanced back and up at his face, eyes very wide, her breathing too rapid. 'I dare say I'll see you tomorrow at the stables.'

'You will.'

With fluttering hands, she pushed at the curtains. He reached over her head and drew them wide.

She tugged at the sash. To no avail.

He stepped behind her and reached for the handles, one on either of the pane's lower frame.

Trapping her between his arms, between the window and him. His fingers brushed hers, clasped about the handles. She sucked in a breath and snatched her hands away. Then froze as she realized he surrounded her.

Slowly, he raised the sash – all the way up.

As he straightened, she straightened, too. Her spine stiff, she turned her head and looked him in the eye. 'I'll bid you a good night.'

There was ice and frost in her words. Turning to the window, she sat on the sill; behind her, Demon smiled, slowly, intently.

She swung her legs over and slipped into the darkness. 'Good-bye.'

Her voice floated back to him; in seconds, she'd become a shadow among many, and then she was gone.

Demon's smile deepened, his lips curving as triumphantly as hers had. She wasn't averse to him – the signs had been there, clear for him to read. He didn't know why she'd pulled back, why she'd shaken free of his hold, but it would be easy to draw her back to him.

And then ...

He stood at the window for a full five minutes, a smile of anticipation on his lips, staring into the night and dreaming – before reality struck.

Like a bolt.

It transfixed him. Chilled him.

It effectively doused his fire.

Face hardening, he stood in the middle of his parlor and wondered what the hell had got into him.

He rose before dawn and headed for the racecourse, for his stables and Carruthers, who was not at all pleased to learn that he'd lost the services of the best work rider he'd ever employed. For once declining to remain and watch his string exercise, Demon left Carruthers grumbling and set his horses ambling back down the road to his farm. The same road led to the cottage.

Fine mist wreathed the hedgerows and blanketed the meadows; it turned golden as dawn tinged the sky. Flick appeared through the gilded haze, a sleepy stable lad atop the plodding cob, heading in for the start of a new day. Demon reined in his bays and waited for her to reach him.

By the time she halted the cob beside his curricle, she was frowning; deep suspicion glowed in her eyes. He nodded, ineffably polite. 'I've tendered your resignation to Carruthers – he doesn't expect to see you again.'

Her frown deepened; to her credit, she didn't ask why. 'But—'

'The matter's simple. If you hadn't resigned, I would have had to dismiss you.' He trapped her gaze and raised a brow. 'I thought you'd prefer to resign.'

Flick studied his eyes, his face. 'Put like that, I don't have much choice.'

The ends of his lips lifted fractionally. 'None.'

'What story did you tell Carruthers?'

'That your ailing mother slipped away, and you'll be joining your aunt's household in London.'

'So I'm not even supposed to be in the vicinity?'

'Precisely.'

She humphed, but without much heat; they'd found Dillon's contact – she was already thinking ahead. 'What about identifying the contact? Have your men turned up anything?'

Because she was watching closely, she saw his hesitation – the swift weighing of his options.

'We've located him, yes.' His gaze swept her consideringly. 'Gillies is currently doing the honors, with strict instructions to miss nothing. If you'd consent to get properly dressed, perhaps we might confer in more conventional style?'

She raised her brows in question.

His smile – a teasing, alluring temptation to dalliance – flashed. 'Go home and change. I'll call at eleven and take you for a tool about the lanes.'

'Perfect – we can discuss how best to go on without any risk of being overheard.' Flick turned the cob and urged him back toward the cottage. 'I'll be ready at eleven.'

Her voice floated back to Demon. The reins lax in his hands, he sat in the strengthening sunshine, watching her bob away from him. His smile deepening, he flicked the reins and set his curricle slowly rolling in her wake.

As promised, she was ready and waiting, a vision in mull muslin, a parasol shading her complexion, when he drew his horses to a scrunching halt before the front steps of Hillgate End.

Tying off his reins, he stepped down from the curricle. Face alight, a soft smile on her lips, she eagerly approached.

She was too slender to bustle – her movement was more a sweeping glide. Demon watched her advance, his every faculty riveted, effortlessly held in thrall.

Luckily, she didn't know it – she had no idea. Secure in that knowledge, he returned her smile. Taking her hand, he bowed elegantly and handed her up to the box seat. She shuffled across; as he turned to follow, Demon caught sight of a maid hovering by the steps. 'I'll return Miss Parteger later in the afternoon – you might mention that to Jacobs.'

'Yes, sir.' The maid bobbed a curtsy.

Climbing up, he took his seat and met Flick's questioning glance. 'Mrs. Shephard packed a hamper so we won't need to return for lunch.'

Her eyes widened, then she nodded. 'It's turning into a lovely day – a picnic is a very good idea.'

Clicking the reins, Demon set the bays pacing, omitting to mention just whose idea it had been.

As he turned out of the drive and the horses stepped out, Flick angled her parasol and glanced at him. 'I take it your men located our quarry?'

Demon nodded, taking the turn to Dullingham in style. 'He's staying at the Ox and Plough.'

'The Ox and Plough?' Flick frowned. 'I don't think I know it.'

'There's no reason you would. It's a seedy little inn off the main road north of Newmarket.'

'Did your man learn the contact's name?'

'He goes by the unenviable name of Bletchley.'

'And he's a Londoner?'

'From his accent, that much seems certain.' Demon slowed his horses as the hamlet of Dullingham came into view. 'Gillies is prepared to swear an oath that Bletchley was born within hearing of Bow bells.'

'Which suggests,' Flick said, turning impulsively to him,

'that the syndicate is London-based.'

'That was always on the cards. The most likely base for a group of rich and greedy gentlemen is London, after all.'

'Hmm.'

When Flick ventured nothing more, Demon glanced at her. She was frowning absentmindedly, her gaze unseeing. It wasn't hard to follow her thoughts. She was considering the syndicate, and the possible need to journey to London to unmask them.

He left her undisturbed, content with her abstraction. As the cottages of Dullingham fell behind, he kept the bays to a steady trot, searching the hedges lining the roadway for the small lane he remembered from years gone by. It appeared on his left; he slowed and turned the bays.

The lane was deeply rutted; despite the strong springs of the carriage, the rocking jerked Flick to attention. Grabbing the front rail, she blinked and looked around. 'Good heavens. Where – *oh*! How lovely!'

Demon smiled. 'It is a pretty spot.'

The lane dwindled to a track; turning the bays onto a stretch of grass, he reined in. 'We'll leave the carriage here.' He nodded to where willows, lit by the sun, hung catkin-draped limbs over a rippling stream. The babble of the brook filled the rustic stillness; sunlight flashed off the water, shooting rainbows through the air. Between the willows, an expanse of lush grass beckoned. 'We can spread the rug by the stream and enjoy the sunshine.'

'Oh, yes! I didn't even know this place existed.'

Alighting, he handed Flick down, then retrieved the well-stocked luncheon basket and a large plaid rug from the boot. Flick relieved him of the rug; holding it in her arms, she strolled beside him to the grassy bank.

Laying aside her parasol, Flick shook out the rug. Demon helped her spread the heavy folds, then handed her onto it. He

waited while she settled, then subsided to lounge, large, lean
– all elegantly indolent – beside her.

She had overheard maids exclaiming how their beaux made
their hearts go pitter-patter. She'd always thought the description a silly nonsense.

Now she knew better. Her heart was tripping in double
time. Definitely pitter-patter.

Reaching for the basket Demon had set by their legs, she
hauled it closer. More definitely between them. It was a
ridiculous reaction – she knew she was safe with him – but
the solidity of the basket made her feel much better. Pulling
out the linen napkins Mrs. Shephard had tucked about the
food, she uncovered roast chicken, slices of beef, and crisp,
fresh rolls. She went to speak, and had to clear her throat.
'Would you prefer a leg, or a breast?'

She looked up; her eyes clashed with Demon's, burning
blue.

Burning?

She blinked and looked again, but he'd looked away,
calmly reaching for the bottle poking out from the basket.

'A leg will do for the moment.'

His voice sounded slightly ... strained. Hiding a frown,
she watched as he eased the cork from the bottle. It popped
free and he looked up, but there was nothing to be read in his
eyes or his expression beyond an easy pleasure in the
moment. He held out a hand for glasses; pushing aside her
uncertainties, she delved into the basket.

Discovering two long flutes, she handed them over; the
wine hissed as he filled them. She took the one he offered her,
studying the tiny bubbles rising through the strawcolored
liquid. 'Champagne?'

'Hmm.' Raising his glass to her, Demon took a sip. 'A
suitable toast to Spring.'

Flick sipped; the bubbles fizzed on her palate, but the wine slid down her throat very pleasantly. She licked her lips. 'Nice.'

'Hmm.' Demon forced himself to look away from her lips – sheening pink curves that he ached to taste. Inwardly frowning at how definite that ache was, he accepted the chicken leg she handed him, a napkin neatly folded about the bone.

Their fingers brushed; he felt hers quiver – was conscious to his bones of the shivery tremble that raced through her. Focusing on the chicken, he sank his teeth into it, then fixed his gaze on the meadows beyond the stream while she busied herself – calmed herself – laying out their repast. Only when she drew in a breath, took a sip of champagne, then fell to eating, did he glance at her again. 'How's Dillon faring?'

She shrugged. 'Well enough.' After a moment, she volunteered, 'I haven't really spoken to him since that evening we learned the truth.'

Demon looked back at the stream to hide his satisfaction; he was delighted to hear that her break with Dillon had not yet healed. 'Who else knows he's there?' He looked at Flick and frowned. 'How does he get food?'

She'd finished her chicken; he watched as she licked her fingers, her wet pink tongue sliding up and around – then she licked her lips. And looked at him.

He managed not to tremble – not to react at all.

'The only one other than us who knows Dillon's at the cottage is Jiggs. He's a footman – he's been at Hillgate End for ... oh, ten years at least. Jiggs takes Dillon food every second day. He told me there's always leftover roast or a pie left wrapped in the larder.' She wrinkled her nose. 'I'm quite sure Foggy also knows Dillon's somewhere close.'

'Very likely.'

They ate and sipped in silence, the tinkling of the brook and the chirp of insects a spring symphony about them.

Replete, Demon dusted his hands, then stretched full length on the rug. Folding his arms behind his head, he closed his eyes. 'Have you told Dillon anything of our discoveries?'

'I haven't told him anything at all.'

From under his lashes, he watched Flick gather up crumbs, then start to repack the basket.

'I decided it wouldn't be wise to tell him we'd found his contact, in case he took it into his head to do something rash – like go into town to see the man himself. It wouldn't do for him to be recognized and taken up for questioning, just when we're making progress.'

Demon suppressed a cynical snort. Dillon was no hothead; he was lazy and indolent. Flick was the one who, with eyes wide open, would rush in where wiser souls feared to tread, supremely confident in her ability to pull things off – to make things happen. To unmask the syndicate.

Loyalty, devotion – and good bottom. Her hallmarks.

The thought slid through his brain and captured his attention. Focused it fully on his angel in disguise.

Lifting his lids a fraction more, he studied her; at the moment, she was all angel – a creation from one of his recent dreams. The sunshine turned her hair to blazing glory, framing her face in golden flames. Her cheeks were delicately flushed – from the warmth of the day and the champagne. As she scanned the meadows, her eyes, soft blue, large and wide, were alive with innocent intelligence.

His gaze dropped – to the slender column of her throat, to the firm swells that filled the bodice of her demure gown, rendering it anything but demure. The fall of her dress hid her waist, the folds swathed her hips and thighs, but having seen her so often in breeches, he didn't need the evidence to conjure the vision.

His smile deepening, he let his lids fall, and he relaxed on the rug. He waited until the basket was neatly repacked and, with her arms wrapped around her knees, her halffilled glass in one hand, she settled to enjoy the view.

'It occurs to me,' he murmured, 'that now we've identified Bletchley and will be following him in earnest, and you no longer need to change clothes and horses morning and afternoon, it would be wise not to go to the cottage at all – just in case Bletchley, or one of his friends, turns the tables on us and follows us back to Dillon. As it's central to our plan to keep Dillon safely hidden, the last thing we want is to lead the syndicate to him.'

'Indeed not.' Flick considered. 'I'll send a message with Jiggs.' Staring at the stream, she narrowed her eyes. 'I'll say that there's no longer any point in me working at the stables – that we think someone from the syndicate is about and don't want to compromise his safety.' She nodded. 'That should keep him at the cottage.'

Sipping her champagne, Flick abandoned all thoughts of Dillon. Dillon was safe at the cottage, and there he could remain until she and Demon had resolved the imbroglio he had mired them all in. On such a lovely afternoon, she refused to dwell on Dillon. A sense of pleasurable ease held her. A curious warmth, like the glow from a distant fire, enveloped her. It wasn't the breeze, for her curls didn't dance, and it wasn't the sun, for it didn't affect all of her at once. Instead, it washed like a warm wave over her, leaving her relaxed, oddly expectant.

In expectation of what she had no idea.

The fact didn't worry her – with Demon, so large, so physically powerful beside her, nothing on earth could threaten her.

The moment was perfect, serene – and strangely intriguing.

There was something in the air – she sensed it with every pore. Which was odd, for she was hardly a fanciful chit. She was, however, abidingly curious – in this case, abidingly interested. Whatever it was that hung in the air, shimmering like a fairy's spell in the bright sunshine, almost of this world but not quite substantial enough for mortal eyes to see – whatever that was, she wanted to know it, understand it.

Whatever it was, she was experiencing it now.

The buzz of the bees, the murmur of the stream, and that undefined, exciting something held her in silent thrall.

Demon slowly sat up and reached for the basket. She turned to see him draw out the almost empty bottle. He refilled his glass, then glanced at hers, almost empty. He looked at her face, briefly searching her eyes, then reached over and tipped the last of the wine into her flute.

It fizzed; she smiled and took a sip.

The bubbles got up her nose.

She sneezed. He looked up; she waved his concern aside. She took another, more careful sip as he returned the bottle to the basket, leaving it by the side of the rug. That done, he lay back again, this time propping on one elbow, his glass in his other hand.

'So,' she asked, shuffling to face him, 'how are we going to follow Bletchley?'

His gaze on the stream, Demon fortified himself with a long sip of champagne, then turned his head and met her gaze, studiously ignoring the expanse of ivory skin, the warm swells promising all manner of earthly delights, now mere inches from his face. 'It's not a hard task. I've got Gillies and two stablemen rotating the watch. It's a small town – now we know what he looks like, and where he's staying, keeping an eye on him shouldn't overtax us.'

'But—' Flick frowned at a nearby willow. 'If we don't learn something soon, won't he notice? Seeing a particular stableman forever about will surely make him suspicious. Newmarket stablemen don't have nothing to do.'

A warm flush swept her shoulders, her breasts. She looked

at Demon; he was looking into his glass, his lids veiling his eyes.

Then he looked at the stream. 'You needn't worry. He'll presumably be at the Heath during morning and afternoon stables – I'll watch him there and in the High Street.' He drained his glass. 'Gillies and the stablemen will watch him in the inns and taverns – they won't be so identifiable in a crowd.'

'Hmm. Perhaps.' Flick stretched her stockinged feet to the sun. 'I'll help, too. About the tracks and in the High Street.' She met Demon's gaze as he looked up at her. 'He won't suspect a young lady of watching him.'

He stared at her for a moment, as if he'd lost the thread of the conversation, then he murmured, 'Very likely not.' His gaze grew intent; he lifted one hand. 'Hold still.'

She froze so completely that she stopped breathing. A vise clamped about her lungs; her heart stuttered, skipped, then raced. She held quiveringly still as his fingers slid through the curls above one ear, ruffling the locks as he disengaged ... something. When he withdrew his hand and showed her a long leaf, flicking it onto the grass, she dragged in a breath and smiled weakly. 'Thank you.'

His eyes met hers. 'My pleasure.'

The words were deep, rumbling; the tone set something inside her vibrating. Her gaze trapped in his, she felt flustered panic rise. She looked down and gulped a mouthful of champagne.

The bubbles hit her again; this time, she nearly choked. Eyes watering, she waved a hand before her face and hauled in a much-needed breath. 'I'm really not used to this.' She lifted her glass. 'This is all new to me.'

Demon's gaze had remained steady, his eyes on hers. His lips lifted lightly. 'Yes, I know.'

Flick felt curiously warm, distinctly light-headed. There was a light in Demon's eyes, an understanding she couldn't fathom.

Demon saw confusion grow in her eyes – he looked away, uncertain of how much of his interest, his curious, newfound obsession with innocence, showed in his. He gestured to the sylvan scene before them and looked at her, his expression easy, controlled. 'If you haven't been here before, you couldn't have strolled the path by the stream. Shall we?'

'Oh, yes! Let's.'

He retrieved her almost empty glass, drained it, then set both glasses back in the basket. Then he rose and held out his hands to her. 'Come. We'll investigate.'

She gave him her hands; he drew her to her feet, then led her to where a beaten path followed the meandering stream. They strolled along; she ambled beside him, sometimes ahead of him, furling her parasol when it limited her view of his face. Demon was grateful – the parasol had prevented him from watching her – any of her. They saw a mother duck with a gaggle of tiny ducklings, all paddling furiously in her wake; Flick pointed and exclaimed, and smiled delightedly. A sleek trout broke the rippling surface, chasing a fat fly; a kingfisher swooped out of the shade, dazzling them with his brilliant plumage. Flick grabbed his arm in her excitement, then sighed as the bird flew on down the stream.

'There's a bronze dragonfly.'

'Where?' She searched the banks.

'Over there.' He leaned close; she leaned closer still, following his pointing finger to where the dragonfly hovered above a patch of reeds. Engrossed, she drew in a breath and held it; he did the same.

The scent of her washed through him, sweet, fresh – quite unlike the cloying perfumes to which he was accustomed, to which he was immune. Her fragrance was light, airy; it reminded him of lavender and appleblossom, the essence of spring.

'Ah.' The dragonfly darted away, and she exhaled.

His head swam.

She turned to him; they were so close that her skirts brushed his boots. If she took another deep breath, her breasts would touch his coat. His nearness surprised her; she looked up, eyes widening, lips parting on a silent gasp as her breath seized. Her eyes met his – for one fleeting instant, pure awareness invested the soft blue. Then puzzlement seeped in.

He saw it, but had too much to do holding his own desires in check to attempt a distraction. For the last hours, he'd delighted in her – in her innocence, in the fragile beauty of a female untouched, unawakened. He'd seen, sensed, her first glimmerings of consciousness – of him, of herself, of their inherent sensuality.

Sensuality was a quality he'd lived with daily for ten years and more; experiencing it anew, through her innocent eyes, had heightened his own far-from-innocent desires.

Her eyes held his; about them, the pulse of burgeoning spring hummed and throbbed. He felt it in his bones, in his blood. In his loins.

She felt it, too, but she didn't know what it meant. When he said nothing, she relaxed, just a little, and smiled, tentatively yet without the slightest fear. 'Perhaps we'd better head back.'

He held her gaze for an instant, then forced himself to nod. 'Perhaps we had.'

His voice had deepened; she threw him another, slightly questioning look. Ignoring it, he took her hand and turned her back along the path.

By the time they regained the swath of green, Flick's puzzlement had grown. Absentmindedly, she helped him fold the rug, then, picking up her parasol, followed him to the curricle.

After stowing the basket and rug, he returned to where she waited by the curricle's side, her frowning gaze fixed on the grass where they'd lain. She looked up as he halted beside her. She said nothing, but her frown was etched in her eyes. He saw it, and read her unvoiced questions with ease.

He had a very good idea what she was feeling – the disconcerting uncertainty, the nervous confusion. She was so open, so trusting, that she thought nothing of showing her vulnerability to him. He knew all the questions crowding her mind – the questions she couldn't begin to formulate.

He knew the answers, too.

She waited, her eyes on his, clearly hoping for some hint as to what it was she sensed. Her stance was both a demand and a plea – a clear wish to know.

Her face was tilted up to him; her tapered chin was firm. Her full lips, tinted delicate rose, beckoned. The soft blue of her eyes, clouded by the first flush of desire, promised heaven and more.

If he'd stopped to think, he would never have risked it, but the web of her innocence held him, compelled him – assured him this was simple, straightforward, uncomplicated.

His eyes locked with hers, he slowly lifted one hand and gently framed her jaw. Her breath caught; deliberately, still moving with mesmerizing slowness, he brushed the pad of his thumb along her lower lip. The contact shook her – and him; he instinctively tightened his hold on his demons. Their gazes held, hers unwaveringly curious.

He drew in a shallow breath and slowly lowered his head, giving her plenty of time to balk. Other than tightening her grip on her parasol, she moved not at all. Her gaze dropped to his lips; she sucked in a breath, only to have it tangle in her throat. Her lashes fluttered, then lowered; her eyes shut on a sigh as his lips touched hers.

It was the most delicate kiss he could remember sharing – a communion of lips, nothing more. Hers were soft, as delicate as they looked, intensely feminine. He brushed them once, twice, then covered them, increasing the pressure only slightly, aware to his bones of her youth.

He was about to draw back, to bring the light caress to an end, when her lips moved beneath his – in clear response, artless, untutored. Enthralling.

She kissed him back – gently, tentatively – her question as clear as it had been in her eyes.

Without thought, he responded, the hand framing her jaw tightening, holding her face steady as he shifted closer, angling his head as he deepened the kiss.

Her lips parted under his.

Just a little – just enough for him to taste her. He ran the tip of his tongue over her lower lip, caressing the soft flesh within, then briefly stroked her tongue, teasing her senses, already taut, quiveringly tight.

They quaked; she shuddered delicately, then stepped closer, so her breasts met his chest, her hips his thighs. Completely trusting, she leaned into him, into his strength.

Demon's head reeled; his blood pounded urgently. The need to close his arms about her – to lock her against him and mold her to him – was almost overwhelming.

But she was too young, too innocent, too new to this game for that.

His demons wailed and demanded – with what wit he had left he fought to deny them.

Even while he fell deeper into their kiss.

Unaware of his problem, Flick reveled in the sudden heat that suffused her, in the heady sense of male strength that surrounded her, in the firm touch of his lips on hers, on the sensual slide of his tongue between her lips.

This was a kiss – the sort of kiss she'd heard maids giggling over, a kiss that slowly curled her toes. It was enthralling, demanding yet unfrightening, an experience of the senses.

The vicar's son had once kissed her – or tried to. That had been nothing like this. There had been no magic shimmering in the air, no skittering sensations assailing her nerves. And none of the excitement slowly growing within her, as if this was a beginning, not an end.

The idea intrigued her, but Demon's lips, firm, almost hard, cool yet imparting heat, effortlessly held her attention, denying all her efforts to think. Leaning against him, her only certainty was a feeling of gratitude – that he'd consented to show her what could be, not just in a kiss but in one glorious afternoon of simple pleasure.

The sort of pleasure a man and a woman could share, if the man knew what he was about. She was immensely grateful to him for explaining, for demonstrating, for enlightening her ignorance. Now, in the future, she'd know what to look for – know where to set her standards.

As for today, she'd enjoyed his tutelage, enjoyed the afternoon – and this kiss. Immensely.

Her unrestrained, open appreciation very nearly overwhelmed Demon. Inwardly shaking with the effort of resisting the powerful instincts that had for so long been a part of him, he finally realized his hand had fallen from her face to her shoulder. Raising his other hand, he gripped her upper arm as well and gently eased her back from him. Then, with gentle care and a reluctance he felt to his soul, he drew back and ended the kiss.

He was breathing too fast. He watched as her lids fluttered, then rose to reveal eyes a much brighter blue than before. She met his gaze; he prayed she couldn't read his state. He attempted a suave smile. 'So now you know.'

She blinked. Before she could speak, he turned her to the curricle. 'Come – we should return to Hillgate End.'

He drove her back directly. To his surprise, she was patently unflustered, sitting beside him, her parasol open, sweetly smiling at the sunwashed countryside.

If anyone was flustered, it seemed it was he. He still felt disoriented, nerves and muscles twitching. By the time he turned the bays through the gates of Hillgate End, he was inwardly frowning, and feeling a touch grim.

He wasn't at all sure what had happened that afternoon, especially not who or what had instigated the proceedings. He'd certainly organized to spend a comfortable, enjoyable afternoon with an angel, but he couldn't remember deciding to seduce her.

Things had not gone according to any plan of his.

Which was possibly not surprising – in this sphere, he was a rank amateur. He'd never dallied with anyone so young, so untouched – so damned *innocent* – before. Which was at least half his problem – half the reason he was increasingly attracted to her. She was a very fresh taste to his definitely jaded palate; awakening her was a rare pleasure, a sweet delight.

But seducing an innocent carried responsibility – a heavy, unavoidable responsibility he'd happily steered clear of for all his years. He didn't want to change – had no intention of changing. He was happy with his life as it was.

The taste of her – apple and delicate spice – returned to him, and had him stiffening. Swallowing a curse, he drew the bays up before the front steps. He tied off the reins and stepped down; rounding the carriage, he helped her down.

She smoothed her skirts, then straightened and smiled – gloriously, openly, entirely without guile. 'Thank you for a delightful afternoon.'

He stared at her, conscious to his bones of a demonic urge to taste her again. It took all his concentration to maintain a suitably impassive mien, to take the hand she held out to him, squeeze it gently – and let go.

With a nod, he turned back to the curricle. 'I'll keep you

informed of anything we learn. Do convey my respects to the General.'

'Yes, of course.'

She watched him drive away, a smile on her lips; as the shadows of the drive enclosed him, a frown settled on Demon's face.

He was still frowning when he reached home.

informed of anything we learn. Do convey my respects to the Admiral.'

'Yes, of course.'

She watched him until he swung away, his limp, as the horses of he .... on .... on Demon's face.

He was still frowning with quite ....d hone

Chapter Six

Demon ran Gillies to earth later that evening in the crowded tap of the Swan; he was nursing a pint and keeping a watchful eye on Bletchley. Their quarry was part of a genial group crowding one corner. Demon slid onto the bench beside Gillies. 'Any action?'

'Nah. He went back to the Ox and Plough this afternoon, seemingly to check the post. He got a letter. Looked like he was expecting it.'

'Did he leave it there?'

Glancing at Bletchley, Gillies shook his head. 'He's got it on him, in an inside waistcoat pocket. He's taking no chances of losing it.'

Demon sipped his beer. 'What did he do after he got it?'

'Perked up, he did, and bustled right out again, back to the Heath for afternoon stables.'

Demon nodded. 'I saw him there – it looked like he had Robinson's string in his sights.'

'Aye – that's my thought, too.' Gillies took another long pull from his pint. 'Robinson's got at least two favored runners in the Spring Carnival.'

'I didn't see Bletchley approach any of the riders.'

'Nor did I.'

'Did he make contact with any gentlemen?'

'Not that I saw. And I've had him in sight since he came

92

down the stairs this morning.'

Demon nodded, Flick's warning in mind. 'Stay at the stud tomorrow. Cross can follow Bletchley to morning stables – I'll take over after that.'

'Aye.' Gillies drained his pint. 'It wouldn't do for him to get too familiar with my face.'

Over the next three days, together with Cross and Hills, two of his stablemen, Demon and Gillies kept an unwavering watch on Bletchley. With activity on the Heath increasing in preparation for the Craven meeting – the official Spring Carnival of the English racing calendar – there was reason aplenty for Demon to be about the tracks and stables, evaluating his string and those of his major rivals. From atop Ivan the Terrible, keeping Bletchley in view in the relatively flat, open areas surrounding the Heath was easy; increasingly, it was Demon who kept their quarry in sight for most of the day. Gillies, Cross and Hills took turns keeping an unrelenting but unobtrusive watch at all other times, from the instant Bletchley came down for breakfast, to the time he took his candle and climbed the stairs to bed.

Bletchley remained unaware of their surveillance, his obliviousness at least partly due to his concentration on the job in hand. He was careful not to be too overt in approaching the race jockeys, often spending hours simply watching and noting. Looking, Demon suspected, for any hint of a hold, any susceptibility with which to coerce the selected jockeys into doing his masters' bidding.

On the fourth afternoon, Flick caught up with Demon.

Disguising her irritation at the fact that since leaving her before the manor steps, he'd made not the slightest attempt to see her – to tell her what was going on, what he and his men had discovered – she twirled her open parasol and advanced determinedly across the grass between the walking pens, her gaze fixed unwaveringly on him.

She was twenty yards away when he turned his head and looked directly at her. Leaning against the last pen's fence, he'd been scanning the onlookers watching his and two other stables' strings exercise. His back against the top rung, his hands sunk in his breeches pockets, one leg bent, booted foot braced on the fence's lower rung, he looked subtly dangerous.

Flick inwardly humphed and dismissed the thought of danger. She was impatient – she wanted to be doing something, not sitting on her hands waiting to learn what had happened long after it had. But she'd dealt with Dillon and the General long enough to know how to approach a male. It wouldn't do to show impatience or anger. Instead, smiling sunnily, she strolled to Demon's side, ignoring the frown forming in his eyes. 'Isn't it a lovely afternoon?'

'Indeed.'

The single word was trenchantly noncommittal; his frown darkened, deepening the blue of his eyes. Still smiling sweetly, she turned and scanned the throng. 'Where's Bletchley?'

Straightening, Demon watched her check through the onlookers, then inwardly sighed. 'Under the oak to the left. He's wearing a scarlet neckerchief.'

She located Bletchley and studied him; against his will, Demon studied her. She was gowned once more in sprig muslin, tiny blue fern fronds scattered over white. The gown, however, barely registered; what was in the gown transfixed his attention, captured his awareness.

All soft curves and creamy complexion, she looked good enough to eat – which was the cause of his frown. The instant she appeared, he'd been struck by an urgent, all but ungovernable, ravenous urge. Which had startled him – his urges were not usually so independent, so totally dismissive, of his will.

As he watched, studied, drank in the sight of her, a light

94

breeze playfully ruffled her curls, setting them dancing; it also ruffled her light skirts, briefly, tantalizingly, molding them to her hips, her thighs, her slender legs. Her heartshaped bottom.

He looked away and shifted, easing the fullness in his groin.

'Has he approached any gentlemen yet? Or they, him?'

Relocating Bletchley, he shook his head. 'It appears his task here – presumably the job Dillon was supposed to do – is to make contact with the jockeys and persuade them to his masters' cause.' After a moment, he added, 'He received a letter some days ago, which spurred him to renewed activity.'

'Orders?'

'Presumably. But I seriously doubt he'll report back to his masters in writing.'

'He probably can't write.' Flick glanced over her shoulder and met his eye. 'So there's still a chance the syndicate – at least one of them – will appear here.'

'Yes. To learn of Bletchley's success, if nothing else.'

'Hmm.' She looked at Bletchley. 'I'll take over watching him for the rest of the afternoon.' She glanced up at him. 'I'm sure you've got other matters to attend to.'

He captured her gaze. 'Be that as it may—'

'As I've already pointed out, he won't expect a young lady to be watching him – it's the perfect disguise.'

'He might not guess that you're watching him, but I can guarantee he'll notice if you follow him.'

She swung to face him; he saw her chin firm. 'Be *that* as it may—'

'No.' The single word, uttered quietly and decisively, brought her up short. Eyes narrowing, she glared up at him; he towered, without apology, over her. 'There is no reason whatever for you to be involved.'

Her eyes, normally so peacefully lucent, spat sparks. 'This

was *my* undertaking – *I* invited you to *help*. 'Help' does not mean relegating me to the position of mere cipher.'

He held her irate gaze. 'You are not a mere cipher—'

'Good!' With a terse nod, she swung back to the Heath. 'I'll help you watch Bletchley then.'

Weaving back to avoid decapitation by her parasol, Demon swore beneath his breath. Falling back half a step, he glared at her back, her hips, the round swells of her bottom, as she stood, stubbornly intransigent, her back to him. 'Flick—'

'Look! He's heading off.'

Glancing up, Demon saw Bletchley quit his position by the oak and amble, with a less-than-convincing show of idleness, toward one of the neighboring stables. Glancing at Flick, already on her toes, about to step out in Bletchley's wake, Demon hesitated, then his eyes narrowed and his lips curved. 'As you're so determined to help ...'

Stepping to her right, he caught her hand and set it on his sleeve, anchoring her close – very close – to his side.

Blinking wildly, she looked up. 'What do you mean?' Her voice was gratifyingly breathless.

'If you want to help me watch Bletchley, then you'll have to help provide our disguise.' He raised his brows at her. 'Just keep that parasol to the side, and as far as possible, keep your face turned to me.'

'But how am I to watch Bletchley?'

He strolled; she was forced to stroll beside him. A smile of definite intent on his face, he looked down at her. 'You don't need to watch him for us to follow him, but we need to see who he's meeting.'

One swift glance ahead verified that Bletchley was heading behind the stable, which, from the horses Demon could see on the Heath, would almost certainly be empty. With Flick's not-exactly-willing assistance, he put his mind to creating a tableau of a couple entirely engrossed with each other, of no possible consequence to Bletchley.

Trapped by his gaze, by the hard palm that held her fingers immobile on his sleeve, by the strength, the power, he so effortlessly wielded, Flick struggled to preserve a facade of normalcy, to slow her breathing and steady her heart. To relax her stiff spine and stroll with passable grace – grace enough to match the reprobate beside her.

The glances he shot ahead, tracking Bletchley, were reassuring, confirming that his intent was indeed to follow the villain and witness any meeting behind the stable. His intent *wasn't* to unnerve her, to send her senses into quiv ering stasis. That was merely an accident, an unexpected, unintended repercussion. Thankfully, he hadn't noticed; she fought to get her wits back in order and her senses realigned.

'Who do you think he's meeting?' she whispered. Her lungs were still not functioning properly.

'I've no idea.' He looked down at her, his heavy lids half obscuring his eyes. His voice had sunk to a deep purr. 'Just pray it's a member of the syndicate.'

His tone and his sleepy expression were disconcerting, of no help at all in reestablishing her equanimity.

Demon looked up. Bletchley had halted at the corner of the stable. As he watched, Bletchley's gaze swept the throng, then fixed on them. Smoothly, unhurriedly, a wolfish smile curving his lips, he looked down, into Flick's wide eyes. 'Smile,' he instructed. She did, weakly. His own smile deepening, he raised his free hand; with the back of his knuckles he brushed her cheek.

Her breath caught – she skittered back and blushed; effortlessly, his smile very evident, he drew her back.

'I'm only teasing,' he murmured. 'It's just play.'

'I know,' Flick assured him, her heart beating frantically. Unfortunately, he was playing a game with which she was unfamiliar. She tried her best to relax, to smile easily, teasingly, back.

From beneath his lashes, Demon glanced ahead; Bletchley was no longer looking their way. After one last scan of the Heath, he turned and lumbered around the building, out of sight.

Flick's eyes widened; she immediately stepped out. He hauled her up short, pulling her to his side. 'No.' She looked up, ready to glare; he leaned closer – nearer – so the ebb and flow of their interaction looked like a seductive game. 'We don't know,' he murmured, his lips close by her temple, 'who he's meeting and where they are. They might be behind us.'

'Oh.' Obedient to his pressure on her arm, Flick, a smile on her lips, steeled herself and leaned against him, her shoulder and upper arm nestling into the warmth of his chest. Then, with the same sweet, inane smile, she eased away as they continued to stroll.

After a moment – after she'd caught her breath – she looked up, into his smiling eyes. 'What are you planning to do?'

His lips quirked, very definitely teasing. 'Join Bletchley and his friend, of course.'

They'd reached the corner of the stable; without pause, Demon continued on, not hugging the shadow of the wall as Bletchley had but strolling on and past, into the clear area behind the stable bounded by a railing fence.

As soon as they had cleared the corner, Flick looked ahead. Demon released her elbow, slid his arm about her waist, drew her against him and kissed her.

She nearly dropped her parasol.

'*Don't* look at him – he'll notice.' Demon breathed the injunction against her lips, then kissed her, briefly, again.

Wits reeling, she hauled in a breath. 'But – '

'No buts. Just follow my lead and we'll be able to hear everything – and see it all, too.' Setting her on her feet, shielded by her open parasol, presently pointed, rather waveringly, at Bletchley, his eyes searched hers, then he added, his voice deep and low, 'If you won't behave, I'll have to distract you some more.'

She stared at him. Then she cleared her throat. 'What do you want me to do?'

'Concentrate on me as if you aren't even aware Bletchley and friend exist.'

She kept her gaze glued to his face. 'Has his friend arrived?' She hadn't been able to see before he'd kissed her.

'Not yet, but I think someone's drifting this way.' Righting her parasol, Demon smiled down at her; his hand resting lightly at her waist, he turned her. Gazes locked, they strolled on, apparently aimlessly.

Bletchley had halted midway along the back of the stable, clearly waiting for someone to join him. From the corner of her eye, Flick saw him frown at them. Demon bent his head and blew in her ear; she squirmed and giggled, entirely spontaneously.

Naturally, he did it again.

With no option but to throw herself into their deception, she giggled and wriggled and squirmed. Laughing, Demon caught her more closely to him, then with a flourish, he whirled her, twirled her – they stopped with him leaning against the railing fence, her before him. His eyes glowed wickedly; his smile was distinctly devilish.

Flick caught her breath on a gasp, a perfectly natural, silly smile on her lips. 'What next?' she whispered.

Screened from Bletchley by her parasol, Demon looked down into her eyes. 'Put your hand on my shoulder, stretch up and kiss me.'

She blinked at him; he raised his brows innocently, the expression in his eyes anything but. 'You've done it before.'

She had, but that had been different. He'd started it. Still ... it hadn't been difficult.

Fleetingly frowning at him, she placed her free hand on his broad shoulder and stretched up on her toes. Even so, he had to lower his head – balanced precariously on the very tips of her toes, she *had* to lean against him, her breasts to his hard chest, to reach his lips with hers.

She kissed him – just a simple, gentle kiss. When she went to draw back, his hands firmed, one spanning her waist, the other closing about her fingers gripping her parasol. He held her steady as his lips closed over hers.

Tilting her and her parasol to just the right angle, Demon held her before him, and, from beneath his lashes, looked out under the parasol's frilled rim. Bletchley, ten yards away, had been slouching, watching them idly – he doubtless considered Demon a reckless blade set on seducing a sweet country miss. But although he watched, Bletchley wasn't interested. Then he straightened, alert, as another man joined him.

Breaking off the kiss, Demon breathed a curse.

Flick blinked, but he didn't shift, didn't let her down.

'No – don't turn,' he hissed as she went to twist her head. 'Who is it?'

His lips, presently at eye level, twisted into a grim grimace. 'Another jockey.' Disappointment laced his tone.

'Perhaps he has a message from the syndicate.'

'Shssh. Listen.'

Balanced against him, she strained her ears.

'Let's see if I got this straight.'

That had to be the jockey; the voice was clear, not scratchy.

'You'll give me three ponies the day before the Stakes, an' two ponies the day after, if I bring Cyclone in out o' the places. That right?'

'Aye – that's the deal,' Bletchley grated. 'Take it or leave it.'

The jockey was silent, presumably ruminating; Demon looked down at her, then his arm slid further around her, better supporting her against him.

'Relax,' he breathed. His lips brushed hers in the lightest of caresses, then the jockey spoke again.

'I'll take it.'

'Done.'

'That's our cue,' Demon said *sotto voce*.

The next instant, he laughed aloud; his arm tightening about her, he swung her around and stood her on her feet. He grinned. 'Come along, sweetheart. Wouldn't do for the local gabblemongers to start wondering where we've got to. Let alone what we've been doing.'

He spoke loudly enough for Bletchley and the jockey to hear. Flick blushed and ignored their audience completely; locking both hands about her parasol handle, she turned back to the Heath with a swish of her skirts.

With another demonic laugh – one of triumph – Demon, his hand lying proprietorially on her back just a little lower than her waist, ushered her around the stable, back into the safety of the racing throng.

The instant they rounded the corner of the stable, Flick wriggled to dislodge his hand. It only pressed closer.

'We can't drop our roles yet.' Demon's murmur stirred the curls above her ear. 'Bletchley's following. While he can see us, we'll need to preserve our act.'

She shot him a suspicious, distracted look; her bottom was heating.

He smiled, all wolf. 'Who knows? An established disguise might come in handy in the following days.'

Following *days*? Flick hoped she didn't look as scandalized as she felt; the laughing, teasing look in Demon's eyes suggested otherwise.

To her consternation, Bletchley returned to stand under the oak beside the Heath – and proceeded to watch the exercising strings for the next hour.

So they watched him, while Demon lived up to his nickname and exercised his rakish talents, using ploy after ploy to ruffle her composure. To make her blush and skitter, and act the besotted miss.

Whether it was due to his expertise or otherwise, it grew increasingly easy to act besotted. To relax and laugh and smile. And blush.

He knew just how to tease her, just how to catch her eye and invite her to laugh – at him, at them, at herself. Knew just how to touch her – lightly, fleetingly – so that her senses leapt and her heart galloped faster than any horse on the Heath. When Bletchley, after approaching one other jockey and getting short shrift, finally headed back into the town, she'd blushed more than she ever had before.

Clinging to her parasol as if it were a weapon, and her last defense, she met Demon's eye. 'I'll leave you now – I'm sure you can keep him in sight for the rest of the afternoon.'

His eyes held hers, their expression difficult to read; for one instant, she thought it was reluctance she glimpsed in the blue – reluctance to set aside their roles.

'I don't need to follow him.' Demon looked to the edge of the Heath and raised his hand. Gillies, lounging against a post, nodded and slipped off in Bletchley's wake.

Demon looked back at his companion of the afternoon. 'Come – I'll drive you home.'

Her gaze trapped in his, she waved to the nearby road. 'I have the groom with the gig.'

'We can send him on ahead.' He raised one brow and reached for her hand. 'Surely you'd rather be driven home behind my bays than the nag harnessed to the gig?'

As one who appreciated good horseflesh, her choice was a foregone conclusion. With an inclination of her head that was almost regal, she consented to his scheme, consented to let him hold her by him – to enjoy her freshness – for just a little while more.

He was seated in the armchair before the fire in his front parlor, staring at the flames and seeing her angelic face, her soft blue eyes, and the curious, considering light that flashed in them from time to time, when, once again, she came tapping on his windowpane. Lips setting, he didn't even bother swearing – just rose, set aside the brandy balloon he'd been cradling, and crossed to the window.

This time, when he pulled the curtains aside, he was relieved to see she was wearing skirts – to whit, her riding habit. He raised the sash. 'Don't you ever use the door?'

The glance she levelled at him was reproving. 'I came to invite you to accompany me to see Dillon.'

'I thought we'd agreed not to see him at all.'

'That was before. Now we know Bletchley's the contact, and that he's wandering about the Heath, we should warn Dillon and bring him up to date, so he doesn't do anything rash.'

Dillon would never put himself to so much bother. The observation burned Demon's tongue, but he swallowed the words. He wasn't at all happy at the notion of Flick riding about the county alone at night, but he knew there was no point trying to talk her out if it. Mentally locating his rid ing gloves, he reached for the sash. 'I'll meet you by the stable.'

Pointy chin resolute, she nodded, then slid into the shadows.

Demon closed the window and went to warn the Shephards he was going out for a few hours.

Atop Jessamy, Flick was waiting by the main stable. Demon hauled open the door. In the dimness inside, lit by the shaft of moonlight streaming in through the door, he located his tack and carried it to Ivan's box. The big stallion was surprised to see him, and even more surprised to be saddled and led out. Luckily, before Ivan could consider and decide to protest, he set eyes on Jessamy.

Noting the stallion's fixed stare, Demon grunted and swung up to his saddle. At least he wouldn't have to exercise his talents on Ivan during their ride through the moonlight – Ivan would follow, intent, in Flick's wake.

She, of course, led the way.

They crossed his fields, the night black velvet about them. The cottage appeared deserted, a denser bulk in the deep shadows between the trees. Flick rode into the clearing behind it and dismounted. Demon followed, tethering Ivan well clear of the mare.

A twig cracked.

Flick whirled, squinting at the cottage. 'It's us. Me and Demon.'

'Oh,' came a rather shaky voice from the dark. After a moment, Dillon asked, 'Are you coming in?'

'Of course.' Flick started for the cottage just as Demon reached her; he followed close on her heels.

'We thought,' she said, ducking through the lean-to and stepping into the main room, 'that you'd want to know what we've learned.'

Dillon looked up, his face lit by the glow of the lantern he'd set alight. 'You've identified one of the syndicate?'

Wild hope colored his tone; settling onto a stool by the table, Flick grimaced. 'No – not yet.'

'Oh.' Dillon's face fell. He slumped down in the chair at the table's end.

Drawing off his gloves at the table's other end, Demon studied Dillon, noting his pallor and the lines the last week had etched in his cheeks. It was as if the reality of his situation, now fully realized, and the consequent worry of apprehension and exposure, were eating away at his childish self-absorption. If that was so, then it was all to the good. Drawing out the last rickety stool, Demon sat. 'We've discovered your elusive contact.'

Dillon looked up, hope gleaming in his eyes. Demon raised his brows at Flick, wondering if she wanted to tell Dillon herself. Instead, she nodded for him to continue. He looked back at Dillon. 'Your man's name is Bletchley – he's a Londoner.' Briefly, he described their quarry.

Dillon nodded. 'Yes – that's him – the man who recruited me. He used to bring me the lists of horses and jockeys.'

Flick leaned forward. 'And the money?'

Dillon glanced at her, then colored, but continued to meet her eyes. 'Yes. He always had my fee.'

'No, I mean the money for the jockeys. How did they get paid? Did Bletchley give you their money?'

Dillon frowned. 'I don't know how they got paid – I wasn't involved. That's not how it worked when I did it.'

'Then how did you do the organizing?' Demon asked.

Dillon shrugged. 'It was simple – the list of jockeys told me how much to offer each one. I did, and then reported if they'd accepted. I wasn't involved in getting their money to them after the race.'

'After the race,' Flick repeated. 'What about the payments before the race?'

Dillon's puzzled frown grew. 'Before?'

'As a down payment,' Demon explained.

Dillon shook his head. 'There *weren't* any payments before the race – only the one payment after the deed was done. And someone else took care of that, not me.'

Flick frowned. 'They've changed their ways.'

'That's understandable,' Demon said. 'They're presently targeting races during the Craven meeting, one of the premier meetings in the calendar. The betting on those races is enormous – one or two fixed races, and they'll make a major killing. That's something the jockeys will know. They'll also know that the risk of being questioned by the stewards is greater – more attention is always paid to the major races during the major meets.'

105

Dillon frowned. 'Last season, they didn't try to fix any truly major races.'

'It's possible they've been building up to this season – or that they've grown more cocky, more assured, and are now willing to take greater risks in the hope of greater rewards. Regardless, the jockeys for the Spring Carnival races would obviously demand more to pull their mounts.' Demon glanced at Dillon. 'The going rate for the two races we've heard fixed is five ponies.'

'*Five*?' Dillon's brows flew up. 'I was only once directed to offer three.'

'So the price has gone up, and they're locking the jockeys in by offering some now, some later. Once the first payment's accepted, the jockey's more or less committed, which is less risky for the syndicate.' Demon looked at Dillon. 'They would, I fancy, be happy to make a down payment to avoid a repetition of what happened in the first race this year.'

Dillon slowly nodded. 'Yes, I see. This way, the fix is more or less certain.'

'Hmm.' Flick frowned. 'Did you ever hear anything from the jockeys you organized about how they got paid?'

Dillon paled. 'Only from one, early last season.' He glanced at Demon. 'The jockey wasn't too happy – his money was left at his mother's cottage. He didn't feel easy about the syndicate knowing where to find his old mum.'

Demon met Dillon's gaze. He didn't like what he was learning. The syndicate sounded disturbingly intelligent – an evil, ruthless and *intelligent* opponent was, in his book, the worst. More of a challenge, but infinitely more dangerous.

That, of course, would normally whet his appetite, stir his Cynster blood. In this case, he only had to look at Flick to inwardly curse and wish the whole damned syndicate to hell. Unfortunately, the way the situation was shaping, it was going to fall to him to escort them there, while simultaneously protecting an angel from the consequences of her almost certain involvement in the syndicate's fall.

While the thought of the syndicate didn't stir his blood, Flick did – in quite a different way, a way he hadn't experienced before. This was not mere lust. He was well acquainted with that demon, and while it was certainly in the chorus, its voice wasn't the loudest. That distinction currently belonged to the impulse to protect her; if he complied with his inner promptings, he'd tie her up, cart her off to a high tower with a single door bearing a large and effective lock, and incarcerate her there until he had slain the dragon she was determined to flush out.

Unfortunately . . .

'We'd better go.' She gathered her gloves and stood, her stool grating on the floor.

He rose more slowly, watching the interaction between Flick and Dillon.

Dillon was looking earnestly at her; she tugged on her gloves, then met his gaze. 'We'll let you know what we discover – when we discover something. Until then, it's best that you stay out of sight.'

Dillon nodded. Reaching out, he caught her hand and squeezed. 'Thank you.'

She humphed and shook free, but without any heat. 'I told you I'm only doing this for the General.'

The statement lacked the force of her earlier rendering; Demon doubted even she believed it.

Dillon's lips twisted rather ruefully. 'Even so.' He looked at Demon and stood. 'I owe you a debt I'll never be able to repay.'

His expression impassive, Demon met his gaze. 'I'll think of something, never fear.'

Dillon's eyes widened at his tone; with a curt nod, Demon turned to Flick.

107

Frowning, she glanced back at Dillon. 'We'll look in in a few days.' Then she turned and led the way out.

Following on her heels, Demon breathed deeply as they emerged into the night. A quick glance at the sky revealed a black pall – the moon had been engulfed by dark clouds. Within the cottage, the light of the lantern dimmed, then died. Eyes adjusting to the dark, Demon looked around as he strode across the clearing; no other human was anywhere about – just the two of them alone in the night.

Flick didn't wait for help but scrambled into her saddle. Untying Ivan's reins, Demon quickly mounted, holding the stallion steady as Flick trotted Jessamy over.

'I'll ride home through the park. I'll see you on the Heath tomorrow afternoon.'

'No.'

Surprised, she stared at him. Before she could scowl, he clarified, 'I'll ride back to Hillgate End with you. It's after midnight – you shouldn't be out riding alone.'

She didn't scowl, but he sensed her resistance. She studied him, then opened her mouth, doubtless to argue, when a breeze wafted through the clearing and set the trees shivering. It moaned, softly, eerily, through the branches, then died away on a sigh, an expiring banshee leaving only the rustling leaves slowly stilling in the deep darkness.

Flick shut her mouth and nodded. 'Yes, all right.'

Shaking her reins she set out; muttering his by now customary oath, Demon wheeled Ivan and set out to catch up. He did in short order; side by side, they rode across the next field – the last bastion of his domain. Beyond its hedge, directly ahead of them, lay the furthest reaches of the former park of Hillgate End.

There was a spot they both knew where the hedge thinned; they pushed through onto an old bridle path. Flick led the way into the dark shadows beneath the trees.

Although some of the park's paths were kept in good condition for riders, notably Flick, to enjoy, this was not one of them. Bushes pressed close on either side, branches flapped before their faces. They had to walk their mounts – it was too dangerous to even trot. The path was deep in leaf mold; it occasionally dipped, creating the added danger of their horses slipping. They both instinctively guarded their precious mounts, alert to every shift in weight, in muscle, in balance, of the beasts beneath them.

The General had no love of shooting, so the park had become a refuge for wildlife. A badger snuffled and growled as they passed him; later, they heard rustling, then the yips of a fox.

'I didn't realize it would be this bad.' Flick ducked beneath a low-hanging branch.

Demon grunted. 'I thought this was the route you used to go back and forth to the cottage. Obviously not.'

'I normally take the path to the east, but that crosses the stream twice, and after last night's rain, I didn't want to risk Jessamy's knees going up and down slippery banks.'

Demon didn't point out that she was risking Jessamy's knees right now – they were deep in the park, with the centuries-old trees forming an impenetrable canopy overhead; he could barely see Flick, let alone any irregularities in the path. Luckily, both Jessamy and Ivan could see better than him. They stepped out confidently; both he and Flick fell back on trust and let their horses find their own way.

After some time had elapsed, he asked, 'Doesn't this path cross the stream, too?'

'Yes, but there's a bridge.' After a moment, Flick amended, 'Well, there *was* a bridge last time I came this way.'

Lips thinning, Demon didn't bother asking how long ago that had been; they'd deal with the rotted and possibly ex-bridge when they came to it.

Before they did, it started to rain.

At first, the light pattering on the leaves high above was of little consequence. But the tattoo steadily grew more forceful, then the forest about them started to drip.

Flick shuddered as a series of heavy drops splattered her. Instinctively, she urged Jessamy on.

'No!' Demon scowled through the night. 'Hold her steady. It's too dangerous to go faster – you know that.'

Her silent acquiescence told him she did. They plodded on, increasingly damp, increasingly cold.

Above them, above the trees, the wind started to rise, to whistle and moan and shake the leaves. Jaw set, Demon searched his memories, trying to gauge how much farther they had to go, but he'd never been on this path before. He didn't know how it meandered, and he couldn't place where it came out. But given the fact that this path crossed the stream only once, and they'd been making very slow progress . . .

He didn't like the answers his estimations suggested. They were still a long way from the manor.

Just how far was revealed when they came to a break in the trees, and he saw before them the stream with a narrow log and plank bridge spanning it. And the charcoal maker's hut in the clearing beyond. *That*, he recognized.

Beneath his breath, he swore.

As if in answer, the heavens cracked; the rain positively teemed. Faced with the sudden torrent – a curtain falling between them and the bridge – Jessamy and Flick balked.

Muttering all manner of dire imprecations, Demon swung down. He tied Ivan's reins to a tree; the stallion, made of stern stuff, seemed unfazed by the downpour. Head up, he sniffed the air and looked toward the bridge.

The bridge that, if not in good condition, would assuredly collapse under his weight.

'Stay back!' Demon yelled at Flick. Pushing past Jessamy,

he strode the three paces to the bridge. Ignoring the rain, he checked the structure thoroughly, in the end standing atop its middle and jumping up and down. The timbers didn't creak; the bridge seemed sound enough.

Ducking back through the rain, he nodded at Flick, then freed his reins and was back in the saddle. Despite the downpour, he wasn't soaked; the bridge itself was protected by a huge oak on the stream's opposite bank.

Flick was looking back at him, her brows high. He nodded again. 'You cross first.'

She nodded and sent Jessamy forward; they clattered across in ordered style. Demon shook Ivan's reins – he bounded forward, keen not to be separated from the mare. His heavy hooves clattered on the planking; in a few swift strides, he was safely across.

Flick was waiting under the spreading branches of the oak; Demon reined in beside her and fixed her with a look calculated to impress on her the unwisdom of arguing with him in his present mood. 'There is no possibility that we can ride on to the manor in this.'

Eyes wide, she looked at him consideringly, then cast a swift glance at the clearing before them, the surface of which was already playing host to myriad tiny rivulets. 'It'll stop soon – these squalls always do.'

'Precisely. Which is why we're going to wait in the hut until it does.'

Flick eyed the hut and immediately thought of dust, and cobwebs, and spiders. Maybe even mice. Or rats. Then she looked at the steady rain coming down and grimaced. 'I suppose it'll only be for an hour or so.'

Demon tightened his reins. 'There's a small stable tacked on the other side – ride straight there.'

Flick shrugged, shook her reins, and did.

A second later, Demon followed.

111

The small stable was only just big enough to house both horses; with the two of them in there as well, laboring in the darkness to unsaddle, space was in short supply. It was impossible not to bump into each other. Arms brushed breasts, elbows stuck into chests. Searching for a loose strap, Flick inadvertently ran her hand up Demon's thigh – she snatched it back with a mortified 'Sorry.'

Which was received in fraught silence.

A minute later, reaching out to locate her so he wouldn't hit her when he lifted his saddle from Ivan's back, Demon found his fingers curving about her breast. An incoherent word of apology was all he could manage, too exercised by the battle to drag his hand away.

Flick's only reply was a muted squawk.

Finally, they were done, and the horses, contented enough, were settled side by side, Ivan with a minimum of rein. Flick joined Demon in the doorway, ducking behind him, into the protection afforded by his broad shoulders.

He glanced around at her, then looked back out, peering along the front of the stone cottage. 'God only knows what state the inside is in.'

'The charcoal makers come every year.'

'In autumn,' he replied incontrovertibly.

She grimaced.

He sighed. 'I'll go and take a look.' He glanced over his shoulder. 'Do you want to wait here? It's perfectly possible I won't be able to get past the door.'

She nodded. 'I'll stay here while you check – call if it's all right.'

He looked back out, then strode swiftly for the cottage door. An instant later, Flick heard wood grating on stone. She waited, looking out at the steady rain, listening to the dripping silence. Beside her, the horses shifted, heaved horsy sighs, and settled. All she could hear was their steady breathing and the soft patter of the rain.

And a hesistant, furtive rustling in what sounded like straw, coming from the rear of the stable.

Flick stiffened. Wild-eyed, she swung around. Visions of munching rats with evil red eyes filled her brain.

She whirled and fled for the cottage.

The door was ajar; without a thought, she slipped through.

'Stop.' It was Demon's voice. 'I've found the lantern.'

Flick stood just inside the door and calmed her leaping heart. He was large – he had large feet. He'd been clomping around in the cottage for at least three minutes – surely, by now, any resident rodents would have departed.

A scrape of a match on tinder broke the stillness; light flared, then softened, throwing a warm glow about the hut as Demon reset the glass.

Letting out the breath she'd held, Flick looked about. 'Well!'

'Indeed.' Demon likewise was taking inventory. 'Remind me to compliment the charcoal makers when next they're by.'

The cottage was neat as a pin, and, bar the inevitable cobwebs, clean. The door had been tight in its frame, and the windows securely shuttered; no unwanted visitors had disturbed the charcoal makers' temporary home.

By extension, however, there was no food left in the cottage to attract vermin. The pots and pans and, most importantly, the kettle, travelled with their owners. There was, however, wood stacked and dry in the woodbox.

Demon glanced at Flick, then moved to the fireplace. 'I may as well get a fire going.' They were both damp, just this side of wet through.

'Hmm.' Flick shut the door, then, rubbing her upper arms, came farther into the cottage. While Demon crouched before the stone hearth, selecting logs and sticks with which to start his blaze, she studied the furniture. There was only one chair

– an old armchair from the manor. Beyond it stood three narrow pallets, each sporting a lumpy, tick mattress. Bending down, Flick grasped the wooden strut at the end of the nearest pallet and tugged until the end of the pallet was positioned before the hearth to one side. Satisfied, she sank down upon it. And sighed as she let her shoulders ease.

Demon glanced back, saw what she'd done, and nodded. The next instant, he had a flame laid in the kindling; busily, he coaxed it into a blaze.

Flick sat and watched the flames grow, watched the bright tendrils writhe, then lick along the dark wood. Patiently, Demon fed the flames, laying branch upon twig until the blaze roared.

Heat billowed out, enveloping her, washing through her, driving away the chill locked in her damp clothes. Contentment rolled through her; she sighed and rotated her shoulders, one, then the other, then settled again to watch Demon's hands, steady and sure, pile logs on the fire.

His hands were like the rest of him – large and lean. His long fingers never fumbled. His grip was strong and sure. His movements, she noted, were economical; he rarely used extraneous flourishes, a fact that enhanced the sense of control, of harnessed power, that invested his every act.

He was, now she considered it, a very controlled man.

Only when the flames were voraciously devouring two huge logs did he stand. He stretched, then turned; large and intensely male, he stood looking down at her.

Her gaze fixed on the flames, Flick knew he was studying her; she felt his gaze on her face, hotter than the heat from the flames. She looked away from the fire, to the nook beside the hearth, gathering strength to look up and meet his eyes.

In the dark corner she saw a flicker of movement, a twitch of a whisker.

A pointy nose and two pink-red eyes.

'*Eeeeeehhh!*'

Her shrill scream split the stillness.

With another shriek, she leapt up, straight into Demon's arms.

They locked about her. 'What is it?'

'*A rat*!' Eyes glued to the dark cranny, she clung, her fingers sinking into his muscles. She gestured with her chin. 'There – by the fireplace.' Then she buried her face in his chest. 'Make it go away!'

Her plea was a panicked mumble. Demon stared at the small field mouse cowering back against the stones. He stifled a sigh. 'Flick—'

'Is it gone?'

This time, he did sigh. 'It's only a field mouse attracted to the warmth. It'll leave in a moment.'

'Tell me when it does.'

He squinted down at her. All he could see was the crown of her curls. Putting his head to the side, he tried to see her face; she had it buried in his chest. She'd somehow insinuated her hands under his coat, and was gripping him, one hand on either side of his back, clinging for dear life.

She was plastered against him, from her forehead to her knees.

And she was trembling.

A faint vibration, the tremor travelled her spine. Instinctively, he tightened his arms about her, then eased his hold to run his hands slowly down and up her back, soothingly stroking.

Bending his head, he murmured into her curls. 'It's all right. It'll go in a minute.'

He could feel her panicked breathing, her breath hitching in her throat; she didn't answer, but bobbed her head to show she'd heard.

So they stood, locked together before the fire, waiting for the still-petrified mouse to make a move.

Demon had imagined waiting patiently, stoically, but within a minute, stoic was beyond him. The fire, a roaring blaze, had dried him; while Flick had been still chilled when she'd rushed into his arms, his body heat was warming her. Warming her breasts, pressed tight against his chest, warming her hips, plastered to his thighs. She, in turn, was heating him – it wouldn't be long before the largest blaze in the room was not the one in the hearth.

Gritting his teeth, he told himself he could endure it. He doubted she was even aware of his susceptibility; he could manage her easily enough.

The heat between them reached a new high, and her perfume rose to waft about him, to wreathe, then snare, his senses. Making him even more aware of the supple softness in his arms, of the warm breasts crushed to his chest, of the subtle pliancy in her frame that beckoned his hardened senses, of the feminine strength in the arms reaching around him. He snatched a breath – and drew her deep, into his soul. Closing his eyes, locking his jaw, he tried to keep his body from responding.

Entirely unsuccessfully. Hard became harder, tighter, tauter. Inexorably, yet in all innocence, she wound his sensual spring notch after notch.

In desperation, he tried to ease her away – she shook her head frantically and burrowed even deeper into his embrace. Teeth gritted, he used just a little of his strength to shift her, so she was more to his side and no longer in danger of learning, graphically, just how much she was affecting him.

He was in pain and helpless to do anything about it. He was paying for his sins in having dallied with her, teased her, enjoyed her.

But he didn't regret a single moment – then, or now.

The realization puzzled him, momentarily distracted him from the physical plane. Grateful for even such minor relief, he followed the thought, trying to unravel the mystery of why, exactly, Flick so attracted him.

He definitely didn't think of her as just another lady with whom he'd like to dally, no different from those who'd gone before. No other lady had made him feel this protective; none other had tapped the surge of feeling she so effortlessly evoked. That, of all things, was what set her apart – that something she made him feel. She could arouse him effortlessly – in itself a shock – but it was that other emotion that came roaring through him simultaneously with the lust that was so new, so addictive.

It was certainly different – something he'd never felt before. It was as if, in her innocence, she could reach into his soul and touch something innocent there as well – something new, bright, something he'd never known existed within him. Something no other had ever reached, ever touched.

He frowned and tried to shift; she immediately gripped him tighter. Demon inwardly sighed – his protective in stincts were well and truly engaged; he couldn't break her hold. Perhaps he should try and think of Flick in the same way he thought of the twins.

That was impossible, yet . . .

Flick the fearless was afraid of mice. He found the thought endearing. Still, as she was truly frightened, the mouse was as good as a dragon. The question was how best to vanquish it – the fear, not the innocent mouse.

Drawing a difficult breath, he grasped Flick's arm and eased her back from him.

'Flick – sweetheart – just look at the mouse. It's a harm-less little mouse – it can't eat you.'

'It might try.'

'Not while I'm here.' He brushed his lips to her temple, nudging her face from his chest. 'Come – look at it. It's so small.'

Warily, she eased her face from his chest; still pressed hard against him, she glanced at the tiny rodent.

'That's right. We'll just watch it until it goes.'

A silent minute passed as they watched the field mouse, still frozen, whiskers twitching nervously. Demon couldn't move to scare it away, not with Flick clinging so tightly – she wouldn't appreciate him moving closer to the mousedragon.

Finally, reassured by their stillness and silence, the mouse started to edge forward. Flick stiffened. Out of the nook the mouse came, hugging the shadow of the hearth's edge. It reached the corner and paused—

A log cracked – sparks spat and showered in the hearth.

The mouse leapt, and dashed back into the cranny, straight to a small gap between two stones. It squeezed its way between and was gone.

'Quick!' Flick released him. 'Block the hole!'

Demon sincerely doubted the field mouse would return, but, snatching a small branch from the woodbox, he swiftly bent and jammed it in the hole. 'There. Now you're safe.' Rising, he turned.

Flick was mere inches away. She'd followed him to look over his shoulder, to check he'd sealed the hole; now she stood, breathing quickly, all but against him once more.

His gaze had risen no further than her breasts, rising and falling in heightened excitement. Only excellent reflexes saved him from reacting – he locked every muscle, gripped every rein. And, slowly, lifted his gaze to her face.

Flick met his gaze and quivered – she told herself it was the remnants of her fright. But the glow in his darkened eyes – the sight of the embers smoldering in the blue – cut off her breathing, leaving her light-headed, swaying with the impulse to return to his arms, not for their safety but for the comfort her senses insisted she would find there.

Eyes wide, lips parted, her cheeks lightly flushed, she literally teetered on the brink of indiscretion –

His lids lowered, steel shutters cutting off the heat in his eyes; an excruciating awareness raced over her skin, from her breasts all the way to her toes. Her nerves flickered; a prickling sensation swept her. Heat washed in its wake.

She dragged in a breath—

He half turned and gestured to the pallet and the chair. 'Which do you prefer?'

She blinked, and struggled to calm her rioting senses, to find her voice. She drew in another breath. 'I'll take the pallet – you can have the chair.'

He nodded; without meeting her eyes, he waved her to her selected seat. Uncertain – of him, of herself, of what shimmered in the air – she went; sitting on the pallet, she shuffled back and drew up her knees so she could balance her boots on the end strut, out of reach of any further rodents. Hugging her knees, she settled her chin atop them, and stared into the flames.

Demon built up the fire, then subsided into the armchair. He, too, fixed his gaze on the flames, denying the urge to gaze at Flick – to look, to wonder ...

That moment of unexpected awareness had very nearly defeated him, nearly overcome the defenses he'd erected between her and himself, between her innocence and his demons. Only her abiding innocence – the innocent confusion, laced with equally innocent, equally open, curiosity, in her blue eyes – had saved them. Given him the strength to resist. The effort had left him aching, far more intensely than before. And inwardly shaking, as if his strength had been depleted to dangerously low levels.

Which meant he was in trouble – that matters between them had gone much farther than he'd thought. Than he'd been aware of.

Even now, although he'd recognized the danger, at least

half his mind was fully engaged in wondering what having an angel beneath him would be like. In fantasizing, as he had so often that afternoon, about how far her delicate blush extended. But his thoughts of her were no longer merely sensual – they were possessively so. Intent, with an underlying, clawing need that he knew no way of easing, bar one. Which, in this case, by extension, meant ...

The very thought made him shudder. *Marriage* was not a word he willingly used, not even in his mind.

A rustling had him glancing her way; he watched as, drowsy, her lids heavy, she turned on her side. Tucking her legs up in her skirts, she settled on the mattress, her gaze still fixed on the fire. Demon forced his gaze to follow hers to the flames. And tried, very hard, not to think at all.

Outside, the drops still pattered down in a steady, soaking rain.

When his mind started to wander, he tried to guess the time, but he had no idea how long they'd taken on the path through the park. An hour? Less?

A soft sigh had him turning, looking – after that, he didn't look away.

She was sleeping.

A hand curled beneath her cheek, her long lashes lay still, brown crescents brushing rose-tinted skin. Her lips, slightly parted, sheened softly, their curves the gentlest temptation imaginable. The firelight gilded her jaw and set golden lights in her hair.

Demon looked, and watched – watched the steady swell and ebb of her breathing reflected in the movement of her breasts, tightly encased in blue velvet, watched the ruffle at her throat rise and fall.

He still wasn't sure how she felt about Dillon, but he'd detected no sign of any sensual awareness between them. He'd initially wondered if they were simply too young, too innocent, to have developed that susceptibility, but he now knew Flick, at least, was more than capable of feeling it.

Which brought him to wondering how she saw him ...

He watched, and pondered. There was no need to look away.

Chapter Seven

He'd seen her face so often in his dreams that he didn't notice when he fell asleep. Her face was his last image before his lids fell – it was the first thing he saw, through the dimness, when he woke.

Frowning, Demon eased his stiff neck and glanced at the fire to see it a pile of cooling ash. He froze, staring at the grey pile, then whipped around to look at the windows.

The heavy shutters were in place, but a thin shaft of pale light edged each slat.

Swearing beneath his breath, he glanced at Flick, still softly sleeping, an angel in repose. Jaw setting, he rose and strode silently to the door. Opening it confirmed his worst fear – the day had dawned.

Drawing the door wide, Demon hauled in a deep breath. The scent of the wet forest flowed into him; he held it in, then slowly exhaled.

A sound behind him had him turning; silent and still in the doorway, he watched Flick awake.

She didn't simply open her eyes. Instead, consiousness slowly invested her features, enlivening her brows, curving her full lips. Eyes still closed, she hummed softly in her throat. Her breasts swelled as she drew in a deep breath, then she stretched languorously, straightening her spine, arching slightly, then she relaxed and her lashes fluttered.

Then, and only then, did her lids slowly rise.

She looked straight at him, then blinked her eyes wide, but no hint of consternation disturbed her content expression. Instead, her lips softened into a sleepily warm smile.

'Is it morning?'

The husky tones of her voice, still drunk with sleep, flowed over him, about him, slid under his skin and seized him. He couldn't speak, couldn't think – he could only want. Want with a searing desire that shocked him, with an absolute possessive need that nearly floored him. Containing that force, reining it in, holding it back, left him rigid. And shaking.

She was still smiling, still waiting for his answer; realizing that, with him framed in the doorway with all light coming from outside, she couldn't see his passion-blank expression, or anything else, he summoned every last ounce of his strength and managed to utter, 'Almost.'

His tone was harsh and uneven; he didn't wait to see her reaction but turned away to ensure she got no chance to study him further, to see the evidence of that rabid desire. Ostensibly surveying the clearing, he cleared his throat. 'I'll get the horses saddled.'

With that, he escaped.

Of course, within a few minutes, she came to help.

Ivan was grumpy and fractious; Demon made that his excuse for barely glancing Flick's way. He felt her puzzled gaze; jaw clenched, he ignored it. He didn't even dare help her saddle Jessamy – if she put her hand on his thigh this morning, he couldn't guarantee his reaction – or rather, his *in*action. As soon as he had Ivan's girths tight, he grabbed his bridle and led the restless stallion out of the tight space.

The charcoal makers' hut had been constructed in that particular clearing because it was the natural confluence of four paths through the park. One was the path they'd travelled last night, another led onward to the manor. A third struck across to join the eastern bridle path Flick usually used to reach the ruined cottage and his farm. Halting Ivan in the middle of the clearing, Demon glanced toward the opening of the fourth path, leading in from a small country lane to the west.

To see Hugh Dunstable, the General's middle-aged steward, ambling up through the morning.

Demon froze.

Dunstable had already seen him; smiling, he raised his hand to his hat. 'Ah! 'Morning, sir.'

Demon nodded easily, urbanely, but he couldn't for the life of him summon a smile. His mind raced while Dunstable's cob plodded closer, ever closer.

''Spect you got caught in last night's squall.' Drawing rein beside him, Dunstable beamed down at him. 'No doubt but it was heavy. Got caught out myself, it came up so quick. I'd been off to the Carters, playing a hand of whist – I was on my way back when it hit. I was drenched by the time I reached home.'

'As you say.' Demon glanced surreptitiously at the shadowed stable. 'It was too heavy to risk riding on.'

Dunstable snorted. 'On these paths? You'd have risked that fine beast.'

The fine beast chose that moment to snort, paw and prance, heavily shouldering Dunstable's cob. Demon swore and drew in Ivan's reins. Settling his placid cob, Dunstable chuckled. 'Aye – riding him must be an adventure. Not hard to see how you came by your name.'

It wasn't his expertise in riding high-bred *horses* that had earned him his nickname, but Demon let the comment pass; he was too busy praying.

Much good it did him. His fervent appeal to the highest authority that Flick would have the sense to remain out of sight was refused; she appeared at that instant, smiling sunnily up at Dunstable as she led Jessamy out.

'Good morning, Mr. Dunstable.'

She glanced up at the sky, and so failed to notice the expression on Dunstable's face – sheer shock to begin with, rapidly transmuting into horror, momentarily displaced by speculation, only to revert to righteous horror again.

By the time Flick looked down and cheerily remarked, 'And a fine morning it seems to be,' Dunstable's features were set in stone, his expression impassive. He mumbled an incoherent reply to Flick; the look in his eyes when he shifted his gaze to Demon was coldly censorious.

Demon reacted in the only way he could – with a high hand. Cool arrogance in his eyes, he met Dunstable's gaze levelly; his expression hard, he raised a challenging brow.

Dunstable, only one step up from a servant, albeit an old and trusted one, was at a loss to know how to respond. Demon regretted putting the old man in his place, but every instinct he possessed refused to let anyone even imagine any ill – any indiscretion – of Flick.

To his relief, she, busy adjusting her stirrups, missed their exchange entirely.

'It looks like the clouds have blown away. I dare say it'll be quite warm by lunchtime.' She straightened and glanced around for a log to use as a mounting block.

Demon dropped his reins and crossed to her side; closing his hands about her waist, he lifted her, setting her lightly on Jessamy's back.

That got her attention; she sucked in a breath and blinked at him, then quickly rearranged her legs and her skirts. 'Thank you.'

Lifting her chin, she fixed her blue eyes on Dunstable. 'I can't believe how overgrown the park has become – we must get Hendricks to cut back rather more. Why, you can barely

125

see the sky, even here, even on such a wonderful morning. I rather think – '

She chattered blithely on, unaware that, with her cheeks still delicately flushed from sleep, her hair tousled and her velvet skirts badly crushed, she presented a perfect picture of a youthful damsel who had recently engaged in an energetic morning romp.

Predictably, she led the way along the path to the manor.

Dunstable followed close behind. To give him his due, while remaining stony-faced, he managed to make the appropriate noises whenever Flick paused in her paean to the morning.

Hands on his hips, Demon watched them amble off, then exhaled through his teeth. Returning to the hut, he secured the door, then mounted Ivan. And paused.

For one long moment, he stared down the path at Flick's and Dunstable's backs. Then, lips thinning, jaw firming, he shook Ivan's reins. And followed.

By the time their party reached Hillgate End, Demon had a firm grip on the situation. There was no doubt that he'd compromised Flick, albeit entirely innocently.

He'd caught up with her and Dunstable, only to hear her gaily state that they'd taken shelter soon after the rain had started. So Dunstable now knew that they'd been at the hut, together and alone, from the dead of night to dawn. Of course, focused on protecting Dillon, Flick had said not a word about what had occasioned her presence, in company with a rake, deep in the park in the middle of the night.

It was no great feat to imagine what Dunstable was thinking. Indeed, it was difficult to conceive of a more damning scenario for a young, unmarried gentlewoman than being discovered at dawn leaving an evening rendezvous in company with a rake of the first order.

Demon had had ample time to consider every facet of their night alone, every nuance, every likely repercussion – their journey to the manor had been slow, the ground very wet, soft beneath their horses' hooves. They'd plodded along, Flick in the lead, followed by Dunstable, with him in the rear. In brooding silence, he'd debated their options – not many – and what that therefore meant, while Flick had entertained Dunstable with her sunny patter.

She'd described the small stable, and exclaimed over the fact that Jessamy and Ivan had been quite dry; she'd continually paused to declaim the wonders of the morning. She had not, however, mentioned the mouse – on consideration, remembering the long moments she'd spent in his arms, he'd decided that was just as well.

God only knew what picture she might paint for Dunstable if she started on that topic.

Finally, they'd reached the manor's grounds; minutes later, they trotted into the stable yard.

Stifling a huge sigh of relief, her mind full of the wonders of a hot bath, Flick reined in. She untangled her legs and skirts from her sidesaddle; she was about to slide to the ground when Demon appeared beside her. He reached for her; his hands closed about her waist, then he lifted her down, and set her on her feet before him.

Quickly catching her breath – she was almost used to the effect of his touch, to the sudden seizing of her lungs – she beamed a sunny smile up at him, and held out her hand. 'Thank you so much for taking pity on me last night and seeing me home. I'm really very grateful.'

He looked at her – she could read nothing in his eyes, in his oddly set expression. He took her hand, but instead of squeezing it and letting go, he wrapped his fingers about hers and turned. 'I'll walk you to the house.'

Flick stared at him – at his back. She would have tugged

and argued, but Dunstable, having dismounted more slowly, was hovering. Demon started walking – stalking; throwing a bright smile over her shoulder at Dunstable, she had to hurry to keep up.

Striding purposefully, Demon headed up the gravel path, ducking under the wisteria to pass beneath the old trees and cut across the lawn to the terrace. He didn't set her hand on his arm and stroll; instead, he kept his hand locked about hers and towed her along.

Flick tried an outraged glare, but he refused to even notice. His expression was set, determined. Determined on what she had no idea.

Glancing back, she saw Dunstable, watching from beneath the stable arch. She flashed him a reassuring smile and wondered what devil had possessed Demon.

He didn't stop until they were on the terrace, before the open morning room windows. Releasing her, he gestured her inside; with a speaking glance, she stepped over the threshold. Swinging her heavy skirts, she faced him as he followed her into the room. 'Why aren't you heading off to the Heath? We have to watch Bletchley.'

Halting in front of her, he looked down at her and frowned. 'Gillies and the others will keep watching until I arrive to take over. At present, I have matters of greater moment to settle.'

She blinked. 'You do?'

His jaw set ominously. 'I need to speak with the General.'

Flick felt her eyes, locked on his, widen.

'What about?' She had no idea why, but she was starting to feel uneasy.

Demon saw her question – her lack of understanding – etched in her eyes. Inwardly, he cursed. 'I need to talk to him about our current situation.'

'Situation? What situation?'

Jaw clenching, he went to step around her; quick as a flash, she blocked his way. 'What are you talking about?'

He caught her eye and frowned even more. 'I'm talking about the past night, which we spent together, alone.' He gave the last two words particular weight; comprehension dawned in her eyes.

Then she blinked and frowned at him. 'So?' Her gaze raced over his face. 'Nothing – nothing *indiscreet* – happened.'

'No,' he agreed, his voice tight, controlled, 'but only you and I know that. All society will see is that the *potential* for indiscretion was present, and that, in society's eyes, is all that counts.'

The sound she made was elementally dismissive. His eyes locked on hers, Demon knew that if she questioned the *potential*, denied it had existed, he'd wring her neck.

She hovered on the brink – he saw it in her eyes. But, after studying his expression, she swung onto a different tack. 'But no one knows. Well' – she waved – 'only Dunstable, and he didn't imagine anything scandalous had happened.'

Stunned, he stared at her. 'Tell me, is Dunstable always so stony-faced?'

She grimaced. 'Well, he is rather taciturn. I always do most of the talking.'

'If you'd done a little more looking this morning, you'd have seen he was shocked to his toes.' Again, he went to step past her; again, she blocked his way.

'What are you going to do?'

He didn't want to lay hands on her – didn't want to risk it in his present state. He pinned her with a glare. 'I am going to speak to the General, and explain to him exactly what occurred.'

'You're not going to tell him about Dillon?'

'No. I'll simply say I came upon you riding alone through my fields late last night, and insisted on escorting you home.' He took a step toward her; to keep his face in clear view, she backed away. 'I'll leave it to you to explain what you were doing in your saddle at midnight.'

She blinked; he pressed his advantage and took another step. She gave ground without noticing. Her eyes, now wide, flicked up to his; before she could interrupt, he stated, 'The General will see instantly that, regardless of what truly transpired at the cottage, all society – certainly every matron of standing in Newmarket – will believe you and I spent the best part of the night heating a single pallet in the charcoal makers' hut.'

A light blush tinged her cheeks; her gaze flickered, then steadied. Abruptly, she stood her ground. 'That's ridiculous.' The statement was emphatic. 'You didn't lay a finge ...' Her words trailed away; her gaze blanked.

'On you?' Demon grinned tightly. 'Not one – all ten.' He trapped her gaze as she refocused. 'Can you deny you were in my arms?'

Her lips compressed, her expression turned mutinous, her chin set like rock. Her eyes – those usually soft orbs – positively flared. 'That was because of a *mouse*!'

'The cause is irrelevant. As far as society's concerned, having spent the night alone with me, your virtue and reputation are in question. The accepted code of behavior decrees I offer you the protection of my name.'

Flick stared at him, then determinedly shook her head. 'No.'

He looked down at her, and coolly raised his brows. 'No?'

'No, that's positively stupid.' Flinging her hands in the air, she swung away. 'You're blowing this up out of all proportion. Society's not going to say anything because they'll know nothing about it. Dunstable won't talk.' Swinging about, she paced back. 'I'll see him and explain – ' Lifting her head, she saw Demon almost at the door. 'No! *Wait*!'

She raced across the room. She would have caught him, but he turned and caught her instead. His hands about her upper

130

arms, he held her away from him. And glared at her.

'There's no point arguing – I'm going to see the General.'

His determination was blazoned in his eyes; Flick couldn't mistake it. Her mind raced; she licked her lips. 'He'll be at breakfast.' Dragging her gaze from his, she sent it skimming down, over his rumpled clothes.

He looked down, too, then frowned; extending one leg, he scowled at the muddy streaks marring his Hessians. And swore. Releasing her, he took stock of his disreputable state. 'I can't go in to see him like this.'

Flick kept her eyes wide and innocent, and held her tongue. Even when – especially when – his gaze, hard and blue, returned to her face.

After a moment, lips compressed, he nodded. 'I'll go home and change – then I'll be back.' Eyes narrowing, he held her gaze. 'And then we can discuss this fully – with the General.'

She merely raised her brows and maintained a strategic silence.

He hesitated, looking into her eyes, then, with a curt nod, turned and stalked out.

Flick watched him go, drifting back to the French doors to watch him stride across the lawn. Only when he'd disappeared into the shadows of the trees did she turn back into the room – grit her teeth, clench her fists, and give vent to a frustrated scream.

'He's *impossible*! *This* is impossible.' After a moment, her eyes darkened. 'He's out of his mind.'

With that, she stalked off to clear the matter up.

Two hours later, Demon drove his bays up the drive of Hillgate End. Under his expert guidance, the curricle came to a flourishing halt immediately before the steps. Handing the reins to the groom who came running, he stepped down. Drawing off his gloves, he strode to the house.

He was perfectly attired in a blue morning coat and ivory breeches, ivory cravat and shirt, with an elegantly restrained blue-and-black-striped waistcoat. His Hessians, another pair, gleamed. His appearance was precisely as he considered it should be, given his errand.

Jacobs opened the door to his knock. Demon returned his greeting with a nod and headed straight for the library. He was somewhat surprised to gain the door without encountering Flick; he'd expected some last-ditch effort on her part to interfere with his plans – his immolation on the altar of the right and proper.

Turning the handle, he opened the door and entered, swiftly scanning the long room for any sign of an angel.

She wasn't there.

The General was, seated as usual at his desk, and sunk behind a huge tome. He looked up as Demon closed the door – and smiled warmly, delightedly.

Demon strolled nearer and saw his mentor's eyes twinkling. Inwardly, he cursed.

The General held up a hand before he could speak. 'I know,' he declared, 'all about it.'

Demon came to a dead halt facing the desk. 'Flick.' His tone was flat. His left hand slowly clenched.

'Eh Oh, yes – Felicity.' The General grinned and leaned back in his chair, waving him to the chair beside the desk. Although Demon moved in that direction, he couldn't sit – he prowled to the window beyond.

The General chuckled. 'You needn't worry. A potential imbroglio it might have been, but Felicity took the bit between her teeth and sorted it all out.'

'I see.' His features under rigid control, his expression utterly bland, Demon turned his head and raised a brow. 'How very helpful of her.' Even to him, his tones sounded steely. 'How did she manage it?'

132

'Well—' If the General was aware of his tension, he didn't show it; he pushed his chair back the better to beam up at him. 'She came straightaway to me, of course, and explained what happened – how she'd felt the need of some air and so gone riding late last night, and forgot the time, and wound up past your farm.' The General's smug expression clouded. 'Have to say, m'boy, I'm not at all sanguine about her riding off like that alone, but she's promised me she won't do it again.' His wide smile returning, he looked up. 'One good thing about this little fright she's had, what?'

Demon said nothing; the General grinned and continued, 'Luckily, this time, you saw her – very good of you to insist on escorting her home.'

'It seemed the least I could do.' Especially as it had been him she'd ridden out to see.

'Silly of her to take that old path – Hendricks gave up on it years ago. As for the rain – I can't tell you how relieved I am that you were with her. Goodness knows, she's a reliable miss, but still, she's young, and inclined to press on regardless. Your decision to stop at the hut until the rain passed was unquestionably correct. After that, of course, all the rest followed – no one's fault it happened as it did. Hardly surprising you both fell asleep.'

The General looked up and frowned – as severely as he ever did – at him. 'And don't think you have to reassure me that nothing happened. I know you – known you from a boy. I *know* nothing untoward occurred. I know my Felicity would be safe with you.'

The unexpected fierceness in the General's eyes held him silent; with a satisfied nod, the General sat back. 'Yes, and she told me about the mouse, too. She's petrified of the silly things – always has been. Just what I'd have expected – you had the sensitivity not to laugh at her, but to soothe her. Nothing scandalous there.'

Glancing at his desk, the General frowned. 'Where were we? Ah, yes. Dunstable. Him coming across you this morning was neither here nor there – he's an old friend and luckily no gabblemonger. Flick insisted on speaking with him after she'd seen me, and he dropped by to see me half an hour ago. Just to reassure me that he would never say a word to harm our Felicity.' Grinning, the General glanced up. 'Dunstable also asked me to convey his apologies to you for jumping to unwarranted conclusions.'

Demon met the General's eye. Flick had plugged every hole, countered every argument.

'So,' the General said, his tone one of conclusion, 'I hope you can see that I'm perfectly convinced there's no reason for any sacrifice on your part. As you haven't in any way harmed Felicity's reputation, there's absolutely no reason you need offer for her, is there?'

Demon held his gaze, but didn't answer; the General smiled.

'It was all perfectly innocent – and now we'll say nothing more about it, what?' He hauled his tome back into position before him. 'Now tell me. I've just been checking these offshoots of the Barbary Arab. What have you heard about this colt, Enderby?'

As if in compensation, the General invited him to lunch. Demon accepted – then, offering to carry word of his joining the table to Jacobs, left the General to his records.

Shutting the library door, Demon paused in the quiet of the corridor, trying, yet again, to regain a sense of equilibrium. He understood what had happened; rationally, logically, he knew all was well. Unfortunately, he didn't feel it. He felt ... deprived.

As if a long-desired object of paramount importance had slipped – been whisked – from his grasp, just as he was about to close his hand.

134

Frowning, he went to find Jacobs.

He discovered him in the butler's pantry; his message delivered, Demon returned to the front hall and, without a heartbeat's pause, set out to hunt down Flick. Feeling very much like a hungry leopard, he prowled through the downstairs rooms. She would be somewhere close, he was sure, just in case he had raised some quibble she hadn't foreseen and the General had sent for her.

He found her in the garden hall.

She was snipping the stems of flowers and slipping them into a vase. Humming, she tilted her head this way and that, studying her creation. Demon watched her for a full minute, taking in her crisp, cambric morning gown, noting her hair, newly brushed, a gilded frame about her face.

After drinking his fill, he quit the doorway; on silent feet, he approached her.

Flick snipped the stem of a cornflower and considered how best to place it. She held it up, her hand hovering—

Long fingers plucked the bloom from her grasp.

She gasped, but even before her gaze collided with his, she knew who stood beside her. She knew his touch – knew the sense of strength he projected. 'Have you seen the General?' she gabbled, frantically trying to slow her racing heart.

'Hmm.' Eyes half-closed, he lazily angled the stem this way, then that, then slid it home into the vase. He surveyed his handiwork, then, apparently satisfied, turned to her. 'I did see him, yes.'

His lazy, indolent – sleepy – expression deceived her not at all; beneath his heavy lids, his eyes were sharp, his gaze incisive. She lifted her chin and picked up the garden shears. 'I told you there was no need for any drama.'

His lips lifted in a slight smile. 'So you did.'

135

Flick stifled a sniff at his tone; she had, indeed, expected his thanks, once he'd had time to consider, to realize what his offer would have meant. She supposed he would marry sometime, but he was only thirty-one, and he definitely didn't want to marry her.

But he made no further comment. Instead, he lounged, shoulders propped against the wall, and, with the same lazy, unnerving air, watched her place her flowers. As the silence stretched, it occurred to her that perhaps he thought she didn't fully appreciate the sacrifice he'd been prepared to make. 'It's not that I'm not grateful.' She kept her gaze firmly fixed on her blooms.

Her comment succeeded in dissipating a little of his indolence. She felt the sudden focusing of his attention.

'Grateful?'

She continued to snip and set. 'For your kind offer to save my reputation. I appreciate it would have entailed a considerable sacrifice on your part – thankfully, there was no need.'

His gaze locked on her profile, Demon fought to remain where he was – and not haul her into his arms and kiss her, just to shut her up. 'Sacrifice? Actually, I hadn't viewed taking you to wife in quite that light.'

'Hadn't you?' She blinked at him in patent surprise, then smiled and turned back to her flowers. 'I dare say you would have, once you'd stopped to think the idea through.'

Demon simply stared at her. He'd never felt so ... *dismissed* in his life.

'Luckily, there was no reason for worry. I did tell you so.'

Luckily for her, what next he might have said, and done, neither of them were destined to learn; Jacobs appeared in the doorway with the information that lunch was awaiting them in the dining parlor.

Flick led the way. Demon no longer expected anything else; he prowled just behind her, making no effort to fully catch up – in his present mood, it was probably wisest if she remained just out of reach.

Lunch was not a success.

Flick grew increasingly impatient with their guest as the meal progressed. He contributed nothing to the conversation beyond answering questions the General threw his way. Instead, broodingly intent, he watched her, as if studying some incomprehensible being of whom he nevertheless disapproved, leaving her to chatter with increasingly feigned brightness until her head ached.

By the time the meal ended and they pushed back their chairs, she was ready to snap at him – if he deigned to give her the chance.

'Well, m'boy – let me know if you detect any weakness in those horses.' The General shook hands with Demon, then smiled at Flick. 'Why don't you see Demon to the stable, m'dear? It's a lovely day out there.' With his usual benign smile, the General waved at the French doors, open to the terrace. 'Enjoy the fine weather while you may.'

Across the table, Flick met Demon's level gaze. The last thing she wanted to do was, all sweet comfort, accompany him to the stable – she was annoyed with him, at the way he was behaving. It was as if he'd been denied something he wanted, for heaven's sake. He was *sulking*! All because things hadn't gone as he'd planned – because she'd rescripted his grand gesture for him, and he hadn't got to play the role he'd expected. That of heroic sacrifice.

Drawing a deep breath, she held it; lips compressed, she held his gaze challengingly. Very nearly belligerently.

He merely raised one brow – even more challengingly, more defiantly; stepping back, he gestured to the terrace.

Flick could almost hear the gauntlet thud down on the table between them.

Lifting her head, she stepped around the table, preceding

137

him out the doors, down the steps and across the lawn. Pacing briskly, irritatedly, she was halfway across the lawn before she realized he wasn't with her.

Abruptly stopping, she glanced back. He was strolling slowly, leisurely, exceedingly unhurriedly, in her distant wake. Gritting her teeth, she waited, and waited, for him to catch up. The instant he did, she turned and, elevating her nose to an angle worthy of her ire, she matched her pace to his, strolling at crawling pace just ahead of him.

Two paces later, a warm flush washed over her nape, exposed above her neckline. The odd sensation drifted lower, spreading across her shoulders, then sliding down her spine. It lingered in the hollow of her waist, then, at a telling pace, washed lower, and yet lower—

She caught her breath and stopped to brush an imaginary wrinkle from her skirts. The instant Demon drew level with her, she straightened and stepped out – at his side – praying her fading blush was no longer visible.

Biting her tongue against all manner of heated phrases, she preserved a tense silence. He strolled calmly beside her and gave her not one opening to snipe at him.

The grooms saw them as they emerged from beneath the wisteria, and they ran to get his bays.

Halting at the entrance to the stable yard, Flick's patience came to an end. 'I can't see why you're not grateful,' she hissed. She kept her gaze on the grooms as they fussed with his horses.

'Can't you? Perhaps that's the problem.'

'There *isn't* any problem.'

'Permit me to disagree.' He paused, then added, 'Aside from anything else, you're glaring.'

She whirled and faced him. 'I'm glaring at *you*.'

'So I noticed.'

'You are *impossible*!'

'*Me*?'

For an instant, his blue eyes blinked wide – she could actually imagine he was sincere in his surprise. Swiftly, his eyes searched hers; his gaze sharpened. 'Tell me,' he murmured, glancing at the lads harnessing the bays, 'do you think to marry Dillon eventually?'

'*Dillon*?' She stared at him, unmindful of the fact that her mouth had fallen open. 'Marry *Dillon*? You *are* out of your mind. As if I'd marry such a ... a ... nobody – an inconsequential boy. A man of no real substance. A *nincompoop*! A—'

'All right – forget I asked.'

'For your information, I have no intention of marrying *any* gentleman unless I want to. I will certainly not marry simply because of some nonsensical social stricture.' Her voice cracked with the effort of screaming in whispers. She drew breath and forged on, 'And as for *your* offer – well, you might as well say I must marry because of a *mouse*!'

The bays came trotting up, led by an eager groom. Tersely, Demon nodded his thanks and took the reins. Climbing to the box seat, he sat and looked at her.

Eyes kindling, she tartly remarked, 'I can't see *why* you aren't grateful – you know perfectly well you don't *want* to marry me.'

He looked down at her, his expression like stone, his eyes hard as blue diamonds. He held her defiant gaze, then his chest swelled.

'You have no idea,' he murmured, his diction frighteningly precise, 'what I want at all.'

He clicked the reins; the bays surged. He swept out of the stable yard and bowled away down the drive.

Chapter Eight

'I wondered if you'd care for a drive?' Gasping, Flick whirled; the large vase she was carrying shook, slipped—

Demon reached out and steadied it; his fingers brushed hers.

Flick trembled. She drew her hands away, leaving him holding the vase. Standing in the sunshine streaming through the gallery windows, she stared at him, disjointed phrases tangling on her tongue. She wanted to rail at him for creeping up on her – again. She wanted to scowl or at least frown – she hadn't forgiven him for his behavior of yesterday.

She wanted to ask what he'd meant by his parting comment. 'A drive?' Her head was still whirling.

He shrugged, his lids veiling his eyes. 'Just a tool about the lanes for half an hour or so.'

She drew in a steadying breath. Twenty-four hours had passed since he'd driven away – twenty-four hours in which she'd thought of little else but him. Swinging to the windows, she looked out on another glorious spring day. Simultaneously, she felt the warm flush she was growing accustomed to slide down her back.

'The breeze is warm. You won't need a spencer.'

Just as well; she didn't have one that wouldn't look hideous with this gown – white mull muslin sprinkled with tiny gold and purple daisies. Flick nodded, determination filling her. 'A drive would be very nice.'

She turned to face him – he was still holding the vase. 'Where do you want this?'

She gestured down the gallery. 'If you'll put it on the table at the end, I'll get my parasol and meet you in the hall.'

She didn't wait for his nod but headed for her room – her steps eager, her heart lighter, even if she'd yet to meet his eyes directly. They had to get past this silly hitch in their friendship, over the hurdle of yesterday – a drive would be a good start.

A good start to what she was no longer sure by the time Demon turned his bays back up the manor drive. She'd imagined they'd simply slide back to their earlier, easy friendship – she'd expected, after the initial, inevitable stiffness evaporated, to once again encounter the teasing light she'd so often seen in his blue eyes.

Instead ...

Angling her parasol, she studied his face as he tooled the curricle up the drive. Shadows from the enclosing trees wreathed his features, but they did nothing to soften the patriarchal lines of his nose and chin. His was an angular face, high cheekbones shadowing the long planes of his cheeks, a broad forehead above large eyes. A hard face, its austerity seductively flavored by the frankly sensual line of his thin lips, the brooding languor of his heavy lids.

She had never really looked, not so deeply. His had been the face of a man she'd thought she'd known. She was no longer so sure of that.

Realigning her parasol, she looked ahead as they swept out of the trees and bowled along beside the lawns. The end of the drive was in sight, and she'd yet to understand why his teasing looks had been replaced by glances much more direct, much more unnerving. Much more intent. She'd yet to determine where he thought they were head ing. Only then could she decide whether she agreed with him or not.

Demon sent the bays into a tight curve so that the curricle fetched up neatly before the steps. He tied off the reins and stepped down, hiding his satisfied smile, along with his awareness of the puzzled looks Flick continued to direct his way.

Strolling around the carriage, he helped her down; releasing her hand, he strolled beside her up the steps. Glancing at her, he met her blue gaze, his expression mild and urbane. 'If you would, tell the General that I'm checking into those horses he mentioned yesterday. I'll call on him tomorrow.'

She searched his eyes, then nodded. 'Yes, of course.'

He smiled easily. 'I hope you enjoyed our drive.'

'Oh – yes. It was very pleasant. Thank you.'

His smile deepened. 'Your enjoyment is all the thanks I need.' Reaching beyond her, he jangled the doorbell. Releasing it, he held her gaze for an instant, then bowed, exquisitely correct. 'I'll leave you then. Good-bye.'

He turned and strolled down the steps, her hesitant farewell drifting after him. The front door opened as he climbed into the curricle and took up the reins; as he wheeled his team, he glimpsed her, parasol still open, standing on the steps watching him drive away.

His lips curved. It wasn't difficult to envision the look on her face – the puzzled frown in her big blue eyes. Smiling more definitely, he whipped up his horses and headed for the Heath.

He returned to the manor at eleven o'clock the next morning, ostensibly to see the General.

Jacobs opened the door to him; Demon crossed the threshold to discover a sermon in progress. Fittingly, it was being delivered by the vicar's wife, Mrs. Pemberton, a trenchantly good-hearted lady. Her venue was the front hall, her audience

Mrs. Fogarty and Jacobs, who, Demon noted, had left the front door wide open. He deduced Mrs. Pemberton was on the point of departure.

His appearance proved a distraction, making Mrs. Pemberton lose her thread. Then she recognized him and regrouped. 'Mr. Cynster! *Perfect*!'

Demon suppressed a wince.

Mrs. Pemberton bustled up. 'I've just been asking after the General – I understand he's presently 'not to be disturbed.' Casting a severe glance at Fogarty, Mrs. Pemberton laid a hand on Demon's sleeve. 'I have a very important message for him – I would take it most kindly if you would convey it to him when next you have the pleasure of seeing him.'

Mrs. Pemberton was no fool. Taking the hand she offered, Demon shook it. 'Only too pleased, ma'am.' He could hardly refuse.

'Excellent. Now my point is this—' She fixed her eye on Fogarty. 'Thank you – I won't need to disturb you further, Mrs. Fogarty.'

Fogarty sent a meaningful look Demon's way, then curtsied and withdrew.

Turning, Mrs. Pemberton fixed her sights on Jacobs. 'Mr. Cynster will see me to the door. Please convey my compliments to Miss Parteger when she comes in.'

Jacobs stiffened but had to bow, close the door, and withdraw, too.

Mrs. Pemberton sighed and met Demon's eye. 'I know they're only trying to protect the General, but *really*! He can't simply go to ground in his library all the time – not when he's the guardian of a young lady.'

Elegantly, Demon gestured to the padded seat lining the alcove at the rear of the hall. Mrs. Pemberton consented to sit. Folding her hands over her reticule, she fixed her gaze on his face as he sat alongside her.

'My purpose in calling is to bring the General to an understanding of his duties in relation to Miss Parteger. It's all gone reasonably well until now, but she's reached an age where he really needs to take a more *active* role.'

Demon raised his brows innocently, encouragingly.

Mrs. Pemberton pursed her lips. 'That girl must be nineteen if she's a day, and she barely sets foot outside this house, at least not in a social sense. We – the ladies of the district – have done all we can in sending invitations to Hillgate End, but, thus far, the General has refused to bestir himself.' Mrs. Pemberton's double chins firmed. 'I'm afraid that's not good enough. It would be a crying shame if that lovely girl is left to molder into an old maid purely because the General won't shake himself out of his library and properly perform his duties as a guardian.'

'Hmm,' Demon replied, entirely noncommittal.

'I particularly wished to speak with him because I'm hosting a small dance at the vicarage – just for the local young people – three evenings from now. We – the other ladies and I – think it absolutely vital that the General puts more effort into taking Miss Parteger about. How else will the poor girl ever find a husband?'

Spreading her hands, she appealed to Demon; luckily, she didn't expect a reply.

'The dance at the vicarage will be just the way to start – not too many people to overwhelm the child. Will you carry my message to the General? And, perhaps, if you could put the argument that he really needs to pay more attention to Miss Parteger's future?'

Demon met her gaze, then nodded decisively. 'I'll see what I can do.'

'Good!' Mrs. Pemberton beamed as Demon walked her to the door. 'I'll be off, then. If you see her, do mention to Miss Parteger that I called.'

Demon inclined his head as Mrs. Pemberton took her leave, considering her parting words.

He would, he decided, tell Miss Parteger she'd called, but not immediately.

Turning, he sauntered toward the library.

Half an hour later, he found Flick in the back parlor. She was ensconced amid the cushions on the settee, her legs curled under her skirts, a dish of shelled nuts on a side table beside her. She was reading a book, utterly absorbed. He watched as, without taking her eyes from the page, she reached out and picked up a nut; without missing a word, she brought the nut to her lips and popped it into her mouth, continuing to read as she crunched.

With Mrs. Pemberton's sermon ringing in his head, he scanned the round blue gown presently concealing Miss Parteger's charms. While her wardrobe would not qualify as 'all the crack,' there was, to his mind, nothing whatever amiss with her simple gowns. Their very simplicity enhanced, underscored and emphasized the beauty of the body within.

Which, he'd decided, was all definitely to his taste.

The body, the beauty, and her simple gowns.

Pushing away from the doorframe, he strolled into the room.

Flick looked up with a start. 'Oh! Hello.' She started to smile one of her innocently welcoming smiles, but as he halted before her, full awareness struck, and the tenor of her greeting changed. She still smiled in welcome, but her eyes were watchful, her smile more controlled.

He returned the gesture easily, inwardly pleased that she was, at long last, starting to see him differently. 'I've finished talking horses with the General. He invited me to lunch and I've accepted. It's lovely outside – I wondered if you'd care to stroll until the gong?'

With him there, large as life, asking, she really had very little choice. While one part of Flick's mind acidly noted that fact, another part was rejoicing, eager to further explore their new, oddly thrilling, not-quite-safe interaction. She didn't understand it – she'd yet to determine where he thought he was headed. But she wanted to know. 'Yes – by all means, let's stroll.'

She gave him her hand and let him pull her to her feet. Minutes later, they were on the lawn, ambling side by side.

'Has anything happened with Bletchley?'

Demon shook his head. 'All he's done is make tentative overtures toward a number of jockeys.'

'Nothing else?'

Again he shook his head. 'They seem to be concentrating on the Craven meeting, and that's still weeks away. I suspect the syndicate will have given Bletchley time to make the arrangements – it's possible his masters won't put in an appearance down here just yet.'

'You think they'll leave it until closer to the meeting to check on Bletchley's success?'

'Closer, but not too close. It takes time to put all the players in place to milk the maximum return from a fix.'

'Hmm.' Pondering that fact, and the likelihood that Dillon would have to remain in the ruined cottage for some weeks yet, Flick frowned into the distance.

'Have you ever been to London?'

'London?' She blinked. 'Only when I stayed with my aunt just after my parents died. I was only there for a few weeks, I think.'

'I confess myself amazed that you've never succumbed to the urge to cut a dash in the capital.'

She turned her head and studied him; to her surprise, he wasn't teasing – his gaze was steady, his expression open – well, as open as it ever was. 'I . . .' She considered, then shrugged. 'I've never really thought of it. It's all so far away and unknown. Indeed' – she raised her brows – 'I'm not even sure what 'cutting a dash' entails.'

Demon grinned. 'Being noticed by society due to one's dress, or exploits.'

'Or conquests?'

His smile deepened. 'That, too.'

'Ah, well. That explains my disinterest, then. I'm not particularly interested in any of those things.'

Demon couldn't restrain his smile. 'A young lady uninterested in dresses and conquests – my dear, you'll break the matchmakers' hearts.'

Her expression as she shrugged said she cared not a whit.

'But,' he continued, 'I'm surprised you don't like dancing – most ladies who enjoy riding also enjoy a turn about the dance floor.'

She grimaced. 'I haven't spent much time dancing. There aren't a lot of balls around here, you know.'

'But there are the usual dances. I vaguely remember my great-aunt prodding me to attend a few many years ago.'

'Well, yes – there *are* dances and the odd ball as one might expect. We do get cards periodically. But the General is always so busy.'

'Does he even see the cards?'

Flick glanced up, but she could read nothing in his very blue eyes. Still ... she tilted her chin. 'I deal with his correspondence. There's no point bothering him with such invitations – he's never attended such affairs.'

'Hmm.' Demon glanced at her face – what he could see beneath her golden halo. Without warning, he reached for her hand; stepping swiftly, he raised it and twirled her, unsurprised that, startled though she was, she reacted smoothly, graceful and surefooted, innately responsive.

He met her wide eyes as she slowed to a halt, her billowing skirts subsiding. 'I really think,' he murmured, lowering her hand, 'that you'll enjoy dancing.'

Flick hid a frown and wondered if that remark was intended to be cryptic. Before she could pursue it, the gong for lunch echoed over the lawn.

Demon offered his arm. 'Shall we join the General?'

They did. Sitting at the dining table with the General to her right and Demon opposite was a familiar, comfortable situation. Flick relaxed; her nerves, in recent times slightly tense whenever Demon was near, eased. Chatting with her usual effervescence, she felt subtlely more in control.

Until the General laid down his fork and fixed her with a direct look. 'Mrs. Pemberton called this morning.'

'Oh?' Flick knew she had – that was why she'd taken refuge in the back parlor. But she was genuinely surprised that the General knew – she, Foggy and Jacobs had a long standing agreement to ensure the local matrons didn't bother him with their demands.

She scanned the room, but Jacobs had withdrawn. Had Mrs. Pemberton bullied her way past their defenses?

'Hmm,' the General went on. 'Seems she's giving a dance for the local young people. Us older folk are allowed to come and watch.' He caught Flick's startled eye. 'I rather think we should attend, don't you?'

Flick didn't – she foresaw all sorts of complications. Including the likelihood of the General learning just how many similar invitations he'd refused in recent times. She glanced at Demon, and was struck by inspiration. 'I really don't have anything to wear.'

The General chuckled. 'I thought you might say that, so I had a word with Mrs. Fogarty – she tells me there's a very good dressmaker in the High Street. She'll go with you tomorrow and see about a dress.'

'Oh.' Flick blinked. The General was smiling at her, a

hopeful question in his eyes. 'Er ... thank you.'

Delighted, he patted her hand. 'I'm quite looking forward to the outing – haven't been about in years, it seems. Used to enjoy it when Margery was alive. Now I'm too old to dance myself, I'm looking forward to sitting and watching you take to the floor.'

Flick stared at him; guilt at having deprived him of innocent enjoyment for years tickled at her mind – but she couldn't quite believe it. He *didn't* like socializing – he'd given his opinion on the *mesdames* of the district, and their entertainments, often enough. She couldn't understand what had got into his head. 'But ...' She grabbed her last straw. 'I don't know any of the local gentlemen well enough to stand up with them.'

'Oh, you won't have to worry about that. Demon here has offered to accompany us – he'll stand up with you, teach you a few steps, and all that. Just what you need.'

Flick didn't think so. Blank-faced, she looked at Demon. He met her gaze, the quality of the smile in his eyes stating louder than words that it was *he* who had got into the General's head.

Despite the fact that his eyes were blue, Flick saw red. But he had her trussed up tight – no matter how she wriggled, the General stood firm. And as it quickly became clear he was, beneath his placid exterior, gruffly worried about her lack of social experience, she found herself acquiescing with a sweetness entirely out of step with her temper.

Her tormentor, of course, beat a strategic retreat once he'd secured his goal. Flick gritted her teeth – she would now have to learn to dance – *with him*. Excusing himself on the grounds that he wanted to be early to the Heath for afternoon stables, he left them at the table.

All her steel went out of her once he'd gone. She chatted easily with the General, while making a very large, very red mental note to tell his prote´ge´ just what she thought of his maneuvering, especially his fostering of the General's worry, the instant she next had a moment alone with him.

That moment did not occur until they were standing by the side of the vicarage drawing room, with every eye in the room upon them. Flick stood, head up, hands lightly clasped, beside the General's chair. Demon, large, lean and hideously elegant, stood immediately by her side.

The stares directed her way, while disconcerting, did not greatly surprise Flick; the vision she presented had stunned her, too. All she'd done was don her new dress and the aquamarine necklace and earrings the General had given her for her last birthday, but the resulting vision that had stared back at her from her mirror had been a revelation.

She'd dutifully gone to the dressmaker with Foggy, a sudden convert to the notion of a dance. The dressmaker, Clotilde, had been surprisingly ready to put aside her other work to create a suitable gown for her. Suitable, Clotilde had insisted, meant pale blue silk, the exact same shade as her eyes. Imagining the cost, she'd demurred, suggesting a fine voile, but Clotilde had waved that aside and named a price that had been impossible to refuse. She'd agreed on the silk, only to be surprised again.

The dress whispered about her, sliding over her in quite a different way from the fine cottons she was used to. It clung, and shifted, and slithered; it was cool and at the same time warm. As for how she appeared in it – she hadn't recognized the slender, golden-haired beauty blinking huge blue eyes at her.

The color of the dress highlighted her eyes, making them appear larger, wider; the texture emphasized curves she normally paid very little attention to.

Demon, on the other hand, had paid a great deal of atten-

150

tion – to her, to those curves, to her eyes. When she'd descended the stairs and found him waiting in the hall, he'd blinked, then slowly smiled. Too intently for her liking. He'd come forward, handing her down the last stairs, then twirling her before him.

As she'd slowed, then halted, he'd trapped her gaze, lifted her hand, and brushed his lips across her fingertips. 'Very nice,' he'd purred, his blue eyes alight.

She'd felt like a blancmange he was just about to eat. Luckily, the General had appeared, and she'd escaped to fuss over him.

Their journey to Lidgate had been filled with the usual discussion of horses, but once they'd entered the vicarage, that subject was, by tacit agreement, not further pursued. Mrs. Pemberton had greeted them with great good cheer – she'd been particularly delighted to welcome Demon.

Flick slid a glance his way; he was idly scanning the room, slowly filling as more guests arrived. The General had insisted they be on time, so they'd been among the first to arrive. But the rest had followed on their heels; since taking up their positions, they'd had no chance to converse, too busy nodding politely as new arrivals nodded at them.

And stared. Half stared at her – the rest stared at him.

Hardly surprising. He was wearing black, a color that rendered his fair hair a brilliant blonde and deepened the blue of his eyes. The severe cut of his coat, pearl satin waistcoat and trousers emphasized his height, the breadth of his shoulders, his long, strong legs. He always looked elegant, but usually in a lazy, negligent way. Tonight, he was every inch the London rake, a predator stepped straight from the ton's ballrooms to prowl the vicarage dance floor.

Flick inwardly grinned at the thought.

As if sensing her gaze, he glanced down at her, then raised a quizzical brow. She hesitated, but with the General so close, she couldn't upbraid him as he deserved for getting her into this – into this room, into this gown, into this situation. With a speaking glance, she elevated her chin and haughtily looked away.

Mrs. Pemberton materialized before them. 'Allow me to present Mrs. March and her family from the Grange.'

Mrs. March nodded approvingly at Flick's curtsy, smiled appreciatively at Demon's elegant bow, then turned to chat with the General.

'And this is Miss March, who we all know as Kitty.'

A young girl in a white dress blushed furiously and curtsied.

'And her friend, Miss Avril Collins.'

The second young lady, a brunette in yellow muslin, curtsied rather more assuredly.

'And Henry, who is squiring his sister and Miss Collins tonight.'

Henry was obviously a March, as fair as his sister. He blushed furiously while executing the stiffest bow Flick had ever seen. 'It's a g-great pleasure, M-Miss Parteger.'

Mrs. Pemberton turned away; a second later, together with Mrs. March, she led the General away to where the older guests were gathering to chat and gossip.

'I say – have you lived in these parts long?'

Flick turned to find Henry March earnestly regarding her. His sister, too, lifting her gaze from a perusal of her blue silk gown, looked interested in the question.

Not so Avril Collins, who was brazenly looking interested in Demon.

'Most of my life,' Flick answered, her gaze on Avril Collins's face. 'I live with the General at Hillgate End, south of the racecourse.'

Avril's pouting lips – they *had* to be rouged – lifted in a little smile. 'I know,' she said on a breathless giggle, one finger reaching out to tap Demon's coat, 'that *you* live in London, Mr. Cynster.'

Flick glanced at Demon's face. He smiled – not a smile she was used to, but one coolly, distantly polite.

'Actually, I live in London only part of the time. The rest of the time I live near Hillgate End.'

'The General keeps a studbook, doesn't he?' Henry March appealed to Flick. 'That must be exciting – do you help him keep track of the horses?'

Flick smiled. 'It is interesting, but I don't help all that much. Of course, all the talk in the house is about horses.'

Henry's eager expression suggested such a household was his idea of heaven.

'Oh, *horses*!' Avril wrinkled her nose and cast an openly inviting glance at Demon. 'Don't you find them the most *boring* of creatures?'

'No.' Demon met her gaze. 'I breed them.'

Flick could almost feel sorry for Avril Collins – Demon purposely let the silence stretch for one exceedingly uncomfortable instant, then turned to Henry March. 'I own the stud farm to the west of the Lidgate road. Stop by some time if you're interested. If I'm not there, my foreman will show you around. Just mention my name.'

'T-thank you,' Henry stammered. 'I'd l-like that immensely.'

Mrs. Pemberton appeared with another group of young people. The fresh round of introductions allowed Kitty March to remove her unfortunate friend. Kitty tugged at her brother's sleeve, but he frowned at her, then returned to his open adoration of Flick.

In that pursuit he was joined by the two male members of the new group, both young gentlemen from nearby estates. Somewhat disconcerted by their soulful looks, Flick did her best to encourage rational conversation, only to be defeated by their patent silliness.

Their silliness, however, was nothing compared to their

153

sisters' witlessness, their vapidity. Flick was not sure which she found more distracting.

'No.' She drew a patient breath. 'I don't watch every race. The Jockey Club sends all the results to the General.'

'Do *you* get to name all the new foals?' One of the young ladies stared wide-eyed up at Demon.

Wearily resigned, he raised his brows. 'I suppose I do.'

'Oh! That must be so *wonderful*.' The young damsel clasped her hands to her breast. 'Thinking up sweet names for all those lovely little foals, staggering around on their shaky legs.'

Flick immediately looked back at her group of swains. 'Do any of you come to Newmarket to see the races?'

She struggled on, racking her brain for topics on which they might have more than two words to contribute. Most of such topics concerned racing, horses and carriages – within minutes, Demon insinuated a comment into their conversation. A minute later, he somehow managed to merge the two groups, which left the young ladies a trifle miffed, but they didn't move away.

Which was a pity, as Mrs. Pemberton arrived with another wave of admirers, both for her and Demon. Flick found herself facing five males, while Demon had his hands full, figuratively speaking, with six young girls. And one not-so-young, not-so-innocent young madam.

'What a delightful surprise, Mr. Cynster, to discover a gentleman of your standing at a gathering such as this. In case you missed my name, I'm Miss Henshaw.'

The throaty voice had Flick quickly turning.

'I say – you ride that pretty little mare, don't you? The one with the white hocks.'

Distracted, Flick glanced back at one of the new male additions. 'Yes. That's Jessamy.'

'Do you jump her?'

'Not especially.'

154

'Well, you should. I've seen conformations like that around the traps – she'll do well, mark my words.'

Flick shook her head. 'Jessamy's not—'

'Dare say you might not know, being a female, but take my word for it – she's got good legs and good stamina.' The bluffly genial youth, the local squire's son, grinned at her, the epitome of a patronizing male. 'If you like, I could organize a jockey and trainer for you.'

'Yes, but—' one of her earnest admirers cut in. 'She lives with the General – he keeps the stud records.'

'So?' Bluff-and-genial raised a dismissive brow. 'What's dusty old records got to do with it? This is horseflesh we're talking about.'

A throaty laugh came from beyond Demon. Flick gritted her teeth. 'For your information' – her tone stopped all argument and made Bluff-and-genial blink – 'Jessamy is an *investment*. As a broodmare, she has arguably the best blood-lines in the country. You may be *very* certain I will not be risking her in any steeplechase.'

'Oh,' was all Bluff-and-genial dared say.

Flick turned to deal with the throaty-voiced Miss Henshaw – and saw a black-haired beauty, smiling and laughing, leaning close to Demon, her face tipped up to his. She was, Flick saw in that one chilling instant, a lot taller than she herself was – so her face, tilted up, was much closer to Demon's, her lips closer to his—

'Now, my dears!'

Every head in the room lifted; everyone looked to where Mrs. Pemberton stood, clapping her hands for attention. 'Now,' she reiterated, when everyone was silent, 'it's time to find your partners for the first dance.'

There was an instant of silence, then a rush as all the young men jockeyed for position. A chorus of invitations and accept-ances filled the air.

155

Flick found herself facing three earnest young men – Bluff-and-genial had been shouldered aside.

'My dear Miss Parteger, if you will—'

'I pray, kind lady, that—'

'If you would honor me with this dance—'

Flick blinked at their youthful faces – they all seemed so *young*. She didn't need to look to know that the seductive Miss Henshaw was batting her long lashes at Demon. She didn't need to look, but she wanted to. She wanted to—

'Actually,' a deep drawling voice purred just above her right ear, 'Miss Parteger's first dance is mine.'

Demon's hand closed firmly about hers; Flick looked up to see him smile with a shatteringly superior air at her youthful admirers. There was no chance in heaven they would argue.

The relief she felt was quite definite, the reasons for it less clear. Luckily, she didn't need to dwell on it. Demon glanced down at her and raised one brow. Gracefully, she inclined her head. He set her hand on his sleeve; the others fell back as he led her onto the rapidly clearing floor.

The dance was to be a cotillion. As Demon led her to a set, Flick whispered, 'I know the theory, but I've never actually danced one of these in my life.'

He smiled reassuringly. 'Just copy what the other lady does. If you wander off in the wrong direction, I'll grab you.'

Despite all, despite her dismissive humph, she found that promise comforting.

They took their positions and the music started; despite her worries, she quickly found the rhythm. The dips and sways and hand-clasped twirls were heavily repetitive; it wasn't that hard to keep her place. And Demon's touch was reassuring – every time his fingers closed about hers, he steadied her, even if she wasn't drifting.

As the dance progressed, she felt increasingly assured – assured enough to stop frowning and smile when her eyes touched his. She laughed up at him, over her shoulder, as he twirled her into their final pose, then she sank into an extravagantly deep curtsy as he bowed, equally extravagantly, to her.

Demon raised her; he wondered if she knew how brightly her eyes were shining, how gloriously unabashed, unfettered in her enjoyment she was. She was so different from the other young ladies in the room, all careful to mind their words, their expressions, if not to artfully deploy them. She was unrestrained in her appreciation – something tonnish ladies rarely were. Exuberance, even if honest, was not the ton's way.

It *was* Flick's way – her wide smile and laughing eyes had him smiling, equally honestly, in reply. 'And now,' he said, and had to draw a deeper breath as he drew her closer and looked into her eyes, 'we must return to our duty.'

She laughed. 'Which duty is that?'

The duty he alluded to was to dance with all the other young people gathered at the vicarage for that purpose. They had barely returned to the side of the room before Flick's hand was solicited for a country dance.

Her other hand still rested on Demon's sleeve. She looked up at him – he smiled reassuringly, squeezed her fingers lightly, then let her go.

As she twirled down the room, Flick noticed Demon twirling, too, with the vicar's daughter. Letting her gaze slide away, she smiled easily at her partner, Henry March.

Dance followed dance, but with time between to allow the dancers to chat. To get to know each other better, to find their feet socially. That was, after all, what the evening was about. The older members of the company sat at the rear of the room, smiling and nodding, watching benignly as their youngsters mingled.

Mrs. Pemberton, her duty as hostess done, sank into a chair beside the General. Luckily, the General was deep in discussion with the vicar; Mrs. Pemberton did not interrupt. Relieved, Flick looked away. Beside her, Demon shifted. Flick looked up, and he caught her eye. And raised a knowing brow. She stared into his eyes, at the comprehension therein, then put her nose in the air and looked away. And struggled to ignore the *frisson* that shot through her when his hand shifted and his fingers brushed hers amid her skirts.

The dances that followed proved a trial. It was increasingly difficult to keep her mind on her steps. As for her eyes, they rarely rested on her partner. Twirling, whirling, she shot glances through the throng, through the constantly moving mass. Looking, searching . . .

She located Demon – he was dancing with Kitty March. Flick relaxed.

The next measure, however, he partnered Miss Henshaw.

Flick collided with another lady in her set, and nearly ended on her bottom. Flustered, she gasped, 'I think' – she didn't have to feign her shaking voice – 'that I'd better sit out the rest of this dance.'

Her partner, a Mr. Drysdale, was only too willing to solic-itously help her from the floor.

By the time Demon returned to her side at the end of the dance, as he had at the end of every dance thus far, Flick had herself well in hand. She'd lectured herself more sternly than she ever had in her life.

It was ridiculous! What on earth was she doing – thinking? Watching over him as if she was jealous. How foolish – making a cake of herself like that. Pray God he hadn't noticed, or he'd tease her unmercifully. And she'd deserve it. There was nothing between them – *nothing*!

She greeted him with a cool smile and immediately looked away.

His fingers found hers in her skirts – and tugged. She had to look up and meet his gaze.

It was serious, exceedingly intent. 'Are you all right?'

His eyes searched hers; God alone knew what he saw. Flick dragged in a breath – and wished she could drag her gaze from his. 'It was just a silly slip. I didn't fall.'

A frown darkened his eyes; his lips firmed, but then he nodded and, very slowly, released her hand. 'Be more careful – this is, after all, your first time at a dance.'

If she'd been feeling at all normal she would have responded to that as it deserved. Instead, the lingering touch of his fingers had blown all her certainties to the wind.

Nothing? If this – the light that turned his eyes dark and smoldering, the sense of protection, of strength, she felt flowing from him, the answering hitch in her breathing, the yearning that grew stronger, day by day, for him – if this was nothing, what would something be like?

More conscious of her heartbeat, of the rise and fall of her breasts than she'd ever been in her life, she looked away.

When she whirled down the next dance, she was conscious of him watching her, aware to her toes of the blue gaze that missed nothing, not a step, not a turn. He was waiting when her partner returned her to the side of the room. As if it was only natural, she slipped into the space beside him.

His gaze swept her face, but he said nothing.

Until the music started up again.

'My dance, I believe.'

His tone brooked no argument – from her potential partners, or her. She inclined her head graciously, as if she'd been expecting his claim. Perhaps she had.

For him to dance with her a second time while there were other young ladies he had not yet favored lent the action a particularity it would otherwise not have had – he was clearly singling her out. Despite her lack of social experience, she knew it – and knew beyond doubt that he did, too.

It was a simple country dance that left them partnered

throughout, without interaction with other dancers; they had no need to shift their attention from each other. From the instant the music started and their fingers touched, their focus was fixed. For her part, she barely heard the music. She moved instinctively, matching his actions, responding to directing touches so light she felt them more with her senses than with her nerves.

His eyes held her. His gaze, as brilliantly blue as a summer sky, wrapped her in its warmth. And she knew – knew that he was squiring her, deliberately, intentionally. Intent as only he could be. He was wooing her – even if the idea seemed so wild and impossible that her mind could not accept it, her senses did. Her first impulse was to step back – to safety, to a point where she could look about and understand. But while she whirled and twirled, her eyes never leaving his, there was no place of safety, nowhere she could hide from the smoldering glow in his eyes – and the very last thing she wanted to do was run.

His gaze held her effortlessly, yet without compulsion; she was fascinated, and that alone was power enough to keep her whirling. The sliding brush of his fingers as their hands met and parted, the gliding caress, so delicate, as he steered her into a sweeping turn – each was planned deliberately, executed with intent. In that single dance, he wove a net about her – one invisible to the eye but very clear to her senses.

Her nerves tingled, tightened; each heartbeat heightened her awareness. Until his every touch held a temptation and a promise, echoed by their movements in the dance.

She swayed closer, looking up as he drew her nearer, and felt the temptation to surrender. To surrender to the conviction of what he was telling her, to give in and believe that he wanted her to be his wife. And would have her.

The dance moved on, and she drew away, until their fingers barely touched. And heard his promise, unspoken, that if she surrendered she'd enjoy – experience – the full pleasures of the flesh.

He was adept at sending that message, expert at making the temptation grow, and the promise shine and beckon like gold.

The music ended. And they stopped. But the temptation and the promise still shone in his eyes.

She felt like Cinderella when he raised her hand and brushed his lips gently across her fingertips.

Chapter Nine

When the next dance commenced, Demon was, courtesy of Mrs. Pemberton, at the opposite end of the room from Flick. Within seconds of their leaving the floor, the vicar's wife had descended on them; with irresistible energy, she'd insisted on taking Demon to introduce him to others of the company.

Her 'others' were the collected matrons of the district; Demon was amused to realize their fell purpose in speaking with him was to subtlely encourage his pursuit of Flick.

'She's such a pretty little thing, and quite assured,' Mrs. Wallace, of the Hadfield-Wallaces of Dullingham, nodded sagely. 'As experienced as you are, you'll have noticed – she's not just in the common way.'

Demon smiled, content to let them convince him of the rightness of his cause. He didn't need convincing, but it wouldn't hurt his campaign to have the matrons' support.

Because of his height, he could track Flick's crowning glory. As the ladies' comments continued, he started to chafe at the bit. He understood very well the reasons behind their reactions – those reasons were gathered about Flick like swarming bees about a honeypot.

Their sons looked set to make cakes of themselves over her – their fond mamas could read the script with ease. It was, therefore, in their best interests to have Demon waltz Flick off her feet, out of reach of their moonfaced sons, so said sons could recover quickly and apply themselves to the real business of the upcoming Season – finding themselves suitable wives.

Flick, of course, was highly suitable, but the ladies had accepted that their sons were not in the running, just as they'd accepted that their daughters had no chance of catching Demon's eye. It was therefore best on all counts to get him and Flick quickly paired and out of contention, before they caused any major disruptions to the good ladies' matrimonial plans.

Such was their strategy. As their plans marched so well with his, Demon was perfectly ready to reassure them as to his intentions. 'Her knowledge of horses is extensive.' He made the comment offhandedly, yet appreciatively. 'And, of course, she is the General's ward.'

'Indeed,' Mrs. Wallace nodded approvingly. 'So very appropriate.'

'A happy circumstance,' Mrs. Pemberton concurred.

With an elegant bow, quite sure they all understood each other well, Demon left them. He ambled down the side of the room, scanning the dancers. He couldn't see Flick.

Halting, he searched more carefully – she wasn't there.

He located the General, chatting with a group of older gentlemen – Flick wasn't with him.

Swallowing a curse directed at milksops who couldn't be trusted to keep a quick-witted girl in line, Demon strolled as swiftly as he could to where he'd last seen her, at the far end of the room. He reached the corner, wondering what had got into her head. Surely her disappearance didn't have anything to do with Bletchley and the syndicate?

The idea that she might have been identified, followed, and lured away chilled him. He shook the thought aside – that was fanciful, unlikely. The main door stood beyond the matrons; he was sure she hadn't gone that way. But the only other doors led deeper into the house.

Where the hell had she gone?

He was searching the throng again when a flicker at the edge of his vision had him turning. The lace curtain over the long window in the corner drifted in a light breeze. The narrow casement was partly open; it extended from head height to a foot above the floor. He couldn't fit through it. Flick, however, was smaller than he.

It took him five minutes to return back up the room, smiling and nodding and avoiding invitations to chat. Regaining the front hall, he slipped out the front door and headed around the side of the vicarage.

The garden beyond the drawing room's corner window was empty. The moon was full; steady silver light illuminated a flagged path and burgeoning flowerbeds edging a neat lawn. Frowning, Demon scanned the shadows, but there were no nooks, no benches set under overhanging boughs – no angel in pale blue communing with the night.

The garden was sunk in silence, the drifting strains of the violins a superficial tune causing barely a ripple in the deep of the night. A lick of fear touched his spine, flicked toward his heart. He was about to turn and retrace his steps, to check she hadn't returned to the drawing room *before* he panicked, when his gaze fell on the hedge lining one side of the lawn.

A path ran beside it, between the lawn and the deep green wall. The hedge was high; he couldn't see over it. Silently, he prowled the wall, searching, wondering if he was wrong in remembering a small courtyard ...

The opening lay in shadow, just a simple gap in the hedge. He stepped into the gap. And saw her.

The courtyard was a flagged square with a raised central bed in which stood an old magnolia, draping its branches over a small pond. Flick paced slowly back and forth before it, the moonlight washing the blue from her gown, leaving it an unearthly silver.

Demon watched her, transfixed by the sway of her hips, the artless grace with which she turned. Until that instant, he hadn't realized how tightly unnamed fears had seized him; he recognized the tension only as it eased, as relief replaced it.

She felt his gaze and looked up, halting, stiffening – then relaxing as she recognized him. She said nothing, but raised a brow.

'In that gown, in the moonlight, you look like a silver sprite.' *Come to steal this mortal's heart.* His voice was gravelly, revealingly deep.

If she noticed, she gave no sign; instead, she looked down at her gown, holding out the skirts to inspect them. 'It *is* a very pale blue. I rather like it.'

He liked it, too – it was the same pale, pure blue as her eyes. The gown was well worth the price he'd paid. Of course, she'd never know he'd offset the gown's cost. Clotilde was an excellent dressmaker; he made a mental note to send some extra token of appreciation her way.

He hesitated ... but they were here, alone in the moonlight, the violins a distant whisper in the dark. Unhurriedly, he strolled forward, his gaze, intent, on her.

Flick watched him approach, large, elegant – dangerous. The moon silvered his hair, rendering his face harsh in its stark light. The angular planes seemed harder, like pale stone; his eyes were deeply shadowed beneath their heavy lids.

How his presence could be reassuring and unnerving simultaneously she didn't know. Her nerves were tightening, her senses stretching ... The yearning she'd felt as they'd danced returned with a rush.

She'd come here to be quiet, to breathe the cool air, to let it soothe her overheated brain, her flushed skin. She'd come here to ponder. Him. Part of her wondered if she'd read him aright. The rest of her knew she had. But she still couldn't bring herself to believe it.

It was like a fairy tale.

Now he was here ... . Her nerves skittered even before she formed the thought. Abruptly, she recalled she was annoyed with him. Folding her arms, she tilted her chin; as he drew near, she narrowed her eyes at him. '*You* conspired with Mrs. Pemberton – Foggy told me she sent her message to the General via you.'

He halted before her. 'Mrs. Pemberton conjured a vision of you moldering into an old maid – that didn't seem a good idea.'

His deep drawl slid over, then under, her skin, effortlessly vanquishing her annoyance. Refusing to shiver, she humphed. 'I can't see how an evening like this is going to change things.' She gestured toward the house. 'I'm certainly not going to find a husband in there.'

'No?'

'You saw them. They're so young!'

'Ah – them.'

His voice deepened; she sensed that net of fascination flow about her again. His lips curved, lifting just a little at the ends, drawing her mentally closer, nearer. 'No,' he said, the word a deep rumble. 'I agree – you definitely shouldn't marry any of them.'

The ensuing pause stretched, then his lids rose and he met her gaze. 'There is, however, an alternative.'

He said no more, but his meaning was clear, written in the planes of his face, in his eyes. He watched her, his gaze steady; the night held them in soft darkness, alive and yet so silent that she could feel her own pulse filling the air.

Then came the music.

Haunting strains drifted over the lawns, flowed over the hedges. The opening bars of a waltz reached them – he angled his head slightly, then, his gaze never leaving her face, he held out his hands.

'Come – waltz with me.'

The net drew tight – she felt its shimmering touch as it settled about her. But he didn't tug; it was her choice to step forward, to accept, if she would.

Flick wondered if she dared. Her senses reached for him – she knew how it felt to be held against his warm chest, how it felt to have his arms close about her, how her hips would settle against his hard thighs. But . . .

'I don't know how.'

Her voice was surprisingly even; his lips curved a fraction more.

'I'll teach you' – a hint of wickedness invested his smile – 'all you need to know.'

She managed not to shiver. She knew very well they weren't talking of a mere waltz – that wasn't the invitation etched in his eyes, the challenge in his stance. Those hands, those arms, that body – she knew what he was offering. And, deep inside, she knew she could never walk away – not without trying, touching. Knowing.

She stepped forward, lifting her arms, tilting her face to his. He drew her to him, one arm sliding possessively about her, the other grasping her right hand. He drew her close, until they touched, until the silk of her bodice brushed his coat. His smile deepened. 'Relax, and let your feet follow where they will.'

He stepped back, then aside; before she knew it, she was whirling. At first, he took small steps, until she caught the rhythm, then they whirled, swooped, swung, trapped in the music, swept up in the effortless energy of the dance.

Then the mood of the music changed, slowed; they slowed, too. He drew her fractionally closer – she leaned her temple against his chest. 'Isn't there some rule that I'm not supposed to waltz before someone or other approves?'

'That only applies in town at a formal ball. Young ladies

have to learn to waltz somewhere, or no gentleman would ever stand up with them.'

She suppressed a sniff – she hadn't stepped on his toes once. They were revolving slowly, the music soft and low.

It was she who stepped closer, fascinated by the slide of silk between their bodies. And by the heat of him.

He didn't step back. His fingers locked about hers, he laid her hand in the hollow of his shoulder. His arm tightened about her, his hand splaying below her waist, locking her to him so that they moved in truth as one.

His hand burned; so did his thighs as they pressed between hers as he steered her through a shallow turn. Her breasts firm against his coat, she laid her cheek against his chest, and listened to his heart.

Eventually, with a minor flourish they ignored, the music died. Their feet slowed, then halted; for one long instant, they simply stood.

Then she lifted her head and looked into his face. His temptation, his promise, were all around her, a shimmering veil, a glow suffusing her skin. She knew she wasn't imagining it; she didn't know enough to imagine this. She knew what was there, what it was, what might be.

She didn't know why.

So she simply asked, her eyes on his, deeply shadowed by his lids, 'Why are you doing this?'

He searched her eyes, then raised one brow. 'I would have thought that was obvious.' After a moment, he stated, 'I'm wooing you – courting you – call it what you will.'

'Why?'

'Why else? Because I want you to be my wife.'

'Why?'

He hesitated, then his hand left hers. His fingers slid beneath her chin, tipping her face up. His lips closed over hers.

It started as a gentle caress. That satisfied neither of them. Whether it was she or he who deepened the kiss was impossible to say – his lips were suddenly harder, firmer, more demanding; hers were correspondingly softer, more beguiling, more inviting.

Greatly daring, she parted her lips, just a little, then more, thrilled to her toes when he took instant advantage. Angling his head, he tasted her, then, like a conqueror, simply took more.

She shivered, and gave, and welcomed him in; his arms tightened about her, impressing her soft flesh with the hardness of his. She sighed, and felt him drink – her breath was his and his was hers; her head reeled as the kiss went on.

Again, it was she who took the next step, who, in all innocence, stretched her arms up, slid her hands to his nape and sank against him. She felt a rumble in his chest – a groan that never made it to his lips.

Their kiss turned ravenous.

Hot. Hungry.

His lips seared hers; his hunger whipped, and licked, and tempted. She sensed it clearly – there – beneath the smooth control, the elegant facade. Ever bold, she reached for it.

He froze.

The next instant, she was standing, unsteadily, on her feet, the air cool between them. Her breasts ached oddly; all her skin felt hot. She blinked, and focused on him – he was breathing every bit as raggedly as she. He was just recovering faster – her wits were still whirling.

His hands fell from her; it was impossible to read his eyes. 'We should get back.'

Before she had time to consider, long before she could gather her wits and think, they were back in the drawing room. They mingled with the other guests while she struggled to find her mental feet. Beside her, he was his usual elegant self, cool and disgustingly controlled, while her lips were tingling, her breathing still too shallow. And she ached, bone-deep, with a sense of having been denied.

The next morning, a stack of books under her arm, Flick stepped out of the side door, looking down as she tugged on her gloves – and ran into a brick wall.

'Ooof!' All the breath was knocked out of her. Luckily, the wall was covered in resilient muscle, and had arms that locked around her, preventing her and her books from tumbling to the ground.

She dragged in a breath, her breasts swelling against Demon's soft jacket, then she blew aside the curls that had tumbled into her eyes. The exhalation ruffled the blonde locks about his ear.

He stiffened. All over.

Rigid, he awkwardly unlocked his arms, grasped her upper arms, and set her back from him.

She blinked at him. He scowled at her.

'Where are you going?'

His tone, that of one having the right to know, was guaranteed to make her bridle; putting her nose in the air, she stepped around him. 'To the lending library.'

He smothered a curse, spun on his heel and followed. 'I'll take you in my curricle.'

Not so much as a by-your-leave! Let alone a 'Good morning, my dear, and how are you?' So much for last night! Entirely unimpressed, Flick kept her gaze fixed stubbornly ahead, ruthlessly denying the impulse to glance at him as he ranged alongside. 'I'm perfectly capable of returning and selecting my novels myself, thank you.'

'I dare say.'

His tone was as stubborn as hers.

She opened her mouth to argue – and caught sight of the

pair of blacks harnessed to his curricle. Her face softened, her eyes lit. 'Oh – what *beauties*!' Her tone was reverent, a fitting tribute to the surely matchless horses impatiently pawing the gravel. 'Are they new?'

'Yes.' Demon strolled in her wake as she circled the pair, exclaiming over their points. When she paused for breath, he nonchalantly added, 'I thought I'd take them for a short outing, just to get them used to town traffic.'

Eyes still round, fixed on the blacks' sleek hides, she wasn't paying attention; seizing the moment, he took her hand and helped her into the curricle.

'They hold their heads so well.' She settled on the seat. 'What's their action like?'

Barely pausing for his answer, she rattled on knowledgeably; by the time she'd run through all her questions and exclamations they were rolling down the drive. Demon kept his gaze on his horses, waiting for her to suddenly realize and berate him for taking advantage. Instead, she set her books on the seat between them and leaned back with a soft sigh.

As the peace unexpectedly lengthened, he shot her a glance; she was sitting easily, one hand braced on the side railing, her gaze fixed, not on the blacks, but on his hands.

She was watching him handle the ribbons, watching his fingers flick and slide along the leather strips. There was an eager light in her eyes, a wistful expression on her face.

He faced forward; a moment later, he clenched his jaw.

Never in his entire career had he let a female drive his cattle.

The blacks, although new, were well broken; thus far, they'd proved well behaved. And he would be sitting beside her.

If he did it once, she'd expect him to do it again.

When riding, she had a more delicate touch on the reins than even he.

171

Turning out of the manor drive, he set the curricle bowling down the road to Newmarket, but he didn't slacken the reins. Instead, drawing in a breath, he turned to Flick. 'Would you like to take the reins for a stretch?'

The look on her face was payment enough for his abused sensibilities – stunned surprise gave way to eager joy, swiftly tempered.

'But ...' She looked at him, hope warring with imminent disappointment. 'I've never driven a pair before.'

He forced himself to shrug lightly. 'It's not that different from a single horse. Here – shift those books and come closer.' She did, eagerly sliding along the seat until her thigh brushed his. Ignoring the heat that shot straight to his loins, he transferred the reins to her small hands, keeping his fingers tensioning the leather until he was sure she had them.

'No.' Expertly, he relaid the reins across her left palm. 'Like that, so you've got simultaneous control over them both with just one hand.'

She nodded, looking so excited that he wondered if she could speak at all. Sitting back, one arm along the seat behind her, ready to grab her if anything did go wrong, he watched her, his gaze flicking ahead now and again to check the road. But he knew it well, and so did she.

She had a little difficulty checking the pair for a curve; he gritted his teeth and managed not to reach out and lay his hand over hers. Thereafter, however, she adjusted; gradually, as the fields rolled past, they both relaxed.

There was, he discovered, one benefit in being driven by a lady – one he trusted not to land them in a ditch. He could keep his gaze wholly on her – on her face, on her figure, in this case, neat and trim in cambric. Her hair, those lovely golden curls, was constantly ruffling in the wind of their passage, a living frame for her delicate face.

A face flushed with pleasure, with an excitement he understood. She was thrilled and delighted. He felt decidedly smug.

She cast him a dubious glance as the first stables by the racecourse came into sight. From there on, there would be other horses, people, even dogs about – all things to which the blacks might take exception. Demon nodded; sitting up, he expertly lifted the reins from her hands. He readjusted the reins, letting the blacks know he had them again.

Flick sat back with an ecstatic sigh. She had always – forever – wanted to drive a curricle. And Demon's blacks! They were the most perfect young pair she'd ever seen. Not as powerful as his champion bays, but so very elegant, with their slim legs and long, sleekly arched necks.

And she'd driven them! She could hardly wait to tell the General. And Dillon – he would be green with envy. She sighed again; with a contented smile, she looked around.

Only then did she remember their earlier words – only then did she realize she'd been kidnapped. Lured away. Enticed into a gentleman's curricle with tempting promises and whisked into town.

She slanted a glance at her abductor. He was looking ahead, his expression easy but uninformative. There was nothing to say he'd planned this – that he'd purposely had the blacks put to that morning just so he could distract her.

She wouldn't mind betting he had.

Unfortunately, after enjoying herself so thoroughly, it would be churlish indeed to cavil. So she sat back and enjoyed herself some more, watching as he deftly tacked through the increasing traffic to pull up before the lending library, just off the High Street halfway through the town.

As was usual, the sight of a magnificent pair had drawn a gaggle of boys in their wake. After handing her to the pavement, Demon selected two and, with strict instructions, left the blacks in their care.

That surprised Flick, but she was too wise to show it;

173

carrying her books, she headed for the library door. Demon followed on her heels; he reached over her shoulder and pushed the door wide.

She walked through into familiar surroundings – the wide front bay where two old gentlemen sat, dozing over their history books, the narrow aisles leading away toward the back of what had once been a hall, each aisle lined on both sides with bookshelves crammed to overflowing.

'Hello, Mrs. Higgins,' Flick whispered to the large, homely woman who presided over her domain from behind a table near the entrance. 'I'm returning these.'

'Good, good.' Perching her pince-nez on her nose, Mrs. Higgins peered down at the titles. 'Ah, yes, and did the General enjoy the Major's biography?'

'He did indeed. He asked me to see if there were any more like it.'

'You'll find all we have in the second aisle, dear – about midway down ...' Mrs. Higgins's words trailed away. Looking past Flick, she slowly raised her hand and removed her pince-nez, the better to take in who had strayed into her castle.

'Mr. Cynster's escorting me,' Flick explained. Facing Demon, she gestured to the chairs in the front bay. 'Would you like to wait there?'

He glanced at the two old gents, then looked back at her, his expression utterly blank. 'I'll follow you.'

He proceeded to do so, strolling directly behind her as she wandered down the aisles.

Flick tried to ignore him and concentrate on the books, but novels and literary heroes could not compete with the masculine presence prowling in her wake. The more she tried to shut him out, the more he intruded on her mind, on her senses. Which was the very last thing she needed.

She was confused enough about him as it was.

174

After spending the hours until dawn reliving their second dance, reliving that amazing waltz, and replaying everything they'd said in the moonlight, over her breakfast toast she'd made a firm resolution to put the entire matter from her – and wait and see.

Wait for him to make the next move – and see if it made any more sense than his last.

She had a very strong notion she was misinterpreting, through lack of experience, reading more into his words, his actions, than he intended. He was accustomed to dallying with sophisticated ladies of the ton. Doubtless, that matter of their second dance, and the waltz, and his warm words in the moonlight – and, of course, that kiss – were all simply tonnish dalliance, the way ladies and gentlemen of his ilk entertained themselves of an evening. A form of sophisticated teasing. The more she thought of it, the more that seemed likely.

In which case, the last thing she should do was place any great emphasis on any of it.

Determinedly, she halted before the bookshelf housing her favorite novels – those of Miss Austen and Mrs. Radcliffe. Ignoring the disapproving humph from behind her, she stubbornly scanned the shelves.

Demon propped one shoulder against a bookshelf, slid his hands into his pockets, and watched her with a distinctly jaundiced eye. If she wanted romance, why the hell was she looking at books?

The fact she was didn't auger well for his plans. He watched as she pulled books out and studied them, returning some, retaining others – and wondered if there was any way he could step up his campaign. Unfortunately, she was young and innocent – and strong-willed and stubborn. Which meant that if he pushed too hard, drove too fast, she might turn skittish and difficult.

175

Which would slow things down all the more. He'd gentled enough high-couraged horses to know the value of patience. And, of course, this time, there was no question of him not succeeding – he intended to get his ring on her finger no matter how long it took.

This time, he refused to entertain any possibility of defeat. Last time, when he'd turned up at the manor, ready to offer himself up on a sacrificial matrimonial altar, he hadn't known what he was about. He hadn't stopped to think – he'd reacted instinctively to the situation about him. Discovering that Flick had made everything right so there was no need for them to marry had brought him up short. He'd been stunned, but not with joy. He had, in fact, been distinctly unamused, and even less amused by that fact.

That had certainly made him think. He'd spent the next twenty-four hours doing precisely that, doggedly separating his real desires from the disguise of convenience he'd wrapped them in, only to discover that, as usual, his instincts hadn't misled him.

He wanted to marry the chit – never mind why – and having her compromised so innocently had been a convenient, if not perfect, avenue by which to stake his claim. His wish to marry her was not at all innocent – his thoughts, even then, had been colored by desire. His disappointment had been so acute that he'd actually felt hurt, which had annoyed him all the more.

No woman had ever made him feel this uncertain, had made him ache with desire with no surety of relief.

His sudden susceptibility – his need for an angel – was something he wanted dealt with quickly. Once he had her safely wedded and bedded, he was sure he'd feel better – back to his usual, assured, self-reliant, self-confident self.

Which was why he proposed to dog her every step until she agreed to marry him. He could only pray it wouldn't take too long.

176

With three books in her arms, she finally quit that book-shelf and strolled farther down the aisle. Pushing away from his resting place, Demon ambled after her. She paused to select a cookbook; he glanced at the title as she lifted it down. *Italian Renaissance Recipes*.

'Are you planning to entertain an Italian count?'

She glanced at him. 'It's for Foggy – she loves reading recipes.' The book was large and heavy; she juggled it, trying to settle it in her arms.

'Here.' He reached for the book.

'Oh – thank you.' With a grateful smile, she handed him the cookbook and her three novels.

Lips setting, Demon accepted them all, reminding himself that none of his acquaintances, not even Reggie, were likely to come in and discover him wandering the aisles at an angel's beck and call, loaded with cookbooks and romantic novels.

Flick's next stop was the biographies. 'The General likes reading about gentlemen connected with horses. The last book I got for him was about a cavalry major.' Frowning, she studied the shelves. 'Do you know of any work he might find interesting?'

Demon glanced at the leather and gilt spines. 'I don't read much.'

'Oh?' Brows rising, she looked up. 'What do you do of a quiet evening?'

He trapped her wide gaze. 'Active endeavors are more to my taste.'

A puzzled frown formed in her eyes. 'You must relax sometime.'

Lips curving, he let his gaze grow intent, let his voice deepen. 'The endeavors I favor are guaranteed to relax.'

A faint blush tinged her cheeks; she held his gaze for an instant, then raised a haughty brow and looked away.

Inwardly grinning, Demon looked back at the books. At

least she no longer viewed him as a benevolent uncle. 'What about this one?' Reaching over her head, he tugged a volume free.

'*Colonel J.E. Winsome: Memoirs of a Commander of Horse*,' Flick read as he put the book in her hands. She opened it and quickly perused the description at the front. 'Oh, yes! This is perfect. It's about the cavalry in the Peninsula War.'

'Excellent.' Demon straightened. 'Can we go now?'

To his relief, Flick nodded. 'Yes, that's it.'

She led the way to the front of the hall.

Mrs. Higgins pursed her lips in silent disapproval as Demon set the books on her desk. Flick appeared not to notice; she chatted blithely as Mrs. Higgins wrote her selections on a card. Stepping back, Demon cast a last glance around – he wouldn't be paying a second visit if he could help it.

One of the old gentlemen in the overstuffed armchairs had woken; he sent a suspicious look his way, frowning direfully from under shaggy brows.

Turning back to Flick, Demon relieved her of the pile of books she'd just settled in her arms. 'Come – I'll drive you home.'

Flick smiled, bid Mrs. Higgins good-bye, and preceded him to the door; Demon followed, his gaze on her hips, his mind busy with plans to cure her of all future need for fictional romantic stimulation.

178

Chapter Ten

For Flick, their journey to the library was the start of a most peculiar week.

Demon drove her back to the manor by the longest possible route, ostensibly to try the blacks' paces. As he consented to let her handle the ribbons again, she refrained from making any comment on his high-handed arrogance – as it happened, she hadn't had anything better to do.

At least, nothing to compare with the sensation of bowling along, the breeze ruffling her hair, the ribbons taut in her hands. The sheer exhilaration of tooling his curricle, well-sprung and built for speed, with the blacks highstepping down the lanes, had worked its addictive magic – she was hooked.

When he drew up before the manor, she was smiling so brightly that she couldn't possibly have admonished him.

Which, from the gleam in his eye, was precisely as he'd planned.

He was back the next morning, although this time, it wasn't her he had come to see; he spent an hour with the General, discussing a line of horses the General was investigating. Of course, the General invited him to stay for luncheon, and he accepted.

Later, she strolled with him to the stable. She waited, but, other than an artful comment about enjoying the view – it was a brisk day and her skirts were flapping – he said nothing.

His eyes, however, seemed unusually brilliant, his gaze especially attentive; despite the breeze, she didn't feel cold.

Day followed day; his visits highlighted each one. She could never be certain when or where he would appear, which was doubtless why she found herself listening for his footsteps.

And it wasn't just his gaze that was attentive.

Occasionally, he would touch her, just a hand at her back, or a sliding of his fingers from her hand to her wrist. Such touches always made her catch her breath – and flush in a most peculiar way.

Her worst moment came when he called one afternoon and inveigled her into joining him to watch the strings exercising on the Heath – he was still watching Bletchley during morning and afternoon stables.

'Hills and Cross are doing the bulk of it these days. They're less identifiable than Gillies or me.'

They were standing by the Heath, she with her hands clasped on the handle of her furled parasol. 'Has Bletchley made any further arrangements – fixed any more fixes?'

Demon shook his head. 'I'm starting to wonder . . . '

When he said nothing more, she prompted, 'What?'

He glanced at her, then grimaced and looked across the close-cropped turf to where his string was going through their paces. Bletchley lounged under his favorite oak; from there, he could see three separate strings working.

'I'm starting to wonder,' Demon mused, 'whether he's got any more fixes to place. He's been chatting up the jockeys, true enough, but lately it's been more in the nature of ingratiating himself with them. Other than those three fixes we know of, all of which are for major Spring Carnival races, he hasn't made any further arrangements.'

'So?'

'So it's possible all the fixes the syndicate want for the

Spring Carnival are now in place – just those three. Considering the races involved, they should clear enough for the greediest of men. I'm wondering if Bletchley is simply whiling away time until his masters are due to check with him, and putting in his hours by learning as much as he can about the race jockeys with a view to making his next round of fixes, most likely in a few months – maybe at the July meeting – easier to arrange.'

Flick studied Bletchley. 'He's looking for weaknesses? Something to give him a hold over the jockeys?'

'Hmm. Possibly.'

She knew the instant he switched his gaze from Bletchley to her, knew precisely when his mind shifted from fixes to ... whatever it was he was thinking about her.

A gentle tug on one curl had her turning her face, only to find him much nearer, closer ...

'Stop staring at him so deliberately – he'll notice.'

'I'm not staring at Bletchley.' She was staring at his lips. They curved, then drew fractionally nearer ...

She stiffened, blinked and dragged her eyes up to his. 'Perhaps we'd better stroll.' Dalliance was all very well, but she was not about to indulge in any of his mindwhirling kisses – not on the open Heath.

His lips quirked, but he inclined his head. 'Perhaps we had.'

He turned her; with her hand on his sleeve, they strolled along the Heath's edge – while she hoped he'd exercise his usual initiative and find an empty stable.

To her unreasoning annoyance, he didn't.

The next morning, he took her into town, so they could savor the scones at The Twig and Bough, which he insisted were a cut above excellent. After their repast, they strolled down the High Street, where Mrs. Pemberton beamed at them from her carriage, exchanging gracious greetings.

Flick was quite sure the vicar's wife had never before looked at her with such patent approval.

Which, more than anything else – far more than the insistence of her silly senses or the wonderings of her illinformed mind – made her question what Demon was about. Really about.

She'd ridden high-bred horses all her life; she'd long ago learned the knack of putting aside all unnerving thoughts and emotions. She had, she thought, been doing an excellent job of ignoring the uncertainties his constant squiring of her had evoked. But after their meeting with Mrs. Pemberton, she could no longer ignore the fact that it really did appear that he was wooing her. Courting her.

Just like he'd said.

Had the moonlight addled his wits – or hers?

The question demanded an answer, not least because his continuing presence was stretching her nerves taut. As it was the same question, albeit in slightly different form, that had been circling in her brain for the past week without answer, there was obviously only one way forward.

And, after all, it *was* Demon – she'd known him nearly all her life. She hadn't shied away from asking for his help with Dillon, and he'd given it. So ...

She waited until they were rolling down the manor drive the next morning for a tool about the lanes so she could hone her driving skills on his powerful bays. He was still holding the reins. Without giving herself time to think, to balk, she asked, 'Why are you behaving like this – spending so much time with me?'

His head whipped around; an incipient frown darkened his eyes. 'I told you. I'm wooing you.'

She blinked; the storm warning in his eyes wasn't encouraging, but she was determined to have all clear. 'Yes,' she admitted, evenly, carefully. 'But that was just . . .' With one hand, she gestured airily.

His frown crystallized; he slowed the bays.

'Just what?'

'Well,' she shrugged. 'Just that night. In the moonlight.'

Demon hauled the bays to a halt. 'What about the past days? It's been nearly a week.' He was appalled. Swearing, not entirely under his breath, he pulled on the brake, tied off the reins and faced her. 'Don't tell me' - narrowing his eyes, he trapped her gaze - 'that you haven't no ticed. That you haven't been paying attention.'

She stared at him, her eyes widening, and widening, as she read the message in his. 'You're serious.'

Her patent astonishment nearly did him in.

'*Serious*?' He clenched one fist on the railing in front of her, slapped the other on the seat behind her and locked his gaze on her face. 'Of *course* I'm serious! What in all creation do you imagine these last days have been about?'

'Well ...' Given the anger vibrating in his tone, Flick decided she'd be wiser not to say. He wasn't yelling - she almost wished he was. His clipped, forcefully enunciated words were somehow more menacing than bellows.

'I am not in the habit of dancing attendance on freshfaced chits just for the pleasure of their innocent smiles.'

She blinked. 'I suppose not.'

'You may be *certain* not.' His jaw hardened to match the rest of his face; his eyes narrowed to slits. 'So what the devil have you been imagining?'

If there had been a way of avoiding the question, she'd have taken it, but the look in his eyes declared he wasn't about to drop the subject. And she had been the one to bring it up - and she did still want to know. Holding his gaze, she carefully said, 'I thought it was just dalliance.'

It was his turn to blink. 'Dalliance?'

'A way to fill in the time.' Spreading her hands, she shrugged. 'For all I know, telling a lady you're wooing her while alone in a courtyard in the moonlight might be standard practice, entirely unremarkable behavior for—'

Caution caught her tongue. She glanced at him; he smiled – all wolf. 'For a rake such as I?'

She suppressed a glare. 'Yes! How am I supposed to know how you go on?'

Narrow-eyed, he studied her face; his softened not at all. 'You may take it from me that when I say I'm courting you, I am.' Turning forward, he started to untie the reins.

Flick straightened. 'Yes, all right. But you still haven't told me why.'

His gaze on his horses, Demon exhaled through set teeth. He released the brake. 'Because I want to marry you, of course.'

'Yes, but that's what I don't understand. *Why* do you want to marry me?'

He was going to throttle her if she didn't leave off with her whys; jaw setting, he flicked the reins – the bays stepped out. He felt her irate glance.

'You can't expect me to believe you've suddenly taken it into your head that you need to marry me. You didn't even know I existed – well, not other than a pigtailed brat – not until you caught me on The Flynn's back.' She swung on the seat to face him. 'So *why*?'

Feathering the turn into the road, he set the bays pacing. 'I want to marry you because you're the right wife for me.' Anticipating her next *why*, he stated, 'You're an eligible parti – you're well-born, your connections are commendable. You're the General's ward – you've grown up around here, and you're remarkably knowledgeable about horses.' He had his excuses down pat. 'All in all, we're an excellent match.' He glanced at her sharply. 'A fact everyone seems to have realized except you.'

She looked ahead, and he turned back to his horses. He wasn't sure he trusted his ears, but he thought she sniffed. She certainly put her nose in the air.

'That sounds horridly cold-blooded to me.'

Cold-blooded? He *was* going to throttle her. Just the *thought* of how heated his blood had been, simmering uncomfortably for more than a week, hot need flaring every time she drew close – and as for those times she'd been in his arms, stretched, flush, body to body against him . . .

He set his teeth and heard his jaw crack. His leader jibbed; dragging in a breath, he held it, carefully resettled his horses, then exhaled slowly.

'I also want to marry you' – he forced the words out through gritted teeth – 'because I desire you.'

He felt her questioning, innocently curious gaze – he wasn't fool enough to meet it – that puzzled look that in vited him to demonstrate, to teach her. She'd perfected that look until it could lure even him into deep waters. His gaze locked on his leader's ears, he kept driving.

'What, *exactly*? . . .'

He hauled in a breath. 'I want you warming my bed.' He wanted her warming *him*. 'The fact that I desire you as a man desires a woman is incidental. It merely adds another element to my wooing of you, and our eventual marriage.' He quickly changed tacks, focusing on the one aspect he suspected had most contributed to her confusion. She was direct and straightforward – she'd misinterpreted his subtlety. She equated subtleties with playing, with teasing – by definition not serious. 'Given your age and lack of experience, as I wish to marry you, a period of courtship is deemed mandatory, during which time my behavior must follow a prescribed pattern.'

He was driving dangerously fast. He didn't want to, but he drew back on the reins, slowing to a safer pace. He'd taken a circuitous route; it wasn't necessary to stop and turn in order to return to Hillgate End. Which was just as well. Stopping with him in his present mood and her in her curious one was the definition of unwise.

She'd been listening carefully; he heard the frown in her voice as she repeated, '*Prescribed* pattern.'

'Society dictates that I can squire you about, but I can't press my suit too openly, certainly not forcefully. That would be improper. I have to be subtle. I shouldn't tell you how I feel outright – that's not the way things are done. I shouldn't seek to see you in any clandestine manner. I shouldn't kiss you – and I should certainly not mention that I desire you – even let you get any hint of that fact. You're not supposed to know about desire.'

He checked the bays for a corner, then set them pacing again. 'In fact, this entire *conversation* shouldn't be occurring – Mrs. Pemberton and company would unhesitatingly class it as *exceedingly* improper.'

'That's ridiculous! How will I know if I don't ask? And I can't ask anyone else about this – only you.'

Demon heard the uncertain note in her voice; much of his tension left him, swamped by a surge of emotion he was growing accustomed to – one Flick and only Flick could evoke. It encompassed an urge to protect, but that wasn't the sum of it.

He sighed, but didn't look at her – he wasn't yet sure how much in control he was, wasn't yet sure he could resist that puzzled, questioning look in her blue eyes. 'It's all right to ask me as long as we're alone. You can say whatever you wish to me, but you must be careful not to let anything we discuss privately influence how you behave when we're not private.'

Flick nodded. The possibility that he might forbid her to question him, especially about subjects like desire, had shaken her – for an instant she'd feared he would erect a wall between them. Thankfully not.

Yet she still didn't entirely understand.

That he seriously wanted to marry her was hard enough to accept. That he wanted to marry her because he desired her – that was beyond her comprehension. She'd assumed she'd always be a child in his eyes. Apparently not.

As the curricle rolled on, she pondered desire. The whole concept, both in general and specifically, intrigued her. She recalled very well the shimmering net he could throw, the temptation, the promise in the moonlight. Her experience beyond that was nonexistent – all she'd known previously came from overhearing maids comparing notes on their swains. But ... there was one point that, no matter how she construed it, remained unexplained.

Drawing a deep breath, her gaze, like his, fixed on the ribbon of lane stretching before them, she asked, 'If you desire me' – she felt her blush heat her cheeks, but she doggedly plowed on – 'as a man desires a woman, why do you go rigid when we touch?'

When he didn't immediately answer, she expanded, 'Like that night in the courtyard when we kissed – you stopped suddenly. Was that due to society's strictures' – she risked a glance at him – 'or something else?'

He went rigid as she looked at him; she could both sense it and see it. Sense the sudden clenching as if it was her own gut, see the muscles beneath his sleeve tense until each band was clearly delineated. As for his face, when she glanced up in surprise, she found it as hard as stone.

Amazed, she lifted a finger and poked his upper arm – it was like stubbing her finger against rock. 'Like that.' She frowned at him. 'Are you sure it's not aversion?'

'It's – *not* – aversion.' Demon didn't know how he got the words out; his hands were locked so tightly about the reins that he could only pray the bays didn't choose this particular moment to act up. 'Believe me,' he reiterated, and had to struggle to draw breath. 'It's not aversion.'

After a moment, she prompted, 'Well?'

He'd told her she could ask. If he didn't get her wed and into bed soon, she might kill him with her questions. He exhaled; his chest felt as tight as a drum. Dredging deep for strength, he took a death grip on his inner demons. His voice almost quavering with the effort of not reacting, he explained, 'That night in the moonlight, if I hadn't stopped when I did – hadn't got you back into the drawing room in short order – you would have found yourself ravished under the magnolia in the vicarage courtyard.'

'Oh?'

Fascinated consideration rang in her tone.

'I'd even worked out how to accomplish the deed. I would have laid you on the stone edging around the tree and lifted your skirts – you wouldn't have stopped me.'

He risked a glance at her; blushing lightly, she shrugged. 'We'll never know the truth of that.'

He bit back a retort; narrow-eyed, he focused his gaze on her.

She glanced up, met it, and blushed more deeply. She looked ahead. After a moment, she wriggled, shifting on the seat. 'All right. I understand about the courtyard, but why does it happen – you freezing like that – now? You even did it yesterday on the Heath when I accidentally bumped into you.' Frowning, she looked up. 'You can't want to ravish me every time we meet.'

Oh, yes, he could. Demon gritted his teeth and let the bays lengthen their stride. 'Desire is like a disease – once you've caught it, every further encounter makes it worse.'

He was exceedingly thankful when she accepted that comment with a humph. She stared ahead, then he felt another of her considering glances.

'I won't break, you know. I won't have hysterics, or—'

'Very likely.' He uttered the words as repressively as he could.

She humphed again. 'Well, I still don't understand. If you want to marry me *anyway* ...'

He couldn't miss her implication – couldn't stop himself from turning his head – and reading, blazoned in the blue of her eyes, her curiosity, and a very definite invitation ...

Swallowing a virulent curse, he swung his gaze back to the lane. Explaining might just have made things worse. He'd thus far managed to hold his demons in check – but what if she picked up the whip?

Oh no, no, no, no, no. He knew what he was, and what she was, and they were literally eons apart. It would take her years – at least an intensive six months – to even come close to comprehending the level of sexual knowledge he possessed. But he could guess what she was thinking, what route her innocent thoughts had taken. He had to head her off, quash any thoughts she had of jumping into that particular sea feet first. It simply couldn't happen like that. At least, not with him.

Unfortunately, at no point had she become wary of him, much to his disgust. She'd somehow gone from regarding him as an uncle to regarding him as an equal. Which was equally erroneous. His jaw ached, along with most of his body. As for his brain, that simply hurt. 'It's not going to happen like that.' The effort of explaining things he didn't want to risk thinking about was wearing him down.

'Oh?'

She had those *Oh*s down to a fine art – they always prodded him to explain.

'Desire leads to physical seduction *but*, in your case – in *our* case – that is not going to translate to any quick, rushed, illicit tumble in a courtyard or anywhere else.'

He waited for her *Oh*; instead, she asked, 'Why?'

189

Because he was going to train her to be his very own fallen angel. He shook aside the thought. 'Because ... ' He struggled, then blinked; if he hadn't been driving, he would have flung up his hands in defeat. Setting his jaw, he reached for the whip. 'Because you're an innocent, and you deserve better than that. And *I* know better than that.' Oh, yes – this impinged on his ego as well. 'I'll seduce you as you deserve to be seduced – *slowly*. Innocence isn't something you should discard like an old shoe. It has a physical value – a passionate value – all its own.'

His frown deepening, he kept his gaze fixed on his leader's ears. 'Innocence shouldn't be tarnished, it shouldn't be crushed. It should be made to bloom. I know.' Those last two words were as much realization as assurance. 'Getting innocence to bloom takes time, takes care and attention and expertise.' His voice deepened. 'It takes passion and desire, commitment and devotion to coax innocence from bud to bloom, to encourage it to unfurl into full flower without a single petal bruised.'

Was he still talking of her innocence, or did he mean something more – something of which he was as innocent as she?

To his relief, she said nothing but sat silently and considered. He considered, too – all that he wanted, the totality of his desire.

He was acutely conscious of her sitting beside him. He could feel his own heartbeat, thudding in his chest, pulsing in his fingertips, throbbing in his loins. For long moments, the only sounds about them were the steady clack of the bays' hooves and the repetitive rattle of the wheels.

Then she stirred.

He shot her a glance, saw her frown – saw her open her mouth—

He jerked his gaze forward. 'And for God's sake, don't you *dare* ask why.'

He felt her glare; from the corner of his eye, he saw her stick her nose in the air, shut her lips, primly fold her hands, and pointedly look over the landscape.

Jaw clenched, he whipped up his horses.

By the time they reached the gates of Hillgate End, he'd regained sufficient use of his brain to remember what he'd intended to tell Flick during the drive.

Setting the bays pacing up the shady avenue, he slanted a glance at her and wondered how much to reveal. Despite his distraction with her, he hadn't forgotten about the syndicate; he knew she hadn't, either.

The truth was, he was growing uneasy. They'd been following Bletchley for weeks and had learned nothing about the syndicate other than that it appeared exceedingly well organized. In the circumstances, he didn't feel happy about fixing all their hopes on Bletchley.

So he'd racked his brain for alternatives. He'd considered requesting help from the rest of the Bar Cynster but had yet to do so. Vane and Patience were in Kent; Gabriel and Lucifer were in London, but needed to keep their eyes on the twins. Richard was, at last report, rather busy with his witch in Scotland. And Devil would be busy with spring planting. Be that as it may, Devil was reasonably close at Somersham. If things got difficult, he'd call on Devil, but, given that all matters to do with racing fell within his particular area of expertise, there seemed little point in summoning aid just yet. He needed to sight the enemy first, before he called in the cavalry.

To which end . . .

He drew the curricle up before the steps with a flourish and stepped down. Taking Flick's hand, he helped her alight, then fell in beside her as she headed for the steps.

'I'm going to London tomorrow – there's some busi ness I need to see to.' He stopped at the base of the steps.

Already two steps up, she halted and swung to face him, a whole host of questions in her eyes.

'I'll be back the day after tomorrow, probably late.'

'But ... what about Bletchley?'

'Don't worry about him.' He trapped her blue gaze. 'Gillies, Hills and Cross will keep an eye on him.'

Flick blinked at him. 'But what if something happens?'

'I doubt it will, but Gillies will know what to do.'

Flick had far less confidence in Gillies than she had in his master. However ... she nodded. 'Very well.' She held out her hand. 'I'll wish you a safe journey, then.'

Taking her hand, he lifted a brow. 'And a speedy return?'

She raised her brows haughtily. 'I dare say I'll see you when you get back.'

He trapped her gaze. His fingers shifted about her hand – raising it, he turned it and pressed his lips fleetingly to her wrist.

Her pulse leapt; she caught her breath.

He smiled devilishly. 'Count on it.'

Releasing her hand, he swept her an elegant bow and strode back to his waiting horses.

Flick watched as he leapt up to the seat, then wheeled the bays with matchless authority and set them pacing down the drive. She watched until he disappeared from sight, swallowed up by the shadows beneath the trees.

A frown slowly forming in her eyes, she turned and climbed the steps. The door was unlatched; she went in, closing it behind her. Crossing the hall, she greeted Jacobs with an absentminded smile, then continued on through the house, out on to the terrace and so onto the lawn. The lawn she had so often in recent times strolled with Demon.

If anyone had told her even three weeks before that the thought of not seeing a gentleman for two whole days would dim her mood – would sap her anticipation for those same days – she would have laughed.

192

She wasn't laughing now.

Not that she was about to succumb to listless lassitude, she had far too much to do. Like deciding how she felt about desire.

She considered the point as she passed beneath the trees and on into the wisteria-shaded walk. Hands clasped behind her, she fell to slowly pacing up and down the gravel.

He wanted to marry her – he intended to marry her. He expected her to say yes – he clearly believed she would.

After this afternoon, and their frank conversation, she at least knew precisely where he stood. He wanted to marry her for all the socially acceptable reasons, and because he desired her.

Which left her facing one very large, formidable question. Would she accept him?

It wasn't a question she'd expected to face. Never in her wildest dreams had she imagined that he, her idol – her ideal gentleman – would want to marry her. Would look at her, a pigtailed brat reborn, and feel desire. The only reason she could state that point, and view the prospect with quite amazing equanimity, was that, deep down, she was still struggling to believe it.

It still seemed like a dream.

But . . .

She knew he was in earnest.

Reaching the end of the walk, she squinted at the clock above the stable arch. There was still an hour before luncheon; all about her was silent, no one else was in sight. Turning, she fell to pacing again, trying to organize her thoughts into a sensible sequence.

The first point she had to consider was obvious. Did she love Demon?

Somewhat to her surprise, the answer was easy.

'I've been secretly in love with him for years,' she

muttered. The admission left her with a very odd feeling in her stomach.

She was so disconcerted, so startled to find her heart had made up its mind long ago and not told her, that she reached the end of the walk before she could set the point aside, accept that it was decided, and move on.

'Next, does he love me?'

No answer came. She mentally replayed their conversations, but there was nothing he'd said that shed light on that point.

She grimaced. 'What if he doesn't love me?'

The answer to that was absolute. If he didn't love her, she couldn't marry him. Her certainty was unshakeable, deeply embedded within her.

To her mind, love and marriage went hand in hand. She knew that wasn't society's view, but it was hers, formed by her own observations. Her parents had loved deeply – it had shown in their faces, in their demeanor, whenever they'd been in the same room. She'd been seven when she'd last seen them, waving good-bye from the rail of their boat as it pulled away from the dock. While their features had blurred with the years, that glow that had always been theirs had not – it still shone strongly in her memory.

They'd left her a fortune, and they'd left her a memory – she was grateful for the fortune, but she valued the memory more. The knowledge of what love and marriage could be was a precious, timeless legacy.

One she would not turn her back on.

She wanted that glow for herself – she always had. She'd grown up with that expectation. From all she'd gleaned about the General and his wife, Margery, theirs, too, had been a union blessed.

Which brought her back to Demon.

Frowning, she paced back and forth, considering his

reasons for marrying her. His socially acceptable reasons were all very well, yet superficial and not essential. They could be dismissed, taken for granted.

Which left her with desire.

One minute was enough to summarize all she knew on that subject. Questions like Did desire encompass love? Did love encompass desire? were beyond her ability to answer. Until this past week, she hadn't even known what desire was, and while she now knew what it felt like, her experience of it remained minimal. A fact their recent discussion had emphasized.

There was clearly much she had to learn about desire – love or no love.

For the next half hour, she paced and pondered; by the time the lunch gong sounded, she'd reached one clear conclusion, which raised one simple question. She had, she thought, as she strolled back to the house, made good progress.

Her conclusion was absolute and inviolable – utterly unchangeable. She would marry with love, or not at all. She wanted to love, and be loved in return – it was that or nothing.

As for her question, it was straightforward and pertinent: Was it possible to start with desire – strong desire – and progress to love?

Lifting her face to the sun, she closed her eyes. She felt reassured, certain of what she wanted, how to face what was to come.

If Demon wanted to marry her, wanted her to say yes when he asked for her hand, then he would need to teach her more about desire, and convince her that her question could be answered in the affirmative.

Opening her eyes, she lifted her skirts; climbing the steps, she went in to lunch.

Chapter Eleven

Demon set out for London just after dawn. He kept the bays up to their bits, eager to reach the capital and the offices of Heathcote Montague, man of business to the Cynsters. After considerable thought, he'd hit upon a possible alternative means of identifying members of the syndicate.

Unbeknown to Flick, he'd visited Dillon and extracted a list of the races he'd fixed. He'd then called in favors from all around Newmarket to get the figures, including various book-makers' odds, necessary to gauge just how much money had been realized through the fixes. His rough estimations had sent his brows rising high – the amount had been startling enough to suggest Montague might be able to trace it. Even a portion of the total should have left some discernible mark somewhere in the financial capital.

It was worth a try.

The road sped beneath his wheels. Demon's thoughts drifted back – to Flick. Impatience gripped him, a restless urge to hurry.

So he could return to Newmarket.

Lips setting, he shook aside the nagging worry – what possible trouble could she get into in two days? He would remain in London for only one night. Bletchley seemed settled; Gillies had his orders. All would be well.

His gaze fixed on the road ahead, he urged the bays on.

Three hours later, neatly garbed in her velvet riding habit and perched upon Jessamy, Flick went riding on Newmarket Heath.

Naturally, she expected to see Bletchley, idly watching the last of the morning gallops as he had for the past week.

To her consternation, she didn't see him. She couldn't find Gillies, Cross or Hills, either. Sitting straight in her saddle, she scanned the gallops – the rising stretches of turf where the last strings were pounding – then turned to survey the surrounding flats. To no avail.

'Isn't that just typical!' Gathering Jessamy's reins, she wheeled the mare and rode straight into town.

Without any idea what to do, Flick walked Jessamy down the paved street. Most of those about belonged to the racing fraternity – stable lads, grooms, trainers, jockeys. Some knew her and bobbed respectfully; all looked Jessamy over with keen professional eyes. Flick barely noticed.

Where had Bletchley been staying? She couldn't remember the inn's name. Demon had said it wasn't in Newmarket, but somewhere to the north.

But what had happened to Gillies and the others? They'd watched Bletchley for this long without mishap – could he finally have identified them and ...

And what? She had no idea.

Doggedly, she headed north up the High Street, an illformed plan of inquiring at the inns to the north of town in mind. Halfway up the street, she came to the Rutland Arms, the main coaching inn. The mailcoach squatted like a huge black beetle before the inn's main door; she glanced at the passengers waiting to board.

A flash of scarlet caught her eye; abruptly she reined in. A curse from behind had her turning in her saddle. 'Oh – I'm so sorry.' Blushing, she drew Jessamy aside to let the racing string she'd impeded pass. The long file of horses with lads atop gave her useful cover; screened by them, she peered across the street.

'Yes!' Eyes lighting, Flick saw Bletchley, his red neckerchief a beacon, clamber up to the coach's roof. Then she frowned. 'Why is he going to Bury St. Edmunds?'

Raising his yard, the guard blew a warning; the next instant, the coach lurched. Overloaded with men, apparently in rowdy mood, clinging to the roof, it ponderously rolled off up the High Street.

Flick stared after it. While she had no idea *why* Bletchley was heading to Bury St. Edmunds, it seemed unlikely he'd stop anywhere en route. There simply wasn't anywhere en route.

She had to find Gillies, and find out what had happened to him and Hills and Cross. She quickly turned Jessamy south, toward the stud farm.

And spied Gillies mounted on a hack not ten yards away. With a muttered exclamation, she trotted Jessamy over.

'Did you see?' She drew rein beside him. 'Bletchley's gone off to Bury St. Edmunds.'

'Aye.' Gillies's gaze drifted up the street in the wake of the departing coach.

'Well' – Flick settled Jessamy as she danced – 'we'd better follow him.'

Gillies's gaze snapped to her face. 'Follow 'im?'

'Of course.' Flick frowned. 'Isn't that what you're supposed to be doing?'

Gillies looked uncertain.

'Where are Hills and Cross?' Flick asked impatiently.

'Hills is at the farm – he was last on watch. Cross is over there.' Gillies indicated with his chin. 'He was watching Bletchley this morning.'

Flick located the lugubrious Cross lounging in a doorway

198

across the street. 'Yes, well, now Bletchley has made a move, we'll need to organize to follow him.'

'We will?'

Flick stared at Gillies. 'What *is* the matter with you? Didn't Demon leave you with orders to follow Bletchley?'

Gillies stared back, then, mute, shook his head.

Flick stared even more; she couldn't imagine what was going on. But Gillies and Cross were out and about. 'What *are* your orders?'

Gillies's face fell; his eyes took on the look of a mournful spaniel's. 'To follow *you*, miss, and keep you out of trouble.'

Only the fact that they were in a crowded public place prevented Flick from giving Gillies her opinion of his master's arrogance. His overweening conceit. His ridiculous male ego.

By the time she, with Gillies and Cross in tow, had retreated to the now empty Heath, she'd calmed down – to simmering. 'I don't care *what* orders he gave before he left, he couldn't have foreseen Bletchley leaving. But he has, so we must improvise.'

Gillies remained blank-faced. 'The master was most particular, miss. He said we was to hold the fort here, and not let – not *make* any rash moves. Anyway, there's no need to follow Bletchley to Bury – chances are, when he wants to hie back to London, he'll come back through here on the coach.'

'That's not the *point*!' Flick declared.

'Isn't it?' Standing beside them, Cross squinted up at Flick. 'I thought that was it – that we was to watch him in Newmarket and see who he talked to here.'

'Not just *here*.' Flick drew a calming breath. 'We need to see who he talks to *wherever* he goes. He might be going to Bury to meet with his masters.'

Cross blinked. 'Nah, he'll be—'

199

Gillies coughed, succumbing to a veritable paroxysm that had both Flick and Cross looking at him in concern. Blinking, he shook his head, waving his hand back and forth in a negative gesture. 'It's all right,' he said to Flick, but his eyes, bright and sharp, were fixed on Cross.

Cross's expression blanked. 'Oh. Ah. Right – well.'

Flick frowned at him. 'We must organize to pick up the watch on Bletchley when he gets to Bury. The mail coach takes hours, so we have a little time.'

'Ah – it's not that simple, miss.' Gillies exchanged a glance with Cross. 'Both Cross here and Hills have duties on the farm – they can't simply up and leave for Bury.'

'Oh.' Flick looked at Cross; he nodded.

'Aye – wouldn't do for us to leave the youngsters unsupervised, like.'

Flick grimaced. It was spring, and the stud farm would be a hive of rather serious activity; taking two senior stablemen away at this time was impossible. Especially not from an enterprise as highly regarded as Demon's. Absentmindedly, she settled Jessamy – tail swishing, the mare was growing increasingly restless.

Glancing up, Flick saw Gillies and Cross exchange a look she couldn't interpret; they almost looked pleased. 'Well,' she stated, 'as we can't afford to let Bletchley roam about unwatched, I'll have to go to Bury myself.'

Gillies's and Cross's reactions to that were easy to read – their eyes went round and their mouths dropped open.

Gillies recovered first. 'But ... but ... you can't go alone.' His eyes looked slightly wild.

Flick frowned. 'No, but I don't want to take my maid.' She looked at Gillies. 'You'll have to come, too.'

The lugubrious Cross shook his head. 'Nah, you don't want to go to Bury just now.' He looked hopefully at Flick.

She looked steadily back. 'As Bletchley has taken himself

200

off, I expect you should get back to the stud.'

Ponderously, Cross nodded. 'Aye, I'd better, at that. I'll tell Hills we don' have no pigeon to watch any more.'

Tight-lipped, Gillies nodded.

As Cross lumbered off, Flick turned back to Gillies. A militant light in her eye, she transfixed him with a glance. 'We had better make some plans over how to watch Bletchley at Bury St. Edmunds.'

Gillies stiffened his spine. 'Miss, I really don't think – '

'Gillies.' Flick didn't raise her voice, but her tone stopped Gillies in his tracks. 'I am going to Bury to watch Bletchley. All you need to decide is whether you'll accompany me or not.'

Gillies studied her face, then heaved a sigh. 'Perhaps, we'd better have a word with Master Dillon. Seeing as it's on his account, an' all.'

Flick frowned harder; Gillies sucked in a quick breath. 'Who knows? Maybe Master Dillon has some idea of what Bletchley's doing at Bury?'

Flick blinked, then raised her brows. 'You're right. Dillon might know – or be able to guess.' She looked around. It was lunchtime; the Heath was empty. 'I'll need to go home for lunch or they'll miss me. Meet me at the start of the track to the cottage at two.'

Resigned, Gillies nodded.

Flick returned the gesture curtly, then loosened her reins, tapped her heels to Jessamy's sides, and raced home.

After polishing off a late lunch at White's, Demon retired to the reading room with a cup of coffee and a large news sheet, behind which he could hide. That last was occasioned by his encounter with the Honorable Edward Ralstrup, an old friend who had joined him for lunch.

'There's a gathering at Hillgarth's tonight. All the usual

crowd, of course.' Eyes bright, Edward had thrown him an engaging grin. 'Nothing like a few highly bred challenges to tune one up for the Season, what?'

'Challengers?' He'd immediately thought of Flick.

Edward's expression was one of blissful anticipation. 'The ladies Onslow, Carmichael, Bristow – need I go on? Not, of course, that you'll need to extend yourself – not with the countess champing at the bit.'

'The countess?' Reluctantly, he'd dragged his mind back from Newmarket and focused on the woman he'd shown to the door before he'd driven north. 'I thought she'd returned to the Continent.'

'No, no.' Edward winked. 'Seems she's conceived an affection for things English, don't you know. Colston had a touch at her – well, word was you'd gone north indefinitely – but it seems she's determined to hold out for ... well, her description was "something rather *more*." '

'Oh.' He'd been conscious of a definite longing for Newmarket.

His less-than-enthusiastic response hadn't registered with Edward. 'After Hillgarth's, if you're still standing, so to speak, there's Mrs. Melton's rout. Quite sure it'll be that, too – plenty of action there. And then tomorrow ... '

He'd let Edward rattle on, while his mind slid back to Newmarket, to the golden-haired angel who was waiting for him, and who didn't know the first thing about matters sensual, let alone 'something rather more.'

'So – what do you say? Shall I pick you up at eight?'

It had taken all his persuasive talents to convince Edward that he wasn't interested – not in the countess or the many other delights that would be offered him about town. In the end, he'd escaped only by assuring Edward that he had to hie north again at dawn and was not about to risk his horses by staying up all night. As his care for his equine beauties was a byword throughout the ton, Edward had finally accepted that he was serious.

'And,' Demon had added, struck by inspiration, 'you might oblige me by letting it be known among the brotherhood that I've relinquished all claim on the countess.'

'Ooh!' Edward had brightened at that. 'I'll do that, yes. Nice bit of sport we should see over that.'

Demon certainly hoped so. The countess was a demanding and grasping woman. While her lush body had provided a temporary distraction, one he'd paid handsomely and generously for, he had no doubt that his interest in her had been just that – temporary. Indeed, it had waned on the day he'd headed north.

Sinking into a deep armchair and arranging the news sheet like a wall before him, he settled to sip his coffee and ponder the discovery that life as he had known it – the life of a rakehell in the glittering world of the ton – no longer held any allure. Somewhat to his surprise, he could still imagine attending balls and parties – just as long as he had a certain angel by his side. He would enjoy introducing her to the ton's entertainments, just to see the expression in her wide eyes.

But the ton without Flick?

Anywhere without Flick?

He took a long sip of his coffee. This, he thought darkly, was what happened when fate caught a Cynster in her coils.

He was sitting in London, a town teeming with uncounted beauties, a surprising number of whom would be easily enough persuaded to reveal their charms to him – and he wasn't interested. Not in the beauties – not in their charms, naked or otherwise.

The only woman he was interested in was Flick.

He recalled imagining that it could never happen – that he'd never be satisfied with one woman. But it had. The only woman for him now was Flick.

203

And she was in Newmarket.

Hopefully behaving herself.

Doing the vases, reading her novels, and twiddling her thumbs.

Possibly thinking about desire.

He shifted in his seat, then frowned. No matter what setting he placed her in, his image of a patient Flick was not convincing.

Ten minutes later, he strode down the steps of White's, his goal the mews close by his lodgings where his bays were presently housed. There was no reason he couldn't leave London immediately. He'd seen Montague that morning, and spent an hour explaining the details of the race-fixing. Montague had done a few quick calculations and concurred with his assessment. The amount of money taken was enormous – it should show up somewhere.

Montague had connections Demon didn't want to know about. He'd left the hard-working agent, who thankfully thrived on financial challenges, with a gleam in his eye. If there was any way to track members of the syndicate through the money they'd taken, Montague would find it.

Which left him free to return to Newmarket, to the watch on Bletchley and his wooing of Flick.

Glancing down, he considered his attire – town rig of trousers, morning coat and shoes. There was no real reason to change. He doubted Flick would even notice, much less make anything of the fact that he hadn't stopped to change before racing back to her side.

Lips twisting wryly, he lengthened his stride and headed straight for the mews.

'Bury St. Edmunds?' Dillon frowned at Flick, then slumped into the chair at the head of the old table. 'Why there?'

Flick pulled up a stool, waving Gillies to the other, wishing he was his master instead. 'We were hoping you might have some clue. Obviously not.'

Dillon shook his head, his expression one of patent bewilderment. 'I wouldn't have thought there was any possible attraction in Bury, not for the likes of Bletchley.'

'So,' Flick stated, her tone businesslike, 'we'll need to go to Bury and find out what 'the attraction' is. Like you, I can't see any reason Bletchley would have gone there, *other* than to meet with his masters.'

Gillies, who'd been listening carefully, and even more carefully sizing up Dillon, cleared his throat. 'There's a prizefight on in Bury St. Edmunds tomorrow morning. That's almost certainly why Bletchley's hied off there. The reigning champion of all England is to take the ring against the latest challenger.'

'Really?' Dillon's lassitude fell away – he was suddenly all eager youth.

'A *prizefight*,' Flick breathed, in the tone of one for whom a light has dawned.

Frowning, Gillies looked from one to the other. 'Aye – so there'll be all manner of bucks and bloods and danger ous blades up from London – the town'll be fair crawling with them.'

'Damn!' Dillon sat back, a frown in his eyes.

Gillies heaved a sigh of relief.

'Fancy a prizefight so close and I daren't show my face.' Dillon grimaced and looked at Flick, clearly inviting her sympathy.

She wasn't looking at him. Grinning, her face alight, she slapped the table. 'That's *it*!'

Gillies jumped. 'What's it?'

'The prizefight, of course! It's the perfect venue for Bletchley to meet with his masters.' Triumph in her eyes, she spread her hands. 'It's obvious – members of the syndicate

205

can come up from London and meet with Bletchley without in any way stepping out of their normal roles, their normal pastimes, the places they would normally be found. A prizefight is perfect.'

Gillies paled. 'No – I don't—'

'You know,' Dillon cut in, 'you just might be right.'

'Of course I'm right.' Flick set her riding gloves on the table. 'Now we need to work out how to keep an eye on Bletchley at Bury, given there's only me and Gillies to keep watch.'

Both Flick and Dillon frowned; Gillies stared at them in patent dismay. 'The master won't want you going to any prizefight.' He made the statement to Flick, then looked at Dillon.

Dillon wrinkled his nose. 'It'll be tricky, but the prizefight must be the venue for Bletchley to meet his masters. Someone's got to watch him.'

Gillies dragged in a breath. 'I'll go.'

Dillon regarded Gillies, then grimaced. 'Without belittling your skills, Gillies, it's damned difficult for one person to keep a full-time watch on a target in a crowd.'

'Indeed.' Flick frowned. 'And besides, what if the meeting is held upstairs at the inn, in a private room? I can go upstairs.' She turned to Gillies. 'You can't.'

'Well,' Dillon put in, 'you won't be able to either, not if you're disguised as a stable lad.'

'I'm not going disguised as a lad.'

Dillon and Gillies stared at Flick – Dillon with interest, Gillies with trepidation. Flick smiled determinedly. 'I'm going as a widow – I have to be able to get a room to stay the night.'

'The night?' Dillon queried. Gillies simply stared.

'Most spectators from London will arrive this evening, won't they?' Flick glanced at Gillies.

'Aye.' His voice was weak.

'Well, then – if a meeting is to be held, it could be held either tonight or tomorrow – which would probably mean after the fight.' Flick frowned. 'If I was doing the organizing, I'd hold the meeting tonight. There's bound to be groups gathering to while away the evening – another group meeting in a private parlor would cause no comment. But if they meet tomorrow, after the fight, it'll seem rather odd, won't it?' She glanced at Gillies. 'I imagine most of the Londoners will leave from the field?'

Woodenly, Gillies nodded.

'Right, then.' Flick nodded curtly. 'The Angel's the major inn at Bury – it's likely everyone will gather there. So that's where I'll stay – we'll make that our headquarters. Between us, Gillies and I should be able to keep Bletchley in sight.'

'The Angel will be booked out,' Gillies protested. 'Won't be any way you'll get a room there.'

Flick's eyes narrowed. 'I'll get a room – don't worry on that score.'

'You said you'd go as a widow,' Dillon looked at her. 'Why a widow?'

Flick's determined smile deepened. 'One' – she ticked her points off on her fingers – 'men always seem to consider young widows to be in especial need of protection, which will help me get a room. Two, widows can wear concealing veils without raising brows. Three, a widow can travel alone – or at least with only her coachman.' She looked at Gillies. 'If you'd rather stay here and await your master, I can get Jonathon to drive me.' Jonathon was the Hillgate End coachman.

Very definitely, Gillies shook his head. 'I'll stick with you.' Under his breath, he grumbled, 'Those were my orders. Necks are going to be wrung enough over this without me sticking mine out.'

Lifting his head, Gillies looked at Dillon and tried one last time. 'The master's not going to like this.'

Flick didn't think Demon would approve either, but she wasn't going to point out the obvious.

Dillon, however, did. 'Pity Cynster's not here.'

'But he's not.' Flick swept up her gloves and stood. 'So it's up to us to manage.' She looked at Gillies. 'Come to the manor stable as soon as you can – I want to leave within the hour.'

In the well-sprung manor carriage, the trip from Newmarket to Bury St. Edmunds did not take long. They rolled into the town as the last traces of the day were fading from the western sky.

They joined the long queue of curricles, carriages, gigs and carts barely crawling along the main street.

Peering out the carriage window, Flick was amazed at the number of conveyances clogging the usually clear road. The clack of horses' hooves, the snap of whips and innumerable ripe curses filled the air. The pavements were awash with surging masses of men – laborers in drab, country squires in their tweeds, and gentlemen of every hue, from the nattily attired sportsman to the elegant rake, to the brash blades and bucks casting their eyes over any female unwise enough to appear in their sight.

Sitting back, Flick was glad of her thick veil. Not only would it hide her face but it would also hide her blushes. Glancing down, she wished she'd stopped to find a more 'widowish' dress – one with a high neckline and voluminous skirts, preferably in dull black. In her haste, she'd donned one of her day gowns, a scooped-necked, high waisted gown in soft voile in her favorite shade of lavender-blue. In it, she didn't look the least like a widow – she suspected she looked very young.

She would have to remember to keep her cloak fully about her at all times whenever she was out of her room. The cloak, luckily, was perfect – voluminous, heavy and dark with a deep hood. An old trunk in the attic recalled from childhood rummagings had yielded the heavy, black lace veil. Old-fashioned it might be, but it was precisely what she needed – it covered her whole head, her hair as well as her face, obscuring all identifiable features, yet it did not interfere too drastically with her vision.

She was going to need to see, and see well, to play the part she would need to play.

With the veil over her head, and her hood up, the whole secured with two pins, she was certain no one would recognize her. As long as she kept her cloak completely about her, all would be well.

Clutching her black reticule, also liberated from the old trunk, she waited impatiently for the sign of The Angel to appear. The carriage rocked, stopped, then rocked and stopped again. The sound of carriage wheels scraping came to her ears – she promptly shut them to the ensuing curses.

Fixing her gaze on the carriage's wall, she reviewed her plans. She had, she thought, managed well thus far. She'd told the General she'd taken a sudden notion to visit a friend, Melissa Blackthorn, who helpfully lived just beyond Bury St. Edmunds. Over the past ten years, she and Melissa had frequently simply visited, without formal arrangements. The General was always at home, and the Blackthorns were always in residence; there was never any danger of not finding a welcome. So she'd claimed she would visit Melissa and, as usual, stay overnight.

Both the General and Foggy had accepted her decision with a little too much readiness for her liking. The General's understanding smile, his gentle pat on her hand, had left her with the distinct – and she was sure not inaccurate – impression that he thought it was Demon's absence that had prompted her visit to Melissa. That his absence was the cause of her restlessness.

Flick wasn't at all sure how she felt about that – irritated, yes, but in a rather odd way. Frowning, she glanced out of the window and abruptly sat up. They were passing the main courtyard of The Angel, already a sea of men and boys all heading in one direction or another. The majority of visitors were still finding places to lay their heads; Flick prayed, very hard, that she'd be successful in carrying out the next phase of her plan. An instant later, the carriage lurched, then turned, and rumbled under the arch into the stable yard of The Angel.

Where pandemonium reigned.

Gillies hauled the horses to a stop, and two inn boys rushed to the carriage. One pulled open the door and let down the steps; the other ran to the boot. Flick allowed the first to take her hand and help her down; as the second, discovering the boot was empty, returned at a loss, she waved him to the carriage. 'My bag is in there.'

Her voice was steady; she'd deepened and strengthened her usual tones so that she sounded older, more commanding. It seemed to work; retrieving her one small bag, the inn boys stood respectfully as, having handed the horses over to the ostlers, Gillies came up.

Lifting her arms wide, palms up to encompass the scene, Flick turned dramatically and launched into her charade. 'Good gracious, Giles! Just *look* at this crowd! Whatever's afoot?'

Gillies simply stared at her.

One of the inn boys shifted his weight. 'It's a prizefight, m'lady. Over on Cobden's field t'morrow mornin'.'

'A *prizefight*!' Pressing a hand to her cloaked breast, Flick fell back a step. 'Oh, how distressing!' She glanced about, then looked at the inn. 'I do hope the innkeeper has a room left – I could not possibly go another mile.'

She stared – beneath her veil she glared – at Gillies.

After a moment, he said rather woodenly, 'Indeed not, ma'am.'

At least he'd remembered to address her as ma'am.

'Come, Giles – we must speak to the innkeeper immediately!' Gesturing dramatically toward the inn's main doors, she picked up her skirts and led the way. Her feminine tones, carrying a hint of imminent distress, had caused more than a few heads to turn, but, as she'd anticipated, the inn boys, responding to her dramatic flair, bustled close, eager to be part of whatever scene was to follow; together with the recently christened Giles, they cleared a path for her to the inn door.

Beyond the door lay a wide reception area fronted by a long counter presently manned by three harassed individuals – the innkeeper, his wife, and his brother. The length of the counter was packed with men – Flick could only catch glimpses of those behind it. Between her and the counter ranged a wall of male shoulders.

It had been years since she'd visited The Angel, but Flick recognized the innkeeper and made a beeline for him, giving wordless thanks when his sharp-eyed wife was called to deal with a customer at the counter's other end. The helpful inn boys, seeing that she'd be swamped, sent up a shout, waving her bag high. 'Make way for the lady.'

Flick could have kissed them.

Gentlemen's heads turned at the mention of a lady; as they took in her dark cloak and veil, those in her path politely stepped back. Between the inn boys and Gillies, she was conducted to the counter; as she fronted it, however, her escort deferentially stepped back, leaving her surrounded by gentlemen.

211

All of whom were studying her rather speculatively.

The innkeeper blinked at her; his expression one of concern, he asked, 'Aye, ma'am?'

Flick took her courage in both hands.

'Kind sir' – her voice hinted at a quaver – 'I have just arrived in your fair town only to discover this crowd before me.' Setting her big black reticule on the counter before her, she clasped her hands tight about it so the innkeeper could not miss the huge square-cut topaz she wore on one gloved finger. It was not an expensive stone, but it was impressive in size and style; the innkeeper's eyes duly widened. Casting an agitated glance about her, she declared, 'I have already travelled far this day – I cannot go further. My horses, too ...' She let the words fade, as if the situation threatened to overwhelm her.

Turning back to the innkeeper, looking into his face, she imploringly put out a hand. 'Oh, dear sir, please say you have one more room left for me?'

Her plea caused a hush.

The innkeeper pursed his lips. 'Hmm.' Brow furrowing, he drew his ledger closer and made a great show of scanning his lists of rooms, all of which Flick knew must already be taken.

Tapping his pencil, he glanced up at her. 'Just you, is it, ma'am?'

Flick drew a deep breath. 'Yes.' She made the word sound very small, very weak. 'I ...' She drew in another breath and clasped her fingers more tightly on the reticule; the facets of the topaz flashed. 'I was recently widowed – well, it's been six months, now, I suppose – I've been travelling ... for my health, you understand.'

She delivered the words in a slightly breathless rush, with what she hoped was just the right degree of feminine fragility. The innkeeper's lips formed a silent *Oh*, then he nodded and looked down.

Exceedingly glad of her veil, Flick glanced about; the innkeeper's eyes were not the only ones in which calculation gleamed.

'I say, Hodges,' one of her neighbors drawled, 'you'll have to find a room for the lady – can't possibly send her out into the night.'

A deep rumble of assent rose on all sides.

'For the honor of Bury St. Edmunds, if nothing else,' some other helpful soul put in.

The innkeeper, who was now scrubbing out and rewriting names on his lists, threw them a distracted frown. That didn't please some of his more arrogant customers. 'Aside from the town's honor, what about this house's honor?' Directing a too-smooth smile her way, one rakish buck leaned on the counter. 'Surely, Hodges, old chap,' he drawled, 'you would-n't want it known that you're the sort of innkeep who turns away helpless widows?'

Flick gritted her teeth and suppressed an impulse to deliver a swift kick to the buck's nearby shin; Hodges was now scowling.

Luckily, he was scowling at the buck. 'No need to take that tone, m'lord. I've found the lady a nice room – I hope I know my duty.'

He shut his ledger with a snap. Turning, he reached for a key hanging with a full score of others on a board behind the counter. To Flick's consternation, all the gentlemen around her leaned forward, squinting at the board to read the number of her room!

She had, she realized, just saddled herself with a large number of champions, some of whom might be entertaining notions of a reward.

But as the innkeeper turned with a key dangling in his hand, she was too relieved to worry.

'If you'll just come this way, ma'am?' He waved to the end

of the counter, to where a wide staircase led upward. Then he turned to the waiting crowd. 'You gentlemen won't mind biding your time until I get the lady settled.'

It wasn't a question. Grinning behind her veil, Flick glided to the staircase. Hodges, despite being a resident of Bury St. Edmunds, was clearly up to snuff.

Gillies returned to her side to briefly murmur, 'I'll go find Bletchley.' Then he melted into the ever-increasing crush as the innkeeper joined her.

'This way, ma'am.'

Five minutes later, with a great deal of graciousness and enough care to make her feel slightly guilty, she was installed in the very best chamber the inn possessed. Hodges admitted as much when she exclaimed over the size of the room and the superior quality of the furniture.

With a gruff suggestion that she might prefer to have her dinner on a tray to avoid the crowd downstairs – a suggestion with which she readily agreed – he left her.

Flick blew out a breath, then returned to the door and threw the bolt. Crossing to the bed, she sank down upon it; extracting her pins, she pushed back her hood and veil.

And grinned triumphantly.

She'd done it! On the eve of a prizefight, she'd secured a room at the most prominent inn.

Now all she needed to do was find Bletchley – and follow him into his masters' presence.

Leaving Newmarket, Demon headed south, past the race-course and his stable and on across the empty Heath. As he tickled his leader's ear, then sent the whip hissing back up its handle, the last glow in the west died. Night came slowly, approaching on silent wings, borne on the shadows that reached over the Heath to enfold the country in darkness. Before him lay his stud farm, with its comfortable parlor and one of Mrs. Shephard's excellent country dinners.

Between him and supreme comfort lay Hillgate End.

It was awfully late to pay a social call, but even before he'd formulated an excuse, he checked the bays and turned them up the manor's drive. Flick would be glad he was back early – she could tell him if anything had transpired in his absence. So could Gillies, of course, but he'd rather hear it from Flick. He'd only stay for a minute, just to assure himself all was well.

He brought the curricle to a scrunching halt in the gravel before the steps. A groom or stable lad – he couldn't see in the gloom – came loping across from the stable.

'I'll only be a few minutes,' he called as he strode up the steps. Just long enough to see Flick's smile – to see her anticipation of tomorrow come alive.

Jacobs opened the door to his knock.

'Good evening, Jacobs.' Crossing the threshold, he drew off his gloves. 'Is Miss Parteger about?'

'I'm afraid not, sir.' Jacobs closed the door and turned. 'She left this afternoon to visit with a friend. I believe she's expected back tomorrow.'

Demon managed to keep the frown from his face – he knew it showed in his eyes. 'A friend.'

'Miss Blackthorn, sir. She and Miss Parteger have been in the way of exchanging visits over the past years.'

'I . . . see.' The proposition that, with Bletchley on the Heath, Flick had abdicated her responsibilities – what she saw as her responsibilities – and had happily gone off to visit a friend, just like any other young lady, was simply too much to swallow. But Jacobs's easy expression declared that he knew no more; with a curt nod, Demon stepped to the door. 'Tell her I called when she returns.'

Jacobs hauled open the door. 'And the General?'

Demon hesitated. 'Don't bother him – I'll call and see him tomorrow.'

215

He went swiftly down the steps and strode to his curricle, every instinct he possessed flickering, every nerve jangling. Accepting the reins with a distracted nod, he stepped up to the box seat and sat. Raising his hands to give the bays the office, he glanced at the groom.

And froze.

He frowned. 'You're the coachman here, aren't you?'

The man bobbed his head. 'Aye, sir.' He jerked his head toward the stable. 'The lads have gone home, so there's just me and old Henderson.'

'But ... if you're here, who's driving Miss Parteger?'

The man blinked. 'Why, your man, sir. Gillies.'

Light dawned – Demon didn't like what he saw. Jaw setting, he nodded to the coachman. 'I see. Thank you.'

He sprang the bays; when he reached the road, he set them flying.

Demon found no joy – no news – waiting for him at the farmhouse. Which, he reasoned, meant Gillies imagined they'd be back before the following evening. That didn't tell him where they were now – where they were spending this evening – and, more importantly, what they thought they were doing.

More specifically, what Flick thought she was doing – he doubted Gillies was behind this escapade. He had, however, given his henchman strict instructions not to let Flick out of his sight; it appeared Gillies was following those instructions to the letter.

Which was some small comfort.

After checking with the Shephards, who knew nothing, he paused only to consign the bays into the hands of his head stableman before swinging up to Ivan's back and riding out into the night. Both Hills and Cross lived in cottages north of the Heath – if he had to, he'd track them down, but first he'd check with Dillon.

If something had happened in his absence, it was possible that Flick had sought counsel with Dillon. Whatever had happened might even involve Dillon – *he* might be the reason Flick had needed a carriage. A host of possible scenarios, none of which he liked, fought for prominence in his mind. He pressed Ivan as fast as he dared over the rough trail to the cottage.

He glimpsed a faint light as he entered the clearing; it disappeared by the time he dismounted.

'It's me – Demon.'

The glow returned, guiding him through the derelict lean-to and into the cottage proper. Dillon was standing by the table, his hands on the lamp; he looked up, his expression open and eager.

Demon met his eyes. 'Where's Flick?'

Dillon grinned. 'She's off gallivanting after Bletchley.' Dropping into his chair, he waved to a stool. 'She's convinced, this time, that Bletchley's going to meet with the syndicate.'

Icy fingers clutched Demon's spine. Ignoring the stool, he halted by the table; blank-faced, he looked down at Dillon. 'And what do you think?'

Dillon opened his eyes wide. 'This time, she might be right.' He glanced up as Demon's gloves hit the table; his engaging grin flashed. 'A pity you weren't here, but Flick'll be there to see—'

A sound like a growl issued from Demon's throat. He grabbed Dillon by his shirtfront, plucked him out of the chair, shook him like a rat, then took one step and slammed him back against the cottage wall.

The chair crashed, the sound echoing in the stillness. The wall shook.

Wide-eyed, unable to breathe, Dillon stared.

Into Demon's slitted eyes.

Dillon was only a few inches shorter, but he was a great deal slighter. There was nine years between them, and it was measured in muscle. Demon knew he could crush Dillon's windpipe with one forearm – from the look in Dillon's eyes, Dillon knew that, too.

'Where is she?' His words were low, slow and very distinct. 'Where is this supposed meeting to take place?'

'Bury,' Dillon gasped. His chest heaved. 'Bletchley went there – she followed. She was going to try to get a room at The Angel.'

'Try to?' The Angel was a very large house.

Dillon licked his lips. 'Prizefight.'

Demon couldn't believe his ears. '*Prize Fight*?'

Dillon tried to nod but couldn't. 'Flick thought it was the obvious – the most *likely* place for the syndicate to meet with Bletchley. Heaps of bucks and blades up from London – all the riffraff and the Fancy, too. Well, you know—' He ran out of breath and wheezed, 'It seemed like sound reasoning.'

'What did Gillies say?'

Dillon glanced at Demon's eyes and paled even more. He dropped his gaze.

When he didn't answer, Demon tensed the muscles in his arms.

Dillon caught his breath in a rush. 'He didn't want her to go – he said you wouldn't like it.'

'And you? What did you say?'

Dillon tried to shrug. 'Well, it seemed like a sensible idea—'

'You call letting a gently reared, twenty-year-old girl go waltzing out to spend the night in an inn filled to the rafters with a prizefight crowd *sensible*?'

A look of petulance passed over Dillon's face. 'Well, *someone* had to go. We needed to learn—'

'*You miserable coward!*'

He didn't crush Dillon's windpipe – he hauled him up, shook him once, then slammed him back against the wall. Hard.

Then he released him.

Dillon collapsed in a coughing heap on the floor. Demon looked down at him, sprawled beside his boots. Disgusted and furious in equal measure, he shook his head. 'When the devil are you going to grow up and stop hiding behind Flick's skirts?' Turning, he swiped up his gloves. 'If I had the time, I'd give you the thrashing you deserve—' He glanced back; when Dillon groggily lifted his head, Demon caught his eye. His lip curled. 'Consider it yet another piece of retribution from which Flick has saved you.'

He stormed out into the night. Vaulting onto Ivan's back, he set course for The Angel.

Chapter Twelve

She'd never seen so many men crammed into one space in her life.

Flick stood at her room window and looked down on the sea of male humanity filling the courtyard of The Angel. She'd been right in guessing that the prizefight crowd would congregate at The Angel; the throng seethed as men entered from the street while others drifted into the bars, returning with jugs and glasses. The courtyard of The Angel was the place to be.

Pitch flares had been placed around the courtyard, their flickering light strong enough for her, up in her chamber at the front of the house, to see faces below clearly. She'd snuffed her candles before parting the curtains. Luckily, the windows were hung with lace as well as the heavier drapes; she could stand close to the glass and peer down without risking anyone seeing her.

The noise was amazing. A multilayered rumble, it rose like a cacophany of deep-toned bells struck and rung without order. The occasional gust of laughter erupted, now from one group, then another. From her vantage point, she viewed the scene like some godlike puppeteer.

She'd been watching for close to an hour. The inn's bars were doing a roaring trade; she was grateful the staff had found time to bring up her dinner on a tray. She'd eaten quickly, then the serving girl had returned and taken away the tray. Since then, she'd been watching Bletchley.

He was halfway down the courtyard out in full view, a heavy figure in an old frieze coat, his scarlet neckerchief a useful feature to distinguish him from the many other older men in unfashionable attire. The fashionable and unfashionable mingled freely, their shared interest transcending social bounds. Bletchley stood, feet wide, his bulk balanced, quaffing ale and nodding as those in his circle expounded their theories.

Gillies was watching him, too. Bletchley had gone into the inn twice – Gillies had followed, sliding away from the group he was part of to slip inside. Each time he'd returned to resume his position as Bletchley did the same, a fresh pint in his hand.

Flick shifted her weight, then folded her arms. She was tired of standing, but if she sat, she wouldn't be able to see into the courtyard. The discussions below were gaining in intensity; in a number of groups, she saw money being waved about. There were gentlemen aplenty, well dressed, with the long aristocratic features that screamed wealth and affluence. Flick studied various hard faces, and wondered if they were members of the syndicate. Perhaps it was a group of blades, the most dangerously irresponsible of the younger gentlemen. She'd heard tales of incredible wagers; such men might well need cash, and they didn't appear to possess overmany scruples. But who? Who?

Her gaze passed over the crowd, then returned to Bletchley to see him squinting at an old watch. Tucking it back into his pocket, he drained his pint, collared a harassed serving boy and handed it to him, then, with a nod, excused himself to his cronies and headed away through the crowd.

Flick straightened. Bletchley wasn't heading inside.

Lumbering through the throng, tacking around groups, he

made his way toward the far end of the courtyard. Flick lifted her gaze past the masses and looked out beyond the flares at the dark expanse of Angel Hill.

She knew that the long, sloping hill led up to the abbey, although she couldn't see it. The light from the flares ended abruptly just beyond the courtyard; Angel Hill was cloaked in the deep dark of a country night.

'Damn!' Flick relocated Bletchley, still struggling through the crowd. She searched for Gillies and found him; he'd seen Bletchley move, and was on his trail.

Flick sighed with relief – then froze. Someone had grabbed Gillies. He struggled to free himself, only to have more men range about him, smiling and laughing. She caught sight of Gillies's face – he was smiling and laughing, too. He also looked desperate.

One man slung his arm about Gillies's shoulders; another grasped his coat in friendly fashion and started talking nonstop. Flick saw Gillies cast a quick look around – saw him try to turn, but his friends wouldn't let him.

'Oh, *no*!' Aghast, Flick glanced to where Bletchley was nearing the far end of the courtyard, bounded by a few scraggly bushes, then she looked at Gillies, trapped and helpless in the middle of the crowd.

From where Gillies was, he couldn't see Bletchley's direction. He also didn't know where she was – that she could, if he looked her way, direct him. Gillies had lost Bletchley, and there was no way she could set him right – she could hardly fling up the window and shout down.

Lifting her gaze, Flick saw Bletchley reach the courtyard's far boundary. He didn't halt; he didn't look around. Pushing through the low bushes, he stepped out purposefully, into the dark. Heading straight up Angel Hill.

To meet with his masters – she just *knew* it!

Smothering a scream, she whirled and grabbed her cloak.

Her veil went flying, disappearing over the edge of the bed; the pins clattered on the floor.

She didn't have time to stop. Dragging the cloak about her, she hauled the deep hood over and down so her face was heavily shadowed. Fingers flicking frantically, she cinched the cloak's laces at her throat, checked to make sure that the cloak was fully about her, then threw the bolt on the door and slipped out, pausing only to lock the door behind her.

Hurrying down the dimly lit corridor, she dredged her memory for all knowledge of the inn. She was on the first floor; the long corridor that crossed hers ended in a side stair leading down to a door just around the corner from the courtyard. Reaching the intersection, she turned and hurried on. Most of the inn's patrons were downstairs; there was no one about. All but running down the narrow carpet, Flick prayed her luck would hold.

She reached the narrow side stair; clinging to the shadows, she descended. The small hall before the side door was empty. She stepped out to cross it –

A door in the wall to her left crashed open. Two maids hurried through, carrying trays of used pots and jugs. They glanced at Flick, plastered back against the wall, but they didn't stop – they rushed on, down the corridor.

Flick dragged in a breath, steadied her pounding heart, and determinedly stepped to the door. It opened easily.

It gave onto a narrow cobbled area around the corner from the courtyard. From her left, noise rolled out and away, into the dark; the flickering flares made little impact on the night beyond.

Closing the door behind her, Flick faced Angel Hill.

Unfortunately, the cobbled area was used to house crates and barrels; it had been extended away from the inn, encroaching on the flank of the hill, where it ended in a high retaining wall. The only way she could gain the hillside and follow Bletchley was to skirt around to her left, cutting through the area dimly lit by the flares.

And risking someone – some man in the courtyard – seeing her.

Flick hesitated. Her back to the wall, safe in her dark cloak in the shadows, she thought of Demon, and Dillon, and the unknown syndicate.

Then she thought of the General.

Drawing a deep breath, she straightened and stepped away from the wall.

She didn't look back – didn't risk the light gleaming on her face or hands. She walked quickly and silently across, skirting the low bushes edging the courtyard and onto the lowest slope of Angel Hill.

Without pause, she walked on, even after the light of the flares had died behind her. Only when the night had swallowed her up and the noise of the courtyard was fading did she stop, draw a deep, reviving breath, and exhale with relief. Then, lifting her skirts, sending fervent thanks to her guardian angel, she hurried on. In Bletchley's wake.

After arranging stabling for Ivan with The Angel's harassed grooms, Demon strolled under the arch separating the courtyard from the stable yard. He stopped and scanned the scene just as Flick appeared briefly in the weak light of the flares on the rising ground on the far side of the courtyard. If he hadn't been looking for her, if she hadn't taken complete possession of his mind, he would have seen nothing more than the outline of a swinging cloak, a shadow against the deeper shadows of the night.

As matters stood, that was enough – he knew it was Flick.

He didn't know where she was going, but that wasn't hard to guess. Swallowing his curses – saving them for later – he stepped into the crowd.

And immediately, inwardly, cursed some more.

He couldn't race after her.

He had more than a few friends there – he'd known of the fight, and would probably have attended if he hadn't been so busy with Flick and her syndicate. His friends, of course, thought he'd come to join them.

'Demon!'

'You took your time. Where're you staying?'

'So – who've you got your money on?'

Adopting an expression of fashionable boredom on his face, Demon answered at random.

If his friends saw him striding into the night, they might follow out of idle curiosity. There was, however, an even greater danger. Many of the young bloods, bucks and blades considered him a man to emulate. If they saw him racing off up Angel Hill, they might send up a hue and cry, and then Flick would find herself enacting the role of fox pursued by a pack of slavering hounds.

Wonderful. This time, Demon vowed, he *would* strangle her.

After he rescued her from whatever danger she was so determinedly marching into.

Mentally gritting his teeth, he smiled and joked; gradually, he made his way to the far side of the courtyard. Only by telling one friend that he was going to join another did he manage to progress at all.

He caught sight of Gillies in the throng; it was instantly apparent his henchman had problems of his own. Demon considered, but detaching Gillies from his mates without attracting attention would prove difficult, and he didn't have the time. Flick had long since disappeared.

Finally reaching the bushes bordering the cobbles, Demon paused to scan the throng. He shifted his weight, first this way, then that, then frowned, turned, surveyed the bushes,

225

then stepped through them. Hopefully, anyone who'd seen him would imagine he was merely caught short and looking to relieve himself.

He walked, definitely but with no panic, out of the circle of the flares.

Then he strode out.

He stopped once the dark had closed around him. He looked back, but could detect no sign of pursuit or interest. Satisfied, he turned back to Angel Hill and the slumbering abbey on the ridge. Somewhere ahead of him Flick was climbing, and, he assumed, ahead of her was Bletchley.

And ahead of Bletchley ...

Lips thinning, Demon set his jaw and climbed faster.

Higher up the slope, Flick had run out of curses. Which was just as well, because she needed to save her breath. She'd climbed Angel Hill numerous times through her childhood, but she'd never climbed it in the dark. What was in full light an easily conquered slope, at night took on the guise of an obstacle course. The overall slope was even, but the terrain was not – there were dips and ridges, foot-sized holes and sudden ledges, all of which seemed to appear beneath her stumbling feet at the moment she least expected them.

And, to top it all, there was the mist.

Before leaving the inn she'd noticed the night was dark – only when she'd left the comforting flares far behind did she realize that it was, in fact, pitch black. Heavy clouds blanketed the moon; there was not even starlight to light her way. Her only landmark was the abbey and the cathedral tower, denser silhouettes on the crown of the hill, outlined against the ink black sky.

Unfortunately, as she left the town and The Angel behind, she ran into more ribbons of mist wreathing the shoulders of the hill. The higher she went, the thicker the mist became, causing her to lose sight of her landmark. Luckily, the cloud cover was not absolute – the moon occasionally shone through, giving her a chance to get her bearings.

During one such fitful illumination, she saw Bletchley laboring up the slope at least two hundred yards ahead of her. Flick thanked her stars she hadn't lost him. She battled on, slogged on, slowing when the moon again disappeared. Another wide band of mist slowed her even more.

Again the moon sailed free; Flick frantically searched the slope ahead, breathing again only when she sighted Bletchley's lumbering form.

He was much higher now, approaching the abbey. Luckily, the mists thinned toward the crest; she could see him clearly. It rapidly became apparent his goal was not the abbey but a thick stand of bushes surounding three trees a little way below and to the west of the abbey wall.

Flick's urgency eased. Bletchley's meeting with his masters would take more than a few moments. There was no need to scramble and risk alerting them to her presence. Far better to take her time and approach silently.

The clouds cooperated enough for her to see Bletchley round the stand of bushes and disappear from sight. In the time before the clouds caught the moon again, she didn't see him reemerge. In the same interval, she scanned the slope all about the bushes, but saw no one else.

Telling herself that Bletchley would definitely be on the other side of the bushes, she forced herself to climb with care, then slipped silently into the bushes' shadow.

Ears straining, she listened. She heard a gruff word, then nothing more. The moon broke free of the clouds and shone down, lighting up the area. Flick took that as a sign. Metaphorically girding her loins – she'd come too far to retreat – she edged to where she would be able to see around the bushes, exercising supreme care to avoid stepping on twigs, or leaves, or doing anything to warn Bletchley and whoever he was meeting of her presence.

She was successful – Bletchley and his companion remained totally unaware of her.

Then again, they would probably have remained oblivious of anything short of a charge of Hussars.

They were decidedly engrossed.

From the corner of the stand of bushes, Flick looked down on the meeting in progress, first in stunned surprise, then with increasing distaste.

The female Bletchley had come to meet lay flat on her back, her skirts rucked up to her waist, exposing chubby, dimpled white thighs, currently clasped about Bletchley's equally chubby, equally dimpled bare buttocks. Said buttocks were rising and falling in a staccato rhythm, quivering and tensing and shaking like jelly as Bletchley strained up and down, plunging himself into the woman's body.

Despite her carnal innocence, Flick knew what they were about. She knew how animals mated, but she'd never seen humans perform the same act. For one long instant, the sight transfixed her – in horrified fascination.

The sounds that reached her were not words about racing, or horses – certainly not the names she wanted to know. Grunts, gasps, pants and moans were the extent of the conversation.

Disgusted yet inhibited from even muttering an oath, she curled her lip, gritted her teeth on her temper, and swung away. Eyes on the ground, she strode back for the inn, heading downhill, directly away from the bushes.

After all her work – all the risks she'd taken! She had half a mind to scream with vexation and hope the sound gave Bletchley a turn. At precisely the wrong moment.

Men!

She strode into the first swath of mist – and ran right into one.

Her nose stubbed against his chest, burying itself in a soft cravat. She sucked in a breath to scream – and recognized his scent. His arms had locked, iron shackles about her, but as her instinctive rigidity eased, he relaxed his hold. She looked up at him.

He glared down at her. 'Where—'

'*Shssh*!' Wriggling free, she tossed her head, indicating the bushes behind her. 'Bletchley's back there.'

Demon studied her face. 'He is?'

Without meeting his eyes, Flick nodded, stepped about him and continued toward the inn. 'He's with a woman.'

Demon looked toward the bushes, then back at Flick, who was stalking down the slope. 'Ah.' His lips twitched, but only momentarily. The next instant, he caught up with her. 'Actually,' he drawled, steel rippling beneath his words, 'I didn't come here to discover what Bletchley was about.'

She didn't immediately reply, but just strode on. 'I followed him here. You were in London. You weren't coming back until tomorrow.'

'I changed my mind – a lucky circumstance. If I'd returned tomorrow, God only knows what trouble you might by then have succeeded in bringing down on your head.' His clipped accents and the underlying force behind his words held a dire, not-at-all-subtle warning.

Unrepentant, Flick sniffed and gestured back at the bushes. 'Obviously, as Bletchley isn't here to meet with the syndicate, I won't be getting into any difficulty.'

'It's not Bletchley you need worry about.' Demon's voice lowered to a dangerous purr. '*He* was never destined to be the source of your trouble.'

A very odd shiver slid down Flick's spine. Demon's fingers closed about her elbow. She considered twisting free, only to feel his fingers tighten into steel shackles. Deciding her wisest course was to ignore him and his hold on her, she haughtily elevated her chin – and allowed him to escort her down the hill.

They covered the distance in silence, a silence that grew increasingly tense as they neared the courtyard. The tone of the gathering had degenerated to raucous, rough and ribald; many of the crowd were weaving on their feet. It was no place for a gently reared lady.

Demon halted beyond the area lit by the flares. 'How did you get out?'

'The side door.' Flick pointed.

He tugged her hood down to her chin. 'Keep your head down.' His arm slid around her waist, and he whisked her across the danger zone, into the shadows by the door.

She barely had time to look up before he bundled her through the door and up the stairs. He followed on her heels. On the first-floor landing, he hissed, 'Where's your room?'

Flick gestured along the corridor. 'Above the main door.'

She led the way, but his arm snaked about her waist and yanked her back, anchoring her to his side.

Flick decided not to argue. Or wriggle. The glimpse she'd had of his face as they'd gone through the door had done very strange things to her nerves. His face was always hard, but it presently appeared fashioned from rock. Uncompromising was the term that leapt to mind.

Sounds of revelry gusted up the stairwell. The corridor leading to the front rooms began just before the stairhead.

Then Demon tensed. Flick looked ahead and saw four gentlemen come staggering unsteadily up the stairs. They were well away, rowdy and boisterous; instinctively, she shrank against Demon. He slowed, stopped, then started to turn toward her, shielding her –

Clapping each other on the back and guffawing, the four lurched off down the corridor in the opposite direction. Without, apparently, seeing them.

More voices drifted up the stairs.

With a barely muffled curse, Demon tightened his arm about her and hurried her on, forcing her to half run.

Flick pressed her lips tightly shut and held back her protest. She knew that if she even murmured, he'd throw her over his shoulder and stride on.

Then her door loomed before them. With a silent sigh of relief, she fumbled in her pocket and drew out the key.

Demon filched it from her fingers; he had it in the lock, turned, and the door swinging wide before she could blink.

Brusquely, he shepherded her over the threshold.

Shutting her mouth, Flick narrowed her eyes, elevated her chin, and swept on into the room. She walked straight to the fireplace, then regally swung about. Clasping her hands before her, spine stiff, head erect, she fixed her selfstyled protector with a challenging glare.

He'd followed her in and closed the door, but he'd paused with his hand on the latch. His blue gaze raked her – from her head to her toes – then returned, sharp and penetrating, to her face.

She showed no hint of maidenly distress – Demon verified that fact with some relief. Whatever she'd seen of Bletchley's endeavors behind the bushes, she wasn't seriously upset. Indeed, her attention appeared to be fixed on him – which was undoubtedly wise. *He* was presently a far greater threat to her serenity than Bletchley would ever be. He captured her gaze. 'Stay here – I'll go and check that Bletchley doesn't go from the arms of his companion to some other meeting.' Even to his own ears, his tone sounded lethally flat. 'And,' he added, 'I'll need to speak with Gillies.'

A hint of color rose to her cheeks, and her chin rose another notch. Her eyes flashed with what could only be defiance. 'The notion to come here was mine – Gillies was good enough to come with me.'

'I know it was your idea.' Demon heard his words and wondered at their evenness; inside him, ungoverned fury raged. 'Gillies would never be such a sapskull as to even suggest bringing you here – into the middle of a *prizefight* crowd.' His anger broke through; ruthlessly, he reined it in. 'Gillies has only obeyed my orders to stay with you at all times. I'm not about to upbraid him.' He held her gaze and quietly stated, 'It's not Gillies I'm furious with.'

He held her wide eyes for an instant longer, then turned to the door. 'I'll be back shortly.'

Opening the door, he stepped out, shut it – and locked it.

Flick heard the bolt click home. Lips parting, arms falling to her sides, she stared at the closed door.

Her temper soared.

Just like that! Put into her room and locked in, while he—!

Clenching her fists, she closed her eyes and gave vent to a frustrated scream.

Demon returned to the dim first-floor corridor at the front of the inn two hours later.

To find two young sprigs, decidedly the worse for the inn's ale, serenading outside Flick's door. His footfalls muffled by the corridor runner, he was upon them before they realized, materializing menacingly beside them.

They jumped like scalded cats.

'*Ooh!*'

'*Aaah!*'

Then they blinked and grinned inanely.

'There's a delightful widow behind the door.'

'We're attempting to entice her to come out and play, don't y'know.'

The first blinked again and stared myopically up at him. 'Have you come to join us?'

With satisfying abruptness, Demon disabused them of that

notion. He sent them fleeing, stumbling on their way, their egos shredded, their ears burning, their rears bruised courtesy of his rather large shoes. He saw them back to the stairs before returning to Flick's door. In the dimness, it took a few tries to get the key in the lock – eventually, he managed it. Straightening, he turned the key, lifted the latch and stepped inside.

Only lightning-quick reflexes allowed him to catch and hold back the heavy earthenware jug that came swinging down from his left.

Stretched on her toes, her hands clamped about the jug, Flick met his gaze. Darkly.

'Oh. It's you.'

Leaving the jug in his hands, she swung away and stalked back across the room. She stopped before the fireplace, before the cheery flames, and swung to face him as she folded her arms.

Demon took in her belligerent stance and mutinous expression, then shut the door. She held her fire while he locked it and set the jug down on a nearby side table.

Then she let loose.

'You locked me in here and left me at the mercy of *those*! . . .' she gestured eloquently. Her eyes flashed. 'I've had to endure *two hours* of nonstop caterwauling – no, no – I mustn't forget the *poems*. How *could* I forget the poems?' She flung her arms to the skies. 'They were hideous! They didn't even rhyme.'

She was unrestrainedly furious. Demon considered the sight.

'Anyway.' Abruptly deserting fury, she fixed him with a narrow gaze. 'Where did Bletchley go?'

Despite her ordeal with badly phrased poems, she was obviously all right.

'The tap, then to his room.' Dropping his gloves on the side table, he pointed upward. 'In the attics.' Shrugging out of his greatcoat, he dropped it on a chair, noting as he did the

233

large number of lighted candles set about the room. Flick had obviously felt in need of light – and reassurance.

She refolded her arms and frowned at him. 'He didn't speak to anyone?'

Glancing around, Demon noted that the chamber was large and commodious, and well-appointed with decent furniture. The bed was long and wide, and made up with pristine linen. 'No one of the ilk we're looking for. He didn't speak to anyone beyond the usual taproom chat.'

'Hmm.' Frowning, Flick watched him as he strolled unhurriedly toward her. 'Maybe he did just come here for the prizefight.'

'So it appears.' His gaze returning to her face, he stopped directly in front of her, trapping her before the hearth. She frowned at him – more with her eyes than her expression. He considered her.

After a moment, she asked, 'What are you thinking?'

How much I'd like to undress you, lay you on the bed and . . . 'I was wondering,' he said, 'what it will take to instill into your stubborn head that it is not acceptable for you to go hying off about the countryside chasing villains. *Regardless* of where I, or anyone else, might or might not be.'

She humphed and tilted her chin at him. Lifting one hand, Demon closed his fingers firmly about her tapering jaw.

Her eyes widened, then spat sparks. 'There's nothing you can say or do that will convince me I don't have as much right as you to go hying after villains.'

He raised one brow; his gaze fell to her lips. 'Is that so?'

'Yes!'

His lips curved – not with humor but with satisfaction at her challenge – a challenge he was only too willing to meet. Tipping her chin up a fraction more, he lowered his head. 'Perhaps we should put that to the test.'

He murmured the words against her lips, hesitated for a

heartbeat to let his warm breath bring her lips alive – then covered them with his.

She held tight for an instant, then surrendered. Her stiffness eased; her lips softened under his. Although still new to this – to kissing, to giving her lips, her mouth, to him – she was eager; her responses flowed instinctively. She had none of the guile of a more experienced woman – she had a fresh enthusiasm, an innocent ardency that delighted him, enthralled him.

He knew precisely what he was doing – distracting her from villains, from Bletchley and the syndicate, by giving her something else to think about. Something more exciting, more intriguing. He would bring her to life, and pique her curiosity so that she spent her time thinking about him, and this, rather than any villain. Sliding one arm about her waist, he drew her against him.

And deliberately deepened the kiss.

She responded sweetly, tipping her head back, parting her lips, welcoming him in. When his arm tightened in response, locking her to him, she eased against him readily, pert breasts pressing tight to his chest, hips sinking against his thighs. He caught his mental breath, locked an iron fist about his demons' reins, and parted her lips further, so he could artfully, skillfully ravish her soft mouth and take what she offered so freely.

The heady taste of her – so light and fresh, so teasingly alluring – went straight to his head, wreathed his senses, and set his demons straining. Wielding expertise like a whip, he held them back and set himself to enjoy the simple pleasure of her even more.

It wasn't anger that drove him, not even the wish to exercise his will over her and insist she stay out of danger. The compulsion steadily rising in his blood was simple desire – nothing more.

During the hours he'd spent watching Bletchley, speaking with Gillies, his anger had dissipated; his inchoate rage over the risks she'd taken had faded. His knowledge was wide, his imagination consequently well-informed; the visions that, even now, formed too readily were guaranteed to set his teeth on edge. But he'd had time to appreciate her thinking, to realize that, from her point of view, innocent of prizefights, coming here had been not only the obvious step but one she'd felt compelled to take.

He could understand. He still didn't approve, but that was another matter, a different aspect of the day's emotions. His anger had died, but the underlying tension hadn't. The anger had been only a symptom of that deeper emotion – one that felt uncomfortably like fear.

Fear was an emotion no Cynster male handled well. He'd had little experience of it – and he definitely didn't like what he was experiencing now. That his fear was centered on Flick was obvious; why it should be so was another of those some-things he preferred not to examine.

If he'd known that deciding to bite the bullet and marry would bring all this down on his head, he would have thought twice. Three times. Unfortunately, it was now too late – the notion of giving up Flick, of retreating from marrying her, was unthinkable.

How unthinkable was borne in on him as he briefly released her lips to drag in a breath. Her scent came with it – apple-blossom and lavender – a fragrance so innocent it touched his soul, so simple it drove through his defenses, caught and effortlessly focused his desire.

To live without this – without her, without the intense satisfaction experience told him could be his with her – *that* was the definition of unthinkable.

Releasing her jaw, he slid his fingers into her curls and held back a shudder at the sensation of pure silk sliding over

236

the back of his hand. His lips firmed on hers; he angled his head, fingers sliding until he cradled her head, holding her steady so he could do as he wished – and take their kiss still deeper. Into realms she'd never experienced, along paths she'd never trod.

He, however, was *supposed* to be in control.

Shocked, he sensed the reins sliding from his grasp, felt his hunger well. Stunned, he pulled back – forced himself to break the all-too-evocative melding of their lips.

Long enough to drag in a much-needed breath. He couldn't remember when last *his* head had spun. 'Umm . . .' He blinked. 'We'll stay until two o'clock. Then we'll leave. I'll take you home.'

He'd worked it all out while watching Bletchley.

Lifting her lids only high enough to locate his lips, Flick nodded, reached up, framed his face, and drew his head back to hers. She knew perfectly well why he was kissing her – he wanted to control her, to render her all weak and limp and acquiescent. She might, indeed, go weak and limp – she might even be a bit distracted – but acquiescent? Just because her body and her wits lost all resolution the instant he had her against him, the second his lips found hers, did not mean her will went the same way.

Which meant that as far as she was concerned, he could kiss her as long as he liked. If he'd decided they had until two o'clock the next morning, she saw no reason to waste any precious minutes.

Being kissed by him was exceedingly nice, exceptionally pleasant. The touch of his lips was enticing, the much bolder caress of his tongue brazenly exciting. It made her feel wild, a touch reckless – oddly restless. That last was due to what lay beyond – all the rest she did not know. His experience was there, in his lips, in the arms that held her so easily, tantalizing, beckoning – simply intriguing.

She offered her lips and he took them again, and her mouth as well. And yet he held back. There was a restraint he placed on his actions, on his hunger, or rather, on letting her see it. She sensed it nevertheless, in his ruthlessly locked muscles, in the tension that held him. But that restraint stood firm, a barrier between her and his greater knowledge. A barrier she could not resist prodding. She was, after all, hardly a chit out of the schoolroom, no matter what he might think.

Brazenly, she leaned into him and wantonly kissed him back – trying this, then that, to see what might best weaken him. Closing her lips about his tongue and sucking was her first success – his attention abruptly focused; his resistance weakened accordingly. Sliding her hands around his neck, locking her fingers at his nape and stretching, sliding, upward against him, worked, too, but—

Abruptly he lifted his head and dragged in a huge breath. He blinked down at her. 'Did the innkeeper see your face?' His voice was not entirely steady; he looked a little dazed.

'No.' She sank deeper into his arms, sliding her fingertips into his hair. 'I was hidden behind my veil the whole time.'

'Hmm.' He lowered his head and brushed his lips over hers. 'I'll go down and pay your shot later. When all's quiet, and there's no one about to hear. There'll be someone at the desk all night tonight. Then we'll leave.'

She didn't bother nodding. Her hands fell to his shoulders as he recaptured her lips, and she met his tongue with hers. She could, she decided, happily spend all night kissing him. Pressing herself to him. The thought prompted the deed, but she couldn't get any closer – she was already locked tight, breast to chest, hips to thighs. But . . .

He hesitated, then his lips shifted on hers. The whirlpool of their kiss dragged her deeper, into a vortex of heady sensations – all beckoning, enticing.

The need to get closer welled, swelled—

His resistance irked. If she wanted to marry him – if he wanted to marry her – then she wanted to know more. Deliberately, she stretched upward, flagrantly inciting, kissing him urgently, as evocatively as she knew how –

His arms shifted, then his hands were on her back – large and strong, they slid down, smoothly sweeping down to her waist, to her hips, then down, over the swells of her bottom. He cupped her, held her tight, her curves filling his hands, then he lifted her.

Up and against him – molding her to him so her soft belly cradled the hard ridge of his erection. She would have gasped – not with shock, but delight, a delight wholly new to her – but with lips suddenly ruthless and a demand she felt to her toes, he ravaged her mouth, took all she offered and searched for more.

There was suddenly hunger enough for two, swirling hotly about them.

Flick sank her fingers into his shoulders and hung on – thrilled to her bones as hot became hotter and hard that much harder. Need, want and desire swam through her – passion swept in in their wake. And caught her.

Excitement – even better than the rush of a winning ride – and an anticipation so keen it hurt flooded her, buoyed her –

Tap! Rat-a-tat-tat!

The sharp tattoo startled them both, ending their kiss. Breathing shallowly, they both stared at the door.

Demon straightened, softly cursing. Whoever it was, he would have to find out. It might be about Bletchley. Sliding Flick down until her feet touched the floor, he reluctantly released her luscious bottom and closed his hands about her waist. He seriously doubted she could stand unsupported.

Glancing around, his gaze fell on the solid dressing table against the wall between the mantelpiece and the bed. He glanced at the door, then steered Flick back so she could lean against the dressing table. 'Stay there – don't move.'

Placed as she was, she couldn't be seen from the door.

She blinked blankly at him, then looked dazedly across the room.

Demon released her; turning, he strode toward the door. Catching a glimpse of himself in the mirror beside the door, he swallowed another curse and slowed, tugging his waistcoat down, resettling his coat and cuffs, then raking his fingers through his hair before reaching for the latch.

He assumed it was Gillies, or one of the inn staff. Whoever it was, he intended getting rid of them fast. Turning the key, he opened the door.

The elegant gentleman who stood on the threshold, an urbane smile rapidly fading, was not a member of the inn's staff. Unfortunately, he was familiar.

Inwardly, Demon cursed, wishing he'd snuffed some of the candles Flick had scattered about the room. At least she was out of sight. Holding the door less than half open, he raised an arrogantly weary brow. 'Evening, Selbourne.'

'Cynster.' Disappointment rang in Lord Selbourne's tone; disgruntlement filled his eyes. His expression, however, remained urbane. 'I—' Abruptly, Selbourne's gaze shifted, going past Demon's shoulder. His lordship's eyes widened.

Demon stiffened, his jaw clenching so hard that he thought it would crack. He didn't, however, turn around.

Lord Selbourne's brows rose, coolly, appraisingly, then he glanced consideringly at Demon. And smiled. '—see.'

The single word carried a wealth of meaning; Demon comprehended its portent only too well. Face set, he nodded curtly. 'Precisely. I fear you'll need to find somewhere else to sleep tonight.'

Selbourne sighed. 'To the victor, the spoils.' With an arch glance directed once again beyond Demon, he turned away. 'I'll leave you, dear boy, to get what rest you may.'

Biting back an oath – an exceedingly virulent one – Demon managed to shut the door without slamming it. Hands rising to his hips, he stared at the wooden panels; after a moment, the tension in his shoulders eased. Shifted. He blinked, then slowly reached out and turned the key.

The sound of the lock falling home echoed gently – a single knell marking an irrevocable step. Demon turned.

And confirmed that Flick had indeed been unable to resist shifting to the other side of the hearth, to peer about him to see who was at the door.

Selbourne had had a perfect view of her – with her hair ruffled, her gown suggestively crumpled, her lips rosy and swollen from his kisses. Most importantly, she hadn't been wearing hood or veil. Demon stared at her.

She stared back. 'Who was that?'

He considered her, then turned back to the door and removed the key. 'Fate. Disguised as Lord Selbourne.'

241

Chapter Thirteen

Flick studied him. 'Do you know him?'

'Oh, indeed.' Slipping the key into his waistcoat pocket, Demon started back toward her. 'Everyone in the ton knows Rattletrap Selbourne.'

'Rattletrap?'

Stopping directly before her, Demon looked into her eyes. 'His tongue runs on wheels.'

She searched his eyes, his face; her lips formed a silent *Oh*.

'Which means,' he explained, 'that at all the balls in London tomorrow evening, the juiciest *bon mot* will be just who the deliciously youthful 'widow' discovered consorting with me at Bury St. Edmunds really was.'

Flick stiffened; her eyes flashed. 'Don't start that again. Just because he saw me doesn't mean I'm compromised. He doesn't know who I am.'

'But he will.' Demon tapped her nose with one finger. 'That's how Rattletrap secures his invitations – the particular niche he's carved in the bosom of the ton. He ferrets out all the indiscretions committed by the rest of us, and whispers them in the matrons' ears.'

He held Flick's gaze steadily. 'He'll find out who you are – you're well known in Newmarket, and that will be the first place he'll look. Gillies described the scene you created to get this room – that's precisely how a lady, living near but not in town, desirous of a room in which to meet her lover, would behave.'

Flick folded her arms and set her chin stubbornly. 'I am *not* compromised.'

'You are.' Demon didn't blink. 'As of the instant Selbourne laid eyes on your face, your situation is the *definition* of compromised.'

She narrowed her eyes. After a moment, she stated, 'Even if, *theoretically*, I am, that changes nothing.'

'On the contrary, it changes a great deal.'

'Indeed? Such as?'

He reached out and tugged her hand free; puzzled, she let him raise it. Catching the other, he lifted both to his shoulders, drawing her nearer. Releasing her hands, he closed his arms about her.

She quickly slid her hands down, bracing them against his chest. 'What are you doing?'

He met her gaze, then lowered his head. 'Demonstrating how much has changed.'

He kissed her – and kept kissing her, not forcefully but persuasively, not ruthlessly but relentlessly, until she surrendered. When she melted against him, he locked his arms about her – and kissed her some more. She responded with her customary eagerness. Steadily, progressively, he retraced their earlier steps until their breathing fragmented, until her hips were pressed tight to his, until heat licked their senses and passion hovered in the wings.

Only then did he lift his head.

Her hands were fisted on his lapels. Her eyes glinted from beneath heavy lids. 'You don't *want* to marry me – not really.'

Flick made the statement without conviction; tight against him, his rampant arousal riding against her, she could hardly claim ignorance of what he wanted. It was a powerful incentive

243

to give in. *But* ... She wanted him to marry her not just for that, no matter how exciting. She wanted him to marry her for more – for at least one other reason. A more important reason.

Tension invested his face. The same tension held her. His eyes remained on hers, his gaze steadfast, unwaveringly blue. Her lips throbbed. Entirely without her permission, her gaze lowered to his lips – clever lips, lean and strong, just like him. They dipped, and brushed hers.

'I do want to marry you.' Again he kissed her – a tantalizing promise as he slid his hands down her back, lifting her against him once more. 'I will marry you.'

His lips closed on hers, and the kiss turned ravenous. And hot. She could cope with ravishment, but the heat – that welling sense of fire and flame – defeated her. He pressed it on her, and she drank it in. It slid through her veins, through her limbs, through her brain.

And she burned, as did he. There was fire in his touch, in his lips – despite the swelling heat, she couldn't get enough. As her limbs melted and resolution evaporated, she clung to her wits and inwardly cursed. How would she get him to love her if he married her like this?

How to stop him?

As if in answer, he deepened the kiss. Her head spun. Boneless, near to spineless, she sank deeper into his arms, into his strength. Into his shocking heat.

'I've dreamed of marrying you.'

The words were a gravelly whisper. He steered her back a few steps; her hips met the dressing table.

'You have?' Breathless, she struggled to lift her lids.

'Mmm-hmm.' Propping her against the dressing table, he eased back.

The sudden loss of his hard body against her, all but around her, left her disoriented. She dragged in a breath, watching as he shrugged out of his coat and waistcoat, tossing

244

them on a nearby chair. He returned to her, his hands sliding, then firming about her waist.

'You've dreamed of our wedding?' She found that hard to believe.

His lips kicked up at the ends; his expression remained driven. 'My dreams were more concerned with our wedding night.'

He drew her to him. Eyes flaring wide, very certain of what she glimpsed in his, she braced her hands against his chest. 'No. You know how I feel about marrying for such a reason.'

He didn't force her closer, didn't pull her against him and simply melt her resistance. Instead, he ducked his head and dotted gentle kisses along her jaw, over her earlobe. Then his lips slid farther, to caress the sensitive skin beneath her ear.

She shivered.

'Would marrying me be such a hardship?'

He breathed the words against her ear, then drew back just enough so that as she turned, her eyes met his.

Their faces were so close that their breaths mingled. Wide-eyed, Flick looked deep into serious blue eyes, into his perfectly serious, well-beloved face. 'No.'

He didn't move, didn't grab her in triumph and crow. He simply waited. She studied his eyes, his face, then drew in a shallow breath. About them, the air shimmered, stirring, alive, invested with power. She felt his temptation, his promise, and more. Lifting one hand, she traced the line from one cheekbone to the corner of his lips. Hauling in another breath, she stretched up on her toes and touched her lips to his.

It was madness – a delicious, heady, compulsive madness – a sudden need that seared her, drove her, impelled her. It was impulse – pure, distilled and potent; she had no idea where it would lead.

245

But she kissed him – invitingly, encouragingly, challengingly. And sank into his arms as they closed about her, sank into his embrace, and into the kiss.

It caught her up, swept her up, and they were back in the fire, back in the flames.

Demon knew very well that she'd simply sprung her horses, that she was riding wild before the wind with no particular goal in mind. It was enough. He was expert enough to ride with her, to set his hand gently on her reins and guide her where he willed.

It took him a moment to work out the details – to plot and plan the where and how. Courtesy of her wildness, her increasingly abandoned kisses, he was already aching, but that was his most minor concern. He'd never made love to an innocent, wild or otherwise – she looked set to test his expertise, his control, to the limit.

Releasing her lips, he firmed his hands about her waist and lifted her, setting her atop the dressing table, giving thanks to whatever rakish god watched over him; the top was the perfect height.

She blinked at him in surprise. Her new position left her face more level with his. Her breasts swelled, then she noticed her skirts straining over her parted knees. She clamped her legs together and quickly shuffled back. Curls in disarray, her lips swollen, her eyes slightly wild, she stared at him. 'What—?' She had to stop and haul in another breath. 'What are you about?'

He let his lips curve reassuringly; he could do nothing about the fire in his eyes. His gaze locked on hers, he stepped forward, his hips meeting her knees, immobilizing her legs. Lowering his gaze to her chest, he reached for the top button of her bodice. 'I'm going to make love to you.'

'What?' Flick looked down as the first button popped free. His fingers caught the next button – she gasped and closed her hands about his wrists. 'Don't be ridiculous.'

She hadn't thought this far. And, thanks to him, her wits were frazzled, her brain was overheated. She certainly couldn't think now. She tugged once, then harder, and shifted his hands not at all. He continued to undo her buttons.

'Since by tomorrow evening we can rely on the entire ton believing that I spent tonight in your bed, there's no reason I can see that I shouldn't.'

Fleetingly, he met her gaze; his was hot, smoldering blue. Temptation and promise – both glowed clearly; Flick found the sight reassuring.

Reassuring? She was losing her mind – he'd already lost his.

'Besides,' he continued, in the same low, sinfully languid tone, 'you made it clear you require something more than social stricture to agree to our wedding.' The last button slipped free; he looked up and met her gaze. 'Consider what follows as my answer to that.'

Raising his hands, he framed her face and drew her lips to his. Flick braced herself to deny him – she would not be won over by main force.

But there was no force in his kiss. He nibbled, kissed, tantalizingly teased until, senses whirling, she grabbed him and kissed him back. She sensed his triumph, but she didn't care – in that instant, she needed his lips on hers, needed to feel the fire and flames again, wanted to know, couldn't live without knowing, more.

And she knew he could – would – teach her.

As if in confirmation, he welcomed her in, drew her deep, then toyed with her – incited her. Ignited her.

Until she was consumed by raging heat too hot to be confined within living flesh.

He eased back, his lips still on hers but their kiss no longer so demanding, no longer the focus of his attention. His hands drifted from her face, long fingers trailing down either side of her throat, then spreading over her shoulders. Unhurriedly, those long fingers skimmed down; with the lightest of touches, they flared over her breasts.

Her flesh came alive. Nerves flickered, unfurled – sensitized, they waited, tightening with anticipation.

He drew back from their kiss. Flick kept her eyes shut and struggled to breathe. Slowly, deliberately, he stroked the upper curves of her breasts, then the lower, through the soft fabric of her gown, then his fingers trailed lightly over the peaks, over nipples now excruciatingly tight.

She gasped – his lips returned, drinking the sound. His hands shifted, firming, palms cupping her curves. Gently but intently – inherently possessively – he closed his hands about the soft mounds.

Her breath hitched; his lips shifted on hers, brushed, caressed, reassured.

She felt her breasts swell even more, felt them heat and firm until they ached.

Demon ached, too, but ignored it. Her breasts were small, pert – they fit snugly within his palms. He closed thumb and forefinger about her nipples, and she gasped, and tensed – and tensed. With his lips on hers, soothing her, distracting her, he played, giving her time to grow accustomed to his touch, ruthlessly denying the impulse to brush aside her bodice and bare her to his senses. Eventually, she sighed into his mouth, the tautness in her frame subtly altered to a tension he recognized very well.

She was awakening.

With every controlled sweep of his fingers, every gentle, encouraging squeeze, he drew her further along the road to fulfillment. Hers. And his.

When he released her lips, drew his hands from her breasts and reached for the edges of her bodice, she didn't stop him.

She did, however, reach up, too, closing her fingers on the edges below his.

She hesitated.

They were both breathing quickly, heated yet in control of their senses, both very much aware. Supremely conscious of the pounding in his blood, the passion he was holding at bay, he drew in a slow breath, locked his jaw and staved off the urge to rush her. And waited.

Her gaze was fixed on his throat; she dragged in a breath, held it, and looked up, into his eyes.

He had no idea what she saw there – what her swiftly searching gaze discovered; he stared down at her, unable to spare the energy to summon any expression, and prayed she wouldn't balk.

Instead, her chin firmed; her lips curved in a smile of pure feminine assurance tinged with her ever-present innocence. In a gesture almost demure, she dropped her gaze from his; tightening her hold on the open flaps of her bodice, she parted them.

Inwardly reeling, he let go and let her do it. That smile, coupled with her action, had hit him with the force of a fist and left him winded. Captured, transfixed, he watched as she wriggled, sliding first one shoulder free, then the other, then drawing her arms from the tight sleeves.

She glanced shyly, questioningly, up at him; he hauled in a breath and took charge again.

He drew the gown down to her waist, then had to pause to look at her – to take in the smooth expanse of creamy skin showing above her demure chemise, to drink in the beauty of her naked shoulders, her sweetly rounded arms, the delicate structure of her collarbone.

His rakish instincts catalogued points for later examination – where her pulse throbbed at the base of her throat, where her shoulder met her collarbone, the outer swells of her breasts. Her breasts themselves remained screened, albeit incompletely; her nipples peaked tightly beneath the fine chemise, but he couldn't appreciate their color. Soft, pure pink was his guess.

Feeling like a drowning man coming up for air, he hauled in a breath. Lifting his hands, he once more framed her face, and brought her lips to his.

Flick sank into the kiss. The heat welled – she welcomed it, then deliberately let go and slipped into the flow, letting it take her on its tide. If there had been a windmill near, and she'd been wearing a cap, she would have shied it into the sky. She'd made up her mind, made her decision.

She knew he desired her powerfully – it was there in his face, in the hard edge passion set to the angular planes, in the fire that smoldered in his eyes. His desire was palpable, a living thing – hot as the sun, it reached for her as his hands, his arms, his whole body did. She recognized it instinctively – she needed no interpreter to tell her what it was. He wanted her as a man wanted a woman. And she wanted him in the converse way.

As for marrying, he hadn't yet answered her question of whether love could grow from strong desire. Nor had she. But she'd expected no easy declaration of love – not from him. If he said it, he would mean it – she could count on that. But he could only tell her if he knew – and she didn't think he did. However ...

There was a light in his eyes, behind the heated glow, behind the passion and desire – there was a sense in his touch, in his kiss, in all his actions. And while that light shone, and while that sense reached her, she was convinced there was hope.

Hope of love – hope for a marriage invested with love, built on love, with him. She was willing to risk all to claim such a prize. Fate had offered her this chance to secure her deepest, all-but-unrecognized dream – she would take it, grasp it with both hands. And do everything she could to make the dream come true.

She would marry him, but on her terms. He would need to do more than seduce her – teach her about passion, desire and physical intimacy – to get her to say yes. She wasn't, however, about to stop and explain. Tonight was for them – their first night together.

Her first time with him.

When next he drew back, she smiled; lifting her arms, she draped them over his shoulders. His eyes met hers as he slid her closer to the dressing table's edge. He studied her face, his own hard, passion-set; wrapping one arm about her hips, he lifted her and stripped her dress away. Excitement shot through her, searing her veins. Clad in her chemise and petticoats, she dared to meet his eyes. He raised his brows slightly, then slid his hands upward and closed them about her breasts. 'Do you like this?'

Her lids fell of their own accord; her head tipped back.

'Yes.' She breathed the word, aware only of his clever hands, his clever fingers, as they stroked and gently squeezed. Although muted by fine lawn, his touch burned. His lips returned to hers. Sliding one hand to her back, he urged her nearer, closer to the table's edge.

She complied without thought – thought was beyond her; all she could do was feel. Her senses gloried in un fettered freedom, freed by her decision, freed by the night.

Freed by him. His kiss anchored her to the world, but it was a world of sensation, a world filled with an excitement she'd never known, and a promise of glory she wanted for her own.

Demon captured her lips and kissed her – ravenously – no longer so gentle, so controlled. She was delectable, and so very nearly his – he wanted to devour her. On the thought,

251

his lips slid from hers, tracing the curve of her throat to where her pulse beat hotly. He laved the spot, then sucked lightly; appeased by her gasp, he moved on, sliding his lips along the curve of her collarbone, then shifting lower to the warm swell of her breast.

Through her fine chemise, one pert nipple beckoned; he closed his mouth over it and heard her shocked gasp. But she didn't try to wriggle back – she didn't tell him to stop. So he settled to feast, to wring more shocked gasps from her. Long before he raised his head, he'd succeeded, drawing a chorus of appreciation from her lips.

He kissed them again, parting them fully, ravishing her softness, taking all – demanding more. She met him eagerly, no match for the brutal strength of his passion but with an open eagerness that nearly brought him to his knees.

Abruptly, he stopped kissing her, amazed to find his own breathing as ragged as hers. Nuzzling aside her curls, he slid his lips into the sweet hollow beneath her ear while his fingers swiftly dealt with the laces of her petticoat.

Speed had suddenly become essential. Imperative.

She sighed, a tense exhalation shimmering with reined excitement; the sound literally shook him. The scent of her, rising to torment him, added to his pain. He glanced down at the soft chemise that hid her body from his sight – he longed to strip it away, but experience warned against it. Sitting naked atop a table in full light might be too much for her this time.

All thus far had gone according to his plan. She'd introduced an odd moment or two, but he'd kept them on track. He intended to seduce her but, this time, he needed to do more. He needed to be gentle, and not just because he was excruciatingly aware, to his very fingertips, of her innocence. He wanted her not just once or even twice – he wanted her for all time. So the moment had to be compelling. As powerfully compelling as he could make it – so she would want him again, as eagerly, as enthusiastically as he knew he would want her.

Another challenge – she was full of them. It was one of the things that so attracted him to her.

The laces of her petticoat came free; he loosened the waistband, pushed it down, then swiftly lifted her and swept the garment down her legs. He freed it from her feet, then flung it after her gown. His cravat and shirt followed – as he stepped back to stand against her knees, he flipped off her shoes.

She was waiting, almost shivering with excitement; she raised her arms, lifted her face and welcomed him back with an open-mouthed kiss. He sank into it and let her lead him where she would while he slipped off her garters, then rolled her stockings down, careful not to touch her bare skin. She was so caught up in their kiss, he wasn't sure she noticed when her stockings slipped away, and she was sitting in the candlelight clothed only in her chemise. The fine garment reached to midthigh; he grasped a fold and tugged – she was sitting on it.

Mentally girding his loins, he filled his lungs and wrested back control of their kiss. When he was sure he had all the reins in his grasp, he set his hands on her hips, simply holding her, giving her a moment to grow accustomed to the feel of his hands there. Her chemise was so fine it was no real barrier – to his touch or his senses.

She skittered a little, but calmed almost immediately; as soon as she did, he let his hands wander. Gliding, soothing, tracing, learning, he caressed her thighs, her knees, her calves. Then, gently but firmly, he grasped her knees and eased them apart.

She no longer had them locked together, but she resisted – for a moment. Then, hesitant but willing, she let him move each thigh outward, until he could step between.

Before he could haul in a triumphant breath, one of her hands slid from his shoulder to his chest. Quivering awareness shot through her – and him – when her fingers tangled in his crisp hair, when her hand came to rest tentatively, warm palm on the wide muscle above his heart.

For one long instant, Demon simply existed, focused totally on her – on holding onto the reins of her seduction. Her awakening was becoming an awakening for him – an introduction to delights more intense than any he'd previously known.

The tension that held her so tight, so taut, was, for all that, so intensely fragile; he felt as if, with one wrong move, one wrong breath, he might shatter it. And her.

When her hand shifted, drifted, then gently traced across his chest, he breathed again. Sealing his demon's reins in a death grip, he subtly altered their kiss, encouraging her to explore, relieved, if more tense, when she did.

Gradually, he eased her forward, closer to him, to the edge of the table. Every inch she slid forward pressed her thighs farther apart, until, beneath her chemise, they were wide-spread, held so by his hips.

She was open to him.

It took him a moment or three to shackle his raging lust – a few more to beat back his demons. What came next had to be perfect – it had to be right. Nothing in his life had mattered so much.

Sliding one hand to the small of her back, he settled it there, solid and sure behind her. Then he raised his head fractionally, breaking their kiss, but leaving their lips a mere inch apart. From beneath his lids, he watched her face as, with the same gentle yet deliberate touch he'd used throughout, he dipped his hand beneath her chemise's hem and slid it slowly up the silken length of her thigh.

Her lids flickered; he glimpsed her eyes, wide pupils circled in startling blue. She trembled; her breath caught, then she slowly exhaled. He stroked her thigh, the long quivering muscle, then the delicate inner face – he stroked upward, brushing her lips when she shuddered, letting her cling when, with the backs of his fingers, he caressed her quivering stomach.

Then, very slowly, he let his fingers glide down, tracing the crease at the top of one thigh, then the other, then, easing back from their kiss, he gently pressed two fingers into the silken curls between her thighs.

She sucked in a breath; a sharp quiver lanced through her. Her eyes were shut, but he watched her face, watched the expressions – anticipation, excitement, sharp delight and flaring need – flow across her features as he caressed her, then parted the soft folds and touched her intimately. She was already hot, already plump and swollen; he played, and damp quickly became wet. He found the tight nubbin hidden in its hood; he circled it with a moistened fingertip – her breath hitched, she shuddered; wildly clutching his shoulders, she sought his lips with hers.

He kissed her, but kept the caress light – he wanted her concentrating on his fingers, not his lips. With his hand at her back, he eased her forward another inch, so she was close, very close, to the edge – instinctively, she raised her knees and gripped his hips for balance.

If he could have grinned triumphantly, he would have.

She was fully exposed – to his touch, to him.

He touched, caressed, then, very gently, probed her slick, soft flesh. He found her entrance – ignoring the sudden heightening of her tension, he eased one finger in, then, in the instant she caught her breath, slid it slowly, inexorably, into her heat.

She dragged her lips from his on a gasp; he felt the shudder that racked her in his bones. Her body closed hotly about his finger. Recapturing her lips, he kissed her – no longer lightly but deeply, evocatively. He stroked her in the same way.

Flick couldn't think, she couldn't reason – she couldn't imagine how she'd survive. She was hot, so hot; her skin felt afire. The flames that had started deep inside had spread to every extremity; her whole skin felt tight. As for her nerves, they were stretched so taut, so tense in anticipation of his next caress, of the next, deeply intimate invasion, that if it didn't come soon she knew she'd fly apart.

If she'd had enough breath left, she would have sobbed.

With pleasure.

She couldn't understand that. She couldn't even think of what he was doing – what she was letting him do to her. Her stunned brain wouldn't hold the mental image. She'd had no idea physical intimacy would prove so shocking. So exciting. So mind-numbing.

So gloriously delicious.

And they hadn't even got to the culmination – the moment when their bodies would join. She knew what that entailed, yet . . .

A little knowledge was a dangerous thing.

Luckily, her lover was experienced – exceedingly experienced if her state was any guide. She was panting, squirming, ready to kill for that next bit of sensation, his next caress, the next experience he had in store.

If he didn't hurry up and give it to her, she was quite sure she'd die.

Demon was well aware of her state – not once had he stopped tracking it. He withdrew his finger from her only to slide another in beside it, deliberately stretching her, preparing her. She squirmed and adjusted instantly. He reached deep – her gasp shuddered into a soft sob. She dropped her forehead to his shoulder; he could feel her soft pants hot against his skin.

He no longer needed to hold her to him – there was no chance she would scoot back. Leaving the hand between her thighs still probing in a slow, repetitive rhythm, with the other he slipped the buttons on his trousers and guided them down his hips. He uttered a wordless thanks to fate that he was in his town rig, with shoes, not boots; he toed the shoes off, let his trousers fall, stepped out of them and kicked them away.

She felt him shift – greedy hands grasped his shoulders, hauling him to her. Momentarily off-balance, he went with her pull – then gasped, biting back a groan as his throbbing erection hit the dressing table's edge.

Her thighs were still wide, her knees clamped to his now naked hips. He drew in a breath, nudged her head up, and found her lips again. He caught her up in the kiss, then drew his hand from her slick heat; one hand at her back, he eased her forward a fraction more – until the broad head of his staff nudged into her hot softness.

Abruptly, she drew back from the kiss. Arms locked about his shoulders, she blinked dazedly as their gazes met. She licked her lips, then glanced at the bed. 'Aren't we? . . .'

'No.' He could hardly speak. The effort of holding still, poised at her entrance, her slickness scalding him like hot honey, was turning his muscles to jelly. 'This way will be easier for you this time.' She was small; to lie beneath him, trapped by his weight, might not be wise – not for her first time.

Her lips formed an *Oh* – she risked a glance down, but her chemise, stretched across her thighs, blocked her view. She cleared her throat. 'How? . . .'

His pained grin never made it to his face. 'Easily. Just – like . . .' He pressed nearer, simultaneously drawing her to the very edge of the table – he sank into her. '*This.*'

The look on her face was one he would treasure all his life – her eyes widened as he entered her, slowly pushing in, stretching her softness. She was oh, *so* tight, but, to his relief, she didn't freeze, didn't tense. He didn't stop – feeling her untried body ease about him, he penetrated her steadily, inexorably filling her until she'd taken him in to the hilt and he was buried in her sweet heat.

Her fractured '*Oh!*' shivered in the air. Her lids fell – she hauled in a huge breath. *Then* she tensed.

Scalding hot, she closed about him, so tight he thought he'd lose his mind.

He trapped her lips and only just managed to catch his reins and haul back on the savage urge to ravish her – her mouth, her hot softness, the luscious vessel of her body. Although reeling himself, he caught her senses and steadied her – in so doing, he steadied himself.

Releasing her lips, dragging in a huge breath, clamping a firm hold on his instincts – where she was concerned, too primal, too raw – he anchored her before him, withdrew, and slid home again.

Her maidenhead had been a mere cobweb. That hadn't surprised him; she'd been riding astride all her life and still did. So there'd been no pain, only pleasure as he'd filled her – as he withdrew and filled her again.

His muscles flickered under the strain, but he kept his rhythm very slow so she could grow accustomed to the intimacy, to the slide of his body into hers, to the flexing, regular rhythm, to the elemental repetition.

His breathing sounded ragged in his ears; he was so tense his lungs felt tight. But now he was, at long last, inside her, and she was so tight and hot, and so accepting, he was determined to prolong the sweet torture to the full.

She was very wet, scalding hot; her thighs eased about him as he loved her. Then she wriggled, pressing closer. Clinging to his shoulders, clamping her knees to his hips, she arched, and picked up his rhythm. She matched him, warm and pliant, a female body more delicious, more rewarding, than any he'd known. They could barely breathe, yet their lips fused and held, melding to the same beat as their bodies, the same beat as their hearts.

She was used to riding; he realized what that meant as she continued to meet him, her body supplely flexing in his arms. She could very likely last as long as he could – which was a thought to make a strong man weak.

It only made him more rigid, more engorged. Her murmur as she adjusted was not one of complaint. So he held her lips with his, held her steady before him, and gave her what she deserved – a long, slow ride to delight.

Flick followed his lead eagerly, delighted to find that she could. That the steady rhythm hadn't overwhelmed her, although at first she'd thought it would. That first instant of feeling him deep within her – even now, she gasped at the sensual memory. She still felt their joining keenly, the internal pressure, the fullness that was so strange, especially as she'd never felt empty there before. But now he was riding so smoothly, so deeply, so effortlessly into her, some part of her wits had reengaged.

Certainly not all of them. It was as if the heat between them had reached a new level, another plane, leaving her reeling in pleasured delight but with enough wit to appreciate the sensation. As for her body . . .

On a gasp, she pulled back from their kiss to draw in a labored breath, aware of her body arching in his arms – aware to her toes of why. Her skin radiated heat, as did his. But aside from the heat, it was very like riding. She hadn't realized it could be done like this – she was finding it quite easy to cope.

He ducked his head; she felt his lips sear her throat. She clung to his broad shoulders and tipped her head away so he could sear as he would. She lifted her heavy lids to regauge their position – she pressed her hips closer, gripped his hips more tightly and splayed her hands over his back.

And caught sight of the mirror on the wall by the door. Directly opposite.

The reflection in the mirror stole her breath, focused her wits and transfixed her attention. In utter fascination.

She could see his naked back, down to his calves, see the flexing of his spine as he drove into her, see his buttocks clench and ease in time with their riding rhythm.

The view was enthralling.

She couldn't help but remember Bletchley in similar circumstance – which left her feeling like the cat who'd secured the prize cream. There was absolutely no comparison – not at *any* level. Not in the long, taut, steely muscles flexing in back and legs, not in the tight muscles that bunched and thrust, not in the steady, effortless rhythm, and certainly not in the powerful result.

Each deep thrust filled her completely, each movement effective, efficient and seemingly effortless – the outcome of harnessed, concerted power. Controlled power.

Bletchley had flailed and thrashed on top of his woman. In complete and stark contrast was the way Demon filled her. Deeply. Relentlessly. And oh, so repetitively.

Watching him thrust, feeling the result deep within her a split second later, focused her mind on the sensation, and drew her back into the maelstrom. Into the heat, and the swirling build of sensation.

Her lids were falling, her eyes almost shut when he changed his movement into a rolling thrust. She saw it – then felt it. She shut her eyes tight to better savor the moment – then quickly opened them again. To watch, and match her anticipation more acutely to his rhythm, to be ready to make the most of each sliding thrust, to shudder in his arms as he drove more deeply – to eventually let her lids fall as their glorious heat reached a new peak.

It was like riding at flat gallop through a fire.

Excitement, tense and searing, gripped her – along with a driving, compulsively *urgent* need. They were both breathing hard, both reaching deep – for the energy, the strength, to make the final dash.

He turned his head and their lips touched, but only briefly; she felt his hand slide, hot as a brand, up under her chemise. Skin to hot skin, he closed his hand about her breast. His fingers shifted; he found her tightly furled nipple. And pressed.

She cried out – the sound, laden with sharp delight, echoed through the room. His hand shifted on her flesh, and she was burning, burning – incandescent within.

Heat and flames were everywhere, raging through her – molten rivers of pleasure and urgent need flowed, a hot tide, from where they joined. The tide swelled, reaching ever higher, consuming her body, buoying her mind, her senses – lifting them high on a rush of pure passion.

Higher – ever higher.

His hand slid over her fevered flesh, from breast to hip, then around to her rear. He caressed her there – with a smothered gasp, she locked her arms about his shoulders and lifted slightly; instantly, his hand slid lower, caressing her bottom knowingly, evocatively, possessively, then reaching further to trace the line beneath the tight globes.

She shuddered – and felt like she was shattering. Blown apart by the heat and the burgeoning frenzy. He set her down and tipped her back, his hands once again at her hips. He angled them; without thought, she lifted her legs and wrapped them about his waist.

Instantly, he filled her deeply, completely; as he drew back, his fingers slid into the damp curls between her wide-spread thighs, straight to the nubbin of flesh he'd earlier teased.

261

He touched her there – and reality shook. She clutched tight – in desperation, she tried to cling to her wits, to her spiralling senses . . .

'Let go.' His lips touched hers briefly – hotly. 'Throw your heart over.'

She heard the raspy order as he touched her again – she obeyed, and soared high.

Her world exploded.

She lost her senses utterly – lost all touch with reality. She was swept up by a force she couldn't describe – hot and powerful, it propelled her into pleasure. Deep, bonemelting pleasure.

It surrounded her like a sea, and left her floating in ecstasy.

To her surprise, her senses returned, heightened but focused solely on him. She felt his hard hands, first gentling, then gripping her, felt the force surge and sweep through his body – and into hers as he drove deep into her molten flesh. She heard his guttural groan as the force caught him, too.

Then he joined her in the void. She felt the warmth of him deep in her womb. Felt the heat of his body beneath her hands as she clung to him, and surrendered.

To the force behind their passion.

Eons later in the depths of the night, she awoke. Slowly, as always. Her mind struggled free of the wisps of sleep, only to slide into mists of confusion.

Her nerves made the dizzying leap from somnolence to excitement – befuddled by sleep, she couldn't understand why. It was full dark. She was lying on her back in the middle of a comfortable bed. A tickling sensation – it had started at the base of her stomach, just above her curls – *that* was what had woken her – was slowly progressing up her body. Over her stomach, past her navel, over her waist, steadily upward.

Some part of her mind was shrieking for her to react – but

her limbs were too weighted – pleasurably weighted – for her to make any rash move. The tickling changed to nuzzling beneath her breasts, then warm kisses followed one curve up and over.

Demon's mouth closed over her nipple.

She sucked in a tortured breath and abruptly came to life. Not, however, quite as her mind intended. Held between his hands, she arched, flagrantly offering her breast – he accepted immediately, laving the tip, then taking it deep in his mouth.

Flick heard a soft, strangled cry – then realized it was hers. The searing wetness shocked her anew. Opening her eyes, she looked down. 'What—?'

She couldn't see him in the dark, but she could feel him. Her heart hitched, then started to canter as she felt his hair-roughened legs between hers, the solid weight of his hips spreading her thighs wide. The heat of his body as he hovered over her, mere inches distant, sent her heart into a gallop. When she realized that her senses hadn't lied – that there was no longer any garment, no matter how fine, between them, that his wicked lips and wickeder mouth were teasing her bare skin, and that, any second, his hard hot body would lie directly, skin to naked skin, on hers – her heart started to race.

'Relax.'

The deep purring murmur came out of the dark as he lifted his head from her breast. After a moment he added, as if to explain, 'I want you again.'

Those four gravelly words went straight to her heart – then straight to her loins. He'd pushed her chemise up to her arms – when he tugged, she dragged in a massive breath, and obliged, lifting her arms and letting him draw the thin garment off over her head.

Leaving her naked beneath him.

What followed was a second lesson in sheer delight. In the dark of the night, in the depths of the bed, he touched her, caressed her, then, when her body was aching with urgent longing, filled her.

She lay on her back and let sensation wash over her – let her mind supply what she couldn't see. The cotton sheets formed a cocoon about them, cool against her fevered skin. The mattress was thick enough to cushion her against the powerful surges of his possession.

Arms braced, he loomed above her, a shadow lover in the night; he held himself over her as their bodies did what seemed to come naturally. To them both.

She couldn't deny she enjoyed it thoroughly, that she joyfully put her heart and soul into the exercise every bit as much as did he. She enjoyed feeling his body merging with hers, enjoyed the deep sense of completion that came, borne on that final surrender.

Enjoyed the weight of him when he collapsed, spent, upon her.

Enjoyed the feeling of having him so deeply within her.

Demon woke as dawn tinged the sky and crept into the room to lay its pale fingers on the bed. In their light he saw an angel – his angel – sprawled asleep by his side.

She was facing away from him, half on her stomach.

For a long moment, he studied her golden curls while vivid memories rolled through his brain. Then, slowly, careful not to jar her, he came up on one elbow, then reached out and gently lifted the sheet, and drew it down.

She was more perfect than he'd thought – more beautiful than his imagination had been able to conjure. As the light about them strengthened, he looked his fill, drank in the sight of firm curves and slender limbs covered in flawless ivory skin – skin he knew felt like silk to his touch.

And would heat with gratifying swiftness if he touched her.

His gaze had fastened on the smooth hemispheres of her bottom. The thought of her responsiveness coupled with the sight brought him swiftly to attention, and too quickly to the brink of pain.

He gritted his teeth – and tried to think. Tried to reason with his overheated flesh.

All he could recall was her eagerness, her enthusiasm, her honest, open, unrestrained passion.

And the fact that he'd exercised great care in taking her the first time, and she hadn't tensed in the slightest when he'd taken her again.

He shouldn't, of course, have been so demanding as to take her a second time mere hours after the first. But he'd been desperate – visited by an ungovernable urge to reassure himself that it hadn't been a dream. That the most sensual woman he'd met in his life was an innocent Botticelli angel.

If he was wise, he wouldn't think about that – about how she'd responded so ardently, adapted so readily, then joined him in a wild ride. A ride rather wilder and certainly longer than he'd intended.

But she'd enjoyed it – and she'd enjoyed their second ride, too.

Perhaps she'd enjoy a third?

His hand had made contact with her bottom before he'd finished the thought.

Flick woke to discover her bottom flushed and fevered, and Demon's hand sliding beneath her hip. He lifted her, and stuffed a pillow beneath her hips, then eased her down, settling her more definitely on her stomach.

Which seemed rather odd. But then, she was still mostly asleep. 'Mmm?' she murmured, making it a question.

He leaned over her, looked into her heavy-lidded eyes, then kissed her shoulder. 'Just lie still.'

She smiled sleepily, and let her lids fall.

His hand returned to her bottom.

To gently but evocatively caress, leaving a tracery of fire on skin already heated and dewed. Her breath came increasingly fast – when she murmured again, an incoherent question, his hand shifted. Long fingers slid between her thighs, into the soft folds of flesh between. He caressed, then probed – she felt him lean over her, the crisp hair on his chest brushing her back, sending tingling shivers racing through her.

All the way to where his fingers delved.

He smothered a curse, then his fingers left her. He shifted, his weight dipping the bed as he lifted over her. With his legs, he nudged hers wide; grasping her right knee, he drew it up, bending that leg, leaving her knee almost level with her waist – he settled his hips in the space created, hard against her bottom.

She blinked her eyes wide – a large hand came down, palm flat by her shoulder, carrying his weight above her.

Her heart throbbed and leapt to her throat as she felt his weight against her bottom – then stopped as she felt a familiar hardness ease into her.

She gasped as he slid powerfully home. All the way.

Holding still, his hips flush with her bottom, he lowered his head and brushed a kiss on her shoulder. 'Are you all right?'

Naked, with him equally naked behind her, joined in a fashion that made her think of stallions and mares, with him throbbing at her center ... shewas more than all right. She was on the brink of ecstasy.

'*Yes*.' The word came out in a rush, laden with a sweet tension she couldn't disguise. He bent his head and touched his lips to her ear.

'You don't have to do anything. Just lie still.'

Then he made love to her until she screamed.

Chapter Fourteen

'Drive on!' Demon climbed into the manor's carriage; a groom shut the door behind him. The carriage lurched, then rumbled out of The Angel's stable yard.

'Are you *sure* Gillies will be able to cope?' Flick asked. 'There's no need for you to escort me all the way to Hillgate End.'

Settling beside her, Demon glanced at her, then leaned back against the squabs. 'Gillies is perfectly capable of locating Bletchley and following him back to London.'

He'd gone down to breakfast and to order a tray to be taken up to Flick, only to find Gillies kicking his heels by the main door. Bletchley, it transpired, had already left for the prizefight field.

'Heard him quizzing the innkeep,' Gillies had said, 'about the special coaches they've put on, running direct from here to London.'

After his lack of activity the previous night, it seemed likely Bletchley had dallied in Newmarket purely to attend the prizefight, but ... they couldn't be certain he didn't have a meeting arranged to take place amid the crowd about the ring. Neither he nor Gillies had believed that – discussing race-fixing surrounded by a crowd containing so many potentially interested ears smacked of rank stupidity, something the syndicate had shown no sign of being. Gillies hadn't followed Bletchley, but waited for orders.

'He went out this morning with the same crew he was chatting with last night, heading straight for the field.'

There was an outside chance of a meeting occurring after the prizefight, although given the aftermath of such events, that, too, seemed unlikely. Still . . .

Demon had rejigged his plans, sending Gillies after Bletchley to watch and to follow, to London if necessary.

'Gillies knows who to contact in London – we'll set up a watch on Bletchley. He'll have to meet with his masters soon.'

Flick humphed impatiently; Demon ignored it. He was relieved that Bletchley was heading south. With him gone, the chances of Flick running headlong into danger were considerably diminished.

With Gillies at the fight, he'd first arranged for a coachman to drive the manor carriage back to Hillgate End, then broken his fast at a leisurely pace, then paid Flick's shot with no explanation whatever, and returned upstairs to escort her, concealingly cloaked and veiled, down to the waiting carriage.

By that time, the fight had started, so there was no one of note left at the inn to witness their joint departure. The only wrinkle in his plan was Ivan the Terrible, presently tied behind the carriage.

Ivan hated being led – especially by a carriage. He was going to be in a foul mood when it came time to ride home.

Demon wasn't, however, disposed to worry about Ivan – before he rode home, he had a number of pressing matters to resolve. The most pressing sat beside him, idly gazing at the scenery, with not the slightest sign of fluster showing in her angelic face.

Which really did surprise him.

He was thirty-one and had bedded scores of women – she was just twenty, and had just spent her first night with a man. Him. Yet her composure was patently genuine. She'd been flustered enough, blushing rosily, when he'd left her in the room and gone to look for breakfast. But by the time he'd returned, she had been perfectly composed, her usual straightforward, openly confident self. Of course, by then, she had dressed.

She'd removed her veil as they'd rolled out of Bury; a quick glance revealed a serene expression, with a slight smile tilting her lips and a soft light in her eyes. As if she was recalling the events of the night and enjoying her memories.

Demon shifted, then looked out of the window – and went over his plans.

Flick was indeed reflecting on the events of the night, and those of the morning, and, further, on how much she'd enjoyed them. She still felt curiously glorious – as if she was glowing all the way to her toes. If this was satiation, she thoroughly approved. Which only made her even more determined on her course.

It seemed clear enough. Demon *could* love her – of that she felt sure. All she needed to do was to make sure he did before she agreed to marry him.

She needed to make him fall in love with her – she would have scoffed at the thought a mere month ago and labelled it an impossible task. Now, however, the prospects looked good. If last night and this morning were any guide, he was already halfway there.

He cared for her – was very careful of her; he clearly enjoyed giving her pleasure. He'd pleasured her to her toes. In a variety of ways. And remained considerate and caring afterward, in his usual overbearing way.

She spent the drive sunk in pleasant memories, but when they rolled through Newmarket, she inwardly shook herself, and sternly told herself to stop thinking of such things. She'd get precious little pleasuring in the days to come – at least until he came to love her.

She slanted a glance at him, then looked away, and rehearsed her plans yet again.

He spoke as they turned through the gates of Hillgate End.

'In case you're wondering, I intend telling the General that, due to an inadvertent circumstance, you and I were seen together in a chamber at The Angel last night by one of the ton's most rabid scandalmongers, and consequently, you've agreed to marry me.'

She turned her head and met his eyes. 'I haven't.'

His face grew hard. 'You've done rather a lot since last evening – precisely what is it you don't believe you've done?'

His tone was precise, his words excessively clipped. She ignored the warning. 'I haven't agreed to marry you.'

The sound he made was frustration incarnate. Abruptly, he sat up. 'Flick – you have been well and truly and very thoroughly compromised this time. You have no choice—'

'On the contrary.' She held his gaze. 'I can still say no.'

Demon stared at her, then narrowed his eyes. 'Why would you want to say no?'

'I have my reasons.'

'Which are?'

She considered him, then said, 'I told you I needed something more than mere circumstance to persuade me to marriage. What you did last night wasn't it.'

He frowned, then shook his head, his expression turning grim. 'Let me rephrase my intention. I'll tell the General what I said before, then, if you still won't agree to our marriage, I'll tell him the rest – how I spent all night in your bed – and half the night in you.'

She raised her brows, considered him steadily, then looked away. 'You know you'll never tell him that.'

Demon stared at her, at her pure profile, at her chin resolutely firm, her nose tip-tilted – and fought down the urge to lay his hands on her.

She was right, of course – he would never do anything to harm her standing with the General, one of the few people she cared about. The General would very likely understand why he'd acted as he had, but he wouldn't understand her refusal. Any more than he did.

Forcing himself to relax, he sank back against the seat and stared out of the window. The horses clopped on.

'What story did you concoct for the household to explain your trip to Bury?' He asked the question without looking at Flick; he felt her glance, then she answered.

'That I was going to see Melissa Blackthorn – her family lives just past Bury. We often visit on the spur of the moment.'

Demon considered. 'Very well. You intended visiting Miss Blackthorn – Gillies offered to drive you in the hope of seeing the fight, but when you reached Bury, the street was blocked with incoming traffic and you got trapped in the melee. It got dark – you were still trapped. Not being *au fait* with prizefights, you sought refuge at The Angel.' He glanced at Flick. 'Hopefully, no one will learn of your disguise or your story to gain a room.'

She shrugged. 'Bury's far enough away – none of the staff have family that far afield.'

Demon humphed. 'We can but hope. So – you were at The Angel when I arrived, intending to stay for the fight. I saw you . . . and then Lord Selbourne saw us. Thus, this morning, I brought you straight home so we can deal with the current situation.' He glanced at Flick. 'Can you see any holes?'

She shook her head, then grimaced. 'I do hate misleading the General, though.'

Demon looked out of the window. 'Given we've struggled to avoid all mention of Dillon and the syndicate thus far, I can't see any point mentioning them now.' It would only upset the General more to know the current imbroglio was a result of Flick's championing Dillon.

271

The shadows of the drive fell behind them; ahead, the manor basked in sunshine. The carriage rocked to a stop. Demon opened the door, stepped out, then handed Flick down. Jacobs opened the front door before they knocked; Demon led Flick into the cool hall, then released her.

Mrs. Fogarty came bustling up, fussing about Flick, who slid around her questions easily. Flick cast a watchful, questioning glance at Demon – he met it with his blandest expression. She frowned fleetingly, but had to reorganize her expression to deal with Mrs. Fogarty. With the housekeeper in close attendance, Flick headed to her room.

Demon watched her go, then his lips lifted, just a little at the ends. Challenges – more challenges. Swinging on his heel, he headed for the library.

'So – let me see if I've got this right.'

In the chair behind his desk, the General sat back and steepled his fingers. 'You and Felicity were *again* caught in an apparently compromising situation, only this time by someone who will take great delight in ruining Felicity's good name. You, however, are perfectly prepared to marry the chit, but she's proving headstrong, and jibbing at the bit. So, instead of pressing marriage on her in such an abrupt manner, you suggest I agree to send her to your mother, Lady Horatia, to enjoy the delights of the Season in London. Under your mother's wing, even without a formal declaration, it will be surmised that she's your intended, but the interlude will give Felicity time to adjust to the position, and accept marriage to you as the sensible course.' He looked up at Demon. 'Is that right?'

Standing before the windows, Demon nodded. 'Naturally, if, in the course of her time in London, she meets any other gentleman and forms a lasting attachment that is returned, I give you my word to release her without complaint. It's her happiness – her reputation – I'm interested in securing.'

'Indeed. Hmm.' The General's eyes twinkled. 'Well then, no reason whatever she should take exception to a sojourn in London. Do her good anyway, to see all she's missed stuck up here with an old man.'

The lunch gong boomed; the General chuckled and rose. 'Capital notion all around. Let's go tell her, what?'

Demon smiled easily. Beside the General, he strolled toward the dining room.

'London?' Flick stared at Demon, sitting directly opposite across the luncheon table.

'Hmm – the capital. My mother would love to have you stay with her.'

It was all so transparent. Flick glanced to her right, to where the General, nodding mildly, was helping himself to more peas. He seemed serenely unconcerned about her reputation, for which she was honestly grateful to Demon; she couldn't have borne it if the old dear had been distressed. Yet she was fairly certain the only reason he was in such fine fettle, knowing her reputation was, if not precisely in shreds, then certainly rather tattered, was because he believed a stay in London under Lady Horatia's wing would make her change her mind and accept his protégé as her husband.

There was a good chance he was right – she certainly hoped so.

And there were a number of good reasons for falling in with Demon's plan. Not least was the fact that Bletchley had gone to London. And while she'd never before felt any interest in tonnish affairs, if she was to marry Demon, then she would need to find her feet in that arena. She was also suddenly insatiably curious as to how, and with whom, he spent his days in London.

Quite aside from all else, if she was going to make him fall in love with her, she needed to be with him.

273

Her eyes locked on his, she nodded. 'Yes – I think I'd like that.'

He smiled. 'Good. I'll drive you up tomorrow.'

'How on earth did that happen?'

Early the next morning, already on the road to London, drawn thence by Demon's powerful bays, Flick swivelled on the curricle's seat and glanced back at Gillies, perched behind. 'I thought you were following him?'

Gillies looked pained; Demon answered. 'We thought Bletchley was planning to take one of the special coaches back to London from Bury – Gillies heard him asking where to catch them. After watching Bletchley throughout the fight – and learning nothing – at the end, Gillies, quite reasonably, moved to the gate leading back to Bury and waited for Bletchley to pass him. He never did.'

'Oh?' Flick glanced back at Gillies.

He grimaced. 'He must have caught a ride on some cart back to Newmarket.'

'And then hired a horse and, bold as you please, came cantering up the manor drive.' Demon set his teeth. That had been too close for his liking – luckily, Bletchley had not seen Flick, nor she, him.

Flick sat back. 'I nearly dropped a vase when Jacobs mentioned he'd called, asking after Dillon.'

'Thankfully, Jacobs sent him on his way.' Demon eased the bays past a farm cart, then let the reins run free. 'Bletchley returned to the Rutland Arms and caught the evening mail to London.'

'So we've lost him.'

He glanced at Flick, relieved to see nothing more than a frown on her face. 'For the moment. But we'll come up with him again, never fear.'

'London's very big.'

'True, but it's possible to keep watch on the likely places Bletchley might meet with a group of gentlemen. The classes don't mix freely at all that many venues. Limmers, Tattersalls, and a few other, less savory haunts.'

'Still, isn't it like looking for the proverbial needle?'

Demon hesitated, then grimaced. 'There might be another way to identify likely members of the syndicate independent of any meeting, which should make it easier, if a meeting does occur, to track someone to it – and so identify all the syndicate.'

'Another way?'

Flick's eyes were firmly fixed on his face. With his gaze on his speeding horses, he outlined his discussions with Heathcote Montague, and what they hoped to discover.

At the end of his explanation, Flick sat back. 'Good. So we haven't given up on helping Dillon – it's just that our investigations have changed direction.'

'Speaking of Dillon, does he know you've left Newmarket?'

'I sent a message with Jiggs – I told him to tell Dillon that we had to follow up clues in London, that I didn't know when we'd be back, but that he should stay in hiding until we returned. I promised I'd write and tell him what we discover. Jiggs will deliver my letters.'

Demon nodded. If nothing else, he'd distanced her from Dillon – while in London, she could concentrate on him, and herself. He was certain his mother would encourage her in that endeavor, while at the same time helpfully denying Flick – a young lady in her charge – the license she would need to pursue Bletchley, the syndicate, or any other villain. Despite the fact both Bletchley and the syndicate were in London, he felt perfectly sanguine about taking Flick there.

As for the danger posed by Lord Selbourne, that was, at least temporarily, in abeyance; his lordship had gone directly into Norfolk to visit with his sister.

The curricle sped south through the bright morning, wheels rolling smoothly along the macadam. Despite losing Bletchley, despite having to revise his plans to accommodate a certain angel's stubbornness, Demon felt in remarkable charity with the world. Their current direction felt right – this was obviously the way to get Flick to say yes. She was, beyond question, already his, but if they had to go through a formal wooing, he was content to remove to London. It was, after all, his home ground. He was looking forward to showing her about – showing her off. Her bright-eyed innocence continued to delight him; through her eyes, he saw aspects of his world he'd long considered boring in an entirely new light.

He slanted a glance at her; the breeze was tugging at her curls, setting her bonnet ribbons twirling. Her eyes were wide, her gaze fixed ahead; her lips, delicate rose, were full, lush, lightly curved. She looked good enough to eat.

Abruptly, he looked ahead, the memory of the taste of her flooding him. Gritting his teeth, he willed the distraction away. He was going to have to keep his demons caged for the foreseeable future – there was no sense in teasing and taunting them. That was the one drawback in placing Flick under his mother's wing – she would be safe from all others, but also safe from him.

Even should she wish otherwise, which was an intriguing, potentially helpful, notion. Mulling over the possibility, he sent his whip out to tickle his leader's ear and urge his horses on.

Beside him, Flick watched the countryside roll past with a keen and eager eye. Anticipation grew with every mile – it was hard to preserve a proper calm. Soon they would reach London; soon, she would see Demon in his other milieu, his other guise. She knew he was considered a rake extraordinaire, yet, until now, her knowledge of him had been restricted to Demon in the country; she had a shrewd notion his tonnish persona would be different from the one she knew. As the miles sped past, she spent the time imagining, envisioning a more graceful, more elegant, more potent presence – the glittering glamor he would assume when in society, a cloak donned over his true character, all the traits so familiar to her.

She couldn't wait to see it.

Despite losing Bletchley, it was impossible to remain sober. Her mood was buoyant, her heart light – she was looking forward to life in a completely new way – facing in a completely unlooked-for direction.

Marriage to Demon – it was a dizzying thought, a dream she had never dared dream. And now she was committed to the enterprise – totally and absolutely. Not that she entertained any doubts about success. In her present mood, that was impossible.

From all she'd heard of London, it would provide the setting – one with the best opportunities – for her to en courage Demon to give her his heart. Then all would be perfect, and her dream would come true.

She sat beside him with barely concealed impatience, waiting for London to appear.

When it did, she blinked. And wrinkled her nose. And winced at the raucous cries. The streets were packed with carriages of every description, the pavements teeming. She had never imagined such close-packed humanity – fresh from the broad plain of Newmarket Heath, she found it disturbing. She felt hemmed in on every side with the sheer weight of humankind. And the noise. And the squalor. And the urchins – everywhere.

She'd lived in London for only a short time before, with her aunt at her London house. She couldn't remember any sights such as those she now saw, but it had, after all, been a long time ago. As Demon concentrated on his horses, deftly tacking through the traffic, she edged closer until she could feel the warmth of his body through her pelisse.

To her relief, the fashionable areas were more as she recalled – quiet streets lined with elegant houses, neat squares with fenced gardens at their centers. Indeed, this part of London was better, neater, more beautiful than her memories. Her aunt had lived in Bloomsbury, which was not nearly as fashionable as Berkeley Square, which was where Demon took her.

He reined in the bays before a large mansion, as imposing as the most imposing she'd seen. As Gillies took the reins and Demon stepped down, Flick stared up at the three-storeyed facade and suddenly knew what 'being not quite up to snuff' felt like.

Then Demon took her hand; stilling her fears, she shuffled along the seat and let him hand her to the ground. Clutching her parasol's handle tightly, she took his proffered arm, and climbed the steps beside him.

If the house was imposing, slightly scarifying, the butler, Highthorpe, was worse. He opened the door to Demon's knock and looked down his beaked nose at her.

'Ah, Highthorpe – how's the leg?' With an affection ate smile at the butler, Demon handed Flick over the threshold. 'Is her ladyship in?'

'My leg is quite improved, thank you, sir.' Holding the door wider, Highthorpe bowed deferentially; he closed it after them, and turned, his starchy demeanor somewhat softer. 'Her ladyship, I believe, is in her sanctuary.'

Demon's smile deepened. 'This is Miss Parteger, Highthorpe. She'll be staying with Mama for the nonce. Gillies will bring her bags around.'

It might have been a trick of the light beaming through the fanlight, yet Flick could have sworn a gleam of interest flashed in Highthorpe's eyes. He smiled as he bowed again to her. 'Miss. I'll mention to Mrs. Helmsley to prepare a room for you at once – I'll have your bags taken there. No doubt you'll wish to refresh yourself after your journey.'

'Thank you.' Flick smiled back – Highthorpe suddenly sounded much more comfortable. Demon drew her on.

'I'll leave you in the drawing room while I fetch Mama.' He opened a door and ushered her inside.

One glance about the elegant blue-and-white room had her turning back to him. 'Are you sure this is a good idea? I could always stay with my aunt—'

'Mama will be delighted to meet you.' He made the statement as if she hadn't spoken. 'I won't be above a few minutes.'

He went out, closing the door behind him. Flick stared at the white painted panels – he didn't come back in. Sighing, she looked around.

She considered the white damask settee, then looked down at her plain, definitely old, outmoded pelisse. Putting one in contact with the other seemed like sacrilege. So she stayed on her feet and shook out her skirts, trying vainly to rearrange them to hide the creases. What would Lady Horatia – the lady who presided over such a wellappointed drawing room – think of her in her far-fromelegant attire?

The point proved academic.

The latch clicked, the door swung wide, and a tall, commandingly elegant lady swept in.

And descended on her, a huge smile on her face, her eyes alight with a welcome Flick could not imagine what she'd done to deserve. But there was no mistaking the warmth with which Lady Horatia embraced her.

'My dear!' Touching a scented cheek to hers, Lady Horatia straightened and held her at arms' length, not to inspect her dowdy pelisse but to look into her face. 'I'm so *very* delighted

279

to meet you, and to welcome you to this house. Indeed' – she shot a glance at Demon – 'I understand it will be my pleasure to introduce you to the ton.' Looking back at Flick, Lady Horatia beamed. 'I couldn't be more delighted!'

Flick smiled warmly, gratefully.

Lady Horatia's smile deepened; her blue eyes, very like Demon's, twinkled expressively. 'Now we can send Harry away and get acquainted.'

Flick blinked, then realized, as Lady Horatia turned to Demon, that she was referring to him.

'You may come back for dinner.' Lady Horatia raised a brow – the gesture appeared haughtily teasing. 'I presume you are free?'

Demon – Harry – merely smiled. 'Of course.' He looked at Flick. 'I'll see you at seven.' With a nod for her and another for his mother, he turned and strolled to the door; it shut softly behind him.

'Well!' Lady Horatia turned to Flick, and smiled exultantly. 'At last!'

Chapter Fifteen

Despite their languid elegance, when Cynsters acted, things happened in a rush. After luncheon, Horatia whisked Flick into her carriage, off to a family afternoon tea.

'Grosvenor Square's not far,' Horatia assured her. 'And Helena is going to be as delighted as I to meet you.'

'Helena?' Flick sifted through the names Horatia had mentioned over luncheon.

'My sister-in-law. Mother of Sylvester, better known as Devil, now Duke of St. Ives. Helena is the Dowager. She and I only had sons – she, Sylvester and Richard, me, Vane and Harry. Sylvester, Richard and Vane are all married—' Horatia glanced at Flick. 'Didn't Harry tell you?'

Flick shook her head; Horatia grimaced. 'He always was one to ignore details. So—' Horatia settled back; Flick dutifully paid attention. 'Sylvester married Honoria Anstruther-Wetherby over a year ago. Sebastian, their son, is eight months old. Honoria's increasing again, so while they'll doubtless come to town for the Season proper, the ducal couple are presently in Cambridgeshire.

'Which brings us to Vane. He married Patience Debbington last November. Patience is increasing, too, so we don't expect to see them for a few weeks, either. As for Richard, he married *quite* unexpectedly in Scotland before Christmas. There was a spot of bother – Sylvester, Honoria, Vane,

Patience and Helena – and a few others – went north, but all seems to have settled comfortably and Helena is in alt at the prospect of more grandchildren.

'However,' Horatia declared, reaching her peroration, 'as neither Honoria nor Patience, nor Richard's Catriona, were young misses in need of help and guidance, neither Helena nor I have *ever* had a young lady to fuss over.' Eyes bright, she patted Flick's hand. 'So I'm afraid, my dear, that you'll have to put up with the two of us fussing over you – you're our last chance in that arena, you see.'

Flick smiled spontaneously. 'On the contrary, I would be glad of your help.' Her gaze drifted over the fashionable ladies and gentlemen strolling the pavements. 'I've no real idea how one should go on in London.' She looked down at her pretty but definitely not chic gown, blushed slightly, and caught Horatia's eye. 'Please do hint me in the right direction – I would be very unhappy to be an embarrassment to you and D – Harry.'

'Nonsense.' Horatia squeezed Flick's hand fondly. 'I doubt you could embarrass me if you tried.' Her eyes twinkled. 'And certainly not my son.' Flick blushed; Horatia chuckled. 'With a little guidance, a little experience, and a little town bronze, you'll do very well.'

Grateful for the reassurance, Flick sat back and wondered how to broach the question uppermost in her mind. Horatia clearly viewed her as a future daughter-in-law, which was what she hoped to be. *But* she hadn't yet accepted Demon, and wouldn't, not until . . . Drawing a determined breath, she looked at Horatia. 'Did D – Harry explain that I haven't *agreed* . . .'

'Oh, indeed. And I can't tell you how grateful I am that you had the wit not to accept him straightaway.' Horatia frowned disapprovingly. 'These things should take time – time enough to organize a proper wedding, at least. Unfortunately, that's not the way *they* see it.' Her tone made it clear she was speaking of the males of the family. 'If it's left to them, they'll sweep you past a cleric and into bed with the barest "by-your-leave!"'

Flick choked; misinterpreting, Horatia patted her hand. 'I know you won't mind my plain speaking – you're old enough to understand these things.'

Flick went to nod and stopped herself; her blush was because she *did* know, and appreciated Horatia's insight – that was certainly how Demon had imagined it. Only, being him, he'd transposed the cleric and the bed. 'I think time – at least a little time – is a necessity in this case.'

'Good!' The carriage rocked, then halted; Horatia looked up. 'Ah – here we are.'

The groom opened the door and let down the steps, then handed Flick, then his mistress, to the pavement. Horatia nodded at the magnificent mansion reached by a sweeping set of steps. 'St. Ives House.'

The afternoon had turned gloriously fine – tables, chairs and *chaises* were set out on the lawn of the enclosed gardens. At Lady Horatia's side, Flick left the house, stepping past the deferential butler and onto the terrace. She saw a small host of well-dressed ladies, ranging in age from very old to a girl barely out of the schoolroom, congregating on the lawn.

There was not a gentleman in sight.

Parasols dipped and swayed above smart coiffures, protecting delicate complexions. Other ladies simply sat back, glorying in the weak sunshine, smiling, laughing and chatting. While substantial, the noise was not overpowering – indeed, it subtly beckoned. There was a gaiety, a relaxed sense of ease pervading the group, unexpected in conjunction with its blatantly tonnish air. This wasn't fashion and brittle frivolity – this was a fashionable family gathering; the distinction was clear.

The large number of guests was a surprise; Horatia had assured her she would meet only family members and a few close connections. Before she managed to fully grasp the reality, a beautiful older woman came sweeping up to meet them as they descended the steps to the lawn.

''Oratia!' The Dowager exchanged kisses with her sister-in-law, but her gaze had already moved on to Flick. 'And who is this?' A glorious smile and bright eyes softened the abrupt query.

'Allow me to present Miss Felicity Parteger – Helena, Dowager Duchess of St. Ives, my dear.'

Flick curtsied deeply. 'It's a pleasure to make your acquaintance, Your Grace.'

As she straightened, Helena took her hand, directing an arrested, inquiring glance at Horatia.

'Felicity is Gordon Caxton's ward.'

With one blink, Helena had the reference pegged. 'Ah – the good General.' She smiled at Flick. 'Is he well?'

'Yes, thank you, ma'am.'

With the air of one who could contain herself no longer, Horatia broke in, 'Harry brought Felicity up to town. She'll be staying with us in Berkeley Square, and I'll be taking her into society.'

Helena's gaze flew to Horatia's face; her smile deepened, and deepened. Looking again at Flick, she positively beamed. 'My dear, I am so *very glad* to meet you!'

Before Flick could blink, the Dowager embraced her enthusiastically, then, one arm about her waist, bustled her down the lawn. With a Gallic charm impossible to resist, the Dowager introduced her to her sisters-in-law first, then the older ladies, and eventually the younger ones, two of whom, clearly twins, were adjured to ensure Flick wanted for nothing, including help with names and relationships.

The pair were the most ravishing blonde beauties Flick had

ever seen. They had skin like alabaster, eyes like cornflower pools and a wealth of ringlets almost as golden as her own. She expected them to hang back – they might be younger than she, but she was definitely not in their social league. To her surprise, they smiled at her delightedly – every bit as delightedly as their mother and aunts had – and swooped forward to link arms with her.

'Excellent! I thought this party would be just the usual thing – pleasant but hardly exciting. Instead, we get to meet you!'

Flick blinked – she glanced from one to the other, trying to remember which was which. 'I've never thought of myself as exciting.'

'Hah! You must be, otherwise Demon would never have looked your way.'

The second girl laughed. 'Don't mind Amanda.' She grinned as Flick glanced around. 'I'm Amelia. You'll get used to telling us apart – we're not identical.'

They weren't, but they were very much alike.

'Tell us,' Amelia urged, 'how long have you known Demon?'

'We ask,' Amanda put in, 'because until the last few weeks he's been severely testing our sanity by watching over us at the balls and major parties.'

'Indeed. So we know he went up to Newmarket a few weeks ago. Is that where you met him?'

'We did meet at Newmarket,' Flick agreed, 'but I've lived there since I was seven, and I've known Demon from the first.'

Both girls stared at her, then Amanda frowned. 'What the devil's he been doing, keeping you hidden away like that?'

'Excuse us for asking, but you are older than us, aren't you? We're eighteen.'

'I'm twenty,' Flick replied. The twins were taller and

certainly more socially assured, but there was a subtle difference; she hadn't imagined herself younger than them.

'So why,' Amanda reiterated, 'didn't Demon bring you down last year? He's not one for dragging his boots – not him.'

'He does tend to drive fast,' Flick grinned. 'He didn't bring me down last year, because ... well, he didn't really know I existed last year.'

That comment, of course, led to further questions, further revelations. Which cleared the way for Flick to ask why Demon had been watching them.

'Sometimes I think it's simply to drive us mad, but truly they can't seem to help themselves, poor dears.' Amanda shook her head. 'It's something in the blood.'

'Luckily, once they marry, they're not such a bother. They'd still interfere if they could, mind you, but Honoria, Patience and Catriona have so far kept Devil, Vane and Richard out of our way.' Amelia looked at Flick. 'And now you'll be here to keep Demon occupied.'

'With any luck,' Amanda added dryly, 'the others will find ladies to dote on *before* we become ape-leaders.'

Flick grinned. 'Surely they can't be *that* inhibiting.'

'Oh, can't they?' the twins chorused. They promptly recounted a series of events illustrating their claim, in the process giving Flick vignettes of Demon within the ton – surrounded by beautiful women. Sensing her interest, the twins dismissively waved aside his London conquests.

'Don't worry about them – they never last long, and now he'll be too busy with you.'

'Watching over *you*, thank heaven!' Amanda raised her eyes to the skies. '*Only* got two more to go.'

Amelia chuckled, and looked at Flick. 'Gabriel and Lucifer.'

'Who?'

The twins laughed, and explained about their older male cousins, the group known as the Bar Cynster.

'We're not supposed to know about the Bar Cynster, so remember not to mention it to Demon,' Amanda warned.

They continued, giving her a potted history of the family – who was whose child, brother, sister. They beckoned the only younger girl over – their cousin, Heather, nearly sixteeen.

'I won't be presented until next year,' Heather sighed, 'but Mama said I could attend the family events this year. Aunt Louise is giving an informal ball next week.'

'You'll be invited,' Amanda assured Flick. 'We'll make sure your name is on the list.'

Amelia stifled a snort. '*Mama* will make sure your name is on the list.'

Minutes later, they were summoned to distribute the tea cups. Flick did her share, moving easily among the company. Although every lady she paused beside spoke with her, beyond the information Horatia had imparted regarding her visit, not one word was said – not one inference drawn. At least, not within her hearing. Every lady made her feel welcome, and if, by dint of subtle questioning, they extracted her entire life history from her, it was no more than she'd expected. But they were the very opposite of nosy, and certainly not judgmental – their warm approval, their ready acceptance, the protection of the group so openly offered very nearly overwhelmed her.

One very old, very sharp-eyed lady closed a claw about her hand. 'If you find yourself in a ballroom, gel, and at a loss what to do, then find one of us – even those flighty flibberti-gibbets' – Lady Osbaldestone's black gaze skewered the twins, then she looked up at Flick – 'and just ask. The ton can be a confusing place, but that's what family's for – you needn't feel shy.'

'Thank you, ma'am.' Flick bobbed a curtsy. 'I'll remember.'

287

'Good. Now you may give me one of those macaroons. Dare say Clara there would like one, too.'

Lady Osbaldestone was not the only one to offer advice and support. Long before the afternoon came to an end and she and Lady Horatia took their leave, amid embraces, waves and plans to meet again, Flick felt she had literally been gathered to the bosom of the Cynster clan.

Settling back in the carriage, Horatia closed her eyes. Flick did the same, and looked back over the afternoon.

They were amazing. She'd known Demon had a large family, but that the Cynsters would prove such a close tribe had been a pleasant surprise. She'd never had a real family – not since her parents had died. She'd never felt part of a continuing whole, a group that had a before and would also have an after, beyond the individual members. She'd been alone since the age of seven. The General, Dillon and the Hillgate End household had become her surrogate family, but this was something very different.

If she married Demon, she would become, once again, part of a real family. One in which there were other women to talk to, to turn to for support; one where, by unspoken accord, the men watched over the young women, even if they weren't their sisters.

In some ways, it was all new to her – in other ways, at some deeper level, it touched a chord that resonated deeply. It felt very right. Opening her eyes, she stared, smiling but unseeing, out of the window, deeply glad at the prospect of becoming a Cynster.

Two mornings later, in a far from glorious mood, Demon gritted his teeth and turned his bays toward the park. For the third time in as many days, he'd arrived at his parents' house only to learn that Miss Parteger was out.

He'd called on the afternoon of the day he'd brought her to

288

town, imagining her sitting alone and forlorn while his mother napped. Instead, they'd been gossiping at his Aunt Helena's – and he knew very well about what. He'd swallowed his disappointment, uneasily surprised that he'd felt it, and reflected that this was precisely why he'd brought Flick to town – so his dear family, especially the female half, could help her make up her mind to marry him. He had no doubt they would do so. They were past masters at engineering weddings. As far as he was concerned, they could exercise their talents on his behalf.

So he'd retired, leaving no message – nothing to alert his too-perceptive mother that he'd been impatient enough to call. He'd arrived promptly for dinner, but discovered that seeing Felicity over a dinner table with his parents present didn't satisfy his appetite.

Yesterday, he'd called at eleven – a perfectly innocuous time. Turning up too close to breakfast would have been too revealing. Highthorpe had looked at him with sympathy and informed him that his mother, his aunt and the young lady had gone shopping.

He knew that meant they'd be away for hours. And they'd be in one of those silly, feminine moods when they returned, wanting to tell him about frills and furbelows, unreceptive to the notion of paying attention to him.

He'd retreated in good order, noting again that this was a part of why he'd brought Flick to town – so she could be seduced by the entertainments available as his wife. Shopping, to the female soul, ranked high as entertainment.

In other arenas, fate was being more helpful; he'd heard on the grapevine that Rattletrap Selbourne had contracted mumps from his sister's offspring and was not expected in town this Season. Selbourne was one complication he could temporarily put from his mind.

Today, he'd arrived at Berkeley Square midmorning, quite

sure he'd find Flick waiting to impress him in one of her new gowns.

His mother had taken her off to the park.

He was seriously considering having a very pithy few words with his mother.

Feathering his curricle through the Stanhope Gate, narrowly missing an approaching landau, he tried to rein in his unreasonable temper and still the urgent pounding in his blood. He was surprised at the strength of his reaction, at the sense of deprivation that had seized him. It was, he reassured himself, simply because he'd got used to seeing her daily, nothing else. The effect would wear off, subside.

It would have to. In town, in the lead up to the Season, he would meet her only briefly, in the park under the watchful eyes of the ton's matrons, or in a crowded ballroom, likewise overseen. Private hours such as he'd grown accustomed to in the country were no longer part of their schedule.

Turning into the Avenue, he replaced his grim expression with his usual, politely bored mask.

He found Flick sitting in his mother's barouche, smiling sweetly at a host of gentlemen who, parading with other young ladies on the lawn, were eyeing her speculatively. His mother was deep in conversation with his aunt Helena, whose landau was drawn up alongside.

Smothering a curse, he angled his curricle in behind his mother's carriage and reined in. Gillies came running to hold the bays' heads. Tying off the reins, Demon jumped down and stalked along the verge.

Flick had heard the curricle pull up, and she'd turned; now she smiled, gloriously welcoming. For an instant, he was lost in her eyes, in her glow – his mask slipped; he started to smile, his usual taunting, teasing smile.

He caught himself just in time and substituted an easy, affable expression and a cool smile. Only his eyes, as they met hers, held any heat. If his mother or his sharp-eyed aunt caught a glimpse of that other smile, they'd know a great deal too much.

Flick held out her hand; he took it, bowing easily. 'Well met, my dear.'

Straightening, he exchanged polite nods with his mother and aunt, then looked back at Flick. He hadn't released her hand. 'Can I tempt you to a stroll about the lawns?'

'Oh, yes!' Eagerly, she shifted forward. Demon suddenly understood her interest in the couples on the lawn: simple envy. She was used to riding every day – she would miss the exercise.

His smile deepening, he opened the carriage door. Over Flick's head, his mother glared at him and mouthed 'new dress.' Inwardly grinning, he helped Flick down, very willing to let his gaze roam. 'Is that new?'

She threw him an ingenuous smile. 'Yes.' Releasing his hand, she twirled, then halted. 'Do you like it?'

His gaze had locked on her body, sweetly encased in lavender-blue twill; now he lifted it to her face – and couldn't find words to answer. His chest had seized, his wits scrambled – the pounding in his blood escalated. The sheer glory of her face, her eyes, didn't help – he'd forgotten what it felt like to be smitten by an angel.

His mother and aunt were watching, eagle-eyed; he cleared his throat and managed to smile urbanely. 'You look ... extremely fetching.' She looked delectable, delicious – and he was suddenly ravenous.

Retaking her hand, he laid it on his sleeve. 'We'll take a turn down to the flowerbeds and back.'

He heard an amused 'humph' from the carriage, but he didn't look back as they strolled onto the lawn, too busy enjoying the sight – and the sensations – of having his angel on his arm again. She smiled up at him – her golden curls

291

caught his eye. 'You've had your hair trimmed.'

'Yes.' She angled her head this way and that so he could appreciate the subtle changes. Her curls had always framed her face, but loosely. Now, by dint of artful clipping, the frame was more complete, more stable – if anything, brighter. 'It suits me, I think.'

Demon nodded. 'It's undeniably elegant.' Lowering his gaze, he met her eyes. 'I expect it complements your new evening gowns well.'

She blinked her eyes wide. 'How did you know? ...'

He grinned. 'I called yesterday and heard you'd gone shopping. As it appears you've visited a modiste, and I know my mother, the rest is easy.'

'Helena came, too. It was ...' She paused, then smiled at him. 'Very enjoyable.'

Content, Demon returned her smile, then looked ahead.

They strolled in silence, as they had so often on the Heath. Neither felt any pressing need of words, deeply easy in the other's company. Flick felt the breeze ruffle her skirts, felt them flap against Demon's polished Hessians. The steely strength of the muscles beneath her fingers, the sense of strength that reached for her, surrounded her and lapped her about, was blissfully welcome.

She'd missed him. Her singing heart told her that; her exulting senses confirmed it. Tipping her face to the sun, she smiled, aglow with an emotion that could only be love.

She slanted him a glance – only to find him watching her. He blinked, a frown forming in his eyes. Even as she looked, his face hardened.

He looked ahead. 'I thought you might like to know what we've discovered about Bletchley.'

Guilt struck. In the whirl of the past days, caught up in her own discoveries, she'd forgotten Dillon and his problems. 'Yes, of course.' Strengthening her voice, she looked ahead.

292

'What have you learned?'

From the corner of her eye, she saw Demon grimace.

'We've confirmed Bletchley arrived on the Newmarket coach. It stops at Aldgate. We checked, but he isn't known in the area.' They reached the flowerbeds and turned onto the gravel path beside the display. 'Montague – my agent – is organizing a watch on the venues gentlemen use to meet with the riffraff they occasionally hire. If Bletchley appears, we'll pick up his trail again.'

Flick frowned. 'Is this Mr. Montague the same man you came down to see before?' Demon nodded; she asked, 'Has he learned anything by looking for the money?'

'Not yet, but there's a large number of possibilities to check. Stocks, bonds, deposits, foreign transactions – he'll check everywhere. He *has* finalized the approximate sums we're looking for – the amounts taken from each fixed race over the autumn season, and the first race this year.'

'Is it a lot?'

Demon met her gaze. 'Enormous.'

Reaching the walk's end, they turned back across the lawn, passing close by a number of other couples. With easy grace, Demon exchanged cool nods, distant smiles and steered her on. Flick mimicked his politesse with a calmly serene expression.

Once they were free, Demon glanced at her, then lengthened his stride. She kept pace easily, but wondered why he was hurrying.

'The total amount taken is simply so huge,' he continued, 'it's utterly inconceivable that it won't show up somewhere. That's one encouraging point. Luckily, we've still got a few weeks before informing the stewards becomes imperative.'

'Is there anything I can do?'

'No.' He glanced down at her, his expression impassive. 'I'll check with Montague in a day or so, if he doesn't contact

293

me.' He hesitated, then added, 'I'll let you know when we learn anything to the point.'

She had to nod – they were almost at the carriage. Glancing at Demon's face, she noted the languidly bored mask that seemed to slide over his features, sensed the steely control that infused his movements, making them appear lazily indifferent. She assumed it was his London persona – his wolf's clothing, as it were.

But she didn't understand why, when he handed her into the carriage and bowed gracefully, he didn't meet her eye.

Horatia tapped his arm. 'You'll receive your invitation to an informal ball Louise is giving today. The ball's early next week – I'll expect you to escort myself and Felicity.'

Demon blinked. 'Won't Papa escort you?'

Horatia waved dismissively. 'You know your father – he'll want to call at White's on the way.'

A grim expression flashed in Demon's eyes, then was gone. Resigned, he inclined his head. 'As you wish.'

As he straightened, his eyes touched Flick's, just for a second, just long enough to reassure her. With a bow to Horatia and Helena, he turned away.

'Don't be late!' Horatia called after him. 'We'll be dining there.'

A wave showed he'd heard. Taking the reins, he leapt into his curricle, then gravel crunched, and he was gone.

Chapter Sixteen

'*Just look at them*!' Amanda hissed disgustedly in Flick's ear, then gracefully twirled away.

Amelia took her place. 'Even if they're dancing, they still sneak looks.' She dipped and swayed, and continued *sotto voce*, 'And there's usually one standing on the sidelines, like Demon is now, so if we rip a flounce or tear a ribbon and try to slip away, they still catch us!'

Flick smiled at her partner and linked hands – she gave no sign of having heard the twins' grumblings. They were whirling and twirling their way through a country dance; about them, Louise Cynster's ballroom was filled with all the family presently in London, together with family friends. As the ball was informal, and most guests related to one another, an air of easy gaiety prevailed. There were many younger people present – girls like Heather and younger males, too – which underscored the feeling of a family celebration.

Flick dipped under her partner's hand and smiled at the innocuous young man; the twins did the same, no sign of their disgruntlement showing in their serene faces.

In the days since she'd first met them, they'd spoken at length on the watchful propensities of their male cousins, but Flick hadn't entirely believed them. Now she did. They did watch – she could see how the twins would find it irksome.

While Gabriel and Lucifer had both taken to the floor, they could occasionally be glimpsed through the press, checking on the twins. As for Demon, he stood at the side of the floor, not even bothering with the guise of chatting, his gaze fixed, distinctly intimidating, on their set.

At first glance, it was a wonder any male with an ounce of self-preservatory instinct would dare invite them onto the floor. However, the younger gentlemen – those not much older than the twins themselves – seemed impervious to any threat. As they were truly innocent of entertaining any impure designs on the twins, they seemed to take it for granted they were safe.

Of course, such innocent young men fell far short of the twins' requirements. Which was what was irritating them so. Flick understood; thus far, she'd danced only with the same sort of youthful gentleman – and was utterly bored.

When the dance ended, and they'd thanked and dismissed their too-youthful cavaliers, she linked arms, a twin on each side. 'They're only trying to protect you – they've met too many bounders, and so want to warn all such men away from you.'

Amelia sighed. 'That's all very well, but their definition of 'bounder' is rather wide.'

Amanda snorted. 'If they think a gentleman has had so much as a single impure thought – a single mental flirt with any less-than-proper idea – then he's a bounder.'

'Which tends to thin the ranks rather drastically.'

'And is absolutely no help in our campaign.'

'Campaign?' Flick stopped beside an alcove hosting three large potted palms.

Amanda glanced about, then took her hand and tugged – they all slipped into the shadowy space behind the palms.

'We've decided . . . ,' Amanda started.

'. . . after discussions with Catriona,' Amelia put in, 'the lady of the vale – a sort of wise woman—'

'That we're *not* going to wait patiently, doing nothing but look pretty while suitable gentlemen look us over and debate whether or not to make an offer—'

'No.' Amelia lifted her head. 'We're going to make our *own* choice.'

Amanda's eyes glittered. 'We're going to look *them* over, and decide who *we'll* choose, not wait to be chosen.'

Flick laughed – an arm about each, she hugged them. 'Indeed, from what I've seen thus far, it would definitely be wise to take the matter into your own hands.'

'So we think,' Amanda declared.

'But tell us.' Amelia drew back to study Flick's face. 'Did you choose Demon, or did he choose you?'

Flick looked across the ballroom to where Demon stood, to her eyes the most superbly handsome man in the ton. He was wearing black, with ivory shirt and cravat; under the glow of the chandeliers, he looked even more dangerous than in daylight. He was chatting to a gentleman; despite that, Flick knew he knew exactly where she was.

Her lips slowly curved – he looked, and to her senses was, the embodiment of her dream, her desire, a far better reflection than any sculpture, any picture in a book.

She glanced at the twins. 'I chose him.' She looked across the ballroom. 'I was only ten at the time, so I didn't really understand, but ... yes, I definitely chose first.'

'Well, there you are.' Amanda nodded decisively. 'That's all of you – Honoria said she didn't choose first, but she definitely chose. Patience and Catriona both said they chose first. And so did you. So *choosing* is obviously the best way forward.'

Flick glanced at them again, at their beautiful faces, and saw the stubborn wills underneath. She nodded. 'Yes, that's probably true.' The twins were very much like her.

'We'd better circulate.' Amelia nudged them from their nook. 'Mama is looking for us.'

Adopting easy smiles, they slid into the crowd.

Smiling, Flick separated from the twins; although she forbade herself to scan the room, her senses searched for Demon. Over the last days, she'd seen him only fleetingly at the park, and once, by accident, in Bond Street. They'd exchanged no more than a few whispered phrases about the syndicate. And not once had his ever-so-slightly bored social mask slipped.

They had, however, been in public.

He'd arrived this evening at precisely the right moment to escort them down to the carriage, so they hadn't had a moment in private to catch up – on anything.

Which was becoming frustrating.

As was the fact she couldn't locate him.

She stopped before a bust of Caesar mounted on a pedestal. Dispensing with subtlety, she stretched on her toes and tried to scan the heads – she knew Demon's was somewhere in the room.

From behind, his hand closed on her arm.

She gasped and swung around.

He was standing beside the pedestal – he hadn't been there a moment before. Swiftly, he drew her to him, then swung and drew her past, until she was standing in the shallow alcove behind the pedestal. He faced her, leaning one arm on the pedestal's top, blocking her view.

Flick blinked. The ballroom possessed three semicircular alcoves; before each stood some arrangement, like the palms or the pedestal, leaving a small area behind. Those desirous of a quiet moment could avail themselves of the spot, partially private but in full view of the ballroom.

Looking into Demon's hard-featured face, she smiled gloriously. 'Hello – I was looking for you.'

His gaze on her face, he hesitated, then said, 'I know.'

She searched his face, his eyes – she couldn't quite place his tone. 'Have you ... ah, learned anything about the money?'

Demon drank in the sight of her, wallowed in the eager, welcoming light in her eyes, basked in the sensual glow that lit her face. She was screened from the ballroom by his shoulders. He drew a deep breath, and shook his head. 'No. But we are making progress.'

'Oh?' Her gaze lowered, and fixed on his lips; briefly, she moistened hers.

Clenching the fist hidden from the room by the bust, Demon nodded. 'Montague has eliminated various securities – financial instruments through which that much money might have been hidden. While so far the results have been negative, we're narrowing our search.'

She continued to stare at his lips, then realized they'd stopped moving; catching her breath on a little hitch, she looked up. And blinked. 'It seems like we've been chasing the syndicate forever. Catching them seems like a dream.' She paused, her eyes softening as they locked with his. Her 'Do you think we ever will?' was softer yet.

Demon held her gaze and fought to remain still, to resist the impulse to lean forward, slide one arm about her and bring her against him. To bend his head, set his lips to hers, and answer the question in her eyes. Her gown, a sheath of silver-blue silk caught beneath her breasts with silver cords, then flaring over her hips into skirts that flirted about her ankles, didn't help. Its only claim to modesty lay in a froth of filmy silk gauze artfully looped about the neckline and over the points of her shoulders. It was an effort to remember her question. 'Yes.' His tone was deep, harsh; she blinked free of his hold, clearly puzzled when she saw his face harden.

The musicians chose that instant to strike up the waltz – he could have cheerfully strangled them with their own strings. Still, that was why they were here, at this moment. He focused on Flick's face, saw the eager light in her eyes, the invitation in her expression. And inwardly cursed. 'That's a . . .' he drew a tight breath, 'very lovely gown.'

She looked down. 'It's from Cocotte.' She spread the silvery skirts and pirouetted in time to the opening bars, then looked at him. 'Do you like it?'

'Very much.' He could state that honestly, convincingly. When he'd first seen her on the stairs in Berkeley Square, he'd felt winded. The gown flattered her figure so well that he was of the opinion it should be outlawed, but he definitely liked it – and what was in it. So much so that it was impossible for him to take her in his arms and waltz beneath the sharp eyes of his too-interested family.

With one hand, he gestured. 'Turn again.' It was no hardship to keep his gaze on her hips as she twirled.

'Hmm.' He kept his gaze on her skirts, not wanting to see the disappointment gathering in her eyes. She'd told him in the carriage that Emily Cowper, a friend of his mother's, had, in light of her years, given her formal permission to waltz. The waltz was now in full swing. 'That's very well cut – slightly different – the way the skirts fall.' He was a past master at seduction – couldn't he do better? Next, he'd be talking about the weather.

'Have you heard anything from Newmarket?'

He looked up – he'd heard the soft sigh that had preceded that question; there was no longer any hint of anticipation in her eyes. She looked resigned, yet still gracious. He straightened. 'Not specifically. But I have heard from a close acquaintance of a member of the Committee that no one has sighted Dillon yet, nor has anyone spoken to the General.'

'Well, that's some relief. I just hope Dillon doesn't do

anything stupid while we're in town. I'd better send him a letter tomorrow.'

She said nothing more but gazed past the bust to where couples were revolving about the floor. Demon pressed his lips tight shut. However badly he felt about making her miss her first London waltz, he couldn't regret it. Unable to dance with her himself, he couldn't have borne standing by the ballroom's side, watching her in the arms of some other gentleman. He would have turned into an incarnation of his nickname – that was certainly how he felt simply at the thought of her in another man's arms.

It was better for her to miss this waltz. 'I heard from Carruthers that The Flynn's shaping well.'

That caught her attention. 'Oh?'

'He's been pushing him morning and afternoon.'

'Carruthers told me he was trying to build his endurance.'

'Carruthers wants me to try him in a steeple.' He glanced at her. 'What do you think?'

Unsurprisingly, she told him. What did surprise him was how detailed her opinion was, how much she understood, how deeply she'd merged with her one-time mount. For the first time in his life, he learned about, and took advice on, one of his horses from a female.

By the time they'd discussed The Flynn's future, and touched on that of the filly Flick had also ridden, the waltz was long over, the next dance about to begin.

A cotillion. Demon turned and beheld a circle of hovering males, all waiting for their chance with Flick. He smiled tightly and turned back to her, still partially hidden by him. His smile softened as he reached for her hand. 'Will you grant me the honor of this dance, my dear?'

She looked up and smiled – the gesture lit her face and flooded her eyes. 'Of course.' She gave him her hand and let him lead her to the floor.

His experience, thankfully, came to the fore – he artfully complimented her, elegantly teased her, all with just the right touch, that of the accomplished rake he was. As only their hands met, and their bodies passed no closer than a hands-breath, she smiled and laughed, but didn't glow. No one watching them, no matter how closely, would have seen anything beyond a young lady responding predictably to an experienced rake's blandishments.

Which was precisely what he wanted them to see.

At the end of the measure, he bowed elegantly and surrendered her to the coterie of admirers, eagerly awaiting their turn. Satisfied he'd weathered the worst of the night and made the best of it, he retreated to the end of the room.

Gabriel and Lucifer joined him there.

'Why do we do this?' Lucifer grumbled. 'Amanda all but ripped up at me, little shrew. Just because I insisted on waltzing with her.'

'I got the ice treatment,' Gabriel returned. 'I can't remember when last I waltzed with an iceberg. If ever.' He glanced at Demon. 'If this is a taste of what the Season will bring, I think I'll take a holiday.'

When Demon, staring over the assembled heads, said nothing, Gabriel followed his gaze to where Flick was holding court. 'Hmm,' Gabriel murmured. 'Didn't see you waltzing, coz.'

Demon didn't shift his gaze. 'I was otherwise occupied.'

'So I noticed – discussing the fate of the Roman legions, no doubt.'

Demon grinned and reluctantly deserted the sight of Flick chatting animatedly. She'd taken to social outings like a duck to water. 'Actually ...' There was a note in his drawl that brought his cousins' gazes to his face. 'I'm investigating a crime.' Briefly, he filled them in, told them all he knew of the race-fixing and the syndicate, all he suspected of who they really were.

'Hundreds of thousands,' Gabriel repeated. 'You're unquestionably right – it's got to show somewhere.'

'But,' Lucifer countered, 'not necessarily where you're looking.'

Demon raised a brow invitingly.

'There's collectibles – jewelry's the obvious, but there's paintings, too, and other artifacts.'

'You could check on them.'

'I'll check – but if those are the sums that should have been appearing over the past months, I'd already have heard.' Lucifer grimaced. 'Despite the possibility, I doubt collectibles are where the money's gone.'

Demon nodded and looked at Gabriel, whose gaze remained distant. 'What?'

Gabriel refocused. 'I was wondering . . .' He shrugged. 'I've acquaintances who would know if money's changed hands underground. I'll put the word out. Then, if Montague's covering the legitimate side of business, we should have all avenues through the city covered.'

Demon nodded. 'Which leaves one large area yet to be canvassed.'

'Indeed,' Lucifer agreed. 'Our own domain, as it were.'

'Hmm.' Gabriel raised a brow. 'So we'll need to flap our ears for any hint of unexpected blunt – old aunts no one heard of before dying, gamblers supposedly under the hatches suddenly resurrected, and so on.'

'Anyone sporting any unexpected blunt.' Demon nodded decisively. His gaze drifted back to Flick.

Lucifer and Gabriel mumured agreement, then a blond in green silk caught Lucifer's eye – he prowled off in her wake. After a moment, Gabriel tapped Demon's sleeve. 'Don't bite – and don't grind your teeth – I'm going to have a word with your guinea-gold delight.'

Demon humphed – the Bar Cynster never poached on each

other's preserves. He wasn't worried about Gabriel.

He was, however, worrying. Gabriel's description validated his concern. Flick was highly visible, even in a crowd. Her crowning glory drew all eyes – her angelic features held them. In sunlight, her hair was bright gold – in candlelight, it glowed richly, a true yellow gold much more distinctive than the twins' pale gold locks.

She drew eyes wherever she was, wherever she went. Which severely compounded their problem. His problem – he didn't want her to know about it.

It was one of the things he delighted in – her openness – the shining honesty of her joy, her feelings, all displayed in her face for anyone to see. She was neither ashamed of her feelings nor frightened of them, so she showed them, openly, straightforwardly. Honestly. Accurately.

Therein lay his problem.

When they were close and she focused on him, the sensual connection they shared *glowed* in her face. The heightened awareness, the sensual anticipation, her glorious excitement and eagerness – and her knowledge – showed all too clearly. He'd seen it in the park, a week ago and more recently; he'd seen it tonight, when they'd met in his mother's front hall. The sight warmed him to his toes, sent a medley of emotions wreathing through him; the very last thing he wanted was to dim it. But . . .

She was too mature, too composed, to imagine she was infatuated. No one who viewed her response to him would believe infatuation was the cause. What they would believe was the truth – that they'd already been intimate – he, a rake of extensive experience and she, a very innocent young lady.

To his mind, all blame – if any was to be laid – should rest squarely at his door. Society, unfortunately, wouldn't see it that way.

Her reputation would be shredded – not even the backing of the Cynsters would protect her. For himself, he didn't care – he'd marry her in an instant, but it would be too late; although the furor might fade, it would never be forgotten. Her reputation would be irreparably tarnished – she'd never be welcomed into certain circles.

Their problem, of course, would not have occurred if she'd married him before they came to town, or even agreed to marry him so they could make some announcement. If such was the circumstance, the ton would turn a blind eye. However, now she was here, under his mother's wing, enacting the role of a virtuous young lady. The ton could be vicious – would delight in being vicious – given that scenario.

Watching her confidently chatting and laughing, her heart obviously light, he toyed with the idea of seeing her tomorrow – alone – and explaining the matter fully. She might not believe him at first, but he could call on his mother, and even his aunts, for verification. *They* wouldn't be horrified, but Flick would. She would, he was sure, agree to marry him immediately.

Which was what he wanted, wasn't it?

Lips compressing, he shifted, and wondered when, and why, a woman's wishes – her tender feelings, her inexplicable feminine emotions – had become so important. An unanswerable question, but there was no ducking the fact. He couldn't pressure her to agree in that way.

Straightening, he drew in a breath. If he told her her expression showed too much, she might recognize the danger and agree to marry him purely to avoid any scandal. Which wasn't what he wanted. He wanted her openhearted commitment – a commitment to him, to their future – not an agreement compelled by society's whip.

But if she didn't realize the deeper implications and opt for marriage, then she would try to hide, to dampen, her instinctive reaction. And she might succeed.

He didn't want that to happen, either.

He'd consorted with too many women who manufactured their emotions, who in reality cared little for anyone or anything. Flick's transparent joy was precious to him – had been from the first. He couldn't bring himself to douse the golden glow in her eyes, not even for this.

Which meant ... he was going to have to find some way to protect her.

He watched her go down a country dance, laughing gaily but without that special delight she reserved just for him. Despite his worry, despite the irony, his lips quirked at the sight. Ambling around the ballroom, his gaze fixed on her – his delight, his desire – he considered how best to protect her good name.

Part of his answer was a drive in the park. Simple, effective – and she wouldn't know enough to realize what he was doing. He drove into Berkeley Square at the earliest possible hour. Ignoring Highthorpe's smugly understanding look, he climbed the stairs to his mother's private parlor, knocked once, then entered.

Seated on the *chaise*, a pair of spectacles perched on her nose, his mother looked up, then smiled. As he'd expected, she was sorting the morning's invitations. Seated on an ottoman before her, Flick was assisting.

'Good morning, Harry – and to what do we owe this pleasure?' Removing her glasses, his mother raised her face for his kiss.

He dutifully obliged, ignoring her teasing look. Straightening, he turned to Flick, who'd quickly risen to her feet. 'I came to ask if Felicity would care for a drive in the park.'

Flick's eyes lit up. Her face was transformed by her smile.

'That would be delightful.' Stepping forward, she held out her hand.

Demon took it – and held it, and her, at a safe distance, ruthlessly denying the urge to draw her – allow her – closer. For one instant, he looked into her face, drank in her eager enthusiasm – then, lids lowering, he smiled urbanely and waved her to the door. 'There's a brisk breeze blowing – you'll need your pelisse.'

Not for a split second had his polite mask slipped; Flick blinked at him, her smile fading slightly. 'Yes, of course.' She turned to Horatia. 'If it's agreeable to you, ma'am.'

'Of course, my dear.' Horatia smiled and shooed; Flick bobbed a curtsy and went.

If Demon had had any doubt as to the reality of the threat posed by Flick's revealing countenance, encountering the suddenly sharp gaze of his mother dispelled it. The instant the door shut behind Flick, Horatia shot him a speculative, potentially rigid, disapproving look – but the question to which she wanted an answer was not one she could ask.

And he was, after all, proposing to drive Flick in the park.

As confusion rose in Horatia's eyes, Demon inclined his head with his usual cool grace. 'I'll meet Felicity downstairs – I need to walk my horses.' Without intercepting Horatia's narrow-eyed look, he turned and made good his escape.

Flick didn't keep him waiting – she came tripping down the stairs as he descended rather more leisurely. Her contempt for feminine preening gave them a rare moment alone. Demon smiled easily, relieved to be able to drop his mask for a moment – he reached for her hand, set it on his sleeve, and drew her close.

She laughed softly, delightedly; smiling gloriously, she turned her face to his. He felt the soft tremor that ran through her, sensed the tensing of her nerves, the tightening of her breathing, the sheer awareness that raced through

307

her as their bodies fleetingly touched. Her eyes widened, pupils distending; her lips parted – her whole face softened. And glowed.

Even in the poor light on the stairs, it was impossible to mistake the sensuality behind the sight. He'd initiated her all too well. She yearned, now, as did he. The temptation to sweep her into his arms, to bend his head and set his lips to hers had never gripped him so hard; need had never driven him so mercilessly.

Drawing an unsteady breath, he glanced down – and spied Highthorpe by the door. He drew back, moving fractionally away, ruthlessly sliding his elegantly bored facade back into place. 'Come – the bays will be cooling.'

She sensed his withdrawal, but then she saw Highthorpe. She nodded, and strolled down the stairs by his side.

Leaving the house, handing her into the curricle, then driving to the park gave him time to reestablish complete control. Flick remained silent – she'd never been one for aimless chatter – but her pleasure in the outing was in her face, displayed for all to see. Luckily, the curricle was sufficiently wide for there to be a good foot between them, so the display was one of simple joy and happiness, rather than of anything more.

'Have you written to Dillon yet?' With a deft flick, he turned his horses through the park gates.

'Yes, this morning. I told him that while we've temporarily lost Bletchley, we're sure to come up with him again, and that meanwhile, we're searching for the money from the fixed races.' Her gaze distant, Flick frowned. 'I hope that will keep him at the cottage. We don't want him imagining he's been deserted and so go investigating himself. He's sure to get caught.'

Demon glanced at her, then looked forward.

The carriages of the *grandes dames* appeared ahead of them, lining the Avenue. 'I've been considering sending The

Flynn to Doncaster. How do you think he'd handle the change of track?'

'Doncaster?' Flick pursed her lips, then launched into an animated answer.

It wasn't hard to keep her talking, speculating, arguing, analyzing all the way down the line of fashionable carriages, then all the way back again. He doubted she truly saw the matrons watching them – she certainly didn't notice the interest their appearance provoked, or the meaningful, smugly approving glances exchanged by the senior hostesses. When the ladies whose opinions controlled the reactions of the ton graciously inclined their heads, he responded with a suavity that confirmed their supposition. Flick, without a blink, inclined her head, too, absentmindedly mimicking him, unaware of how her following his lead so smoothly appeared.

'If you're serious about developing The Flynn as a 'chaser,' she concluded, 'you're going to have to move him to Cheltenham.'

'Hmm, possibly.'

Turning the bays' heads for the gates, Demon was seized by a sense of triumph. He'd pulled it off – done the deed – made his declaration, albeit unspoken. Every matron they'd passed had heard it loud and clear.

And it hadn't, somewhat to his surprise, abraded his sensitivities – if anything, he felt immeasurably relieved to have so definitively staked his claim. Every matron who mattered now understood he fully intended to marry Miss Felicity Parteger. All would assume there was an understanding between them. Most importantly, the good ladies would see it as entirely proper that he, being so much older than she, with so much more worldly experience, would declare his hand in this fashion, then allow her to enjoy her Season without keeping by her side.

No one would now think it odd if he kept a safe distance between them.

'I'll take you back to Berkeley Square, then I'll call on Montague and see what he's learned.'

Flick nodded, the joy in her eyes dimming. 'Time is getting on.'

Chapter Seventeen

Time was indeed passing, but not as Flick had hoped. Four evenings later, she sat in the shadows of Lady Horatia's carriage and tried not to feel let down. Any other young lady would be enjoying herself hugely, caught up in the frantic whirl. She'd been to Almack's, to parties, balls, musicales and soirees. What more could she possibly want?

The answer was sitting on the seat opposite, clothed in his usual black. As the carriage rocked, his shoulders swayed. She could see his fair hair, and the pale oval of his face, but not his features. Her mind, however, supplied them – set in his customary social mask. Ineffably polite with just a touch of cool hauteur, that mask conveyed mild boredom. No hint of interest, sensual or otherwise, was ever permitted to show.

Increasingly, Flick wondered if such interest still existed.

She virtually never saw him in daylight. Since that drive in the park, he hadn't called again, nor had he appeared to stroll the lawns by her side. She appreciated he might be busy with other matters, but she hadn't expected him to bring her here, then leave her so terribly alone.

If it wasn't for the twins' friendship and the warmth of his family, she'd be lost – as alone as she'd been when her parents had died.

Yet she got the distinct impression he still wished to marry her – that everyone expected they'd soon wed. Her words to the twins haunted her; she'd chosen, but she'd yet to declare her choice. If that choice meant leading a life like this, then she wasn't at all sure she could stand it.

The carriage halted, then rocked forward, then halted again, this time under the brilliantly lit portico of Arkdale House. Demon uncoiled his long legs – the door opened and he stepped down, turned and handed her down, then helped his mother from the carriage. Horatia shook out her skirts, smoothed her coiffure, then claimed the butler's arm and swept inside, leaving Demon to lead Flick in.

'Shall we?'

Flick glanced at his face, but it was his mask she saw; his tone held the same boredom. Studiously correct, he offered his arm; inclining her head, she rested her fingertips on his sleeve.

She kept a sweet smile on her lips as they progressed through the door and on up the curving staircase – and tried not to dwell on his stiff stance, his bent arm held away from his body. It was always thus, these days. No longer did he draw her close, as if she was special to him.

They greeted Lady Arkdale, then followed Horatia to a *chaise* by the wall. Demon immediately requested the first cotillion and the first country dance after supper, then melted into the crowd.

Stifling a sigh, Flick held her head high. It was always the same – he assiduously escorted her to every ball, but all that ever came of it was her laying her hand on his sleeve on the way in, one distant cotillion, one even more distant country dance, a stilted supper surrounded by her admirers, a few glimpses through the crowd, then her placing her hand on his sleeve as they departed. How anyone could imagine there was anything between them – anything with the potential to lead to marriage – she couldn't comprehend.

His departure was the signal for her court to gather. Infusing her features with appropriate delight, she set her self to manage the youthful gentlemen who, if she let them, would fawn at her feet.

In no way different from the evenings that had preceded it, this evening, too, rolled on.

'I say – careful!'

'Oh! I'm *so* sorry.' Flick blushed, quickly shifted her feet, and smiled apologetically at her partner, an earnest young gentleman, Lord Bristol. They were swinging around the floor in a waltz; unfortunately, she found dancing with anyone but Demon more a trial than a delight.

Because, if she wasn't dancing with him, she was forever trying to catch glimpses of him as he stood conversing by the side of the floor.

It was a dreadful habit, one she deplored, one she lectured herself on constantly. To no avail. If he was there, her eyes were drawn to him – she was helpless to prevent it. Luckily, the ton's ballrooms were large and excessively crowded; a quick glimpse was all she ever caught. Her partners, as far as she knew, had not noticed her fixation.

Even when she stepped on their toes.

Inwardly wincing, she sternly told herself to pay attention. She hated the taste her silly behavior left in her mouth. Once again, she was a besotted girl peering through the banisters for a glimpse of him. Her idol. The one man she'd wanted but who'd been out of her reach. More and more, she was starting to feel he was still out of her reach.

She didn't like watching him, but she did – compulsively. And what she saw brought no joy. There was inevitably a woman by his side, some hideously beautiful lady, head tilted as she looked into his face, her own creasing into smiles as she laughed at some risque' quip. It only needed a glimpse for her to take it all in – the languidly elegant gestures, the saber-witted remarks, the arrogantly seductive lift of a brow.

The women pressed close, and he let them. Some even lifted their white hands to his arms, his shoulders, leaning against him while he charmed and teased, employing the seductive wiles he no longer used on her.

Why she kept looking – fashioning a whip for her own back – she didn't know. But she did.

'Do you think the weather will hold fine tomorrow?'

Flick refocused on Lord Bristol. 'I suppose so.' The skies had been blue for a week.

'I was hoping I might prevail upon you to honor me and my sisters with your presence on a drive to Richmond.'

Flick smiled gently. 'Thank you, but I'm afraid Lady Horatia and I are fully committed tomorrow.'

'Oh – yes, of course. Just a thought.'

Flick let regret tinge her smile – and wished it was Demon who'd asked. She didn't care a fig for the constant round of entertainments; she would have enjoyed a drive to Richmond, but she couldn't encourage Lord Bristol to imagine he had any chance with her.

Supper had come and gone; Demon had coolly claimed her, stiffly escorted her into the supper room, then sat by her side and said not a word as her court endeavored to entertain her. This waltz had followed immediately; she performed without thought, waiting for their revolutions to bring them once more in sight of her obsession. He was standing at the end of the room.

Then Lord Bristol swung her into the turn. She looked – and nearly gasped. Whirling away, she dragged in a breath, struggling to mask her shock. Her lungs constricted; she felt real pain.

Who was she – the woman all but draped over him? She was stunningly beautiful – dark hair piled high over an exquisite face atop a body that flaunted more sumptuous curves than Flick had imagined possible. Much worse, her cloying closeness, the way she looked into his face, positively screamed their relationship.

Blissfully unaware, Lord Bristol swung her up the room. Blankness descended, blessed relief from the clawing, shrieking jealousy that had raked her. The change left her dizzy.

The music faded, the dance came to an end. Lord Bristol released her – she nearly stumbled, only just remembering to curtsy.

Flick knew she was pale. Inside she was trembling. She smiled weakly at Lord Bristol. 'Thank you.' Turning, she walked into the crowd.

She hadn't known he had a mistress.

That word kept repeating in her mind – incessantly. As she tacked through the crowd all but blind, instinct came to her aid; she headed for a group of potted palms. There was no alcove, but in the shadow cast by the large fronds close by the wall, she found sanctuary.

Not once did she question the correctness of her assumption; she knew she was right. What she didn't know was what to do. She'd never felt so lost in her life.

The man she'd just glimpsed, heavy lids at half-mast as he traded sensuous quips with his mistress, was not the man she'd met on Newmarket Heath – the man to whom she'd willingly given herself in the best bedchamber at The Angel.

Her mind wouldn't work properly – bits of her problem surfaced, but she couldn't see the whole.

'Can't see her at present, but she's a pretty little thing. Quite suitable. Now that Horatia's taken her under her wing, all will, no doubt, go as it should.'

The words came from the other side of the palms, in accents of matriarchal approval. Flick blinked.

'Hmm,' came a second voice. 'Well, one can hardly accuse him of being besotted, can one?'

Flick peeked through the fringed leaves – two old ladies were leaning on their sticks, scanning the ballroom.

'As it should be,' the first intoned. 'I'm sure it's precisely as Hilary Eckles said – he's had the sense to recognize it's time for him to take a wife, and he's chosen well – a gently reared chit, ward of a friend of the family. It's not a love match, and a good thing, too!'

'Indeed,' the second old biddy nodded decisively. 'So tiresomely emotional, these love matches. Can't see the sense in them, myself.'

'Sense?' The first snorted. 'That's because there isn't any to see. Unfortunately, it's the latest fashion.'

'Hmm.' The second lady paused, then, with a puzzled air, said, 'Seems odd for a Cynster to be unfashionable, especially on that point.'

'True, but it appears Horatia's boy's the first one in a while to have his head screwed on straight. He may be a hellion but in this, he's displayed uncommon sense. Well' – the lady gestured – 'where would *we* have been if we'd allowed love to rule us?'

'Precisely. There's Thelma – let's see what she says.'

The two ladies stumped off, leaning heavily on their canes, but Flick no longer felt safe behind the palms. Her head was still spinning; she didn't feel all that well. The withdrawing room seemed her safest option.

She slipped through the crowd, avoiding anyone she knew, especially any Cynsters. Reaching the door to the corridor, she stepped into the shadows. A little maid jumped up from a stool and led her to the room set aside for ladies to refresh themselves.

The room was brightly lit along one side, which was lined with mirrors, leaving the rest of the room heavily shadowed.

Accepting a glass of water from the maid, Flick retreated to a chair in the gloom. Sipping the water, she simply sat. Other ladies came and went; no one noticed her in her dim corner. She started to feel better.

Then the door swung wide, and Demon's mistress stepped through. One of the ladies preening before the mirrors saw her; smiling, she turned. 'Celeste! And how goes your conquest?'

Celeste had paused dramatically just inside the door; hands rising to her voluptuous hips, she scanned the room. Her gaze stopped, briefly, on Flick, then lifted to her friend. She smiled, a gesture full of feminine sensuality. 'Why it goes, *cherie* – it goes!'

The lady before the mirrors laughed; others smiled, too.

In a sensuous glide that focused attention on her bounteous hips, tiny waist and full breasts, Celeste crossed the room. Stopping before a long mirror, hands on hips, she critically examined her reflection.

Exchanging glances and raised brows, the other ladies departed, all except Celeste and her friend, who was artfully rerouging her lips.

'You have heard, have you not,' Celeste's friend murmured, 'the rumors that he's to wed?'

'Hmm,' Celeste purred. In the mirror, her eyes sought Flick's. 'But why should that worry me? I don't want to *marry* him.'

Her friend snickered. 'We all know what you want, but he might have other ideas – at least once he marries. He is a Cynster after all.'

'I do not understand this.' Celeste had a definite accent, one Flick couldn't place; it only made her purring voice more sensual, more evocative. 'What matter his name?'

'Not his name – his family. Not even that, but ... well, they've all proved remarkably constant as husbands.'

317

Celeste made a moue; she tilted her head – from beneath half-closed lids, her eyes glinted. Deliberately, she leaned toward the mirror, trailing her fingers tantalizingly across the full curves and deep cleavage thus revealed. Then she straightened, gracefully lifting her arms and half turning to examine her bottom, superbly displayed by her satin gown. Then her gaze locked with Flick's. 'I suspect,' she purred, 'that this case will prove an exception.'

Feeling more ill than when she'd entered, Flick rose. Summoning strength from she knew not where, she crossed to the table by the door. Shakily, she set the glass down – the click drew the attention of Celeste's friend. As she slipped through the door, Flick glimpsed a horrified face and heard a moaned '*Oh, Lord*!'

The door closed; Flick stood in the dim corridor, the impulse to flee overpowering. But how could she leave? Where could she go? Drawing in a huge breath, she held it and lifted her chin. Defying the sick giddiness that assailed her, refusing to let herself think of what she'd heard, she headed back to the ballroom.

She'd gone no more than three paces when a figure materialized from the shadows.

'There you are, miss! I've been chasing you for hours.'

Flick blinked – into the pinched features of her Aunt Scroggs. Clinging to the tattered remnants of her dignity, she bobbed a curtsy. 'Good evening, Aunt. I hadn't realized you were here.'

'No doubt! You've been far too busy with those young blighters that surround you. Which is precisely what I want to speak to you about.' Wrapping thin fingers about Flick's elbow, Edwina Scroggs looked toward the withdrawing room.

'There are ladies in there.' Flick couldn't bear to go back, much less explain why.

'Humph!' Glancing around, Edwina drew her to the side,

hard against the tapestry-covered wall. 'This will have to do then – there's no one about.'

The comment sent an unwelcome chill through Flick; she was already inwardly shivering. Lady Horatia had helped her locate her aunt; she'd visited her early in her stay. There was, however, nothing more than duty between them – her aunt had married socially beneath her and now lived as a penny-pinching widow, despite being relatively affluent.

Edwina Scroggs had been paid by her parents to take her in for the short time they'd expected to be away. The minute news of their deaths had arrived, Mrs. Scroggs had declared she couldn't be expected to house, feed and watch over a girl of seven. She'd literally flung Flick onto the mercy of the wider family – thankfully, the General had been there to catch her.

'It's about all these youngsters you've got sniffing at your skirts.' Putting her face close, Edwina hissed, 'Forget them, do you hear?' She trapped Flick's startled gaze. 'It's my duty to steer you right, and I'd be lacking indeed if I didn't tell you to your face. You're staying with the Cynsters – the word around town is that the son's got his eye on you.'

Edwina pressed closer; Flick's lungs seized.

'My advice to you, miss, is to make it his *hands*. You're quick enough – and this is too good a chance to pass up. The family's one of the wealthiest in the land, but they can be high in the instep. So you take my advice and get his ring on your finger the fastest way you know how.' Edwina's eyes gleamed. 'Seems Cynsters are prime 'uns, always ready to take what they can get. That house is monstrous enough – no difficulty to find a quiet room to—'

'*No!*' Flick pushed past her aunt and fled down the corridor.

She stopped just outside the swath of light spilling from the ballroom. Ignoring the surprise in the little maid's eyes, she pressed a hand to her chest, closed her eyes and struggled to breathe. To hold back the silly tears. To still the pounding in her head.

Cynsters are prime 'uns, always ready to take what they can get.

She managed two breaths, neither deep enough, then heard her aunt's heels tapping, tapping, nearer . . .

Sucking in a breath, she opened her eyes and plunged into the ballroom.

And collided with Demon.

'*Oh!*' She managed to mute her cry, then ducked her head so he couldn't see her face. Reflexively, he caught her, his hands firm about her arms as he steadied her.

In the next heartbeat, his grip tightened. 'What's wrong?'

His tone was oddly flat. Flick didn't dare look up – she shook her head. 'Nothing.'

His grip tightened, his fingers iron shackles about her upper arms. 'Dammit, Flick—!'

'It's *nothing.*' She squirmed. Because of his size, and because they were standing just inside the door, thus far they'd attracted no attention. 'You're hurting me,' she hissed.

Immediately, his grip eased. His hands remained on her upper arms, holding her away from him but sliding soothingly up and down, warm palms to her bare skin, slipping beneath the silk folds that formed her sleeves. His touch was so evocative – so tempting; she was wracked by the urge to sob and launch herself into his arms—

She couldn't do that.

Stiffening her spine, she hauled in a breath and lifted her head. 'It's nothing,' she restated, looking past his shoulder to where couples were milling on the dance floor.

Eyes narrowed, Demon stared over her head, into the shadows of the corridor. 'What did your aunt say to upset you?' His voice was even – too even. It sounded deadly, which was precisely how he felt.

Flick shook her head. '*Nothing*!'

He studied her face, but she wouldn't meet his eyes. She was as white as a sheet and ... fragile was the word that leapt to mind. 'Was it one of those puppies – the ones yapping at your heels?' If it was, he'd kill them.

'*No*!' She shot him a venomous look; her chin set. 'It was *nothing*.'

The effort she was making to pull herself together was visible. He didn't move – while he stood before her, she was screened from curious eyes.

'It was nothing,' she repeated in a steadier voice.

She was trembling, more inside than outwardly – he could sense it. His impulse was to drag her off to some quiet room where he could wrap her in his arms, wear down her resistance and learn what was wrong – but he didn't trust himself alone with her. Not in his current state. It had been bad enough before. Now ...

He drew in a breath and seized the moments she needed to calm herself to steady his own wracked nerves. And reshackle his demons.

The cross he'd fashioned and willingly taken up was proving much heavier than he'd expected. Not spending any time with her – even by her side in a ballroom – was eating at his control. But he'd set the stage; now he had to play his part and stick by the script he'd written.

For her good, for her protection, he had to keep his distance.

That sentence was hard enough to bear – he didn't need anyone adding to his burden. Bad enough that he'd had to force himself to swallow every instinct he possessed and watch as she waltzed with other men. Until she agreed to marry him and they made a public announcement, he didn't dare waltz with her in public. And, given who he was – a much older, infinitely more experienced rake – and the fact that she was transparently innocent, they could never be private, not until they were formally engaged.

Straightening, he let his arms fall – she shivered at the loss of his touch. Jaw clenching, he drew in a patient breath and waited.

How long he could wait, he didn't know. Every night, the ordeal of the waltz grew worse. Those who'd previously been his partners had tried to tease him onto the floor, but he had no desire to waltz with them. He wanted his angel and only her, but he'd used the others for distraction – not his, but the ton's.

Tonight, it had been Celeste – he'd almost managed to distract himself by giving the salacious countess her *congé* in no uncertain terms, for she'd proved she understood nothing else. Miffed, she'd peeled herself from him and swanned off in a snit, from which he sincerely hoped she never recovered. For one moment, he'd felt good – buoyed by success. Until he'd glanced up and seen Flick in that puppy Bristol's arms.

Half-turning, his gaze raked the dance floor. Couples were forming sets for the next country dance, the second of the dances he permitted himself with Flick. As far as he could tell, all her puppies were somewhere on the floor. So who had upset her?

He looked back at her; she was calmer – a touch of color had returned to her cheeks. 'Perhaps we should stroll, rather than dance.'

She shot him a startled look. 'No! I mean—' Shaking her head wildly, she looked away. 'No, let's dance.'

She sounded suddenly breathless; Demon narrowed his eyes.

'I owe you a dance – it's on my dance card.' Gulping in a breath, she nodded. 'That's what you want from me, so let's dance. The music's starting.'

322

He hesitated, then, using his grace to camouflage her state, he bowed and led her to the nearest set.

The instant he took her hand in his, he knew he'd been right to acquiesce – she was so brittlely tense, so fragile, that if he pressed her she'd shatter. She was holding herself together by sheer force of will – all he could do was support her as best he could.

It was just as well he was there. He could perform any dance with his eyes closed, but she'd only learned the steps in the last weeks. She needed to concentrate, but that was presently beyond her. So he guided her as if she was a nervous filly with his hand on her reins. For most of the dance, their hands were locked – by squeezing her fingers, this way or that, he directed her through the figures.

He'd never seen her clumsy before, but she nearly stumbled twice, and bumped into two other ladies.

What the devil was wrong?

Something had changed, not just tonight but gradually. He'd been watching her closely; he wasn't mistaken. There'd been a joy in her eyes, a delight in life, that had, over the past days, slowly faded. Not the sensual glow he fought to avoid eliciting, but something else – something simpler. It had always been there, vibrant, in her eyes. Now, he could barely detect it.

The music ended with a flourish; the dancers bowed and curtsied. Flick turned from the floor and drew in a breath – he knew it was one of relief. He hesitated, then took her hand and placed it on his sleeve. 'Come,' he said, as she looked up at him. 'I'll take you to my mother.'

She, too, hesitated, then acquiesced with a small nod.

He didn't let her go until he'd planted her beside the *chaise* where his mother was chatting. Horatia looked up fleetingly, noting Flick's return, but turned back to her conversation immediately. Demon would have said something to her, if he could have thought of what to say. He glanced down at Flick; she still wouldn't meet his eyes. She was still very tense – he didn't dare press her.

Girding his loins for the inner battle he fought each time he left her, he stiffly inclined his head. 'I'll leave you to your friends.' Then he moved away.

Her court gathered around her almost instantly. Retreating to the wall nearby, Demon studied the group but could detect no reaction on Flick's part; he could discern no threat from any one of her admirers. Indeed, she seemed to treat them as the puppies he'd labelled them, managing them with an absentminded air.

He wanted to stride back and disperse them, but it was hardly acceptable behavior. His mother would never forgive him and Flick might not, either. He couldn't even join her circle; he'd be too utterly out of place within her youthful court, a wolf amidst so many sheep.

The evening, thank God, was nearly over.

Stifling a grunt, he forced himself to stroll farther away, and not stand there staring quite so hungrily at her.

Fate had one last trial in store for him that evening.

He was propping up the wall, minding Flick's business, when a gentleman, every bit as languidly elegant as he, caught sight of him, smiled, then strolled over.

Demon ignored the smile. Grimly, he nodded. 'Evening, Chillingworth.'

'One would never imagine it a good one from your expression, dear boy.' Glancing over the intervening heads to where Flick was passing the time with an enjoyment more apparent than real, Chillingworth's smile deepened. 'A tasty little morsel, I grant you, but I never thought you, of them all, would saddle yourself with this.'

Demon decided not to understand. 'This what?'

'Why—' Chillingworth turned his head and met his eyes.

'This torment, of course.'

Demon held back a glare, but his eyes narrowed; Chillingworth grinned and looked again at Flick. 'Devil, of course, was doomed to run the full race, but the rest of you had far greater latitude. Vane had the sense to avail himself of it and marry Patience away from the ton. Richard – I always considered him the most sane – married his wild witch in Scotland, as far from the mad whirl as it's possible to get. So—' Pondering Flick, Chillingworth mused, 'I have to ask myself why – why you've put yourself in line for such punishment.' Amused understanding in his eyes, he glanced at Demon. 'You must admit it's hardly comfortable.'

Demon was not about to admit anything, and certainly not that. That his inner demons were howling with frustration. That he was hardly sleeping, barely eating, and as physically uncomfortable as it was possible to be. He met Chillingworth's gaze steadily. 'I'll live.'

'Hmm.' Chillingworth's lips curved into a full smile. 'Your fortitude leaves me quite ...' Turning, he studied Flick. '*Envious.*'

Demon stiffened.

'As you know,' Chillingworth murmured, 'young innocents have never been my cup of tea.' He glanced back and met Demon's stony stare. 'However, I've always been in remarkable accord with your family's taste in women.' He looked back at Flick. 'Perhaps—?'

'*Don't.*'

The single word rang with lethal warning. Chillingworth's head snapped around; he met Demon's eyes. For one instant, despite their elegance, the scene turned primitive, the force resonating between them both primal and violent.

Then Chillingworth's lips curved; triumph gleamed in his eyes. 'Perhaps not.' Smiling, he inclined his head and turned away.

Inwardly cursing, Demon was damned if he'd let him escape unmarked. 'If Devil was doomed, and he was, then so will you be.'

Chillingworth chuckled as he strolled away. 'Oh, no, dear boy.' His words floated back. 'I do assure you, *this* will never happen to me.'

'Thank you, Highthorpe.' After handing over his gloves and cane, Demon strode down the corridor and swung into his parents' dining room.

And came to a dead halt.

His mother's brows rose. 'Good morning. And what brings you out this early?'

Surveying the empty chairs about the table, Demon inwardly grimaced. He'd asked for his mother, assuming Flick would be with her. Returning his gaze to Horatia's face, he raised his brows. 'Felicity?'

Horatia studied him. 'Still abed.'

It was past ten. Flick, Demon was certain, would be up at the crack of dawn, regardless of how late she'd been up the night before. She was used to riding early – morning stables started at dawn.

The impulse to ask Horatia to check on her gnawed at him. He resisted only because he couldn't think of any reason for such a peculiar request.

Horatia was watching him, waiting to see if he'd do anything revealing. He actually considered letting her guess. It wouldn't take much to have her leap to the right conclusion; she knew her sons well. But ... there was no guarantee, regardless of how understanding she might be, that she wouldn't, however unintentionally, pressure Flick into accepting him. And he didn't want her to be pressured.

Lips compressing, he nodded curtly. 'I'll see you this evening.' He was supposed to escort them to a party. He swung on his heel – then paused, and looked back. And met Horatia's eye. 'Tell her I called.'

Then he left.

He stopped on the pavement, drew in a deep breath, then looked down and pulled on his gloves. In the wee hours, when he'd been lying in bed wracking his brains, he'd remembered Flick's *'that's what you want from me.'*

They'd been talking about a dance – at least, he had. So what had she meant? He didn't want her for a dance partner – at least, not primarily – not for that sort of dance.

He sighed and looked up, tightly gripping his cane. His mind was running hard in predictable grooves. Restraining his impulses, his instincts, never stronger than where she was concerned, was proving harder, more debilitating, day by day. Just how close to the edge of control he was had been demonstrated last night – he'd overheard two of her youthful swains referring to her as 'Their Angel.' He'd nearly erupted – nearly kicked them and the other yapping puppies away from her skirts, and told them to go find their own angel. She was *his*.

Instead, he'd forced himself to grit his teeth and bear it. How much longer he could manage to do so he really didn't know.

But he couldn't stand on the pavement outside his parents' house for the rest of the day.

Grimacing, he reached into his coat pocket and hauled out the list Montague had drawn up for him in between searching for clues left by the money. Checking the addresses on the list, he set out for the closest.

It was all he could think of to do – to distract himself, to convince himself that it would all work out in the end. The only thing that might give him a smidgen of ease – make him feel he was doing something definite, something meaningful, to further their matrimonial plans.

They would need a house to live in when in London.

A town house, nothing too large, with just the right com bination of rooms. He knew what he was looking for. And he knew Flick's tastes ran parallel to his – he felt confident enough to buy her a house for a surprise.

Not a house – a home. Theirs.

328

Chapter Eighteen

Yet another ball – Flick wished, very much, that she was back at Hillgate End, Demon was back at his stud, and life was simple again.

'Miss Parteger, Framley's composed a smashing ode to your eyes. Are you sure you wouldn't like to hear it?'

'Quite sure.' Flick fixed Lord Henderson with a severe glance. 'You know my feelings about poetry.'

His lordship looked suitably abashed. 'Just thought, perhaps, as it is *your* eyes . . .'

Flick raised a brow and gave her attention to the next member of her youthful court seeking to dazzle her. In dealing with the many admirers she'd gathered without the slightest effort, she tried hard not to be unkind, but they were so young, so innocuous, so incapable. Of anything, but most especially of awakening her interest.

Another had done that, very effectively – and then deserted her. She felt her eyes narrow and quickly forced them wider. 'Indeed, sir.' She nodded agreement to Lord Bristol's comment on the rain. Maintaining an expression of polite interest, she pretended to listen to the chatter while her mind remained focused on the long, lean figure lounging indolently against the opposite wall of Lady Henderson's ballroom. She could see him from the corner of her eye, as usual, along with the beautiful lady fluttering her lashes at him – also as usual.

Admittedly, the lady had a different face every night, but that didn't, to her mind, change anything; she now viewed such women as challenges – to be conquered and obliterated.

He wanted to marry her – this morning, lying late abed, she'd decided she definitely wanted to marry him. Which meant he was going to have to learn to love her, regardless of what Celeste, Aunt Scroggs or any old biddies might think. He'd dangled her dream before her eyes. She'd grabbed it, and wasn't about to let go.

She couldn't relieve her feelings by glaring at him. She toyed with the idea of doing something rash. Like waiting until a waltz started, striding across the room, displacing his lady for the evening, and demanding that he waltz with her.

What would he do? How would he react?

Her fantasies were interrupted by a gentleman who, in a neat maneuever, replaced Lord Bristol at her side.

'My dear Miss Parteger – a pleasure.'

Reflexively, Flick gave him her hand; he held it rather longer than necessary. He was older than her other admirers. 'I'm afraid, sir' – she retrieved her hand – 'that you have the advantage of me.'

He smiled. 'Philip Remington, my dear, at your service. We met briefly at Lady Hawkridge's last week.'

Flick placed him, and inclined her head. At Lady Hawkridge's ball, he'd merely noticed her, though he hadn't shown any particular interest. His gaze had been momentarily arrested by her face, before, with a polite nod, he'd moved on. Now his gaze was much more intent. Not frighteningly so, but she certainly wouldn't confuse him with the callow youths surrounding her.

'I've a question, my dear, if I might be so bold. I fear the ton too easily turns supposition into truth. Confusion is a byword, which makes life unnecessarily complicated.'

He delivered the speech with a conspiratorial smile; Flick

returned it readily. 'Indeed, I often find tonnish ways confusing. What is it you wish to know?'

'A somewhat delicate matter, but ... if I don't ask, how will we ever know?' His gaze caught hers. 'I wish to know, my dear, whether rumor is correct, and you and Harry Cynster are engaged.'

Flick drew in a breath and lifted her chin. 'No. Mr. Cynster and I are not engaged.'

Remington smiled and bowed. 'Thank you, my dear. I must admit to being very glad to hear that.'

His meaning glowed in his eyes. Flick inwardly cursed, even though her pride responded to the warmth; Remington was a distinctly handsome man.

Their words had riveted the attention of other gentlemen idling at the periphery of her circle; like Remington, they were older than her puppies. One pushed through to her side, displacing Lord Henderson. 'Framlingham, Miss Parteger. Seeing you amidst the Cynster household, well – we simply assumed, don't you know?'

'I'm a friend of the family,' Flick replied repressively. 'Lady Horatia has been kind enough to take me around town.'

'Ah!'

'Indeed?'

Other gentlemen closed in, relegating her fawning puppies to the outer ranks. Flick stiffened, but, flanked by the courteous and subtly protective Remington and the gruff Framlingham, she quickly realized that her new court was far more entertaining than the last.

Within minutes, she found herself laughing spontaneously. Two other young ladies joined the circle; the conversation shifted to a new level, one of more scintillating repartee.

Stifling a giggle at one of Remington's dry remarks, Flick threw a glance across the room – Demon, she knew, would have appreciated the joke.

He was looking down – into Celeste's face.

Flick caught her breath and swung her gaze back to Remington. After a moment, she exhaled, then drew in another breath, straightened her spine, lifted her chin, and smiled on her new cavaliers.

The next morning, the instant Lady Horatia's carriage halted by the verge of the Avenue, it was swamped.

'Your Grace. Lady Cynster.' At the head of a group of six gentlemen and two ladies, Remington bowed to Helena and Horatia, then with a warm smile, bowed to Flick. Straightening, he addressed Horatia. 'Could we persuade you, ma'am, to allow Miss Parteger to stroll the lawns in our company?' His gaze switched to Flick. 'If, of course, we can tempt her to join us?'

If Demon had been anywhere in sight, Flick would have sat in the carriage and prayed he'd speak with her – but he wasn't. He hadn't appeared in the park in the last week. She'd sent another reassuring letter to Dillon that morning, increasingly worried that he would set out to chase Bletchley himself, and get caught. The General would be devastated. Unfortunately, it wasn't Demon standing before her, ready to reassure her. It was Remington, who knew nothing about her life. Nevertheless, if she walked with Remington, at least she would get to stretch her legs. Returning his smile, she glanced at Horatia. 'If you don't mind, ma'am?'

Having shrewdly assessed the group on the lawn, Horatia nodded. 'By all means, my dear. A walk will do you good.'

'We'll keep within sight of the carriage,' Remington assured her.

Horatia nodded, watching as Remington helped Flick to the ground. Flick turned and bobbed a curtsy, then put her hand on Remington's sleeve and joined the others waiting.

'Hmm.' Beside Horatia, Helena watched the group as they

332

moved off. 'Is that wise, do you think?'

Her eyes on Flick's bright curls, Horatia smiled grimly. 'As to that, I can't say, but it should get some action.' Turning to Helena, she raised a brow. 'Don't you think?'

As had been his habit for the past weeks, Demon spent his day at White's. Montague and the people he'd hired to watch for Bletchley called on him there – he acted as a general, coordinating their searches. For all their efforts, they'd precious little to show. Both the money and Bletchley had to be somewhere – they'd yet to discover where. And time was running out.

Worrying at the problem – not at all enamored of having to admit defeat and inform the Committee about the fixes planned for the Spring Carnival, simultaneously handing Dillon over without any evidence to support his tale – Demon dropped into an armchair in the reading room, picked up a news sheet and opened it in front of his face.

And tried to relax. At least one or two muscles.

He sighed, too aware that every nerve was taut, every muscle half-tensed. He had a serious illness, caused by a Botticelli angel. The cure was obvious, but, given their present state, he was likely to suffer for some weeks yet.

He still had no idea what had upset her; she seemed, however, to have recovered. Unfortunately, there was now a certain coolness in her attitude to him. She seemed to be watching him measuringly. Which made no sense at all. She'd known him for years – she even knew him in the biblical sense – what more did she think to discover?

Suppressing a snort, he flicked out the news sheet. Dealing with that too-revealing glow of hers *had* to be his primary concern. Some might see it as mere encouragement, but only those with poor eyesight. As matters now stood, she was safe from self-incrimination. Reestablishing their previous relationship would simply be a matter of wrapping her in his arms and kissing her witless, once she'd come around to the idea of marrying him. There was no need to worry on that score.

There was no reason to reverse direction and start hovering over her, even had that been an option. The best thing to do was to hold the line – to keep his distance even more rigidly. Just as he had for the last two nights.

Setting his jaw, he forced himself to read the news.

'Hmm – interesting.'

Demon looked up; Chillingworth stood beside his chair, regarding him quizzically.

'I have to confess to supreme envy at your coolness under fire.'

Demon blinked; every muscle hardened. He searched Chillingworth's face. 'What fire?'

Chillingworth's brows rose. 'Why, the raging interest in your sweet innocent, of course. Haven't you heard?'

'Heard what?'

'That Remington – you've heard that his acres are mortgaged to the hilt and his pockets entirely to let?'

Demon nodded.

'Apparently he did the unthinkable. In the middle of a ballroom, he asked your dear delight whether she and you were engaged.'

Demon swore.

'Precisely. Combined with the fact that supposedly impeccable sources credit her with an income of not less than ten thousand a year, and, well ...' Demon looked up; Chillingworth met his gaze. 'I do wonder, dear boy, that you have time to read the news.'

Demon held his gaze for a pregnant instant, then swore viciously. Crumpling the paper, he stood and shoved it at Chillingworth. 'My thanks.'

Chillingworth smiled and took the paper. 'Don't mention

it, dear boy. Only too glad to help any of your family into parson's mousetrap.'

Demon heard the words, but he didn't waste time thinking of a riposte – there was someone he wanted to see.

'Why the *hell* didn't she – you – *someone* tell me she was a damned heiress? *Ten thousand a year!*' Pacing his mother's parlor, Demon shot her a far from filial look.

Sitting on the *chaise*, engrossed in sorting silks, Horatia didn't see it. 'As that's a paltry sum compared to what you have, I can't see why it so concerns you.'

'Because she'll have every fortune hunter in town hanging about her!'

Horatia looked up. 'But ...' She frowned. 'I was un der the impression there was an understanding between Felicity and yourself.'

Demon gritted his teeth. 'There is.'

'Well, then.' Horatia looked back at her silks.

Fists clenched, Demon hung on to his temper – already sorely tried – and absorbed the fact that his mother was baiting him. 'I want to see her,' he ground out. Only then did it occur to him that to find Horatia without Flick in attendance at this time of day was odd. A chill touched his spine. 'Where is she?'

'The Delacorts invited her to a picnic at Merton. She went down in Lady Hendricks's carriage.'

'You let her go *alone*?'

Horatia looked up. 'Good heavens, Harry! You know that crew. They're all young, and while both Lady Hendricks and Mrs. Delacort might have sons in need of wealthy wives, as you and Flick already have an understanding, what harm can there possibly be?'

Her blue eyes, fixed on his face, dared him to tell her.

Teeth gritted so hard that his jaw ached, Demon nodded curtly, swung on his heel, and left.

335

He couldn't do a damned thing about it – the sudden rush of picnics, alfresco luncheons and daytime excursions that swept into the more youthful stratum of the ton.

Standing, arms crossed, against a wall in Lady Monckton's ballroom, Demon eyed the circle gathered about Flick, and only just managed not to glare. It had been bad enough watching a group of helpless puppies fawning about her skirts; the gentlemen now about her were of a different calibre. Many would rank as eligible, some had titles; the majority, however, needed money. And they were all a good few years younger than he. They could, with society's blessing, dance attendance on her, court her assiduously by attending all the picnics and innocent gatherings – all things he could not.

Whoever heard of going on a picnic and taking your own wolf? It simply didn't happen.

For the first time in all his years within the ton, he felt like an outsider looking in. The area of society Flick inhabited was not one he could enter. And she couldn't come to him. Thanks to her unfailing honesty, the distance between them was widening to a chasm.

And he was helpless to prevent it.

He'd been tense before. Now ...

Securing two dances with her was impossible now; he'd settled for the country dance after supper – it would follow the waltz just starting. Her present partner, he grimly noted, was Remington, one of those he trusted least. Flick didn't share his opinion; she often waltzed with the bounder.

He no longer cared if people noticed he was watching her, but he was nevertheless grateful for the tonnish quirk that held grossly overcrowded ballrooms to be the mark of a successful hostess. This evening, Lady Monckton was an unqualified success, which lent him a little cover.

The idea of using that cover to whisk Flick away, to take

336

her in his arms and kiss her drifted through his mind. Reluctantly, he let the idea go – it was another thing he simply couldn't risk. If anyone saw them, despite his extreme care to date, questions would be asked.

Without conscious direction, his eyes tracked her through the whirl of dancers, fixing on her glorious halo. As he focused on her, she laughed and smiled at Remington. Demon gritted his teeth – unbidden, unwelcome, his promise to the General replayed in his mind. What if ...

His blood ran cold – he couldn't even finish the thought, couldn't let it form in his brain. The prospect of losing Flick paralysed him.

Abruptly filling his lungs, he shook aside the thought – swiftly replaced it with the image of 12 Clarges Street, the house he'd viewed that morning. It was perfect for him and Flick. It had just the right number of rooms, not too large . . .

His gaze on Flick, his thoughts slowed, stopped, in time with the music. On the other side of the room, Flick and Philip Remington halted; instead of turning toward the *chaise* where Horatia sat, Remington cast a quick glance about, then led Flick through a door. Out of the ballroom.

Demon straightened. 'Damn!'

Two matrons beside him turned to glare – he didn't stop to apologize. Moving easily, apparently unhurriedly, he crossed the room. He knew very well the implication of Remington's swift look. Who the hell did the bounder think he was?

'Ah – *darling*.'

Celeste stepped into his path. Dark eyes glinting, she lifted a hand—

He stopped her with one look. 'Good evening, madam.' With a terse nod, he stepped around her and continued on. From behind, he heard a lewd curse in French.

Gaining the corridor that lay beyond the ballroom, he was

just in time to see the door at its end close. He paused to dredge up his memories of Monckton House – the room at the end was the library.

He stalked down the corridor, but halted before he reached the end. There was nothing to be gained by rescuing Flick before she realized she needed rescuing.

Opening the door of the room before the library, he entered. Eyes quickly adjusting to the dark, he crossed it, silently opened the French door, and stepped onto the flagged terrace beyond.

Standing in the middle of the library, Flick scanned the pictures on the walls, then looked at her companion. 'Where are the etchings?'

The library was made dark by paneling and bookshelves packed with brown books, but a small fire burned cheerily in the grate. Lighted candelabra stood on a table beside the sofa and on a side table by the wall, casting a glow about the room, their flames flickering in the breeze sliding through the French doors open to the terrace. Completing a second survey of the walls, Flick turned to Remington. 'These are all paintings.'

Remington's smile flashed; she saw his hand shift, heard a click as the door's lock engaged. 'My sweet innocent.' There was gentle laughter in his voice as he advanced, smiling, toward her. 'You didn't really believe there were any etchings here, did you?'

'Of course, I did. I wouldn't have come otherwise. I'm fond of etchings ... ' Her voice faded as she studied his face, then she stiffened and lifted her chin. 'I think we should return to the ballroom.'

Remington smiled winningly. 'Oh, no. Why? Let's just dally here for a short while.'

'No.' Flick fixed him with a steady, unblinking stare. 'I

wish you to return me to Lady Horatia.'

Remington's expression hardened. 'Unfortunately, my dear, I don't wish to do so.'

'Don't worry, Remington – I'll escort Miss Parteger back to my mother.'

Lounging against the frame of the French doors, Demon drank in their reactions. Flick whirled – relief softened her face, softened her stance. Remington's jaw dropped, then he snapped it shut and glowered belligerently.

'Cynster!'

'Indeed.' Straightening, Demon swept Remington a taunting bow. His gaze was steely, as were the undercurrents in his voice. 'As you're unable to show Miss Parteger the etchings you promised her, might I suggest you depart? Not just this room, but the house.'

Remington snorted, but eyed him uncertainly. Which was wise – Demon would happily take him apart given the slightest provocation. 'I'm sure,' he drawled, 'you can see that's the best way.' Strolling forward, he stopped beside Flick and trapped Remington's now wary gaze. 'We wouldn't want there to be any whispers – if there were, I'd have to explain how you'd misled Miss Parteger over the existence of etchings in the Monckton House library.' Raising his brows, he mused, 'Difficult to find a rich wife if you're not invited to the balls any more.'

Remington's expression didn't succeed in masking his fury. But he was a good deal shorter and slighter than Demon; swallowing his ire, he nodded, bowed curtly to Flick, then swung on his heel and stalked to the door.

Beside Demon, grateful for his intimidating, reassuring presence, Flick frowningly watched the door close behind Remington. 'Is he a fortune hunter?'

'*Yes*!' With an explosive oath, Demon lifted both hands, then appeared not to know what to do with them. With

339

another oath, he swung away, pacing. '*He* is! Half those about you are – some more so than others.' His blue gaze stabbed her. 'What *did* you imagine would happen once you let it be known how much you're worth?'

Flick blinked. 'Worth?'

'You can't be *that* innocent. Now the news is out that you come with ten thousand a year in tow, they're all flocking around. It's a wonder you haven't been mown down in the rush!'

Understanding dawned, along with her temper – she swung to face him. '*How dare you!*' Her voice quavered; she drew in a huge breath. '*I* didn't tell anyone *anything* about my fortune. I haven't spoken about it at all.'

Demon halted; hands on hips, he looked at her. Then he scowled. 'Well you needn't look at me. I'm hardly likely to fashion a rod for my own back.' He started to pace again. 'So who spread the news?' He spoke through clenched teeth. 'Just tell me, so I can wring their neck.'

Flick knew exactly how he felt. 'I think it must have been my aunt. She wants me to marry well.' She wanted her to marry Demon, so her aunt had let it be known that she was an heiress. She assumed, avaricious as she was, that the news would prompt him to grab her, regardless of how wealthy he was.

'Was that what she said to upset you at that ball?'

She hesitated, then shrugged. 'In a way.'

Demon glared at her. First his mother, now her aunt. Elderly ladies were lining up to make his life difficult. That, however, wasn't the cause of the black, roiling, clawing rage that filled him, fighting to get loose, spurred by the knowledge of what would have happened if he hadn't been watching her so closely.

'Whatever – *whoever*.' He bit off the words. Towering over her, his hands on his hips, he captured her gaze. 'Bad enough you're surrounded by a gaggle of fortune hunters – that doesn't excuse your behavior tonight. You know damn well not to go anywhere alone with any man. What the *hell* did you think you were doing?'

Her spine stiffened; her chin rose. Her eyes flashed a warning. 'You heard. I happen to like etchings.'

'*Etchings!*' Jaw clenched, he only just managed not to roar. 'Don't you know what that means?'

'Etchings are prints made from a metal plate on which someone has drawn with a needle.'

She capped the comment by putting her pert nose in the air; Demon tightened his fingers about his hips against the urge to tighten them about her. He bent forward, lowering his face so it was closer to hers. 'For your information, a gentleman offering to show a lady etchings is the equivalent of him inviting her to admire his family jewels.'

Flick blinked. Puzzled, she searched his eyes. 'So?'

'*Aargh!*' He swung away. 'It's an invitation to intimacy!'

'It is?'

He swung back to see her lip curl.

'How like the fashionable to corrupt a perfectly good word.'

'Remington was looking to corrupt *you*.'

'Hmm.' She looked at him, her expression stony. 'But I do like etchings. Do you have any?'

'Yes.' The answer was out before he'd thought. When she raised a brow, he grudgingly elaborated, 'I have two scenes of Venice.' They hung on either side of his bed. When he invited ladies to see his etchings, he meant literally as well as figuratively.

'I don't suppose you'd invite me to see them?'

'No.' Not until she agreed to marry him.

'I thought not.'

He blinked, and scowled at her. 'What's that supposed to

341

mean?' Her cryptic utterances were driving him crazy.

'It means,' Flick enunciated, her accents as clipped as his, 'that it's become increasingly clear that you want me merely as an ornament, a suitable, acceptable wife to parade on your arm at all the family gatherings. You don't want me *powerfully* at all! That doesn't impress me – and I've been even less impressed by your recent behavior.'

'Oh?'

The single, quietly uttered syllable was a portent of danger; she ignored her reactive shiver. 'You're never *there* – never about! You don't deign to waltz with me – you've driven me in the park precisely once!' Looking into his face, fists clenched, she let loose her pent-up frustrations. '*You* were the one who insisted on bringing me to London – if you thought this was the way to get me to marry you, you've seriously miscalculated!'

Her eyes narrowed as she looked into his. 'Indeed, coming to London has opened my eyes.'

'You mean it's shown you how many puppies and fortune hunters you can have at your beck and call.'

His growl was a grating rumble she had to concentrate to hear; her reply was a sweet smile. 'No,' she said, her tone that of one explaining a simple matter to a simpleton. 'I don't want puppies or fortune hunters – that wasn't what I meant. I meant I've seen the light about *you!*'

Eyes mere slits, he raised one brow. 'Indeed?'

'Oh, indeed!' Buoyed on an outrush of pure release, Flick gestured wildly. 'Your women – ladies, I'm sure. Particularly Celeste.'

He stiffened. 'Celeste?'

There was demand in his tone, along with a clear warning. Flick heeded the first but not the second. 'You must remember her – dark hair, dark eyes. *Enormous*—'

'I *know* who Celeste is.' The steely words cut her off.

'What I want to know is what you know of her.'

'Oh, nothing more than anyone with eyes knows.' Her own eyes, filled with fury, told him precisely how much that was. 'But Celeste is by the way. At least, if we're ever to marry, she will certainly have to be 'by the way.' My principal point, however, is this.'

Halting directly in front of him, she looked into his face, and hissed, '*I am not your cousin, to be watched over in this dog-in-the-manger way*!'

He opened his mouth – quick as a flash, she pointed a finger at his nose. 'Don't you *dare* interrupt – just listen!'

He shut his mouth; the way his jaw set, she felt reasonably sure he wouldn't open it again soon. She drew in a deep breath. 'As you well know, I *am not* some eighteenyear-old innocent.' With her eyes, she dared him to contradict her; his lips thinned ominously, but he remained silent.

'I want to talk, walk, waltz and drive – and if you wish to marry *me*, you'd better see it's with *you*!'

She waited, but he remained preternaturally still. A sense of being too close to something dangerous, something barely controlled, tickled her spine. Hauling in a breath, she kept her eyes steady on his, unusually dark in the weak candlelight. 'And I will *not* be marrying you unless I'm convinced it's the right thing for me. I will *not* be browbeaten, or pressured in any way.'

Demon heard her words through a smothering fog of seething rage. Muscles in his shoulders flickered, twitched – his palms itched. The injustice in her words whipped him. He'd done nothing for any reason other than to protect her. His body was about to explode, held still purely by the force of his will, which was steadily eroding.

She'd paused, searching his face; now she drew herself up and coolly stated, 'I will not be managed by you.'

Their gazes locked; for one long moment, absolute silence

held sway. Neither moved – they barely breathed. The conflagration within him swelled; he locked his jaw, and endured.

'I *refuse—*'

He reached out and pulled her into his arms, cutting the statement off with his lips, drawing whatever repudiation she'd thought to make from her mouth, then he plundered, searched, took all she had and demanded, commanded, more.

He drew her against him, hard against the unforgiving rock his body had become. His mind was a seething cauldron of emotions – rage colliding hotly with passion and other, more elemental needs. He was coming apart – a volcano slowly cracking, outer walls crumbling, blown asunder by a force too long compressed. Only dimly did he recall that he'd wanted to shut her up, wanted to punish her – that wasn't what he wanted now.

Now, he simply wanted.

With a desire so primitive, so primally powerful he literally shook. For one instant, he stood on the cusp, quivering, the last shreds of restraint sliding through his grasp – in that moment of blinding clarity he saw, understood, that he'd asked too much of himself, too much of who he really was. Remington had provided the last straw, piling it on top of more amorphous fears – such as what he would do if she fell in love with someone else. How he would cope if she did.

He'd assumed he could control the thing that was inside him – the emotion she and only she evoked. In that quivering, evanescent instant, he knew he'd assumed wrong.

With the last shreds of his will, he forced his arms to ease just enough to give her leeway to pull away, to escape. Even in extremis, he didn't want to hurt her. If she struggled, or even remained passive, he could fight, hold back, endure, and eventually releash his demons.

She grabbed the chance and pulled her arms from between them; something inside him howled. He braced himself for her shove on his chest – whipped himself to let her go –

Her hands caught his face, framed it. Her lips firmed, then angled under his; her fingers slid into his hair.

She kissed him hungrily. Voraciously. As powerfully demanding as he.

His head spun. Desire exploded. He was lost.

So was she – no angel, now, but a woman wild, demonically demanding, flagrantly inciting—

Madness.

It caught them up – set them free.

Flick gloried in the rush, gloried in the sense of being impossibly alive. Gloried in the hard body against hers, the chest like rock against her aching breasts, the thighs like pillars trapping hers. His lips bruised hers and she exulted; his hard hands held her brutally close, lifting her, rocking her – she only wanted to be closer.

She wanted him more than she wanted to breathe. Flinging her arms about his shoulders, she levered herself up in his punishing embrace, then held tight so their faces were closer, nearly level. His hands wrapped over her bottom, he held her high against him; she could feel the hard ridge of him grinding against her mound.

She wanted him inside her. Here. Now. Immediately. His tongue plundered remorselessly, his lips more ruthlessly demanding than ever before – she had no breath to tell him. Her skirts were just wide enough for her to grip his hips with her thighs; she did, then moved against him.

His breathing hitched; muscles tensed, then quivered. Beneath her hands, he felt like tensile steel, coiled, compressed, ready to let fly.

She moved again. He caught his breath and resumed his heated ravishing of her mouth. But his hands on her bottom shifted; supporting her with one hand, he reached down, caught the hem of her gown, and flicked, sliding first one hand under, then, palm to her bare bottom, changing hands and slipping the other, too, under her silk skirts.

Her fine chemise was short – no impediment. His hands were beneath it from the start. Hauling in a breath, she gripped tighter with her thighs, locked her arms about his neck, and flagrantly wriggled in his hands.

He got the message – his hands drifted, his touch driven, demanding, over the backs of her splayed thighs, over the globes of her bare bottom, then, holding her high with one hand, he slid the other down and around, hard fingers ex ploring the soft, slick folds between her thighs.

He found her entrance – one finger slid deep.

She gasped and arched lightly. The finger left her – a second later, two returned, pressing deep, drawing back, then stabbing once, twice, hard and deep.

She couldn't catch her breath – heat raged beneath her skin. Her body quivered, ready to fly apart. But that wasn't what she wanted.

Locking one arm about his neck, she slid her other hand between them – down to where his engorged flesh throbbed, rampant and hard as iron. She closed her fingers greedily, sliding them down as far as she could—

He groaned. And shuddered. '*God*—!'

Voices reached them. Footsteps steadily approached the library. Panting, senses screaming, Flick turned her head and stared at the door. The unlocked door.

Like the procession of thoughts said to presage death, Demon saw in his mind's eye Remington closing the door behind him. Saw the image he and Flick would present to those nearing the library. They were both beyond dishevelled, barely able to breathe; Flick's arms would never release in time – nor would his.

Three giant strides had them at the French doors; with two more, he got them out of sight.

346

The library door opened.

Swinging Flick against the wall, he pressed her into the soft creeper – the scent of jasmine wafted about them. Chest heaving, he leaned into her, pinning her there, physically wracked by the effort of exerting his will. His entire body had been focused on doing only one thing – burying himself inside her.

Voices from inside reached them clearly; he couldn't separate the sounds through the drumming in his ears.

He tried to think, but couldn't. Flexing every mental muscle, he tried to pull back from the soft body his rockhard limbs were holding fast against the creeper-covered stone. And failed. Just thinking about that soft body had hurled him back into the volcano of his need.

Molten desire rose, battered at his senses, broke and consumed his will.

His breathing harsh in the moonlit night, he slowly lifted his head, raised his lids and looked into her face. He expected to see shock, fright – even fear – surely he had to be scaring her? Even fear of discovery – a real possibility – would do; anything to help him hold back from doing what he would do.

Instead, he saw a face sultry with desire, heavy-lidded eyes fixed hungrily on his lips. Saw her swollen lips part, her tongue briefly lick the lower. She felt his gaze and looked up – her eyes searched his briefly, then her chin firmed. 'Now.'

The demand reached him on a determined whisper. Her lips curved – he could have sworn in ruthless triumph. Then he felt her hand, still trapped between them.

She closed it, slid her fingers down, then up – he closed his eyes and shuddered. Her wicked chuckle was a warm breath against his lips as she trailed her fingers higher – to his waistband. She'd worn male attire herself; in seconds, she'd slipped the buttons and had him free. He leapt in her palm, iron hard, ready to explode.

347

With a gasping groan he only just suppressed, he reached between them, caught her hand and hauled it up, leaning even harder into her, teeth gritted against the sensation of her silk skirts sliding over his sensitized flesh.

He met her eyes, mere inches from his. If he could have glared, he would have. But his features were set, graven – impossible to shift – hers looked the same way. Driven, muscles locked and quivering, he teetered on the brink—

She met his hard gaze directly, challengingly. 'Do it!' she hissed against his lips. Then kissed him ravenously.

The conversation inside the library droned on; mere yards away, in the moonlight on the terrace, hot and frenzied needs held sway. A bare second was all it took for him to lift her skirts, to smooth them up, out of the way. His staff slid seeking between her thighs; she gripped him hard and pulled him to her.

He found her entrance and plunged – drove into her heat – straight into a vortex of shattering need.

His – and hers.

The combination was too powerful for either of them to control; it buffeted them, battered them, drove them. Their bodies bucked and strained, desperate for release, locked in a battle with no foe.

Lips frantically locked to stifle the sounds that clawed their throats, they took all they could, grabbed and held on, clutched for each precious moment – there, against the wall in the moonlight.

The sounds from the library washed over them, gentle, soothing, heightening their awareness.

Of the heated slickness where they joined, of skin too hot to touch, of the raging tide in their blood – of the driven fusing of their bodies.

Crushed blossoms released perfume in a cloud about them – an evocative scent as deeply illicit, deeply intimate as their

348

mating. Gasping, Flick dragged the scent deep. Demon's hips flexed again, ruthlessly driving into her. His lips cut off her glad cry as he plunged. Again and again he filled her – a sword slamming into its sheath. She gripped him lovingly and gloried in the power – the power that drove them both.

The ride was wild – wilder than she'd imagined anything could be. She clung tight, drunk on that power, delirious with speed, drugged with pleasure. Then the peak was before them – they rode faster, gripped by compulsive urgency.

And then they were there – the mountain exploded, erupted, melting them in its massive heat.

No! Don't leave me! Flick silently begged, clinging tightly for one heartbeat, then, accepting that he would have to, she sighed and relaxed her hold.

He withdrew from her; she closed her eyes against the sudden emptiness. Cool air slid between them, chilling her flushed skin. She gripped his shoulder as he shifted, sliding her down, carefully guiding her back to earth.

Her slippers touched cold stone; he flicked her skirts down. They fell easily. She glanced down and was amazed – they were only slightly crushed. He didn't move away; one arm about her, he angled his body, shoulder to hers as he roughly straightened his clothes.

The murmur of voices still flowed from the library; as the pounding in her ears subsided, she could hear two older men swapping tales of long gone battles. The doors to the terrace stood wide, the candlelight a pale swath on the grey flags. If anyone had come to the threshold ...

Luckily, no one had.

Heat still lapped her; warmth still flowed in her veins. She felt both exhilarated and disappointed – and confused that that was so.

Tightening his arm about her, Demon steered her along the

terrace to the next set of doors, also open. Without a word, he helped her over the step and into the dark room.

Her heart leapt – instantly, she stilled it. What was she thinking? Just because she still wanted to hold him, to feel his body naked against hers, to hear his heart beating under her ear, to snuggle close – feel close – to cling – just because she wanted, didn't mean they could. They were at a ball, for heaven's sake!

He drew away from her, quickly tucking in his shirt, doing up his trousers, straightening his cravat and coat. Breathless, giddy, her heart still pounding, she shook out her skirts and smoothed them, wriggled her chemise straight, fluffed out the organza ruffle that traced her neckline and formed her transparent sleeves.

She looked up to discover Demon looking at her; she stared at him hungrily, conscious to her toes of a compulsion to reach out and touch him. Hold him. Although her body hummed with satiation, some other part of her felt ... deprived. Denied. Still yearning.

Even through the dimness, Demon saw the need in her eyes; he felt it in his gut. He cleared his throat. 'We have to go back.'

She hesitated, then nodded.

'Do you know where the withdrawing room is?' He spoke in a hushed whisper, conscious of those next door.

'Yes.'

'Go there – if anyone comments on you coming from the wrong direction, just say you went out of the other door and got lost.' He surveyed her critically. 'Put cold water on your lips.' Reaching out, he tucked one unruly curl back behind her ear. Ruthlessly squelching the impulse to trail his fingers along her jaw, to fold her in his arms and simply hold her, he lowered his hand. 'I'll go directly back.'

She nodded, then turned to the door. He opened it, glanced

out, then let her through, retreating back into the gloomy room to wait until she'd passed out of sight.

He needed to talk to her, explain things, but he couldn't do it now – not tonight. Thanks to her wantonness, and his, he couldn't think straight – and they had to get back to the ball.

Chapter Nineteen

Desperate needs called for desperate deeds. Flick knew her needs qualified as desperate, especially after last night. She needed much more from her lover – her prospective husband. She knew what she wanted. The big question was: How to get it?

Surrounded by her court, in the middle of Lady Ashcombe's drawing room, she pretended to listen while inwardly she plotted. She'd come to London with one clear aim: to make Demon fall in love with her. If he'd been going to look at her face and fall down smitten, it would have happened long ago. As it hadn't, she was going to have to do something – take some active steps – to achieve her desired goal.

Insisting he spend more time with her was the logical next step. She'd made a start last night, although they'd got distracted. She'd enjoyed the distraction, as far as it had gone, but that had only made her more determined, more stubbornly set on her course. Such distractions, and the subsequent empty yearning, provided yet more reasons to act soon. She didn't want to find herself in the situation of *having* to agree to his suit. That would leave her with absolutely no leeway to secure her dream. And she definitely wanted to ease the desolate, empty feeling their interlude outside the library had left about her heart.

She was still convinced he could love her if he tried. They had so many things in common. She'd enumerated them at length in her cold bed last night; she felt confident the possibility of love was there.

The first step to making it a reality was to ensure that he spent more time with her. To do that, she needed to speak with him alone. She also wanted to talk to him about Dillon. Recalling how the previous night's interlude had come about, she eyed her would-be suitors measuringly.

Demon saw her proposition Framlingham. His mental imprecations as he strolled to the side door to cut off their escape should have set her ears aflame.

'Oh, ah! Evening, Cynster.'

'Framlingham.' With a perfunctory nod to Flick, he met his lordship's eyes. 'Dissatisfied with her ladyship's entertainments?'

'Ah—' Although bluffly genial, Framlingham was not slow. He shot a glance at Flick. 'Miss Parteger needed a breath of fresh air, don't you know.'

'Indeed?'

'Indeed,' Flick verified. 'However, now you're here, I won't need Lord Framlingham's kind escort.' She gave Framlingham her hand and smiled sweetly. 'Thank you for coming to my aid, my lord.'

'Any time – er.' Framlingham glanced at Demon. 'Pleased to have been of assistance, my dear.' With a nod, he beat a hasty retreat.

Demon watched him go, then slowly turned his head and met Flick's limpid gaze. 'What are you about?'

She opened her eyes at him. 'I would have thought that was obvious. I want to speak with you.'

So she'd jerked his leash. Demon clenched his jaw and fought to preserve some semblance of debonair aloofness.

She swung to the door. 'Is the garden this way?'

Along with the terrace. 'I find it difficult to believe you're in need of fresh air. You're not the wilting sort.' She certainly hadn't wilted last night.

'Of course not, but we need to speak privately.'

'Indubitably.' He bit the word off. 'Not, however, out there.' He wasn't about to risk a repeat of last night.

Meeting his gaze, she tilted her chin. 'Where, then?'

One challenge to which he had an answer. 'There's a *chaise* in an alcove over there.'

He caught her hand, placed it on his sleeve, and led her through the crowd. Although this was only a party, there were still too many guests crowding the room. It took them some minutes to cross it, time in which his anger faded to resentment – at her action, his reaction, and the ever present, irritating confusion that dogged him.

Never in his life had he had so much trouble with a woman. As on horses, so too in the ballrooms. He was widely acknowledged as clever in the saddle, yet for all his experience, Flick was forever running her own race, perpetually relegating him to following at her heels. He was constantly having to reassess, rethink, readjust, which was not what he'd expected. Unfortunately, there seemed little else he could do.

He had to follow, and *try* to keep *his* hands on their reins. And ignore the nagging feeling that he was out of his depth with her.

Deep inside, he knew it, but he couldn't accept it – he was infinitely more experienced than she. But this was not the young chit he'd made blush under the wisteria, the innocent miss he'd kissed by the banks of the stream, and taught to love at The Angel. This Flick was a conundrum, one he'd yet to work out.

The alcove was deep but open to the room. If they kept their voices down, they could talk freely, but in no real sense were they private.

He handed her to the *chaise*, then sat beside her. 'Do you think, next time you wish to speak with me, you could dispense with manipulation and simply send a note?'

She looked him in the eye. 'From someone who has so consistently tried to manage me, that's definitely a case of the pot calling the kettle black.' Her voice was even but her eyes spat blue sparks.

He waved a hand at the crowd. 'Face forward and look bored. Make it appear we're idly chatting while you rest.'

Her eyes flared, but she did as he said. '*See*?' she hissed.

'Look bored, not irate.' He looked down; her fists were clenched in her lap. 'Relax your hands.' Despite his irritation, he'd lowered his voice to a cajoling murmur; after an instant's hesitation, her fingers uncurled.

Looking ahead, he drew in a breath, intending to explain, simply, succinctly, that in this sphere he was infinitely more experienced than she, that he knew precisely what he was doing and if she'd only deign to follow his lead, all would be well—

'I want you to spend more time with me.'

The demand made him bridle, but he preserved his bored facade. His instinctive response to any outright demand was resistance, but in this case, resistance was tempered by desire. It was a shock to realize he was not at all averse to spending the bulk of his days by her side. He felt his features harden as the implication sank in, while all the reasons he couldn't do so replayed in his mind.

Not least was that sensual glow of hers – if they were frequently together, he'd never preserve a safe distance. And she'd react. On top of that, there was a quality in their interactions now that simply shouldn't be there. For instance, if he leaned closer, she would turn to him, not draw away as an innocent would. Physically, she was completely at ease in his company – womanly, seductively alluring, not nervous and skittish as she should be.

Drawing in a breath, he considered telling her, but . . . the very last thing he wanted was for her to change.

'No.' He spoke decisively. After a moment, he added, 'That's not possible.'

She didn't, to his surprise, react – didn't turn her head and glare. Instead, she continued to study the room.

It took Flick some time to absorb his words. She'd made her demand expecting an argument, not bald denial. Yet she'd sensed his stiffening the instant the words were out – she'd braced herself to hear something she'd rather not. Nevertheless . . . she had trouble taking it in. Trying to understand. What was he telling her?

A sudden premonition swept her – last night she'd accused him of wanting her solely as an ornament. She'd said it to prod him to deny it. He hadn't. Forcing in a breath, she concentrated on not gripping her fingers and wringing them. Had she, from the first, completely misread him – completely misunderstood what this something between them was?

Had she fooled herself into believing he might, one day, love her?

The cold started in her toes and flooded upward; her lungs froze – she felt giddy. But she had to know the truth. She glanced at his face. His features were set, determined. It wasn't his social mask that watched her, but another more stony, more ruthless. She searched his eyes, steady crystalline blue, and found no softness there either. 'No?'

The word trembled on her lips. Abruptly, she looked away, struggling to mask the effect of that word – a blow to her unwary heart.

He tensed, shifted, then sat back. After a moment, he said in an even voice, 'If you agree to marry me, then I can spend more time with you.'

Flick stiffened. 'Indeed?' First a blow, then an ultimatum.

In the same controlled tone, he continued, 'You know I

wish to marry you – that I've been waiting for you to make up your mind. Have you done so?'

She turned her head further away so he couldn't see the fight she waged to keep her hurt from showing.

Demon swallowed a curse. Her agitation reached him clearly, leaving him even more confused than before. But he couldn't reach out and force her to face him – force her to tell him what the devil was wrong. Kept going wrong between them.

He now wished he hadn't pressed for her answer. But he wanted her, and the agony got worse every night. His gaze locked on her curls, he waited, conscious to his bones of that deep wanting, of the contradictions between his mask, his behavior, and his feelings. He wanted to press her, wanted to reassure her. He desperately wanted to tell her the right answer.

One of her curls, the same one he'd often tucked back, had come loose. Raising one hand, he caught it, adjusted it.

And saw his hand shaking.

The sight shook him even more, forcing the vulnerability he'd tried to ignore to the forefront of his mind. His face set; his jaw clenched. A moment later, he demanded, his tone harsh, 'Have you decided?'

Flick looked at him, forced herself to meet his hard blue eyes, tried to see behind the ruthless mask. But she could catch no glimpse of what she searched for – this was not the man she loved, the idol of her dreams, the man who'd made long slow love to her all night at The Angel. The man she'd hoped would learn to love her.

Looking away, she drew in a shaky breath and held it. 'No – but I think I've made a dreadful mistake.'

He stiffened.

She hauled in a tight breath. 'If you'll excuse me?' Briefly inclining her head, Flick stood. Demon stood as she did, so

357

winded he wasn't able to speak. He wasn't able to think, let alone do anything to stop her. Stop her leaving him.

Flick walked back to the group she'd earlier left. Within seconds she was surrounded by eligible gentlemen. From the side of the room, Demon watched her.

The word 'mistake' burned in his brain. Who had really made it – her, or him? Her rejection – how else was he to take it? – seared him. His eyes narrowed as he saw her nod graciously to some man. Perhaps, this time, he should swallow his pride and take her at her word?

The thought was like acid, eating at his heart.

Then he saw her smile fleetingly – a huge effort all for show; the instant the gentleman looked away, her smile faded, and she glanced surreptitiously his way.

Demon caught that glance – saw the hurt, haunted look in her eyes. He swore and took an impulsive step forward, then recalled where they were. He couldn't cross the room, haul her into his arms and kiss her senseless, much less swear undying devotion.

Suppressing a snarl, rigidly schooling his features to a cast that would allow him to move through the throng, he swung on his heel and left the house.

Every time he tried to manage her, things went wrong.

She refused to run in his harness; she never reacted predictably to the reins. He'd expected to be in control, but that wasn't the way it would be.

Lounging in the doorway of the nursery at 12 Clarges Street, the house he dreamed of bringing Flick to as his wife, Demon looked around the room. Set beneath the eaves, it was of a good size, well lit, well ventilated. As in the light, airy rooms downstairs, he could see Flick here, her curls glowing brighter than the sun as she smiled, shedding her warmth about her.

358

The house would be cold without her.

He'd be cold without her. As good as dead.

He knew she wanted something from him – something more than a few hours every day. He even knew what that something was. If he wanted to convince her that she'd made no mistake, that her heart was safe with him, he was going to have to give rather more than he had.

He didn't need to hear her say she loved him – he'd known that for some time, at The Angel if not before. But he'd thought of her feelings as a 'young' love, youthful, exuberant, relatively immature – easy for him to manage and fulfill without having to expose the depth of his own feelings. He'd even used the mores of the ton to assist him in hiding those – the emotions that at times raged so powerfully he couldn't contain them.

He certainly couldn't manage them. Or her.

His chest swelled as he drew in a deep breath, then slowly exhaled. What lay between them now was an obsession – deep and abiding and impossible to deny – not on her part, or his. She was meant for him and he for her, but if he didn't confront the one thing he most feared, didn't surrender and pay the price, he would lose her.

A prospect the Cynster in him could never, ever accept.

He stood for long moments, gazing unseeing at the empty room. Then he sighed and straightened. He would have to see her alone again, and find out what, precisely, he was going to have to do to get her to agree to be his.

That evening, together with Horatia, Flick attended Lady Merton's musicale. Musicales were the one social event Demon had flatly refused to attend. Slipping into the room just as the soprano started to wail, Flick winced and tried to block out the thought that her reaction to such music was something else she and Demon shared. They didn't share the most important trait, which was the only one that mattered.

Setting her chin against a deplorable tendency to quiver, she looked along the rows of seats, hunting for an empty one. She'd taken refuge in the withdrawing room to avoid the twins – one look at their bright, cheery expressions and their far-too-sharp eyes and she'd fled. She possessed no mask solid enough to hide her inner misery from them.

She'd expected to sit with Horatia, but she was now surrounded, as were the twins. Looking along the edge of the room, she tried to spot a vacant seat –

'Here, gel!' Clawlike fingers gripped her elbow; surprisingly strong, they drew her back. 'Sit and stop flitting – it's distracting!'

Abruptly sitting, Flick found herself on one end of a love seat, the rest of which was occupied by Lady Osbaldestone. 'Th-thank you.'

Hands crossed over the head of her cane, her ladyship fixed Flick with a piercing black gaze. 'You look quite peaked, gel. Not getting enough sleep?'

Flick wished she had a mask to hold in front of her face; the old eyes fixed on hers were even sharper than the twins'. 'I'm quite well, thank you.'

'Glad to hear it. When's the wedding to be, then, heh?'

Unfortunately, they were sufficiently distant from other guests not to have to remain silent. Shifting her gaze to the singer, Flick fought to quell the tremor in her lips, in her voice. 'There isn't going to be a wedding.'

'Is that so?' Her ladyship's tone was mildly curious.

Keeping her gaze on the singer, Flick nodded.

'And why is that?'

'Because he doesn't love me.'

'Doesn't he?' That was said with considerable surprise.

'No.' Flick couldn't think of any more subtle way to put it – even the thought was enough to overset her. Breathing evenly, she tried to ease the knot clutched tight about her heart. It had constricted the previous evening and still hadn't loosened.

Despite all, she still wanted him – wanted desperately to marry him. But how could she? He didn't love her, and wasn't expecting to. The marriage he intended would be a living mockery of all she believed, all she wanted. She couldn't endure being trapped in a loveless, fashionably convenient union. Such a marriage wasn't for her – she simply couldn't do it.

'Humor an old woman, my dear – why do you imagine he doesn't love you?'

After a moment, Flick glanced at Lady Osbaldestone. She was sitting back, calmly waiting, her full attention on her. Despite feeling remarkably close to Horatia, Flick could hardly discuss her son's shortcomings with her kind and generous hostess. But ... recalling her ladyship's first words to her, Flick drew breath and faced forward. 'He refuses to give me any of his time – just the polite minimum. He wants to marry me so he'll have a suitable bride – the right ornament on his arm at family gatherings. Because we suit in many ways, he's decided I'm it. He expects to marry me, and – well, from his point of view, that's it.'

A sound halfway between a snort and a guffaw came from beside her. 'Pardon my plain speaking, my dear, but if that's all you've got against him, I wouldn't, if I was you, be so hasty in your judgments.'

Flick shot a puzzled glance at her elderly inquisitor. 'You wouldn't?'

'No, indeed.' Her ladyship sat back. 'You say he won't spend much time by your side – are you sure that shouldn't be *'can't'*?'

Flick blinked. 'Why 'can't'?'

'You're young and he's much older – that alone restricts

361

the arenas in which your paths can cross in town. And an even greater restriction stems from his reputation.' Her ladyship fixed her with a direct look. 'You know about that, do you not?'

Flick colored, but nodded.

'Well, then, if you think about it, you should see there are precious few opportunities for him to spend time with you. He's not here tonight?'

'He doesn't like musicales.'

'Yes, well, few gentlemen do – look around.' They both did. The soprano screeched, and her ladyship snorted again. 'I'm not even sure *I* like musicales. He's generally been squiring you to your evenings' entertainments, hasn't he?'

Flick nodded.

'Then let's think what else he could do. He can't dance attendance on you, because, being who he is, and you who you are, society would raise its brows censoriously. He can't hang about you during the day, in the park or elsewhere – he most certainly can't haunt his parents' house. He can't even join your circle of an evening.'

Flick frowned. 'Why not?'

'Because society does not approve of gentlemen of his age and experience showing their partiality too openly, any more than it approves of ladies wearing their hearts on their sleeves.'

'Oh.'

'Indeed. And Harold, just like all the Cynsters, lives and breathes society's rules without even thinking of them – at least when it comes to marriage, specifically anything to do with the lady they wed. They'll happily bend any rule that gets in their high-handed way, but not when it comes to marriage. Don't understand it myself, but I've known three generations, and they've all been the same. You may take my word for it.'

Flick grimaced.

'Now, Horatia mentioned you haven't accepted him yet, so that simply lays an extra tax on him. Being a Cynster, he would want to stick by your side, force you to acknowledge him, but he can't. Which, of course, explains why he's been going around tense as an overwound watchspring. I have to say he's toed the line very well – he's doing what society expects of him by keeping a reasonable distance until you accept his offer.'

'But how can I learn if he loves me if he's never near?'

'Society is not concerned with love, only its own power. Now, where were we? Ah, yes. Not wanting to make himself, or you, or his family appear outre´, and very definitely not wanting society to view your relationship askance, restricts him to half-hour calls in Horatia's presence – and only one or two a week, to meetings in the park, again not too frequently, and escorting you and Horatia to balls. Anything else would be construed as bad ton – something no Cynster has ever been.'

'What about riding in the park? He knows I like riding.'

Lady Osbaldestone eyed her. 'You're from Newmarket, I believe?'

Flick nodded.

'Well, riding in the park means you'll be walking your mount. At the most, you can break into a trot for a short stretch, but that's the limit of what is considered appropriate stimulation for a female on horseback.' Flick stared. 'So are you surprised he hasn't taken you riding in the park?'

Flick shook her head.

'Ah, well, now you appreciate the intricacies Harold's been juggling for the past weeks. And from his point of view, he doesn't dare put a foot wrong. Most entertaining, it's been.' Lady Osbaldestone chuckled and patted Flick's hand. 'Now, as to whether he loves you or not, there's one point you've obviously missed.'

'Oh?' Flick focused on her face.

'He drove you in the park.'

'Yes.' Her expression said 'So?'

'The Bar Cynster never drive ladies in the park. It's one of those ridiculously high-handed, arrogant, oh-somale-Cynster decisions, but they simply don't. The only ladies any of them have ever been known to take up behind their vaunted horses in the park are their wives.'

Flick frowned. 'He never said anything.'

'I imagine he didn't, but it was a declaration, nonetheless. By driving you in the park, he made it plain to the ton's host-esses that he intends to offer for you.'

Flick considered, then grimaced. 'That's hardly a declara-tion of love.'

'No, I grant you. There is, however, the small matter of his current state. Tight as a violin string about to snap. His temper's never been a terribly complacent one – he's not easygoing like Sylvester or Alasdair. His brother Spencer is reserved, but Harold's impatient and stubborn. It's a very revealing thing when such a man willingly and knowingly submits to frustration.'

Flick wasn't convinced, but ... 'Why did he make this declaration?' She glanced at Lady Osbaldestone. 'Presumably he had a reason?'

'Most likely to keep more experienced gentlemen – his peers, if you will – at a distance, even if he wasn't by your side.'

'To warn them away, so to speak?'

Lady Osbaldestone nodded. 'And then, of course, he kept watch from the other side of every ballroom, just to make sure.'

Flick felt her lips twitch.

Lady Osbaldestone saw and nodded. 'Just so. There's no reason to have the megrims just because he's not beside you.

In terms of his behavior, he's handled this well – I really don't know what more you could want of him. As for love, he's shown possessiveness and protectiveness, both different facets of that emotion, facets gentlemen such as he are more prone to openly demonstrate. But for the facets to shine, the jewel must be there, at the heart. Passion alone won't give the same effect.'

'Hmm.' Flick wondered.

The singer reached her finale – a single, sustained, piercingly high note. When it ended, everyone clapped, including Flick and Lady Osbaldestone. The audience immediately stood and milled, chatting avidly. Others approached the love seat; Flick rose.

Lady Osbaldestone acknowledged Flick's curtsy. 'You think of what I told you, gel – you'll see I'm right, mark my words.'

Flick met her old eyes, then nodded and turned away.

Lady Osbaldestone's comments cast matters in a new light, but ... as Horatia's carriage rumbled over the cobbles, Flick grimaced, thankful for the deep shadows that enveloped her. She still didn't know if Demon loved her – could love her – would ever love her. She'd settle for any of those alternatives, but for nothing less.

Looking back over the past weeks, she had to acknowledge his protectiveness and possessiveness, but she wasn't certain that in his case those weren't merely a reflection of his desire. *That* was strong – incredibly, excitingly powerful. But it wasn't love.

His frustration, which she'd recognized as steadily escalating, was to her mind more likely due to frustrated desire, compounded by the fact that she'd yet to accept his offer. She couldn't see love anywhere, no matter how hard she looked.

And while Lady Osbaldestone had explained why he couldn't spend time with her in town as he had in the country, she hadn't explained why, when he was by her side, he still kept distance between them.

As the carriage rumbled through the wide streets, lit by flickering flares, she pondered, and wondered, but always came back to her fundamental question: Did he love her?

Heaving a silent sigh, grateful to Lady Osbaldestone for at least giving her hope again, she fixed her gaze on the passing scenery and considered ways to prod Demon into answering. Despite her usual habit, she balked at asking him directly. What if he said no, but didn't mean it, either because he didn't realize he did, or did realize but wasn't willing to admit it?

Either was possible; she'd never told him how important having his love was to her. It hadn't escaped her notice that he'd got into the habit of using that one small word with her – on this subject, she couldn't risk it. If he said no, her newfound hope would shrivel and die, and her dream would evaporate.

The carriage swung around a corner, tilting her close to the window. Beyond the glass, she saw a group of men standing outside a tavern door. Saw one raise a glass in toast – saw his red neckerchief, saw his face. With a gasp, she righted herself as the carriage straightened.

'Are you alright, dear?' Horatia asked from beside her.

'Yes. Just . . .' Flick blinked. 'I must have dozed off.'

'Sleep if you will – we've still got a way to go. I'll wake you when we reach Berkeley Square.'

Flick nodded, her mind racing, her troubles forgotten. She began to ask Horatia where they were, but she stopped, unable to explain her sudden need of street names. She kept her eyes glued to the streets from then on, but didn't see any signs until they were nearly home.

By then, she'd decided what to do.

366

Masking her impatience, she waited. The carriage rocked to a halt outside the Cynster house; handed to the pavement, she matched her pace to Horatia's and unhurriedly ascended the steps. As they climbed the stairs, she smothered a yawn. With a sleepy goodnight, she parted from Horatia in the gallery and turned toward her room.

As soon as she'd turned the corner, she picked up her skirts and ran. Hers was the only occupied room in that wing, and she'd forbidden the little maid who helped her to wait up. So there was no one about to see her fly into her room. No one to see her tear to her wardrobe and delve into the cases on its floor. No one to see her shed her beautiful gown and leave it lying on the rug.

No one to see her climb into attire that would have made any lady blush.

Ten minutes later, once more Flick the lad, she crept downstairs. The door was left unlatched until Demon's father came in, usually close to dawn. Until then, Highthorpe polished silver in his pantry, just beyond the baise door. Flick inched down the hall. The front door opened noiselessly – she eased it back just far enough to squeeze through, worried that a draft might alert Highthorpe. Only after she'd closed it again and gently set the latch down did she breathe freely.

Then she darted down the steps and into the street.

She stopped in the shadow of an overhang. Her first impulse was to retrace the carriage's journey, find Bletchley, then follow him through the night. This, however, was London, not Newmarket – it was hardly wise, even dressed as she was, to slink through the streets in the dark.

Accepting reality she headed for Albemarle Street.

Chapter Twenty

Luckily, Albemarle Street wasn't far. She found the narrow house easily enough – Horatia had pointed it out when they'd driven past. Demon lived alone with only Gillies as his general factotum, for which Flick was duly grateful – at least she wouldn't have to cope with strangers.

Slipping through the shadows to the front steps, she noted a lone carriage a few doors down the street. The coachman was shuffling on the box, settling under a blanket; thankfully, his back was to her.

Flick crept up the steps. She reached for the brass knocker, steeling herself to tap gently, but the door gave, just an inch. Catching her breath, she stared at the gap. Splaying her fingers, she gently pushed – the door swung enough for her to slip through.

In the dimness beyond, she looked around, then eased the door closed. She was in a narrow hall, a flight of stairs directly before her. The wall to her right was shared with the next house; to her left lay a closed door, presumably to the parlor. A narrow corridor ran back beside the stairs.

Demon might not be home – there was no light showing beneath the parlor door. Looking up, Flick discerned a faint light low on the landing above. The room upstairs was probably his bedroom.

She bit her lip and considered the narrow stairs.

And heard a sudden scuffle, then the scrape of chair legs on polished boards.

Followed, quite distinctly, by a purring, feminine, highly accented voice: 'Harrrrry, my demon . . . '

Flick's feet were on the stairs before she knew it.

From above came a vibrant oath. Then, 'What the *devil* are you doing here, Celeste?'

'Why, I've come to keep you company, Harrrry – it's cold tonight. I've come to keep you – *all* of you – warrrrrrm.'

Another oath, as heated as the last, answered that. Then came, 'This is ridiculous. How did you get in here?'

'Never mind that – *here I am*. You should, at the very least, reward me for my enterprise.'

In the shadows on the landing, hard by the door, Flick heard a deep, aggravated, very masculine sigh.

'Celeste, I know English isn't your first language, but no is no in most tongues. I told you at least four times! It's over. *Finis*!'

It sounded as if the words were forced through gritted teeth.

'You don't mean that – how can you?'

Celeste's tone conveyed a purring pout. The soft shushing of silk reached Flick's straining ears – she pressed close, one ear to the panel.

An explosive expletive nearly rocked her on her heels.

'*Dammit*! Don't do that!'

A brief scuffle ensued. A confused medley of muttered oaths mixed with Celeste's increasingly explicit cajoling had Flick frowning –

The door was hauled open.

'*Gillies*!'

Flick jumped – and stared, wide-eyed, into Demon's face, watched his snarling expression transform in a blink to utter blankness.

In utter, abject disbelief, Demon stood in his shirtsleeves on the threshold of his bedroom, fury still wreathing his faculties, one hand imprisoning the wrists of his importuning ex-mistress, his gaze locked with the wide blue eyes of his innocent wife-to-be.

For one definable instant, his brain literally reeled.

Flick, thank heaven, was as stunned as he – she stared up at him and uttered not one peep.

Then Gillies shuffled into the hall. 'Yessir?'

Demon looked down the stairs. Behind him, Celeste hissed and clawed at his hands. He filled the doorway so she couldn't see Flick, now shrinking back into the corner of the tiny landing, tugging her cap low, pulling her muffler over her face.

Hauling in a breath, he stepped forward and turned, squashing Flick into the corner behind him. 'The countess is leaving. *Now.*' He yanked Celeste out of his room and released her; stony-faced, he gestured down the stairs.

Celeste paused for one instant, black eyes spitting fury, then she uttered three virulent words he was quite happy not to understand, stuck her nose in the air, hitched her cloak about her shoulders, and swept down the stairs.

Gillies opened the door. 'Your coach awaits, madam.'

Without a backward glance, Celeste swept out of the house. Gillies shut the door.

Behind Demon, Flick grinned, having watched the entire proceedings from under his arm.

Then she jumped, plastering herself against the wall as he swung on her and roared, '*And what the damn hell do* you *think you're doing here?*'

'Heh?' Stunned, Gillies looked up. 'Good God.'

Considering what she could see in Demon's eyes, Flick didn't think God would be much help to her. She could barely remember the answer to his question. 'I saw Bletchley.'

He blinked and drew marginally back. 'Bletchley?'

She nodded. 'On one of the corners we passed on the way home from the musicale.'

'From Guilford Street?'

She nodded again. 'There was a tavern on the corner – he was drinking and chatting to some grooms. *And'*— she paused dramatically—' *he* was in livery, too!'

Which, of course, explained why they hadn't found him, why he hadn't appeared at any of the usual places to meet with the gentlemen of the syndicate. He was, quite possibly, in the household of one of the syndicate.

Demon studied Flick's face while his mind raced. 'Gillies?'

'Aye – I'll fetch a hackney.' Pulling on his coat, he went out.

Straightening, Demon drew in a huge breath, his gaze steady on Flick's eyes. 'Which corner was it?'

'I don't know – I don't know London streets very well.' She tilted her chin and looked straight back at him. 'I'd know it if I saw it again.'

He narrowed his eyes at her; she widened hers and stared back.

Muttering an oath, he spun on his heel. 'Wait there.'

He fetched his coat, shrugged into it, then escorted her down the stairs and into the hackney. At his order, Gillies came too, scrambling up onto the seat beside the driver.

'Guilford Street. As fast as you can.' Demon pulled the door shut and sat back.

The jarvey took him at his word; neither Demon nor Flick spoke as they rattled through the streets and swung around corners. On reaching Guilford Street, Demon told the jarvey to head for Berkeley Square, following the directions he relayed from Flick. Sitting forward, she scanned the streets, unerringly picking out their way.

'It was just a little farther – *there*!' She pointed to the little

371

tavern on the corner. 'He was there, standing by that barrel.'
Bletchley wasn't, unfortunately, there now.

'Sit back.' Demon tugged her back from the window, then
ordered the jarvey to draw up after the next corner. As the
coach rocked to a halt, Gillies swung down and came to the
door. With his head, Demon indicated the tavern. 'See what
you can learn.'

Gillies nodded. Hands in his pockets, he sauntered off,
whistling tunelessly.

Sinking back against the leather seat, Flick stared into the
night. Then she looked down and played with her fingers.
Two minutes later, she drew in a deep breath and lifted her
head. 'The countess is very beautiful, isn't she?'

'No.'

Startled, she looked at Demon. 'Don't be ridiculous! The
woman's gorgeous.'

Turning his head, he met her gaze. 'Not to me.'

Their eyes locked, silence stretched, then he looked down.
Lifting one hand, he reached out, tugged one of hers from her
lap, and wrapped his long fingers about it. 'She – and all the
others – they came before you. They no longer matter – they
have no meaning.' He slid his fingers between hers, then
locked their palms together.

'My taste,' he continued, his tone even and low as he
rested their locked hands on his thigh, 'has changed in recent
times – since last I visited Newmarket, as a matter of fact.'

'Oh?'

'Indeed.' There was the ghost of a smile in his voice.
'These days, I find gold curls much more attractive than dark
locks.' Again, he met her eyes, then his gaze drifted over her
face. 'And features that might have been drawn by Botticelli
more beautiful than the merely classical.'

Something powerful stirred in the dark between them –
Flick felt it. Her heart hitched, then started to canter. Her

lips, as his gaze settled on them, started to throb.

'I've discovered that I much prefer the taste of sweet innocence, rather than more exotic offerings.'

His voice had deepened to a gravelly rumble that slid, subtly rough, over her flickering nerves.

His chest swelled as he drew breath. His gaze lowered. 'And I now find slender limbs and firm, svelte curves much more fascinating – more arousing – than flagrantly abundant charms.'

Flick felt his gaze, hot as the sun, sweep her, then it swung up again. He searched her eyes, then lifted his other hand, shoulders shifting as he reached for her face. Fingers closing about her chin, his gaze locked with hers, he held her steady, and slowly, very slowly, leaned closer.

'Unfortunately' – he breathed the word against her yearning lips – 'there's only one woman who meets my exacting requirements.'

She deserted the sight of his long, lean lips – lifting her lids, she looked into his eyes. 'Only one?'

She could barely get the words out.

He held her gaze steadily. 'One.' His gaze dropped to her lips, then his lids fell as he leaned the last inch nearer. 'Only one.'

Their lips touched, brushed, molded –

Gillies's tuneless whistle rapidly neared.

Smothering a curse, Demon let her go and sat back.

Flick nearly cursed, too. Flushed, breathless – absolutely ravenous – she struggled to steady her breathing.

Gillies appeared at the door. 'It was Bletchley, right enough. He's somebody's groom, but no one there knows who his master is. He's not a regular. The place is the local haunt for the coachmen waiting for their gentlemen to finish at the—' Gillies stopped; his features blanked.

Demon frowned. He leaned forward, looked out at the

street, then sank back. 'Houses?' he suggested.

Gillies nodded. 'Aye – that's it.'

Flick glanced along the row of well-tended terrace houses. 'Maybe we could learn which houses had guests tonight, then ask who the guests were?'

'I don't think that's a viable option.' Demon jerked his head; Gillies leapt at the chance to scramble up top. 'On to Berkeley Square.'

The carriage lurched forward. Demon sat back and pretended not to notice Flick's scowl.

'I can't see why we couldn't ask at the houses – what harm could there be?' She sat back, folding her arms. 'They're perfectly ordinary residences – there must be some way we can inquire.'

'I'll put some people onto it tomorrow,' Demon lied. Better a lie than have her decide to investigate herself. That particular row of ordinary residences hosted a number of high-class brothels, none of which would welcome inquiries as to the identity of their evening's guests. 'I'll see Montague first thing tomorrow, and swing all our people into the fashionable areas.' Inwardly, Demon nodded. Things were starting to make sense.

Flick merely humphed.

Demon had the hackney drop them off just around the corner from Berkeley Square, then take Gillies on to Albemarle Street. He checked the Square, but it was late – there was no one about to see him bring Flick the lad home. He only hoped he could sneak her past Highthorpe.

'Come on.' He strolled along the pavement; Flick strolled beside him.

As they climbed the steps to his parents' door, he glanced down at her. 'Go straight up the stairs as silently as you can – I'll distract Highthorpe.' He gripped the doorknob and turned it – 'Damn!' He turned the knob fully and pushed.

Nothing happened. He swore. 'My father must have come home early. The bolts are set.'

Flick stared at the door. 'How will I get in?'

Demon sighed. 'Through the back parlor.' He glanced around, then took her hand. 'Come on – I'll show you.'

Striding back down the steps, he led her down the narrow gap between his parents' house and the next, into a lane running along the backs of the mansions. A stone wall, more than seven feet tall, lined the lane.

He tried the gate in the wall; it, too, was locked.

Flick eyed the wall and groaned. 'Not again.'

''Fraid so. Here.' Demon linked his hands. Grumbling, Flick placed her boot in them – he threw her up. As in Newmarket, he had to slap his hand under her bottom and heave her over – she grumbled even more.

Demon caught the top of the wall, hauled himself up, then dropped down to join Flick in the bushes below. Grabbing her hand, he led her through the rhododendrons, across the shadowed lawn, and onto the back terrace. He signalled her to silence, then, using a small knife, he set to work on the French doors of the back parlor. In less than a minute, the lock clicked and the doors swung open.

'There you are.' Pocketing the knife, he gestured Flick in. Hesitantly, she crossed the threshold. He stepped in behind her to get off the open terrace –

She clutched his sleeve. 'It all looks so different in the dark,' she whispered. 'I've never been in this room – your mother doesn't sit here.' Her fingers tightened; she looked up at him. 'How do I get to my room?'

Demon stared at her. He wanted to see her alone – to talk to her privately – but a more formal setting in daylight was imperative, or he'd never get out what he had to say. Not before he forgot himself and kissed her. Screened by the dark, he scowled. 'Where's your room?'

'I turn left from the gallery – isn't that the other wing?'

'Yes.' Stifling a curse, he locked the French doors, then found her hand. 'Come on. I'll take you up.'

The house was large, disorientating in the dark, but he'd slipped through its corridors on countless nights past. He'd grown up in this house – he knew his way without looking.

Flick bided her time, trailing him up the stairs and into the long gallery. The curtains at the long windows were open; moonlight streamed in, laying silver swaths across the dark carpet. She waited until they drew abreast of the last window, then she tripped, stumbled—

Demon bent and caught her—

Quick as a flash, she straightened, lifted her arms, framed his face and kissed him, wildly, wantonly – she wasn't going to wait to learn if he was planning to kiss her. What if he wasn't?

Her preemptive action rendered Demon's plans academic. Curses rang in his head – he didn't hear them. Couldn't hear them over the sudden pounding of his blood, the sudden roar of his needs. Her lips were open under his; before he'd even thought, he was deep inside, tasting her, exulting in the sweet mystery of her, drinking her deep.

And she met him – not tentatively or shyly, but with a demand so flagrant it left him giddy.

He pulled back from the kiss to draw in a huge breath, conscious to his toes of the firm swells of her breasts compressed against his expanding chest. He straightened; hands sliding to his nape, she held tight. Eyes glinting under heavy lids, she drew his lips back to hers.

He went readily, urgently hungry for more heady kisses, his pulse pounding in anticipation of the deeper satiation her body, pressed to his in sweet abandon, promised. His arms had locked about her, but it was she who sank against him, a simple surrender so evocative he shook.

Pulling back, he dragged in a breath; dazed, he looked into her face, subtly lit by the moonlight. From under heavy lids, she studied him, then with one finger, traced his lower lip.

'Lady Osbaldestone said you've been keeping your distance because that's what society demands.' She arched one fine brow. 'Is that right?'

'Yes.' He went back for another taste of her, so sweetly intoxicating she was making him drunk. She gave her mouth freely, sliding her tongue around his, then drawing back.

'She said by driving me in the park you made a declaration.' She whispered the words against his lips, then kissed him.

This time, it was he who gave, then drew back, rakish senses alert to some subtle shift in the scene. He blinked down at her. Inwardly swearing, he fought to realign his spinning wits. She was, as usual, setting the pace. And he was left scrambling in her wake.

Reaching up, she drew his lips down to hers for another slow, intimate kiss that left them both simmering.

'Did you intend the drive in the park as a declaration?'

'Yes.'

His lips were back on hers. She pulled away. 'Why?'

'Because I wanted you.' Relentless, he drew her back.

For long moments, silence reigned; locked together, they heated, then burned. When next they broke for breath they were panting. Hearts racing, eyes dark and wild under heavy lids, they paused, lips not quite touching.

'Lady Osbaldestone said you would have wanted to pressure me – why didn't you?'

He shuddered; the supple strength of her, so much less than his, struck through to his bones and left him weak. Aching to have her. 'God knows.'

He went to kiss her, but she stopped him – by running one hand down one locked bicep, then up, across his shoulder and his chest. Stopping with her palm over his heart, she splayed her fingers and tried to press them in – they made no impression on the already tensed muscle.

'She said you were frustrated.' She looked up into his eyes. 'Is she right?'

He sucked in a breath and tensed even more. 'Yes!'

'Is that why you won't let me close – near – even when we're together?'

He hesitated, looking deep into her eyes. 'Put that down to the violence of my feelings. I was afraid they'd show.' He was never, *ever*, going to tell her she glowed.

As if in vindication, she did. He swooped and took her mouth – she surrendered it eagerly, sinking deeper against him, openly, joyously, feeding his need. Her lips were soft under his, her tongue ready to tangle; he took what she freely gave and returned it full-fold.

'I couldn't bear to see you surrounded by those puppies – and the others were even worse.'

'You should have rescued me – carried me off. I didn't want them.'

'I didn't know – you hadn't said.'

Where the words were coming from, he didn't know, but they were suddenly flowing. 'I hate seeing you waltz with other men.'

'I won't – not ever again.'

'Good.' After another searching kiss, he added, 'Just because I'm not forever by your side doesn't mean that's not precisely where I want to be.'

Her 'Mmm' sounded deeply content. She softened in his arms; his breath hitched, his wits reeled – even in her breeches, her body flowed with the promise of warm silk over his erection. He gritted his teeth and heard himself admit, 'I nearly went mad thinking you would fall in love with one of them – prefer one of them – over me.'

378

She drew back. In the moonlight he saw surprise and shock in her face, then her expression softened; slowly, she smiled at him – glowed at him. 'That won't ever happen.'

He looked into her eyes, and thanked God, fate – whoever had arranged it. She loved him – and she knew it. Perhaps he could leave it at that, now he'd admitted so much, and soothed her silly fears that his caution had been disinterest, that his towering restraint had been coolness. He studied her eyes, basked in her glow. Perhaps he could leave things to ease by themselves ...

A second later, his chest swelled; he bent his head and kissed her – deeply, demandingly, until he knew her head was spinning, her wits in disarray. Then he drew back and whispered against her lips, 'I wanted to ask ...'

Drawing back a fraction further, he drank in the sight of her angelic face – the finely drawn features, smooth ivory skin, swollen, rosy lips, large eyes lustrous under heavy lids, her bright curls gleaming gold even in the moonlight. Her cap had disappeared, as had her muffler. As had his wits. 'I hadn't meant it to be like this. You had engagements all day today – I was going to call on you tomorrow to speak to you formally.'

Her lips curved; her arms tightened about his neck. 'I prefer this.' Arching lightly, she pressed against him; he caught his breath. 'What were you going to ask?'

Flick waited, and wondered, with what little wit she still possessed. She felt so happy, so reassured. So wanted. Deeply, sincerely, uncontrollably wanted.

His eyes held hers – she both sensed and felt him steeling himself.

'What will it take to make you say yes?' After a moment, he clarified, 'What do you want from me? What do you want me to do?'

She wanted his heart – she wanted him to lay it at her feet.

Flick heard the words in her head, which was suddenly spinning much too fast. She dragged in a too-shallow breath –

'Just tell me.' His voice was so low she felt it more than heard it.

Eyes wide, she held his darkened gaze and dazedly considered it – considered asking the one question she'd told herself she never could. Searching his face, she saw his strength, and a new, more visible devotion, both unswerving, unfailing – there for her to lean on. Neither surprised her. What did – what made her breath catch and her head swim – was the raw hunger in his eyes, in the harsh planes of his face; for the first time, she saw his naked need. She shivered, deeply thrilled by the sight, shaken by its consequence.

He'd asked for the price of her heart. She would have to tell him it was his.

Drawing in a deep breath, she steadied, calmed. This was, without doubt, the highest fence she'd ever faced. She felt his arms about her, felt his heart thudding against her breast. Her eyes locked with his, so dark in the night, she drew in a last breath, and threw her heart over. 'I need to know – to believe – that you love me.' Her lungs seized; she forced in a quick breath. 'If you love me, I'll say yes.'

His expression didn't change. He looked at her for a long, long moment. She could feel her heart thudding in her throat. Then he shifted, one arm sliding more completely around her, holding her locked against him; with the other, he lifted her hand from his shoulder. He held her gaze, then carried her hand to his lips.

His kiss seared the back of her hand.

'I could say 'I love you' – and I do.' Raising his lids, he met her gaze. 'But it's not that simple ... not for me. I never wanted a wife.' He drew in a breath. 'I never wanted to love – not you, not any woman. I never wanted to risk it – never wanted to be forced to find out if I could handle the strain. In my family, loving's not easy – it's not a simple sunny thing that makes one merely happy. Love for us – for me – was always going to be dramatic – powerful, unsettling – an ungovernable force. A force that controls me, not the other way about. I knew I wouldn't like it – ' His eyes met hers. 'And I don't. But ... it isn't, it appears, something I have a choice about.'

His lips twisted. 'I thought I was safe – that I had defenses in place, strong and inviolable, far too steely for any mere woman to break through. And none did, not for years.' He paused. 'Until you.

'I can't remember inviting you in, or ever opening the gates – I just turned around one day and you were there – a part of me.' He hesitated, studying her eyes, then his face hardened, his voice deepened. 'I don't know what will convince you, but I won't ever let you go. You're mine – the only woman I could ever imagine marrying. You can share my life. You know a hock from a fetlock – you know as much about riding as I do. You can be a partner in my enterprises, not a distant spectator standing at the periphery. You'll stand at the center of it all, by my side.

'And I'll want you there always, by my side – in the ton as much as at Newmarket. I want to build a life with you – to have a home with you, to have children with you.'

He paused; Flick held her breath, very conscious of the steely tension investing his muscles, of the brutal strength holding her gently trapped, of the power in his voice, in his eyes, so totally focused on her.

Releasing her hand, he tucked one stray curl back behind her ear. 'That's what you mean to me.' The words were gravelly, raw, compelling. 'You're the one I want – now and forever. The only future I want lies with you.'

Demon drew breath and looked into her eyes, and saw tears welling bright against the blue. He inwardly quaked, unsure if they meant victory or defeat. He swallowed and asked, his voice barely audible, 'Have I convinced you?'

She searched his face, then smiled – glowed. 'I'll tell you tomorrow.'

His hands, one at her waist, the other at her hip, tightened – he forced them to relax. Disappointment welled, but ... she seemed happy. Deeply content. If anything, her glow had reached new heights, new depths.

He studied her eyes, hard to read in the silvery light, then forced himself to nod. 'I'll call on you midmorning.' He raised her hand and pressed an ardent kiss to her palm. If he had to wait, that was all he dared do.

Steeling himself, he eased his arms from her.

Instantly, she clutched – her eyes flew wide.

'No! Don't go!' Flick locked her eyes on his. 'I want you with me tonight.'

She didn't want to tell him her decision in words – she could never match his exposition. She intended telling him in a more direct fashion – in a manner she was sure he'd understand. Words could wait until tomorrow. Tonight ...

He grimaced lightly. 'Flick, sweetheart, much as I want you, this is my parents' house, and—'

She cut him off with a kiss – the most potent one she could muster.

Long before she stopped for breath, Demon had forgotten the point of his argument – he'd lost the reins of their carriage long ago. The only point he was capable of contemplating lay at the juncture of her thighs, but ... deeply ingrained honor forced him to pull back, catch his breath –

She touched him.

Inexpertly, not firmly enough – but she was learning. He shuddered, groaned – and caught her hand. 'Flick—!'

She wriggled – he had to move quickly to catch her other hand before she reduced him to quivering helplessness.

'Dammit, woman – you're supposed to be innocent!'

Her warm chuckle was the very opposite. 'I gave you my innocence at The Angel – don't you remember?'

'How could I forget? Every damned minute of that night is engraved on my brain.'

She grinned. 'Like an etching?'

'If an etching can convey sensations as well, then yes.' The memories had warmed him, tortured him, for weeks.

Her grin widened. 'In that case, you must recall that I'm not a sweet innocent any more.' Her expression softened, and glowed. 'I gave you my innocence. It was a gift – won't you accept it?'

Demon stared into her lovely face – he couldn't think.

She dropped her gaze to his lips. 'If you won't stay with me here, I'll come back to your lodgings.'

'No.'

'I'll follow you – you can't stop me.' Her lips curved; she met his eyes. 'I want to see your etchings.'

Demon looked down into eyes so blatantly full of love he wondered how he could have doubted her answer. She loved him, and always had, regardless of whether he loved her. But he did love her – desperately. Which meant they'd marry soon. Why was he holding her away?

He blinked. The next instant, he released her hands, wrapped his arms about her, and pulled her hard against him. 'God, you are so *stubborn*!'

He kissed her – powerfully, passionately, deliberately letting the reins go – feeling her tug them from his grasp and fling them aside.

At some point in the subsequent heated exchange, they surfaced long enough to turn the corner of the gallery and find the door to her room. Once inside, he leaned back against the door – and let her have her way with him. It was a new experience, and oddly precious – to have a woman so wantonly, ravenously, set on ravishing him.

383

He reveled in it, in the hot kisses she pressed on him, in the greedy clutch of her fingers on his naked chest. She'd wrecked his cravat, crushed his coat and waistcoat – his shirt had lost buttons. When she hummed in her throat and reached for his waistband, he summoned enough strength to back her to the bed. 'Not yet.' Catching her hands, he stayed her. 'I want to see you first.'

Despite having had her more than once, he hadn't, yet, had a chance to sate his senses as he wished, and view her totally naked. He wanted that – and he wanted it now.

She blinked as he sat on the bed and drew her to stand between his thighs. 'See me?'

'Hmm.' He didn't elaborate – she'd catch on soon enough. At The Angel, he'd seen her naked back, but not her naked front – not in any degree of light. Her male attire made undressing her easy – he had her clad only in a whisper-fine chemise in less than a minute.

By then her eyes were round.

He stood. She stepped back, swiftly scanning the room, noting the lighted candles on her dresser and bedside table, the flickering glow cast by the fire. Dispensing with his coat, cravat, waistcoat and shirt took a minute – his boots and stockings took one more.

Then he sat on the bed again, thighs wide. She turned to look at him, then shyly smiled. All but swaying with the force, the steady pounding, of desire, he went to move – to reach out and draw her to him—

She moved first.

With that same, shy smile on her lips, she grasped the hem of her chemise, and slowly drew it off over her head.

His chest locked – if his life had depended on not looking at her – not visually devouring her – he'd have died.

He wasn't sure he hadn't – he couldn't breathe, couldn't think – he certainly couldn't move. Every muscle had seized, poised, ready ... It took enormous effort to drag in a breath, to drag his gaze upward from the lithe sweeps of her thighs, from the golden nest of curls at their apex, over the smooth curve of her stomach, up over her waist – one he could span with his hands – to the swells of her breasts, high, pert, and tipped with rose.

Her nipples puckered as his gaze touched them; he felt his lips curve, and knew his smile was hungry.

He was ravenous – aching to have her, to haul her into his arms and possess her, sink his throbbing staff deep into her softness, to ride her into sweet oblivion.

She still held her chemise in one hand, but she didn't clutch it close, didn't try to hide from his hot gaze. She shivered, but let him look his fill; when his gaze reached her face, she met his eyes.

There was no mistaking her glow – it was invitation and known delight – it held a siren's allure, and the confidence of a woman well-loved.

If she ever looked at another man like that she would break his heart. The vulnerability washed over him – he acknowledged it, accepted it and let it pass. Reaching out, he took her chemise from her, let it fall to the floor, then curved his hand about her hip.

He urged her to him and she came – shy but not hesitant. Her hands came to rest on his shoulders; he slid his about her waist and held her, sensing the supple strength of her, then he looked up, trapped her gaze, and slid both palms down, over her hips, over the firm spheres of her bottom. He spread his fingers and cupped her, caressed her, kneaded gently – within seconds, her skin dewed and heated. Her pupils dilated, her lids half lowered; she caught her breath and tensed slightly.

Holding her gaze, refusing to let her break the contact, he left one hand evocatively fondling, tracing the smooth curves and hidden valleys, brushing the backs of her thighs. His other hand he placed palm flat on her belly. She sucked in a breath, and tensed even more. Ruthlessly holding her gaze, he slowly slid his hand up, brushing the sensitive underside of one breast with the backs of his fingers, then closing his hand about the firm mound.

She gasped softly; her lids fluttered, then fell. He smiled and kneaded, stroked and tweaked, all the time watching desire flow across her face. Her lips parted. Her tongue slipped out to moisten them; her breath came in little rushes, not yet pants, but with urgency building. Her lashes fluttered as she felt him learn her, explore her.

With a wolfish smile, he bent his head.

Her shocked gasp rang through the room. She clutched his head, fingers gripping tight as he rasped his tongue over the nipple he'd suckled, torturing it even more. She was soon panting in earnest, the sound sweetly evocative.

He drew back. Desire had flooded her, changing her skin from flawless ivory to rose. Sliding his hand down over her waist, he watched her face as he gently kneaded her taut belly, then reached lower, spearing his fingers through her soft curls, pressing into the soft flesh behind.

She was already wet, swollen and ready – he stroked, and she shuddered. And leaned against one thigh, caught his shoulder for balance.

Before he could blink, she hauled in a breath, opened her eyes, and reached for his buttons. Her nimble fingers slid them free; she reached in—

He closed his eyes and groaned.

She closed her hand and he shuddered. His hands fell from her; head bowed, hands fisted, he endured as she eased her hold and went searching, exploring.

He gritted his teeth. He didn't want to open his eyes – his lids still lifted, just enough so he could see her slender arm, wrist-deep in his open breeches, fine muscles flexing as she stroked and squeezed.

386

Then she reached deep.

The groan she ripped from him was one of real pain – he was achingly hard, throbbing fit to explode.

Her other hand pushed at his chest. 'Lie back.'

He did, falling flat on his back, chest heaving as he struggled for breath – control was far beyond him. Her hand left him – he cursed the loss of her touch.

'Just a minute.'

In disbelief, he felt her tugging at his breeches. This was nothing like what he'd had planned, but ... with a defeated groan, he lifted his hips and let her strip them from him. She got them halfway down, then froze.

Only then did he recall she'd never seen what she'd so successfully accommodated four times thus far.

Oh, God! He levered his lids up – she was standing between his thighs, completely naked, staring, absolutely mesmerized, at his groin. At his rather large member, thick as her wrist, which was presently standing at full attention out of its nest of brown hair.

Stifling a groan, he tensed to sit up, to grab her before she jumped away – to calm her, soothe her, reassure her—

In that instant, the stunned look on her face dissolved into a glorious smile – a wicked, purely sensual, blatantly eager light danced in her eyes. Releasing his breeches, she reached for him—

'*No!*'

Chest heaving, he lay on the bed and gazed at her in absolute horror. Her fingers had stopped mere inches from his staff, which was growing more painfully rigid by the second. He glanced at her face.

She opened her eyes wide and raised her brows back. She didn't get close to looking innocent – it was pure sensual challenge that flashed in her eyes. When he didn't immediately respond – just lay there looking at her, stupefied and at her mercy – her chin firmed.

He hauled in a breath. 'All right – but for God's sake get these off me first.'

She chuckled wickedly and did, quickly easing the tight breeches down his long legs, then hauling them off his feet.

He used the moment to gather his strength – she was going to kill him.

His breeches hit the floor; the next instant, she clambered eagerly onto the bed – and surprised him again. He'd assumed she'd come to his side – instead, she climbed up between his thighs, settling herself on her knees directly before what was clearly her present obsession.

He sucked in a breath – it got trapped in his lungs; they seized as she seized him. Too gently. On a groan, he reached down and closed his hand about hers, showing her how much pressure to exert. As in all things, she learned quickly. After that, all he could do was lie back and think of England. Of Lady Osbaldestone – of anything that might distract him. Not that anything did – it was utterly impossible to detach himself from her touch, from her increasingly explicit caresses. With the fingers of one hand wrapped about his rigid length, she reached to his chest, running her warm hand over taut muscles that tensed and tightened even more.

Then she leaned over him – she couldn't reach his mouth – she did reach his flat nipples. When he jerked, she chuckled – when he moaned, she only licked harder. With gay abandon, she spread hot, wet, open-mouthed kisses across his chest, then nibbled her way down, over his ridged abdomen.

He went rigid when she nuzzled along the trail of hair leading down from his navel—

And nearly died when she closed her hot mouth about his head.

He caught her, gripping her arms tight, fighting a desperate battle not to buck and push himself deeper. Dizzy, almost faint, he clenched his jaw, and hauled in three deep breaths, even while he gloried in the intimate caress.

Then he slid his hands further, gripped and lifted her.

Her eyes went wide as he held her briefly above him while he brought his legs inside hers.

'Didn't you like it?'

He met her gaze briefly. 'Too much.' He bit the words off – he wasn't up to talking. He set her down astride his hips. 'I need to be inside you.'

He was nudging into her as he spoke, muscles bunching, flickering, veins cording as he fought to be gentle. He should have readied her more, eased her more, but ...

He glanced up – she met his gaze, studied his eyes fleetingly, then she smiled, gloriously wanton, and gave her wicked little chuckle. Setting her hands on his chest for balance, she leaned forward, just a little.

She flowered and opened for him. Before he could catch his breath and thrust upward, she sank down, not in a rush – he was too big for that – but slowly. Her lids fell; her breath caught. Frowning in concentration, her lower lip caught between her teeth, she eased herself down on him, inch by steady inch, even tucking her rear deeper to take him all. She enveloped him in hot, wet silk, slick with her own passion; when she was fully impaled, she released the breath she'd held – and tightened firmly about him.

After that, he couldn't remember anything clearly – just startling moments of achingly sweet sensuality, a delight he'd never experienced before. As she rode him, loved him, used her body to pleasure him, he lay back, conquered – defeated – and surrendered and simply took. He let her set the pace, let her gallop, rush, or amble as she would. While she moved over him, rising and falling, he let his hands roam, refreshing his memory, learning more – feasting on the knowledge, reveling in the intimacy.

And when, flushed and panting, she convulsed about him, collapsing, sated, into his arms, he decided this had to be heaven. Only an angel could have given him so much.

He held her, soothed her, waited until she'd caught her breath before he rolled her beneath him. Pushing her thighs wide, he thrust heavily, deeply; she caught her breath and opened wide, then clung.

She stayed with him as he rode her, reaching up to stroke his chest. Briefly meeting his eyes, she smiled – a cat who'd savored a whole bowlful of cream. 'I love you.' Her eyes drifted shut on the whisper; her smile remained on her face.

'I know,' he murmured, then closed his eyes and concentrated on loving her back.

A soft, smug smile flirted about her lips. Two minutes later, it died.

She blinked, and shot him a surprised look, immediately wiped from her face as she gasped and arched beneath him. He stifled a groan as she tensed, and tightened about him once more. He was fully engorged and so deeply inside her he was going to lose his mind.

She lost hers first, coming apart in a series of small explosions, a shatteringly long, rolling release.

He continued to ride her, hard and deep, waiting until she eased, until all tension leached from her limbs, until, open and possessed, she lay beneath him, her body accepting him with no resistance – in that instant just before she started drifting, just before he joined her in the void, he leaned down, and kissed her gently.

'I love you, too.'

Chapter Twenty-One

The instincts of years hadn't died – Demon woke long before anyone else in the house. And instantly remembered his last words. He tensed, waiting for horror to engulf him – instead, all he felt was a warm peace, a subtle sense that all was right in his world. For long moments, he simply lay there, luxuriating in that feeling.

A ticking inner clock finally prompted him to move. It wasn't yet dawn, but he had to leave soon. Turning on his side, he studied the angel snuggled beside him. He'd fallen asleep still inside her; during the night, he'd woken and disengaged, then gently settled her to sleep by his side.

How she woke was one of the delights already imprinted – etched – on his mind. Smiling, he gently tugged the sheet from her slack grasp and lifted it.

Flick woke to the sensation of him parting her thighs, to the sweet stroking of his finger in the soft flesh between. She never woke quickly – she simply couldn't do it. By the time her breathing had accelerated enough for her to lift her lids, she was hot and wet, aching and empty. In the instant before she would have tensed to move, he shifted over her, one hand pressing beneath her bottom to tilt her up, his hard thighs pressing hers wide.

He entered her – solid and hard and hot. He pushed in, and stretched her, filled her until she gasped, clutched and clung.

He rode her and she joined him, their bodies locked together, driven and driving, seeking, climbing, racing until their hearts almost burst and glory rained upon them.

Flat on her back, gasping in the aftermath, she felt him still high and hard inside her. He hung over her, on his elbows, head bowed, chest working like a bellows. They were both hot, skins slick. The hair on his chest abraded her nipples – in her sensitized state, she could feel his hair elsewhere – on his forearms and calves, on his stomach, at his groin. Their limbs touched – everywhere; they were as intimately joined as it was possible to be. She had never been more physically aware of him – or herself.

His heart, thudding against her breast, slowed. Raising his head, he looked at her. 'Have I convinced you?'

She lifted her lids and looked into his eyes, then deliberately tensed, tightening all about him, smiled, and let her lids fall. 'Yes.'

He groaned, moaned, dropped his forehead to hers – and predictably convinced her all over again.

As he left her room in a rush, flitting through the corridors like a thief to slip out of the side door before any maid caught sight of him, Demon swore on his soul that he'd never again underestimate an angel.

His morning was busy, but he was back in Berkeley Square by eleven, confident that now the Season was in full swing, his mother would not yet be down. As he'd requested before he'd left, Flick was waiting – she came gliding down the stairs as Highthorpe opened the door.

The light in her eyes, that glow in her face, took his breath away. As she crossed the hall toward him, the sun shone through the fanlight full upon her – it was all he could do not to pull her into his arms and kiss her senseless. If Highthorpe hadn't been standing in silent majesty beside him, he would have.

Flick seemed to sense his thoughts; the glance she shot him as she glided straight past and out of the door was designed to torment.

'We'll be back late in the afternoon.' Demon threw the comment back at Highthorpe as he followed her down the steps. He caught her on the pavement and lifted her into his curricle.

Flick glanced at the empty pillion. 'No Gillies?'

'He's off visiting his peers all over town.' Retrieving the reins and rewarding the urchin who'd held them, Demon joined her; he set the bays pacing smartly. 'I spoke to Montague – we've people everywhere. Now we know where to look, we'll find Bletchley. And his masters.' He took a corner in style. 'And not before time.'

Flick glanced at him. 'I had wondered . . .'

The Spring Carnival was next week. Demon grimaced. 'I should have gone back and seen the Committee this week, but . . . I kept hoping we'd find something – at least one link, one fact, to support Dillon's story. As things stand, we should locate Bletchley by tomorrow evening at the latest – if he's anywhere within the ton, he won't be able to hide. As soon as we have any further information, I'll go back to Newmarket – at the very latest, on Sunday.' He glanced at Flick. 'Will you come with me?'

She blinked and opened her eyes wide. 'Of course.'

Suppressing a grin, he looked to his horses. 'We haven't found any trace of the money – not anywhere – which is odd. We now think it has to be moving through the ton as wagers and overt expenditure. But no one's been throwing large sums around unexpectedly.'

He flicked the reins; the bays stretched their legs. As they passed the gates of the park, he added, 'I'd assumed the syndicate was too clever to use their own servants, but it's possible that, when both Dillon and Ickley declined to provide the necessary services so close to the Spring Carnival, they had no choice but to send someone already to hand – someone they trusted.'

'So Bletchley's gentleman might be a member of the syndicate?'

'Possibly. Bletchley's a pawn, but he may still be being used at a distance. As a gentleman's groom, he'd have plenty of opportunity to meet with other gentlemen – just a word here and there wouldn't register as odd. There'd be no need for formal meetings.'

Flick nodded. 'I'll write to Dillon and tell him we'll be back by Sunday.' Relief rang in her tone. A moment later, she realized her surroundings weren't familiar. 'Where are we going?'

Demon glanced at her. 'There's a sale at Tattersalls – carriage horses mostly. A pair of high-steppers I wouldn't mind picking up. I thought you might like to watch.'

'Oh, *yes*! Tattersalls! I've heard so much about it, but I've never been there. Where is it?'

Her continuing eager queries left Demon in no doubt that he'd discovered the one woman in all England who would rather watch a horse auction than stroll down Bond Street. When, incapable of hiding his appreciation, he said as much, Flick blinked at him in blank bemusement.

'Well, of course – don't be ridiculous. These are *horses*!'

By mutual agreement, he bid on a pair of sweettempered, high-stepping greys, rather too finely boned for his taste – he didn't tell Flick they were for her. When they were knocked down to him, she was absolutely thrilled – she spent the time while he arranged to have them delivered to Newmarket making their acquaintance. He all but had to drag her away.

'Come on, or we'll never make it to Richmond.'

'Richmond?' Consenting at last to let him lead her from the yard, she stared at him. 'Why there?'

394

He looked down into her eyes. 'So I can have you to myself.'

He did, throughout a glorious day filled with simple pleasures, simple delights. They went first to the Star and Garter on the hill, to partake of a light luncheon. Settling her skirts at a table for two by a window overlooking the parklands, Flick noted that the other diners were definitely noticing them. She raised a brow at Demon. 'Shouldn't we have some sort of chaperon for this type of outing?' Her tone was merely curious, certainly not complaining.

He met her gaze, then reached into his pocket. 'I took this to the *Gazette* – it'll be run tomorrow.' He handed her a slip of paper. 'I didn't think you'd object.'

Flick smoothed out the slip, read the words upon it, then smiled. 'No – of course not.' Refolding it, she handed the paper back – it contained a brief statement of their engagement. 'So does that mean we can go about alone without trampling on society's toes?'

'Yes, thank heaven.' After a moment, he amended, 'Well, within reason.'

Reason included a long ramble in the park, under the huge oaks and beeches. They fed the deer, then, hands locked, ambled on through the sunshine. They walked and talked – not of Dillon and the syndicate, or society – but of their plans, their hopes, their aspirations for the shared life before them. They laughed and teased – and shared brief, stolen, tantalizing kisses, screened by the trees. Those kisses left them trembling, suddenly too aware; in unstated accord, they turned back to the carriage and their talk turned to their wedding, and when it was to be.

As soon as possible was their unanimous decision.

As Demon had expected, his mother was waiting when they returned to Berkeley Square.

'Her ladyship is in the upstairs parlor,' Highthorpe

intoned. 'She wished to see you immediately you returned, sir.'

'Thank you, Highthorpe.' Still smiling, Demon ignored Flick's questioning look; taking her hand, he led her up the stairs.

Reaching Horatia's private parlor, he knocked, then opened the door and sauntered through, towing Flick behind him.

Horatia, head already raised, fixed him with a look so severe – so filled with menacing portent – he should have been struck to stone.

Demon grinned. 'How long does it take to arrange a wedding?

The next afternoon, Flick went for a drive in the park with Horatia and Helena. The notice of her engagement to Demon had appeared that morning; Horatia was in alt. Indeed, she'd been so happy and excited on their behalf last night that they'd cancelled their evening's plans and dined unfashionably *en famille* so they could discuss their impending nuptials. As Demon's only stipulation was that it had to be soon, and she had nothing more to add, Horatia was beside herself with plans.

Naturally, Helena had been immediately informed – she'd appeared in Berkeley Square for breakfast, ready to join in the fun. She was presently seated in the carriage beside Horatia; both were regally dispensing information to the senior matrons of the ton, all of whom made a point of stopping by the carriage to comment, and compliment, and graciously bestow their approval.

Flick sat back, endeavored to look pretty, and smilingly accepted the ladies' good wishes. According to Helena and Horatia, that was all she was required to do.

Thus mildly occupied, Flick scanned the scene and wondered if Demon would appear. She doubted it – he didn't seem enamored of this facet of the ton. Indeed, she'd got the distinct impression that as soon as they were wed, he intended to whisk her back to Newmarket, to his farmhouse, and keep her there for the foreseeable future.

That plan met with her complete approval.

Lips quirking, she glanced at the carriageway, at the high-perch phaeton bowling smoothly toward them along the Avenue. The horses caught her eye; she viewed the high-stepping blacks with educated appreciation, then glanced at the carriage – spanking new, black picked out with gold – not showy but exceedingly elegant.

Idly wondering, she lifted her gaze to the gentleman holding the reins, but she didn't know him. He was older than Demon, brown hair curling tightly above a face that was startling in its cold handsomeness. His features were classical – a wide brow and patrician nose set between thin cheeks; his skin was very white. His eyes were cold under their heavy lids; his thin mouth was unsmiling. Overall, his expression was of overweening arrogance, as if even those blue bloods lining the Avenue were beneath his notice.

Flick mentally raised her brows as the equipage swept past; she was about to look away when her gaze touched the liveried groom up behind. *Bletchley*!

Flick turned to Horatia. 'Who is that gentleman – the one who just drove past?'

Horatia looked. 'Sir Percival Stratton.' She waved dismissively. 'Very definitely not one of our circle.' She returned to Lady Hastings.

Flick smiled at her ladyship, but behind her demure facade, her mind raced. Sir Percival Stratton – she remembered the name. It took her a moment to recall from where – an invitation sent to Vane Cynster's house, redirected to his parents as Vane and Patience were still in Kent.

Sir Percival was giving a masquerade that evening.

Flick could barely contain her impatience. The instant she and her two soon-to-be relatives regained the Cynster front hall, she excused herself and quickly climbed the stairs – then rushed to reach the parlor ahead of Horatia and Helena. Quickly shutting the door, she raced to the mantelpiece and rifled through the pile of cards set on its end. She'd been helping Horatia answer the invitations; she'd seen Sir Percival's while sorting the cards one morning, and put it with the others for Vane and Patience. Finding it, she tucked it into the folds of her shawl, then sank down on a chair as the door opened and Helena and Horatia swept in. Flick smiled. 'I thought, after all, that I might join you for tea.'

She did, then excused herself, saying she would rest. Helena would soon leave, then Horatia would rest, too. They all had a full evening of engagements – a dinner and two balls.

That gave her a few hours in which to think what to do.

On the window seat in her bedchamber, she studied the heavy white card, inscribed with bold, black lettering. The invitation was addressed to Mr. Cynster, not Mr. and Mrs. Cynster; Sir Percival must not have realized that Vane had married. Sir Percival's masquerade was to commence at eight o'clock. Unfortunately, it was to be held at Stratton Hall, at Twickenham.

Twickenham was beyond Richmond, which meant it would take hours to get there.

Jaw firming, Flick jumped up, crossed to the bellpull, and sent a footman in search of Demon.

The footman returned, not with Demon but Gillies. He joined Flick in the back parlor.

'Where's Demon?' she asked baldly the instant the door shut behind the footman.

Gillies shrugged. 'He was meeting with Montague, and then had some business in the city – he didn't say where.'

Flick mentally cursed and fell to pacing. 'We're due at a dinner at eight.' Which meant there was no reason Demon would hurry home before six. She shot a glance at Gillies. 'How long will it take for a carriage to travel from here to Twickenham?'

'Two and a half, perhaps three hours.'

'That's what I thought.' She paced back, then forth, then halted and faced Gillies. 'I've found Bletchley. But ...' Quickly, she filled him in. 'So you see, it's absolutely imperative that one of us is there from the start, in case the syndicate decide to meet. Well' – she gestured – 'a masquerade – what more perfect venue for a quiet meeting on the side? And even if the syndicate don't meet, it's vital we move quickly – we'll need to search Stratton's house for evidence and this is the perfect way to gain entry, the perfect opportunity to poke around.'

When Gillies simply stared at her as if he couldn't believe his ears, she folded her arms and fixed him with a stern look. 'As there's no way of knowing when Demon will return, we'll have to leave a message and go on ahead. One of us must be there from the start.' She glanced at the mantel clock – it was already after four. 'I wish to leave promptly at five. Can you arrange for a carriage?'

Gillies looked pained. 'You sure you wouldn't like to reconsider? He's not going to like you hying off on your own.'

'Rubbish! It's just a masquerade, and he'll follow soon enough.'

'But—'

'If you won't drive me, I'll take a hackney.'

Gillies heaved a put-upon sigh. 'All right, all right.'

'Can you get a carriage?'

'I'll borrow her ladyship's second carriage – that's easy enough.'

'Good.' Flick considered, then added, 'Leave a note saying where we've gone and why in Albemarle Street – I'll leave one here, too. One for Demon, and another for Lady Horatia. That should make all smooth.'

Gillies's expression was the epitome of doubtful, but he bowed and left her.

Gillies returned driving Lady Horatia's second carriage, a small, black, restrained affair; he handed Flick into its dimness at just after five o'clock.

Settling back, Flick mentally nodded. Everything was going according to plan. By the time she'd convinced Gillies and returned upstairs, her little maid had returned from the attics with a full black domino and a wonderful, fanciful, feathered black mask. Both were now lying on the seat beside her. The evening was warm, heavy clouds hanging oppressively low. She would don her disguise when they reached Stratton Hall; she was sure no one would see through it.

Indeed, the mask looked quite nice on her, the black heightening the gold of her hair. She grinned. Despite the seriousness of what she was doing, of the syndicate and the danger, she felt a welling thrill of excitement – at last, they were close. At last, she was doing.

With mounting anticipation, she considered what lay ahead. She'd never been to a masquerade before – while such entertainments had once been commonplace, they didn't, it seemed, feature much these days. Idly, she wondered why, and put it down to changing fashions.

Regardless, she was confident that she'd cope. She'd been to heaps of balls and parties; she knew the ropes. And Demon would follow as soon as he got home – there was very little chance of anything going wrong.

Thunder rumbled, low, menacing, yet still distant. Closing her eyes, Flick smiled.

400

Gillies had stated that Demon wouldn't like her going into danger. Lady Osbaldestone had warned her that he was protective – she already knew that was true. She rather suspected she would be hearing a sound just like that thunder much nearer at hand once he caught up with her.

Not that she was shaking in her slippers. She sincerely hoped he never realized that his reaction was no deterrent. If there was something she felt she needed to do, she would do it – and gladly pay his price later. Ease and soothe his possessiveness. Just as she had at The Angel.

Swaying as the carriage rocked along, she wondered what his price would be tonight.

Demon returned home just after six, with a silly grin on his face and the deed to 12 Clarges Street in his pocket.

Only to find, stoically rigid on his doorstep, one of the footmen from Berkeley Square. The message the footman carried was almost hysterical.

He strode into his mother's parlor five minutes later. 'What's the matter?' She hadn't said in her note – mostly a bleat about him never forgiving her, which was so out of character that he'd been seriously alarmed. The sight of her prostrate, sniffing what looked suspiciously like smelling salts, didn't ease his mind. 'What the devil's going on?'

'I don't *know*!' Verging on the tearful, Horatia sat up. 'Felicity's gone off to Stratton's masquerade. Here – read this.' She waved a badly crushed note at him. 'Oh – and there's one for you, too.'

Demon accepted both. He barely glanced at hers before setting it aside and opening the missive Flick had left for him. As he'd expected, it was much more informative.

'She asked me who Stratton was this afternoon in the park, but I never *dreamed—*' Horatia lifted both hands in the air. 'Well – who would have? If I'd known she'd take such a silly

401

notion into her head, I would never have let her out of my sight!'

Demon returned to the note Flick had left her. 'What have you done about your evening's entertainments?'

'She suggested I excuse her on the grounds of her having a headache – I've excused us *both* on the grounds of *me* having a headache – which I have!'

Demon glanced at her. 'Stop worrying. She'll be all right.'

'How do you know?' Suddenly noticing his relative calm, Horatia narrowed her eyes at him. 'What's going on?'

'Nothing to get in a flap about.' Returning her note, Demon pocketed his. Flick had told Horatia she'd been seized by a desperate longing to attend a masquerade, so had gone to Stratton Hall, expecting him to join her there. 'I know what Stratton's masquerades are like.' The admission made Horatia narrow her eyes even more; imperturbably, he continued, 'I'll go after her immediately – she'll only be there an hour or so before I catch up with her.'

Although clearly relieved, Horatia continued to frown. 'I thought you'd be ropeable.' She snorted. 'All very well for *me* not to worry – why aren't *you* worried?'

He was, but ... Demon raised his brows resignedly. 'Let's just say I'm growing accustomed to the sensation.'

He left his mother with her brows flying, and returned to Albemarle Street. Gillies's note gave him more details. Pausing only to extract his own invitation to Stratton's masquerade from the edge of his mantelpiece mirror, and to unearth his old domino and a simple half-mask, he hailed a hackney, and, once again, set out in Flick's wake.

Within two minutes of haughtily sweeping into Stratton Hall, Flick realized that no amount of tonnish balls and parties could ever have prepared her for Sir Percival's masquerade.

Two giant blackamoors wearing only loincloths, turbans,

and a quantity of gold, each carrying a wickedlooking cutlass, stood guard, arms akimbo, in the front hall, flanking the main doors to the ballroom. Inside the enormous room running the length of the house the scene was similarly exotic. Blue silk flecked with gold stars draped the ceiling; the walls were an Arabian Nights' dream of silks, brocades and brass ornaments.

Mindful of her disguise, she didn't pause on the threshold and stare – spine straight, chin tilted at an imperious angle, she stepped straight into the crowd.

In the room's center, an elaborate fountain splashed; Flick saw guests filling glasses with the water – then realized it was champagne. The fountain was ringed with tables displaying delicacies galore; other tables elsewhere were similarly loaded with the most expensive fare – seafood, pheasant, caviar, quails' eggs – she even saw a roast peacock stuffed with truffles.

Wine was flowing freely, as were other spirits – the spirits of the guests were rising in response. Nearing the room's end, she heard a violin, and glimpsed a string quartet playing in the conservatory beyond the ballroom.

There were guests everywhere. Even behind their masks and cloaked in dominos, the women were remarkable – she'd yet to see one who was less than stunning. The men were gentlemen all – she heard it in their accents, invariably refined, and saw it in their clothes – many wore their dominos loose, more like a cloak, in some cases thrown rakishly back over one shoulder.

From the end of the room, Flick circled, searching for Stratton. The long windows giving onto the terrace had been left open to the sultry night. Black clouds raced, roiling across the sky. Thunder rumbled intermittently, but the storm was still some distance away.

'Well, well . . . and what do we have here?'

Flick whirled – and found herself pinned by Stratton's cold eyes.

'Hmm ... a woodland sprite, perhaps, come to enliven the evening?' His thin lips curved but there was no warmth in his smile.

His gaze left her face to openly rove over her; Flick quelled a shiver. 'I'm searching for a friend.'

A calculating gleam entered Stratton's eyes. 'I'll be happy to oblige, my dear, once the festivities begin.' He lifted a hand. Flick instinctively recoiled but he was too fast. He caught her chin and tilted her face this way, then that, as if he could see through her mask. He was certainly aware of her resistance; it seemed to please him. Then he released her. 'Yes – I'll keep an eye out for you later.'

Flick didn't even attempt a smile. Luckily, Stratton's attention was claimed by some other lady; Flick seized the moment and slipped away.

The swelling crowd was growing restive. Flick plunged into it, purposefully crossing the room, leaving Stratton before the windows. In addition to the main ballroom door, there were three other doors leading into the house. Guests were arriving via the main door; thus far, she'd seen only footmen using the other doors. The masquerade was getting underway – while the noise exceeded that of the usual ton ball, it had yet to reach raucous.

Flick halted midway down the inner wall, with the fountain and its surrounding melee directly between herself and Stratton. He was reasonably tall – she could see him. She hoped he couldn't see her. From where she stood, she could keep watch on the doors leading into the house – if any meeting was to be held, she doubted it would be convened in the increasingly crowded ballroom.

Until Demon joined her, watching for any sign of a suspicious gathering was the best she could do. Her heart slowing, she relieved the urge to scrub at where Stratton had touched her chin. Settling against the wall, she kept a wary eye on him.

The gathering before her grew increasingly licentious – the guests might be wealthy and well-born, but she was quick to see why masquerades no longer found favor with the *grandes dames*. Even after spending two nights in Demon's arms, some of what she saw still shocked her. Luckily, there were rules of some sort. Despite the way some other ladies were behaving, letting gentlemen freely grope beneath their dominos, all the gentlemen present *were* gentlemen – those who paused to speak with her as she stood quietly by the wall treated her with courtesy, albeit, like Stratton, with a certain predatory intent.

She recognized that intent well enough, but most moved on once she made it clear she was in immediate expectation of being joined by her particular gentleman.

Unfortunately, there were exceptions to every rule.

'I say – your gentleman not here yet?' One predatory rogue lounged close. 'Just realized you're still waiting – a pity to waste time, such a pretty little thing like you.'

He reached out and flicked a feather on her mask; Flick swayed back, her frown concealed by the mask.

'Indeed.' The rogue's friend appeared on her other side, his gaze trailing speculatively down her length. 'What say we retire to one of the rooms along the hall, and you can show me and my friend here just how pretty you are, hmm?' He looked up, cool eyes searching hers. 'You can always come back and meet your gentleman later.'

He moved closer, as did the first rogue, crowding her between them. 'I don't think my particular gentleman would like that,' Flick stated.

'We weren't suggesting you tell him, sweetheart,' the first all but whispered in her ear.

Flick turned her head to him, then had to turn the other way as his friend did the same thing.

'We wouldn't want to cause any ructions – just a friendly bit of slap and tickle to keep my friend and me going until the orgy starts.'

Orgy? Flick's jaw dropped.

'That's it – just think of it as a case of mutual tummyrubbing. Here we are, with our peckers twitching but the action some way off—'

'And here *you* are, a plump little pigeon just waiting to be plucked, but with your chosen plucker not yet in sight.'

'Right – a bit of hot fumbling and a few good pokes would ease things all around. What do you say?'

They both leaned closer, voices low, increasingly hoarse as they whispered, in quick fire exchanges, a stream of suggestive suggestions directly into Flick's ears.

Behind her mask, her eyes grew rounder, and rounder. Toes? *Tongues*? Rods ...

Flick had had enough. First Stratton, now these two. They'd pressed close; jerking both elbows outward, she jabbed them in the ribs. They fell back gasping – she whirled on them. 'I have never met with such arrogant presumption in my life! You should be ashamed of yourselves – propositioning a lady in such terms! And without the slightest invitation! Just think how horrified your poor mamas would be if they ever heard you speaking like that.' They stared at her as if she'd gone mad; Flick glared, then hissed, 'And as for your twitching appendages, I suggest you take them for a long walk in the rain – *that* should cure them of their indisposition!'

She glared one last time, then swung on her heel—

And collided with another male.

Hers. His arms closed about her before she bounced off. Clutching his domino, she looked up into his masked face.

For a moment, his gaze remained levelled over her head, then he glanced down.

Flick frowned. 'How did you recognize me?'

She was the only woman there with hair like spun gold and she drew his senses like a lodestone. Demon narrowed his eyes. 'What in *heaven* possessed you—'

'Ssh!' Her eyes darted about. 'Here – kiss me.' Stretching on her toes, she did the honors. As their lips parted, she whispered, 'This appears to be a bacchanalby-another-name – we have to do our best to fit in.' Sliding her arms beneath his domino, she sank against him.

Demon gritted his teeth and backed her into the space she'd recently vacated.

'Those two gentlemen who were talking to me – you'll never guess what—' She broke off. 'Where did they go?'

'They suddenly remembered pressing engagements elsewhere.'

'Oh?'

She shot him a glance. Demon ignored it, and her distraction. 'What I want to know is why you thought fit—' He broke off on a hiss, sucking in a breath as she twined her arms about his neck and shifted her hips against him.

He stared blankly down at her – she smiled, and laid her head on his chest.

'I found Bletchley. He's Sir Percival's groom.'

He studied her eyes, lit with anticipation, with expectant excitement, and inwardly sighed. 'So your note said.' Gathering her more comfortably into his arms, he shifted so he could view the room. 'I suppose you've decided the syndicate will meet tonight.'

'It's the perfect occasion.'

He could hardly disagree – looking over the sea of heads, he noted the spontaneous distractions arising here and there in the crowd. 'Those attending wouldn't even risk being recog-

407

nized.' He looked down and met her gaze. 'Let's take a look around – Stratton's occasions are always open house.' Aside from anything else, he wanted her away from the center of activity, although, as things went, Sir Percival's masquerade had a long way yet to go.

Boldly curving a palm about her bottom, he steered her toward the nearest door. Glancing down, he met her shocked glance, and raised a far from innocent brow. 'We have to do our best to fit in.'

He flexed his fingers – behind her mask, her eyes flared, then a dangerous glint entered the soft blue. Before he could stop her, she swayed close, slipped one slim hand through the opening of his domino and stroked, tantalizingly, up his length.

Sucking in a breath, he froze; she chuckled wickedly. Catching his hand, she swung to the door. 'Come along.' The look she threw him as she led him out would have convinced the most suspicious observer that her fell aim was entirely in keeping with Sir Percival's masquerade.

Drawing a steadying breath, Demon went along with her charade while considering a few elaborations to her scheme. Once in the corridor, he drew her closer, settling her within his arm, his hand returning to its former, stridently possessive position. Any others coming upon them in the dimly lit corridors would simply see two revellers searching for a quiet nook.

Many others were doing the same. Pausing before every door, Demon urged Flick to kiss him, then opened the door and half stumbled in, scanning the room without releasing her, mumbling an incoherent apology and swinging straight back out again if it was already occupied. All the downstairs rooms were, some hosting groups; despite his best efforts, it was impossible to completely screen Flick from the frolics in progress. At first, she stiffened with shock – by the time they'd covered all the downstairs rooms, her reaction had changed to one of curiosity.

A fact he tried not to think about. Some of what she was seeing she was definitely not up to. Yet.

'No meetings,' Flick murmured as they turned back to the front hall. 'Couldn't we just watch Stratton, then follow when he leaves the ballroom?'

'That might not help us. Remember what I said about Bletchley's employer not necessarily being one of the syndicate?'

Flick frowned. 'Stratton's phaeton is brand new – his horses would have done you credit.'

'Maybe so, but while Stratton's a deuced cold fish, he's also exceedingly wealthy.' Demon gestured to their surroundings. 'He inherited a massive fortune.'

Flick grimaced. 'He seemed such a promising candidate.'

'Yes, well—' Reaching the hall, Demon turned her up the stairs. 'I think we should check all the rooms.'

Other couples, flushed and subtly dishevelled, laughing breathlessly, were descending the stairs as they went up. Demon drew Flick suggestively close as they climbed – with her one step ahead of him, their bodies slid against each other as they ascended.

They reached the gallery. Flick paused and whispered breathlessly, 'Shouldn't we be checking outside? If it's not Stratton but some of his guests come to meet with Bletchley, wouldn't they use the garden?'

'It's raining – it started as I arrived. I think we can assume no meeting had taken place earlier. Now, it'll have to be held indoors – in some area open to the guests.'

They continued their search. Some of the bedrooms and suites were occupied, others were empty. While they stumbled upon meetings aplenty, none were of the type they sought. Flick's shoulders had slumped long before they reached the last door at the end of the last corridor.

Demon tested the handle, then carefully turned it fully and tried the door. 'It's locked.' He started to turn back; Flick stood in the way, frowning at the locked door.

'Why locked?' She glanced back up the corridor. 'His bedroom wasn't locked.' She looked at the door behind which two couples were engaged in an energetic romp on Stratton's huge bed. 'Nor was his dressing room or study.' She nodded at each of those doors, then turned to stare at the last door. 'Why would he lock this room and not any other in the house?'

Demon looked at her face, at her stubbornly set chin, and sighed. Placing his ear to the panel, he listened, then glanced down at the bottom of the door; no telltale strip of light showed. 'There's no one in there.'

'Let's look,' Flick urged. 'Can you unlock it?'

Demon considered reiterating that Stratton was not a good candidate for race-fixer, but her sudden excitement was infectious. He drew out the small tool he carried everywhere – a multi-pronged pick and knife useful for destoning horses' hooves. In less than a minute, he had the door open. The room within was empty; standing back, he let Flick in. Glancing back up the corridor, he confirmed it was empty, then shut the door behind them.

A warm glow suffused the room. Flick adjusted the wick on a lamp set on a wide desk, then reset the glass. They both looked around.

'An office.' Demon glanced at ledgers and books of accounts filling one bookshelf. It wasn't a large room. A padded leather chair stood behind the desk; a wooden chair faced it. One wall was filled with windows looking out over the river – they presently displayed a landscape of driving rain and thick grey clouds backlit by sheet lightning. Thunder rumbled, drawing nearer.

'Half a library, too.' Flick considered the wall of book-shelves opposite the windows. 'I wonder why he keeps them up here. The library was barely half full.'

Demon turned from the elemental rage outside and saun-tered to the shelves. Scanning the titles, he found familiar volumes on various games of chance, and a few not so famil-iar on card-sharping techniques and ways of weighting the odds in some forms of wagering. Frowning, he looked more closely, eventually hunkering down to read the titles of the volumes on the lowest shelf. 'Interesting.'

His voice had changed – he read the titles again, then rose and turned to the desk, his frame radiating purpose.

Flick looked at him questioningly. He met her gaze as he joined her behind the desk, shrugging off his domino, slipping off his mask.

'Those' – with his head he indicated the bottom shelf of books – 'are the full race records for the past two years.'

Flick blinked. 'The *full* records?'

Demon nodded and pulled open the top desk drawer. 'Not something one finds in your usual library. *I* don't even have a set.'

'How? . . .' Without finishing her question, Flick drew out the top drawer on her side of the desk.

'A set went missing last year – never to be found. But he's also added the most recent volumes – those from last season.'

'A most useful tool for fixing races.'

'Indeed. Look for anything that even mentions horses.'

They were the ideal team for the task – they both knew the names of all recent winners, as well as those expected to win in the upcoming season. They sifted through every drawer, examined every single piece of paper.

'Nothing.' Blowing an errant curl from her forehead, Flick turned and sat on the desk.

Grimacing, Demon dropped into the padded chair. Without

411

enthusiasm, he lifted the last item from the bottom drawer, a leather-bound ledger. Propping it on the desk, he opened it and scanned the entries. After a moment, he snorted. 'That phaeton is new, and he paid a pretty penny for it. As for the horses, he definitely paid too much.'

'Anything else?'

'Caviar's gone up two pounds an ounce in the last year – his account-keeping habits are as stultifyingly rigid as he is. He enters every single transaction – even the lost wagers he's paid.'

Studying the grim set of his face, Flick grimaced. 'No entries under race-fixing, I take it?'

Demon started to shake his head, but he froze as one particular figure danced before his eyes. Slowly straightening, he flicked back a page, then another . . .

'What is it?'

'Remind me we owe Montague an enormous bonus.' If it hadn't been for the agent's accuracy, he'd never have seen it. 'Those amounts we were looking for – the sums cleared from each fixed race?'

'Yes?'

'They show up here. According to this, they're his main source of income.'

'I thought you said he was rich.'

Flicking back through the ledger, Demon bit back a curse. 'He was – he must have lost it.' He tapped an entry. 'His income from the Funds was miniscule last year, then it ends. There've been huge debts paid – Hazard, at a guess.' He looked up. 'He never went to the wall – no one realized he'd been rolled up because he substituted income from race-fixing to cover his lost investment income. He's always been a lavish spender – nothing appeared to have changed. He simply carried on as he always had.'

'Except he corrupted and blackmailed Dillon, and jockeys,

412

and goodness knows what happened to Ickley.'

'Or any others.' Demon studied the ledger. 'This is too wieldy to smuggle out.' He flicked through the pages, then laid the book on the desk and ripped out five pages.

'Will that do?'

'I think so – they show the amounts from three fixed races going in, and five major purchases that can be traced to Stratton, as well as four very large debts paid to members of the ton who I'm sure will verify from whom they received those sums. On top of that, his writing's distinctive.' He scanned the pages, then folded them and stowed them in the inner pocket of his coat. He returned the ledger to the bottom drawer. 'We'll take the pages to Newmarket tomorrow – with any luck, he won't notice they're missing.'

He shut the drawer and looked at Flick.

A board creaked in the corridor – footsteps paused, some way away – then quickly, purposefully, strode toward the office.

Chapter Twenty-Two

What occurred next happened so quickly that to Flick it was
just a blur. Demon stood, shifted her to the desk's center, her
back to the door, yanked the neck ties of her domino free, and
flung the garment off so it pooled about her. He tugged – a
button on her bodice popped, then he hauled her gown and
chemise down, dragging her sleeves down her arms, fully
exposing her shoulders and breasts.

'Free your arms – lean back on them.'

His words were a sibilant hiss – instinctively, she obeyed.
He sat before her, throwing her skirts up, pushing her knees
wide.

The door opened. He clamped his mouth over one nipple;
Flick gasped – his mouth was hot!

He licked, and suckled, and slid his hand between her
thighs, slid his long fingers into her soft flesh, stroking, then
probing ...

Flick moaned; her arms locked. She let her head roll back,
helplessly arching as he suckled and probed simultaneously.

Then he lifted his head, looking beyond her. She forced her
lids up – in the glow from the lamp bathing her bare breasts,
sheening the skin showing above her garters, his eyes were
glazed, dazed, as he blinked at the door.

'Problem, Stratton?'

Flick didn't look around – Demon's fingers were still

414

playing teasingly between her thighs. It wasn't hard to imagine the tableau their host was seeing as he stood in the doorway. From her quivering back it must be clear she was bare to the waist, and that, with her skirts rucked up so, she must, to Demon, be exposed below as well. The only thing she was still truly wearing was her feathered mask.

She could barely breathe, all too conscious of the slick wetness Demon's long fingers were reveling in. Her heart thudded in her throat; excitement sizzled in her veins.

Sir Percival's hesitation was palpable. In the stillness, she heard the rain pelting the windows, heard her own ragged breathing. Then he shifted, and drawled, 'No, no. Do carry on.'

The door clicked softly shut; Flick hauled in a relieved breath – and promptly lost it as Demon's mouth closed over her nipple again. He suckled strongly – she barely restrained her shriek. 'Demon?' Her voice shook.

He suckled more fiercely.

'*Harry*!'

Two fingers slid deep, probing evocatively.

She arched – on a long, shuddering gasp, she managed, '*Here*?'

'Hmm.' He stood, easing her back to lie across the desk.

'But . . .' Flat on her back, she licked her dry lips. 'Stratton might come back.'

'All the more reason,' he whispered, leaning over her, cupping her breasts as he kissed her. She parted her lips and he surged within; he kneaded her aching flesh, fingers tightening momentarily about her ruched nipples before his hands drifted away.

Clinging to her senses, her tongue sliding about his, she felt him unbutton his trousers, then his hands closed about her hips, anchoring her as he stepped closer, between her wide-spread thighs. She felt the pressure as his rigid flesh parted her swollen folds, then found her entrance.

'All the more convincing,' he purred against her lips. Straightening, he looked down at her, the wicked curve to his lips elementally male.

Dazed, she stared up at him. 'Stratton might be dangerous!'

Curtailing his perusal of her quivering body held taut between his hands, he met her gaze and lifted a brow. 'Adds a certain recklessness to the situation, don't you think?'

Think? She couldn't think.

He grinned. 'Don't tell me you're not game?'

'Game?' She could barely gasp the word. With him poised just inside her, she was frantic. One step away from spontaneous combustion. But game? Lips and chin firming, she dragged in a breath, lifted her legs and wrapped them about his hips. 'Don't be ridiculous.'

She pulled him to her – then gasped, arched – frantically gripped his forearms as he pushed steadily, inexorably, all the way in until he filled her.

That sense of incredible fullness was still new, still startling. She caught her breath and clamped down, feeling him hot and hard, buried deep within her. His lids fell, his jaw locked, then, fingers tightening about her hips, he eased back, then surged anew.

As usual, he was in no hurry – he teased her, tormented her – tortured her. Held before him, virtually naked but for her mask, she squirmed, panted, moaned, then screamed as the world fell away and she was consumed by glory. The storm beyond the windows swallowed her wild cries as he flicked a sensual whip and drove her on, into a landscape of illicit delight, of pleasures honed to excruciating sharpness by the very real presence of danger.

His hands roamed, hard and demanding; she writhed and begged, wanton in her pleading.

And when she came apart for the last time, senses fragmenting beneath his onslaught, he followed swiftly, joining her in that delicious void – only, too quickly, to draw her back. He drew away from her; chest still heaving, he straightened his clothes, then hers.

Struggling to coordinate her wits, let alone her limbs, she helped as best she could. If they didn't reappear in the ballroom soon, Stratton would notice – and start to wonder.

They returned downstairs, Demon holding her close against him. They reentered the ballroom, but didn't go far – propping his shoulders against the wall, Demon cradled her against him, her cheek against his chest, then bent his head and kissed her. Soothingly, calmingly.

Distractingly. Despite that, as her senses returned, Flick heard catcalls, whistles, suggestions called out – clearly to some exhibition at the room's center. From the associated sounds, and some of the suggestions, it wasn't hard to imagine what that exhibition entailed. With Demon's arms around her, she couldn't see – she didn't try to look.

After fifteen or so minutes, when their hearts had slowed to their normal pace, Demon glanced around the room, then looked down at her. 'We've been seen and duly noted,' he murmured. 'Now we can leave.'

They did in short order, their bodies still thrumming, their spirits soaring, the evidence they'd sought for weeks at long last in their possession.

Demon called in Berkeley Square at eight the next morning; Flick was waiting in the front hall, her packed bags at her feet, a glorious smile on her face. Within minutes, they were away, the bays pacing swiftly, Gillies up behind.

'You were right about your mother stopping her scolding when I told her we'd rely on her and Helena to make all the wedding arrangements.'

Demon snorted. 'That was a foregone conclusion – she

could hardly scold while in alt. It's her dream come true – to organize a wedding.'

'I'm only glad, after all her worrying, that we could leave her so happy.'

Demon merely snorted – distinctly unfilially – again.

Two minutes later, in a quiet street, he drew in to the curb, tossed the reins to Gillies, and jumped down. Flick looked around. 'What? ...

Demon impatiently waved her to him; she shuffled along the seat and he lifted her down. 'I want to show you something.' Taking her hand, he led her up the steps of the nearest house – a gentleman's residence with a portico held aloft by two columns. In the portico, he pulled a set of keys from his pocket, selected one, opened the front door, and pushed it wide. With an elegant bow, he waved her in, merely lifting his brows at her questioning look.

Wondering, Flick entered a pleasant rectangular hall – from the echoes and absence of furniture it was apparent the house stood empty. Pausing in the middle of the hall, she turned and raised her brows.

Demon waved her on. 'Look around.'

She did, starting with the reception rooms opening from the front hall, then on up the stairs, going faster and faster as excitement gripped her. The pleasant, welcoming aura that hung in the hall recurred throughout the rooms, all airy and gracious, the morning sun streaming in through large windows. The master bedroom was large, the other bedrooms more than adequate; she eventually reached the nursery, under the eaves.

'Oh! This is wonderful!' She darted down the corridor that led to the small bedrooms, then crossed to peek into the nanny's domain. Then, her heart swelling so much she thought it would burst, she turned and looked at Demon, lounging, all rakish elegance, in the doorway, watching her.

She met his gaze, smiling but watchful.

He studied her face, then raised one brow. 'Do you like it?'

Flick let her heart fill her eyes; her smile was ecstatic. 'It's wonderful – perfect!' Reining in her excitement, she asked, 'How much is it? Could we possibly? . . .'

His slow smile warmed her. Drawing his hand from his pocket, he held up the keys. 'It's ours – we'll live here while in town.'

'*Oh*!' Flick flew at him, hugged him wildly, kissed him soundly – then raced off again. She didn't need further explanation – this would be their home – this the nursery they would fill with their children. After the last weeks, she knew family was a vital part of him, the central concept around which he was focused. Even if he didn't know it, she did – this, from him, was the ultimate declaration – she needed no further vows. This – the home, the family – would be *theirs*.

Demon grinned and watched her. He still found her joy deeply refreshing, her open delight infectious. As he trailed her once more through the house, he wryly admitted he could now understand why so many generations of his forebears had found pleasure in indulging their wives.

That had been an abiding mystery before – it no longer was. He – Demon by name, demon by nature – had been vanquished by an angel. He no longer viewed her as innocent and youthful in the sense of being less able than he. After last night, he knew she could match him in any venture, any challenge. She was the wife for him.

And so here he was, trailing in her wake. She led – he followed, with his hand oh-so-lightly on her reins. What he'd found with her he'd found with no other – she was his and he was hers, and that was how it had to be. It was that simple. This was love – he was long past denying it.

Regaining the drawing room, she stopped at its center. 'We'll have to shop for furniture.'

Demon quelled a shudder. He followed her in, slid one arm around her waist, drew her against him, paused for one instant to watch the sudden flaring of awareness in her eyes, then kissed her.

She sank into his embrace; he tightened it about her. The kiss deepened – and they said all they needed with their lips, their bodies, their hearts. For one long moment, they clung, then he lifted his head.

The evidence he carried in his pocket crackled.

His chest swelled as he drew in a breath; she looked up – he met her eyes. 'Let's take these to Newmarket.' So they could get on with the rest of their lives.

She nodded briskly. They disengaged, straightened their clothes, then hurried out to the curricle.

By ten o'clock, they were bowling northward, the enclosed spaces of London far behind. Joyfully, Flick breathed deep, then turned her face to the sun. 'We'll have to go to Hillgate End first – to tell the General and Dillon.'

'I'll drive to the farm. We can leave your things there for the moment, ride to the cottage and collect Dillon, ride on to the manor and tell the General, then go straight on to the Jockey Club. I want to get that information before the Committee as soon as possible.' His face hardened; he reached for the whip.

Flick wondered if his grim urgency stemmed from concern for the industry he'd so long been a part of, or from the nebulous feeling that they hadn't, yet, defeated Stratton. That feeling hadn't left her since Stratton had walked in on them last night – like a specter, it hovered at her shoulder, growing blacker, weightier. As they rounded a curve, she looked back, but there was no one there.

They drove through Newmarket in the early afternoon and headed straight for the farm. While Demon organized their

420

horses, Flick hurried upstairs and changed into her riding habit. In less than half an hour, they were riding into the clearing behind the ruined cottage.

'It's us, Dillon,' Flick called as she slid from the saddle. 'Me and Demon. We're back!'

Her excitement rang in her voice. Dillon appeared through the lean-to, struggling to contain the hope lightening his haggard features.

One glance was enough to tell Demon that Dillon had changed – somewhere, somehow, he'd found some backbone. He said nothing, however, but joined Flick as she headed for the cottage.

Even before she reached him, Dillon stiffened. Demon had never seen him stand so tall, so determined. Fists clenched at his sides, he met Flick's gaze directly. 'I've been to see the General.'

She blinked and stopped before him. 'You have?'

'I told him all about it – the whole story – so you don't need to lie for me – cover up for me – any more. I should have done that at the start.'

He looked Demon straight in the eyes. 'Papa and I decided to wait until tomorrow in case you found anything, but we'll be going to see the Committee regardless.'

Demon met his eyes and nodded, his approval sincere.

'But we *have* found something.' Flick gripped Dillon's arm. 'We've learned who the syndicate is and we've enough proof to show the Committee!'

One hand at her back, Demon urged her in. 'Let's take our revelations indoors.'

Neither Dillon nor Flick argued. If they had, Demon couldn't have explained who he thought might overhear. But he was edgy, and had been since he'd looked into Stratton's cold eyes the previous evening.

That Stratton had noticed them the instant they'd regained

the ballroom had him worried. Stratton was known as cold and detached – he might well prove a formidable enemy. If there had been any way to safely leave Flick somewhere well out of the action, he'd have snatched the opportunity. But there wasn't. That being so, the safest place for her was with him.

In the cottage, Dillon faced them. 'I've written a detailed account of my involvement, first to last – just the bare facts.' He looked grim. 'It's hardly pleasant reading, but at least it's honest.'

Flick smiled. Her inner happiness radiated from her, all but lighting up the cottage. She laid a hand on Dillon's arm. 'We've proof of the syndicate.'

Dillon looked at her, then at Demon; his expression said he hardly dared hope. 'Who are they?'

'Not they – that was our error. It's a syndicate of one.' Briefly, Demon explained. 'I have to hand it to him – his execution was almost flawless. Only his greed – the fact he fixed too many races – brought the scheme to light. If he'd been content with the money from one or two major races a year . . .' He shrugged. 'But Stratton's lifestyle calls for rather more blunt than that.'

Reaching into his pocket, Demon drew out their evidence. 'This was the key.' He smoothed out a sheet on the table. Flick hadn't seen it before; together with Dillon, she crowded close.

'I gathered all the details I could about the betting on the fixed races, and my agent, Montague, worked out the amounts cleared from each one. He's a wizard. If he hadn't got it right – very close to exact – I would never have recognized the figures in Stratton's ledger.'

Unfolding the sheets he'd torn from Stratton's account book, Demon laid them alongside Montague's sheet. 'See?' Tapping various figures in Stratton's income column, he pointed to similar figures on the other sheet. 'The dates match, too.' Both Dillon and Flick glanced from one sheet to the others, nodding as they took it in.

'Can we prove these are Stratton's accounts?' Dillon looked up.

Demon pointed to certain entries in the expenditure column. 'These purchases of a phaeton, and here the pair to go with it – and even more these – lost wagers paid to gentlemen of the ton – can be proved to have been Stratton. With virtually the exact money from the races listed as income on the same pages, it's hard to argue any case other than it was Stratton behind the race-fixing. These' – he gestured to the papers – 'are all the evidence we need.'

Heeeee – crash!

With a tearing scream, the main door flew in, kicked off its rusting hinges to slam down on the floor. The whole cottage shook. Demon grabbed Flick as they backed up, eyes watering, coughing as dust reared and washed over them.

'How exceedingly foolish of you.'

The words, clipped, precise and totally devoid of all feeling, came from the man silhouetted in the doorway. The bright sunlight outside haloed him; they couldn't see his features. Flick and Demon recognized him instantly.

Eyes on the long barrelled pistol in Stratton's right hand, Demon tried to push Flick behind him. Unfortunately, they'd backed up against the hearth with its low chimney coping.

'Just remain where you are.' Stratton stepped over the threshold. He barely glanced at the papers lying scattered on the table, evidence enough to put him in Newgate, a long way from the luxury to which he was accustomed.

Demon tensed, praying Stratton would look at the papers – take his eye off him just for an instant . . .

Stratton hesitated, but didn't. 'You've been far too clever. Much too clever for your own good. If I didn't have such a suspicious nature, you might even have succeeded, but I checked my ledger at four o'clock this morning. By six, I was on the road to Newmarket. I knew you wouldn't dally. It was just a matter of time before you appeared.'

'And if we'd gone directly to the Jockey Club?'

'That,' Stratton admitted, 'would have been exceedingly messy. Luckily, you drove straight through. It was easy to follow you on horseback. Equally easy to guess that, if I was patient, you'd lead me to the one player still eluding me.' He inclined his head toward Dillon, but the pistol, aimed directly at Flick's chest, didn't waver. He studied her for a moment, then sighed. 'Such a pity, but after that little exposition, I fear I'll have to make away with you all.'

'And how,' Demon asked, 'do you imagine explaining that?'

Stratton raised a brow. 'Explaining? Why should I explain anything?'

'Others know I've been investigating you in connection with the race-fixing.'

'Do they now?' Stratton remained very still, his eyes steady on Demon's face, his aim never faltering from Flick's chest. Then his thin lips eased. 'How unfortunate – for Bletchley.'

Stratton's jaw set. He lifted his arm, straightening it, aiming the pistol at Demon –

Flick screamed.

She flung herself at Demon, clinging to his chest, shoving him back against the chimney.

Stratton's eyes widened – his finger had already tightened about the trigger.

Dillon stepped across Flick – the pistol discharged. The explosion echoed deafeningly between the cottage walls.

Demon and Flick froze, locked together before the chimney. Demon had frenziedly tried to wrestle Flick to the side, knowing he'd be too late—

They both continued to breathe, each searingly conscious the other was still alive. They turned their heads and looked—

Dillon slowly crumpled to the floor.

'Damn!' Stratton dropped the pistol.

Demon released Flick. She dropped to the floor beside Dillon. His face a mask of vengeance, Demon went for Stratton and nearly fell as his boots tangled in Flick's skirts. He grabbed the table to steady himself and saw Stratton pull another, smaller pistol from his greatcoat pocket, saw him aim at him –

'Here! Wait a minute!' Ducking through the lean-to, Bletchley lumbered in. 'What's this about things being unfortunate for me?'

Belligerent as a bull, he made straight for Stratton.

Without a blink, Stratton swung his arm farther and shot Bletchley.

Demon vaulted the table.

Stratton swung to face him, raising his riding quirt—

Demon's right cross snapped his head back with a satisfying *scrunch*. He followed up with a left, but Stratton was already on his way down. His head hit the flags with a thud. After one glance at Bletchley's slumped form, Demon leaned over Stratton.

He was unconscious, his aristocratic jaw at an odd, very painful-looking angle. Demon considered, but restrained himself from rearranging any more of his features. Wrecking Stratton's cravat without the slightest compunction, he dumped him on his face, hauled his arms back, secured them, then tied them to his ankles. Satisfied Stratton was no longer a threat, Demon glanced over the table. Flick was staunching a wound on Dillon's shoulder.

Turning to Bletchley, Demon eased him onto his back. Stratton had been rushed, his aim fractionally off. Bletchley would live, hopefully to sing of his master's infamy. Right now, all he could do was moan.

Demon left him to it – he wasn't bleeding badly enough to be in any real danger.

From what little he'd glimpsed, Dillon was.

Rounding the table, Demon joined Flick, on her knees beside Dillon. She'd eased him onto his back. Her face white as a sheet, she struggled to contain her trembling as she pressed her wadded petticoat down hard on his wound. Demon glanced at her face, then looked at Dillon. 'Ease back – let me see the wound.'

Relaxing her arms, she leaned back. Demon lifted the wad and quickly looked, then replaced it. His face easing, he looked at Flick as she reapplied pressure to the wound.

'It's bad, but he'll live.'

Blank-faced, she looked at him. Demon put his arm around her shoulders and hugged. 'Stratton was aiming for me. Dillon's shorter than I am – the ball's in his shoulder; it hasn't even touched his lung. He'll be all right once we get the doctor to him.'

She searched his eyes; some of the cold blankness left her face. She looked down at Dillon. 'He's been such a fool, but I don't want to lose him – not now.'

Demon hugged her tighter and pressed a kiss into her curls. He wasn't all that calm himself, but he knew what she meant. If Dillon hadn't come good at the last – hadn't become man enough to, for once, shield Flick rather than expecting the reverse, Flick would have died.

His arm still about her, his cheek against her golden curls, Demon closed his eyes tight and again told himself – the being who dwelled deep inside – that it really was all right, that Flick was still with him, that he hadn't lost his angel so soon after finding her. Flick was a lot shorter than he was – if Dillon hadn't shielded her, Stratton's bullet would have hit her in the back of her beautiful head.

He really couldn't think of it – not without coming apart – so he pushed the image away, locked it deep inside. Lifting his head, he looked down at Dillon, to whom he now owed more than his life. Flick was still staunching the flow of blood, but it seemed to be easing. Demon considered, then looked into her face. She was still pale, but composed.

Part of him wanted to shake her – to swear and rant at her for throwing herself across him; the saner part realized there really was no point. She would simply set her little chin and get that stubborn look on her face and refuse to pay the slightest attention. And she'd do it again in a blink.

The realization only made him want to hug her, hold her tight, keep her forever safe in his arms.

Drawing a deep breath, he reached out and gently tugged her hands from the bloody pad. 'Come.' She turned to him; he met her gaze. 'Leave that to me – you're going to have to ride for help.'

Sorting it out took the rest of the day. Flick rode to the farm – Gillies and the Shephards took over from there, summoning the doctor, the magistrate and constable while Flick rode to Hillgate End. She stayed with the General, soothing and reassuring, until the doctor's gig arrived from the cottage with Demon driving and Dillon in the back.

They got Dillon inside – the doctor, a veteran of the Peninsula Wars, had extracted the bullet at the cottage, so Dillon was quickly made comfortable. He was still unconscious – the doctor warned he probably wouldn't wake until the next day. Mrs. Fogarty installed herself at his bedside; the General, after seeing his son still breathing, and hearing from both Flick and Demon of Dillon's bravery, finally consented to retire to the library.

The magistrate and the constable met them there; the

members of the Committee, at Newmarket for the Spring Carnival that week, joined them. Tabling Dillon's account, then an explanation of the investigations that had resulted in Montague's estimations, then laying out Stratton's accounts for all to see, Demon led the assembled company through the details of Sir Percival's race-fixing racket.

While Dillon's involvement was frowned upon, in light of the greater crimes involved and his clear repentance, his misdemeanors were set aside, to be dealt with later by the Committee, once he was fully recovered. At present, they had greater fish to fry – the extent of Stratton's manipulation of their industry fired them with fury. They left, faces stiff, vowing to make an example of him. An aim Demon openly supported.

The instant they'd gone, the General slumped. Flick fussed and fretted and worried him into bed; Jacobs assured her he would watch over him. Leaving the General propped on his pillows, Flick paused in the corridor; shutting the General's door behind him, Demon studied her face, then walked to her side and drew her into his arms.

She stood stiffly for an instant, then the iron will and sheer stubbornness that had kept her going until then dissolved. She sank into his arms, sliding hers about him, laying her cheek against his chest.

Then she started to shake.

Demon carried her downstairs and coaxed a small glass of brandy past her lips. Her color improved marginally, but he didn't like the distant look in her eyes. He racked his brain for something with which to distract her.

'Come on.' Abruptly standing, he drew her to her feet. 'Let's go back to the farmhouse. Your luggage is there, remember? Mrs. Shephard can feed us, then you can look around and decide what changes you'd like to make.'

She blinked at him. 'Changes?'

He towed her to the door. 'Remodelling, redecorating – how should I know?'

They rode back. He watched her every step of the way, but she was steady in her saddle. His staff were very pleased to see them; it instantly became clear Gillies had spread their news. Which was probably just as well, as Demon had every intention of dining alone with his angel.

Mrs. Shephard was on her mettle, laying a nourishing meal quickly before them. Demon was relieved to note Flick's appetite hadn't evaporated. They sat quietly as the evening lengthened, making comments at random, slowly winding down.

Finishing his port, Demon rose, rounded the table, and drew Flick to her feet. 'Come – I'll give you the grand tour.' He showed her all around the ground floor, then climbed the stairs; his tour ended in his bedroom, above the parlor at whose window she used to come a-tapping.

Much, much later, Flick lolled, utterly naked, in Demon's big bed. She had, she decided, never felt more comfortable, more at peace, more at home, in her life.

'Come on.' A sharp smack on her bottom followed. 'We'd better get dressed and I'll drive you home.'

Flick didn't look around. She didn't lift her head – she sank it deeper into the pillow and shook it. 'You can drive me home early in the morning, can't you?'

Lounging beside her, as naked as she, Demon looked down at her – what he could see of her – the tousled guinea gold curls gilding his pillow, one sweetly rounded shoulder and delicately curved arm, one slender leg, and one firm, absolutely perfect buttock, all clothed in the silkiest ivory skin, presently lightly flushed. All the rest of her – all that he'd enjoyed for the past several hours – was provocatively draped in his satin sheets.

She was going to be a never-ending challenge, demanding

all his skill to let her run as free as she wished, with only the very lightest hand on her reins.

A slow smile curved his lips as he reached for the sheet. 'Yes – I suppose I can.'

Epilogue

April 30, 1820
St. Georges Church, Hanover Square

Everyone attended. The Duke and Duchess of St. Ives sat in the first row, with the Dowager beside them. Vane, of course, was best man; he and Patience had returned to London the week before. Of all the family and its myriad connections, only Richard and Catriona hadn't been able to attend, and that only because of the short notice.

The twins were Flick's bridesmaids, with Heather, Henrietta, Elizabeth, Angelica and little Mary as flower girls. Such a crowd had been needed, Demon had discovered, to manage Flick's long train. But from the instant she'd appeared and walked down the nave to join him, to the moment they were pronounced man and wife, he couldn't recall any detail beyond the sheer beauty of her angelic face.

Now, beside him on the pavement before the ton's favored church, an angel in truth in pearl-encrusted silk, she glowed with transparent joy; he couldn't have felt more proud or more favored by fate. Crowds of well-wishers flocked about them as they paused before their carriage. All the family and much of the ton had turned up to see yet another Cynster tie the knot – they were all about to adjourn to Berkeley Square for the wedding breakfast.

His mother was in tears – positive floods of happiness.

Halting before him, she stretched up to place a motherly kiss on his cheek, then she sniffed, and quavered, 'I'm so glad I made you promise not to marry in any hole-andcorner fashion.' She dabbed at her overflowing eyes. 'You've made me so happy,' she sobbed.

Helplessly, he looked at her, then looked at his father.

Who grinned and clapped him on the back. 'Play your cards right, and you'll be able to live on this for years.'

Demon grinned back, shook his hand, then glanced again at Horatia. Today had been the happiest, proudest day of his life – one he wouldn't have missed for the world. Despite his earlier view of marriage, he was now much wiser. But he wasn't fool enough to tell his mother that – instead, he leaned down and kissed her cheek.

Instantly suspicious, she stopped crying and stared at him; his father chuckled and drew her away.

Grinning, Demon turned to have a word with the General and Dillon, standing beside Flick on his other side. Dillon was a far cry from the petulant youth of only a few months ago; now he stood straight and tall, unafraid to meet any man's eye. The Committee had agreed that in reparation for his crime – one against the industry – he would act as a clerk to the Jockey Club, and assist in keeping the breeding register up to date. In his spare time, of his own accord, he'd taken up the task of managing the General's investments, giving his father more time for his research. Seeing them together now, father and son side by side as they chatted with Flick, Demon sensed a closeness, a bond that hadn't been there – or not openly so – before.

Sliding his arm around Flick, he smiled and held out his hand to Dillon.

Above the bustle, lounging against one of the pillars of the church porch, Lucifer looked down on the gathering. In

432

particular, on the twins. 'They're going to be much worse after this, you realize.'

'Hmm.' Beside him, Gabriel resignedly raised his brows. 'I've never understood what it is about weddings that so excites the mating instinct of females.'

'Whatever it is, you only need to look at them to see its effect. They look ready to grab anything in breeches.'

'Luckily, most of us here are related.'

'Or, in their view, too old to count.'

They continued watching the twins, perfect pictures of delight in cornflower blue gowns the same color as their eyes, their pale ringlets dancing in the breeze. They'd been hovering not far from Flick. Now they pushed forward to hug her frantically as she and Demon prepared to enter the waiting carriage. Flick returned their hugs affectionately – even from the porch, it was easy to discern her reasssuring words: 'Your time will come – never doubt it.'

To Gabriel and Lucifer, those words held a different ring.

Gabriel quelled an odd shiver. 'It's not going to be easy, now it's just you and me.'

'Devil and Vane will help out.'

'When they're allowed to.'

Lucifer's dark blue gaze shifted to Honoria and Patience, standing chatting to one side. 'There is that. Still, we should be able to manage it – don't you think?'

Gabriel didn't answer, well aware they hadn't been talking solely about the twins.

At that moment, Demon handed Flick into the carriage. A cheer went up from all the onlookers. Demon turned to acknowledge it – to exchange a round of last comments with Devil and Vane. They laughed, and fell back; Demon reached for the carriage door.

Then he looked up, directly at them – the last unmarried members of the Bar Cynster. A slow, rakish, too-knowing smile lit his face; holding their gazes, he raised a hand and saluted them, paused for one last instant, then turned, ducked and entered the carriage.

Barely hearing the cheers and huzzahs as the carriage rumbled off, Gabriel stood in the porch as if turned to stone. In his mind rang the words *Your time will come – never doubt it*. Not, this time, in Flick's soft voice, but in Demon's much more forceful tones.

He blinked and shook aside the horrendous thought, then shivered in earnest as a chill touched his spine.

Exactly as if someone had walked on his grave.

Disguising his shiver as a wriggle of his shoulders, he resettled his cuffs, then glanced at his brother. 'Come on – we'd better do the honors *vis-a`-vis* the twins, before they find some bounder to accompany them instead.'

With a nod, Lucifer followed him down the church steps.

In the carriage rocking over the cobbles toward Berkeley Square, Flick was in her husband's arms. 'Demon! Be careful!' She tried vainly to right her headdress. 'We'll be greeting our guests soon.'

'We're ahead of them,' Demon pointed out, and kissed her again.

Flick inwardly sighed and forgot about her headdress, forgot about everything as she sank into his embrace. Possessive, protective, passionately loving – he was all she'd ever wanted. She loved him with all her soul. As she kissed him back, she felt the glow her parents had always had infuse her and Demon, enfolding them in its warmth. With this marriage, this man, this husband and lover, she'd seized her parents' legacy – now, they'd make it their own.

Author's Note

Dear Reader,

The Bar Cynster - a group of arrogant Regency rogues - domineering, autocratic, rakish - what more need one say? Writing about them - their lives, their loves and about the wider Cynster family with its strong, willful women - has been a delight. What especially attracted me to write about the Bar Cynsters was what I see as the ultimate strength in strong, arrogant, warrior males - the fact that their very nature compels them to seek their own family to protect and defend. And in order to establish that family, ah well - they need a wife. But Fate, a willful woman herself, has reserved a special destiny for every Cynster: to love and be loved by said wife. To surrender to love - to willingly do so - takes courage, determination, and commitment. As Demon recognizes at the beginning of this book, marrying the lady one loves - being forever at the mercy of a woman who holds one's heart, soul, and future in her small, delicate hands - is a fate baneful enough to make the strongest warrior blanch. Although each of them blanches, and clearly recognizes the danger, every member of the Bar Cynster ultimately makes his fateful choice. First Devil, in *Devil's Bride*, then Vane in *A Rake's Vow*, followed by Richard in *Scandal's Bride*, and now Demon in *A Rogue's Proposal*. Each choose love, family, and a lifetime of commitment over all else their wealthy world has to offer.

To me, that willing choice is the very essence of romance in the Regency.

Recording how each Cynster falls has been my privilege, watching as Fate lays her snare for each one. The next in line is Gabriel. He receives a summons from a mysterious countess and meets her in the mists at St. Georges, Hanover Square. Even cloaked and veiled, the lady raises much more than his interest. She wishes to recruit his talents to expose a financial scam. Gabriel agrees, intent on exposing much more than that. But the countess proves a creature of night and shadow. What Gabriel finally reveals when he rips aside her last veil rocks him to his very foundation. That, however, is just the start of his problems.

I hope reading my work brings you as much joy as creating it gives me. A big thank-you to all my readers – your letters, cards and email provide a constant stream of support. I write to entertain you, and hope to do so for many years yet!

Stephanie Laurens

436

Watch out for more

fabulous titles

from

Stephanie Laurens

now available from

Piatkus . . .

A SECRET LOVE

Stephanie Laurens

When a mysterious lady, her face hidden by a black veil, begs Gabriel Cynster for his help, he cannot refuse her plea. For despite her disguise, Gabriel finds the woman alluring and he is powerless to deny her. But he exacts payment as only a Cynster would demand: with each piece of information he uncovers, she must pay him – in the form of a kiss.

Lady Alathea Morwellan knows Gabriel is intrigued, but despite the sparks that fly between them, they have never passed a civil moment together. Yet as the stakes get higher, so does Gabriel's desire for payment. And with each overpowering kiss, each passionate embrace, Alathea knows that she will not be able to resist his ultimate seduction . . . but what will happen when she reveals the truth?

'Her lush sensuality takes my breath away!'
Lisa Kleypas

978-0-7499-3720-1

ALL ABOUT LOVE

Stephanie Laurens

Six notorious cousins, known to the ton as the Bar Cynster, have cut a swath through the ballrooms of London. Yet one by one, each has fallen in love and married the woman of his heart, until only one of them is left unclaimed . . .
Alasdair Cynster

Known to his intimates as Lucifer, Alasdair had decided to rusticate in the country before the matchmaking skills of London's mamas become firmly focused on him, the last unwed Cynster. But an escape to Devon leads him straight to his destiny in the irresistible form of Phyllida Tallent, a wilful, independent beauty of means who brings all his masterful Cynster instincts rioting to the fore. Lucifer tries to deny the desire Phyllida evokes – acting on it will land him in a parson's mousetrap, one place he's sworn never to go. But destiny intervenes, leaving him to face the greatest Cynster challenge – wooing a reluctant bride.

'Laurens is one of my favourites!'
Linda Howard

978-0-7499-3721-8